Back to Willow

MEL VERAN

Copy-edited by Kirsty McQuarrie
Proofread by Valentini Amaxopoulou
Cover design by Rotoscope Design
First printed version: October 2024
Paperback ISBN: 978-989-33-6749-0

PREFACE

The pandemic has changed the world forever and mine was no exception. Amidst such terrifying events, I found comfort inside a new world I had never thought to be a part of. Writing became an escape and a way to better deal with everything else around falling apart.

From the corners of my brain, Liam and Willow's story came to life. What you need to know about their path is that, while there are painful parts, this story is about having hope and healing. How, even if one's world is turned upside down, even if one's life is ripped apart, it isn't the end. And we should hold on to it.

There are mentions to some sensitive subjects, such as depression, SA and the aftermaths of it. Despite that, you will also find faulted characters, who make mistakes but love unconditionally. Some of them are very unique and will provide some funny moments.

It was an honour to bring Willow, Liam and Dylan to life. In the end, I hope this book fills your heart the same way it did mine.

You are more than what happens to you.

Playlist

Alex& Sierra – Little do You Know
Alexander Stewart – If you only Knew
Alexander Stewart – Day I die
Alie Gatie – It's you
Ali Gatie – What if I told you that I love you
Benson Boon – To Love Someone
Benson Boon – Little Runaway
Benson Boon – Let me go
Catch your Breath – Dial tone
Cian Ducrot (ft. Ella Henderson) – All for you
Finneas (ft Ashe) – 'Till forever falls apart
Here At Last – Ordinary Life
Lauren Daigle – You Say
Mat Hansen – Better off Without Me
Morgan St Jean – Not All Men
New West – Home
New West – In Good time
New West - Lovely
New West – Panick Attack
New West – Those Eyes
Slander – Love is Gone

PROLOGUE

Liam

THE BRISK RUSH OF AIR WORKS AS AN ANXIETY SUPPRESSANT, lowering my body temperature and solidifying my state of alert. I'd still be going downhill if I stayed inside, suffocating in that sea of dancing bodies. The crazy lights swirling around the club are gone, and the deafening music is now muffled by the back exit of the building. It was getting too loud and overwhelming, too much for me to take.

I hate nights like this when the anxiety creeps in at the most inopportune moments. For the past few years, I've been nothing but focused on finishing my degree and starting work as a doctor. I knew staying busy was the only way to keep going, and it has worked so far. It's like every time I treat myself with any kind of leisure, Karma comes knocking on my door to yell, "Not tonight, bitch!"

All I know at this point is that life is miserable. While I know my coping mechanisms throughout the years haven't always been the healthiest, I had hoped that by now, things would be better. Besides being close to finishing my master's degree and starting residency, I often ask myself, what am I even here for? Because nothing else makes sense.

Not without her.

I must be stupid to have thought tonight would be different from all other nights, where copious amounts of alcohol helped me take my mind off...her. Today would have been our seventh anniversary, and going through it sober is torture.

"Fuck, no," I grit to the emptiness of the dimly lit alley. "No thinking about this. She doesn't fucking deserve it."

It's no fun, though. Ever since I started University, everything has been different. The assignments I am completing throughout the beginning of the residency are giving me little to no time to wallow in my shit—thankfully. In a way, not having time to remember the past has made me feel better. Like she isn't the centre of the universe anymore.

It's frustrating as hell that the few moments I have some free time to have fun, she comes crawling back all over again. Like a plague on my brain, body, heart, and soul.

Sometimes, if I focus too hard, I can still smell her flowery scent. It used to calm my heart and rebellious soul. Her soft eyes are engraved in my mind, tearing at the pain even more. They used to be so full of love and affection, and it filled me up so much. But now? It just eats me alive.

Every now and then, when I wake up groggy from exhaustion or hangovers, I can still feel those silky chocolate waves against my face and hands from when we had fallen asleep after long study sessions. My heart still skips a beat if someone looks remotely similar to her. Even if, deep down, I know it won't ever happen again.

She made the choice to disappear from my life without a word. I won't be the one to search for her either. *Not anymore.*

All the time I wasted begging my parents for help, and all the times I chased Jacob around with the hopes of getting somewhere. A word, just a "she's fine" or a "here, you can have her number." But nothing.

Fucking nothing.

The whole family closed as tight as clams and shut me out, aiding her in the pain she caused. She not only broke my heart, she also had her family step on it until it withered away to ashes.

"Why are you here alone with such a cool party raging inside?" The sultry feminine voice that sounds behind me makes me turn around.

The first word that comes to mind: hot. Golden-tanned skin and subtly muscled legs and arms. She's wearing a short sparkling-silver dress, giving me a decent view of her full cleavage. Her dark hair is locked behind her head in an updo, showing off her slender shoulders and long neck.

With hooded hazel eyes and plump lips, the girl is gorgeous. Not the sweet and gentle kind of beautiful she was. But still very attractive.

"Just needed a breather," I tell her, keeping my armour intact.

I've given up on telling anybody what's going on inside me. People never understand, especially because most have never found a love like this—one that's strong and all-consuming.

It's always the same old talk of "time heals everything" and the most common "you'll get through it." It's all a fucking lie. After all of these years, I haven't gotten over it—especially not over her. There hasn't been anyone who caught my attention or made me forget her for more than a few crazy hours of hot sex. She broke me for everyone else.

"It's a shame that such a handsome guy is out here, all alone..."

The woman trails off with a tilt of her head and arms crossed over her chest, pushing those tempting breasts up and making them pop. She's beautiful, and even though I know she doesn't stand a chance in the long run, maybe I could try and have some fun—get my mind off of her.

With a new goal set for tonight, I flash her one of my best dazzling smiles. I was never cocky about my looks, but over the years, I've noticed the effect I have on women. And with how misguided I have been, I admit I've often used it to my advantage.

There's no misleading here, though. I've been direct with every woman I've been with, making it clear about what I want, and there has never been a problem with it.

"Why don't you keep me company, then?" I beckon her to me.

Her breath hitches right before my eyes, and her teeth press against her lower lip as she considers my offer. I can't help but think of how sexy this expression looks on her, how big the urge is to release that lip and bite it myself.

The girl before me seems to have made up her mind as her long, toned legs finally move, slowly walking towards me with hips swaying rhythmically. I know, right here and now, I've got her.

Is it presumptuous of me? Yes. Am I ashamed of it? Maybe if this girl was her instead, I would. But right now, with this desperate need to get rid of this torment eating me alive, I don't care. If I have to use my looks for an escape once more...I will.

I lean against the wall, and she mirrors my position against the railing in front of me.

"Now, what brought you out here to the point of having you curse to yourself?"

Wow. I guess she was here for longer than I realised. Still, I don't let my mask waver.

"Nothing to be worried about."

I give her a small smile, and she nods, understanding my unwillingness to talk.

Good, because there's no way we're talking about this.

"I've never seen you around. Are you from here?" Her bold hand rises and starts teasing the top buttons of my white shirt.

She is interested.

I let her play with them and smirk back, which she takes as a sign to be even more forward, unbuttoning the top two and exposing a little bit of my chest. To be honest, it feels good to have her touch me and talk to me.

The perfect distraction.

"Not really," I answer honestly with a shrug of my shoulders. "I moved here for University five years ago."

Her eyes widen, and I use the moment to watch her intently. They are warm and inviting like melted caramel, and her skin is flawless. A light slap on my arm wakes me from my hazy session.

"What? No way," she exclaims playfully. "I am starting Uni here, too. Which one do you go to?"

Starting? No wonder she looks younger than me.

"Porto's Medicine Faculty," I answer.

"Oh!" Her whole face lights up, and my stomach coils with her reaction. "That's close to mine. I am taking translation and literature. What year are you?"

I need this, and I should want this, so why do I feel guilty for giving this girl the time of day? It has been like this with everyone else. I haven't been able to feel the same—or more—ever since.

But if I don't push against this, against the shadow of her, I will never move on.

So, I answer her question, "Entering the last year of my master's degree. Currently finishing up my thesis while I start my residency."

Curiosity is visible in her eyes and body language as she takes a step closer and asks, "Well, which speciality are you choosing after the residency?"

"Cardiology, I think." I shrug my shoulder, still not exactly certain which way to go.

"So, you're what, twenty-four?"

"No, I finished high school a year early, so twenty-three." I try to contain the pride that threatens to drip off my voice. "You?"

"Nineteen, almost twenty." She smiles seductively, not showing any signs of being intimidated by me being a little older.

"Quite bold of you to strike up a conversation with a stranger in a dark and empty back exit," I tease, my hand lifting slowly to grab a strand that fell free from her updo and lock it behind her ear.

"I had my eyes on you from the moment you walked into the building. I saw an opportunity, and I took it."

"Yeah?" I breathe out, stepping even closer. "Seizing the moment, are we?"

She chuckles, and from up close, I can see the glistening skin of her chest rising with every breath. She looks slightly dishevelled but in a good way. Her hair has a few wild pieces sticking out. She must have been hot from dancing for a while. Without being able to control myself, my index finger shamelessly grazes along her collarbone towards her shoulder, where her dress strap has fallen to her arm. Carefully, I slide my finger under it and drag the fabric back up where it should be.

This captivating girl in front of me shivers but doesn't attempt to move away from my touch. Instead, she gifts me a seductive smile, and I suddenly feel like I've had enough small talk.

"You're smooth." She chuckles. "At least tell me your name."

"Liam," I whisper, moving closer to her as my hand sits on her neck.

Her skin prickles under my touch as goosebumps spread across her skin, and a light blush settles on her cheeks. She's not afraid to call me out on my shameless attitude. I know what I want, and I've never been afraid to show it. And yet, she responds immediately to every touch or word of mine.

Subtly, but I can see she wants this as much as I do.

Maybe for different reasons, but the goal is the same tonight.

"That's a good name."

"Right?" I grin while tilting her chin up. "And yours?"

"Johanna."

"Hmm, Johanna," I muse, my lips grazing hers.

She shudders under my hold, and the moment my free arm wraps around her waist, her body moulds into mine, hands splaying across my chest as if she magically has lost the strength in her legs.

"I like hearing you say my name," she whispers back, her white teeth biting on those tempting lips again.

"How about we find out the different ways we can say each other's names?"

"Sounds good to me," she answers in a sensual tone.

It's all the confirmation I need. As soon as the words roll off her tongue, I crash my mouth against hers.

Here's to forgetting.

ONE

Willow

"MUMMY, I DON'T WANT TO GO." DYLAN KICKS THE AIR WITH A HUFF, and I roll my eyes.

This boy of mine is not a morning person.

Just a few months were enough to forget how hard it is to get a kid up in the early hours of the morning to get ready. Those were hard, long days during my last two years of high school that I sure don't miss. And yet again, here I am at bloody six in the morning, fighting this little devil's terrible temper so I can get him to kindergarten before I head to school.

I've genuinely received a few hits from his tantrums in the past, but I have been relentless in getting him to control his impulsive temper. Thankfully, he's gotten better at it with time, slowly learning to explain what he's feeling or what he wants instead of throwing fits. But I can see it's starting to develop more as a personality trait, to often act without thinking. *Just like someone I used to know...*

"Dylan, what did I tell you about kicking and hitting just because you don't get what you want? What if you had hit me, huh?"

At my words, he sits up straight and looks at me wide-eyed. I know he doesn't mean to hurt anybody with it, but still, he needs to start growing out of it.

"No, no, no! Sorry, Mummy! I didn't mean to hit you, but I am just so, so sleepy," he whines, burying his head in my chest and faking a sob.

Kids these days turn into professional manipulators at an early age. Thank god I don't fall for it anymore.

"If you had done as I told you yesterday, you wouldn't be tired right now. Tonight, you'll go to bed earlier," I scold.

Dylan groans into my chest but makes no move from the position we're in.

"Come on. Let's get you ready." I tap his shoulder but don't attempt to move either. "We have our first day of school today, and we can't miss it."

"Aren't you old for my school?"

"I have explained it to you," I answer him with a light chuckle. "Mummy's not going to your school. Remember that I told you I paused everything when you were born? You were very little and needed a lot of care and attention..." It was difficult to accept I had to stop studying; the only bright side of it was taking care of him. Dylan quickly consumed my thoughts, leaving my studies on the back burner. When he nods, I continue. "Well, now you're older and ready to go play with other kids, and I can finally finish my studies."

"Then what kind of school is it?"

"It's called college. A kind of grown-ups school."

His eyebrows twist in confusion as his mouth forms an 'o'. "Is it important?" I nod, giving him a patient smile. "Why?"

"Because Mummy wants to be a teacher, like the ones you'll meet today. And for that, I need to study some more, so I can do what I love."

I did it. It may be four years later than usual, but I still did it and am so proud of myself. I will be able to show my baby boy that even as a teenage mother, I didn't give up on my dream; that his existence encouraged me even more to be a good example to follow.

"Will I need to go to college, too?"

"If you want to." I smile gently.

"I don't know..." He trails off.

"And that's alright." I chuckle. "You're too young to decide now. Let's focus on the school for your age and get ready, eh?"

"I don't want to go," he grumbles.

"Why?"

"I don't know anyone at this school." He tilts his head to peek one eye at me. It's so freaking hard to stay mad at that adorable face. I couldn't even if I wanted to.

"Don't be silly, baby. You've spent the last two weeks playing with the next-door girl, Abby. She's your friend already and going to be in your class today."

Dylan straightens and blushes slightly but keeps what should be a serious expression I find too cute to take seriously before answering me. "But she's a girl. The boys will make fun of me for being friends with a girl." He crosses his arms over his chest and huffs.

I just laugh.

"Nonsense, Dylan. What did I tell you about this kind of behaviour? Just because other kids like to be mean, it doesn't mean you have to be the same as them to be accepted. Because..." I prolong the last word to let him finish for me.

"Because they are in the wrong. You don't hurt or hit anyone, not even with a flower," he continues in a monotone voice.

Ever since he started making friends, I've been trying to teach him not to do what others do or tell him to just because it's cool, especially if it means treating girls poorly. I don't want my son to be a bully, disrespectful, or even worse...

Changes are always hard for kids, and this one—moving—is his biggest yet. And while it was hard at first, children are resilient and adapt quickly. Once we got settled, he met Abby and got less and less resistant to his new reality.

"Exactly, and what do you do if other kids taunt or hurt you?" I ask.

"I defend myself." He puffs his chest, and I stifle a laugh.

"How so?" I push him. I want to hear him say the correct words.

I want my boy to be good but not too good. I don't want him to take shit from anyone.

"Well, if it's with words, I just tell them off, but if they hit me, I hit them back." He tries doing what could be a kung-fu move but ends up falling to the mattress on his back.

"No, Dylan. You defend yourself and only hit if you need to," I press. "Got it?"

"But if I can't show off the moves Uncle Jake taught me, why did I learn them?"

"To defend yourself and no more. Yes?"

"Okaaaayy." He rolls his eyes while dragging the word with a snarky tone.

"Good. Now, go get dressed. Do you need help?"

"No, Mum. I'm a big boy!"

"Okay. I'll be downstairs making breakfast. Call me if you need help."

Ten minutes after, when I am almost done with breakfast, Dylan shows up in the kitchen, jumping around ecstatically–the complete opposite of the boy whining because he was sleepy just before. This kid is a ball of energy; I can only imagine how it is going to be when he grows up.

"Mummy, do I look good or what?" He poses in front of me with both hands on his hips, head cocked to the side, and a cocky expression on his face.

This boy couldn't be more like *him*, even if I wanted him to be, and it tugs my heart. A ton of memories that are buried in the back of my mind threaten to be released and dampen my mood. That is until I notice how his T-shirt is inside out, and his little jeans are unbuttoned.

I can't control the loud cackle that comes out of me, making Dylan frown at my reaction before looking at himself.

"Come here, you silly." I beckon him, then take the T-shirt off and put it back correctly, and then button his jeans up.

"Thanks, Mummy," he chirps and runs off to his seat at the table.

We eat breakfast, and I help him so he doesn't get stains on his clothing before taking him to school.

Abby is already waiting for him by the gate, and as soon as we exit the car, she's waving excitedly. Dylan grins at her and prepares to run but hesitates and looks up at me for permission.

I extend my hand, hinting for him to hold it. There's a road we have to cross, and I won't risk it, even though it's right in front of the school and drivers are usually careful, but you never know.

The walk to the gate is quick but not quick enough for my son, it seems. With each step that isn't as fast as he's expecting, he tugs on my hand, trying to speed me up. I chuckle silently at his antics, and when we finally reach Abby and her mother, Dylan lets go of my hand and gives the girl a huge, tight hug.

My heart melts when it reminds me of easier times. Times when I, too, had a best friend like Dylan who would hug me and stand by me for everything. The fact that I no longer have that hurts, making me aware of how great the void in my heart is. A void that even the love of my son can't fill. But whatever happened, it gave me what I have today, and I wouldn't change having my son for anything in this world.

"Good morning," I greet Abby's mum, forcing myself out of my thoughts. She replies kindly with another good morning, and we fall into an easy conversation about how the weekend was and how excited the kids are for school.

One of the teachers comes outside, letting me know it's time for them to go in, and I crouch to Dylan's level for my hug. He comes without hesitation, hugging me tightly.

"Remember to be kind, okay? Voice what you're feeling. I will be back later to pick you up." I kiss him on the cheek, and he nods at me before turning back to Abby.

He picks her hand up, tangling their fingers together, and they go inside as the teacher accompanies the big group of kids.

Never glancing away from his small stature, I force myself to take a deep calming breath with my fingers twisting continuously and my brain repeating to my heart that it'll be alright. That he'll be back home at the end of the afternoon.

You would think separation anxiety would improve as the years went by. *It doesn't.* When he was little, he was the only comfort for my loneliness, and when the time came that I had to start to work to help Nana and put him in school, I really struggled.

I used to bawl my eyes out every time I left him at daycare and spent the days on edge, waiting for a call saying something bad had happened or that his father's family had found out about him and taken him. It never happened, and slowly, I got used to the brief time we had to spend apart.

"It'll get easier," Abby's mum, Nina, says to me.

"You think?" I chuckle nervously.

"Just try and enjoy the hours he is away. Focus on yourself." She nods alongside her words. "We often forget to take care of ourselves when kids come into our lives. We matter, too."

Don't I know it?

"I get you," I start slowly, still unsure if I should disclose what my life is at the moment. "But I'm not sure I'll have a moment to myself with both work and college mixed in the middle."

Nina's eyes widen for a second before she clears her throat. "That sounds like a lot."

I already feel the pressure of it, and I haven't even started properly. I can only hope that with Nana's help—which she has made clear she is one hundred percent free for—I'll be able to manage.

Though it worries me because, at her age, she should be relaxing and enjoying life, and yet, here she is, helping me get my life straight.

"I applaud you," Nina offers, catching my attention. "To do that... all on your own. It's really brave."

Brave is the last word I'd use to describe myself. If it weren't for my brother and grandmother, I don't know where Dylan and I would be right now. I probably would have given in to the pressure my parents put on me to get an abortion.

"Thank you," I answer. However, her words trigger a reaction, and I add, "But I'm not alone."

With an understanding smile, she nods before saying her goodbyes and leaving me to my thoughts.

After everything that has happened, Dylan became the blessing I needed at a time when I hit my lowest point. A beacon of light where all that existed around me was darkness.

And maybe doing all of this at the same time is not ideal, but sometimes we just have to keep moving forward. People usually say that if life throws you lemons, make lemonade, and that's exactly what I'm doing.

But for now, it's one day at a time.

Since I've already visited the college grounds before, I've got all the documents and information needed. A member of the Student Council, a girl graduating this year, has already shown me around and answered all my questions and addressed my doubts.

After navigating the long halls and up the staircases, I finally find the first class of today: Portuguese.

In this degree, we not only have to relearn the grammar side in a way that'll make us understand how to teach it but also the literature part of it. I'm unbelievably excited about all of it.

When I was younger, I wanted to be a biologist, but Dylan opened my eyes to my true calling. It was like a lightbulb switched in my brain when I realised the joy I had and still have when teaching him. *I fell in love*–at least, in the only way I still can.

Helping kids and giving them—as much as I can—the right tools to use in their adulthood fills what's left of my heart.

When I reach the classroom, I am met with plain white walls and a brown wooden floor. On one half of the room, tables and chairs are lined up, while just one single desk sits on the opposite side in front of a whiteboard and a projector.

I notice a few seats still available, so I head to the vacant ones around the middle area. Within a few minutes, the room slowly fills up as more students arrive and sit down.

I've got my head in my notepad when a girl stops at the seat right next to mine. "Hey, is this seat taken?"

"Oh, no. Go ahead." I encourage her with a smile.

"Are you a freshman?"

"I'm Willow. And yes." I chuckle. "I'm a freshman, and you?"

"Oh god, yes. Can't you tell? I'm so nervous." She giggles too, and it makes me smile in response. "Aren't you?"

"I guess I should be? But oddly enough, I'm not." She's taking her notebook out of her bag, so I take a moment to glance at her.

Dark chocolate locks frame her tanned face, and plump red lips compliment her flawless makeup. She is gorgeous, that's for sure. While I am much smaller and on the thinner side, this girl is all long legs and toned muscles.

People often tell me I look frail and ill, even though I'm not. It seems like raising a toddler, working, and being busy preparing everything to study took a toll on me. I wonder what adjective they'll add when my exams start...

"So, are you from here?"

Her question pulls my attention back to her. "Em, no. I come from the south, a town called Évora. Do you know it?"

"Yes," she exclaims. "My grandmother is from there. I used to spend a lot of my summers there growing up."

I am not from Évora. Though, it has been my home ever since I was sixteen.

"How come we've never met?" she asks.

"Uhm, I didn't go out much because I...I have been working full time for a few years now." I stumble a little on my words, not overly keen on disclosing my life story just yet.

I may have grown stronger throughout the years in some regards, but I'll still avoid confrontation like the devil runs away from the cross. He was the strong one in that department. He wasn't afraid to tell someone—no matter who it was—to fuck off. Unfortunately for my pathetic personality, conflict is still one of the few things that makes me anxious. Panic attacks are no longer as frequent, but they do still come out once in a while.

"Work?" Her eyebrows furrow. "For how long have you been working? I mean, your whole stance is so mature, but you seem so young!" Her ability to be invasive in an innocent way is really sweet.

"I am twenty two," I answer. "I know it's kind of late to start college, but life got in the way, and I had to postpone." When the silence stretches, I add, "I made it, though."

"Hell yes, girl," she exclaims with a pump of her fist. "That's what women are made of; we persevere and never give up!" she hollers a little too loud at the same time the professor enters the classroom. I don't look around, but I bet everyone is glaring at us.

"Shhh!" someone hisses from behind us.

I can't help but turn around to the thick-glasses framed face and smile guiltily. Her face is twisted in an annoyed glare, her greyish eyes throwing darts at me with sleek but dark makeup, giving her big round eyes a smoky and cat-like aesthetic. Her straight hair is jet black, completely matching the hues of her clothing—the only exception being the greyish jeans. She is intimidating.

"Sorry," I whisper.

Next to her sits a guy. He is the complete opposite, with dark brown hair and honey-coloured eyes. Loose and light blue jeans, topped with an oversized T-shirt and a tiny hoop earring. He is leaning back with a relaxed stance and a smirk gracing his lips. He's cute and charming, to an extent.

"It's fine, *Willow.*" He smiles back, earning an elbow from the girl right next to him.

My cheeks burn from the embarrassment. So, they just heard our *entire* conversation.

"I'm Ethan, and this is my cousin, Hazel."

"Nice meeting you guys." The brunette on my side greets them, too, loudly once again.

I wince, feeling all eyes on us. My body automatically turns back around to the front, and I am met with the most menacing glare from the professor. But his glare quickly changes into an expression of surprise. It doesn't last long because he shakes his head, willing back a neutral expression.

I have to admit, he's made an impression on me. He is daunting—domineering, even. And young. It may sound pretentious, but I was expecting a much older and less attractive person in his place. It might be good, though, to have a teacher who is easy on the eyes.

"Good to know that this year's students are so much more invested in this class," he mentions before turning back to his desk, where he starts to settle himself. If sarcasm was visible, I'd see it dripping from his mouth and down his chin. The embarrassment has me sinking further down in my chair.

That tongue is as sharp as his jaw, that's for sure.

"Damn, girl. That man is hot as fuck," she whispers too loudly, with her breath close to my face and her brown locks brushing my shoulder.

"Shhh." I try to shut her up, but he still looks up at us with a cocked eyebrow, and all I can do is blush, madly.

Oh god, I hope he doesn't start to pick on me. I was a real nerd in high school. If this is the kind of professor that puts you aside, no matter the effort you make, I might be screwed.

"Very well," he starts after clearing his throat. "Good morning. I am Professor Adell, and I'll be your teacher for the semester. Not Mr Adell, nor my name if you end up finding it out. Especially not Sir or Mr."

His eyes sweep the classroom once more, lingering on me.

Why is he lingering on me?

"You can only call me Professor Adell—it'll save you and me a lot of trouble. Believe me."

A light murmur echoes throughout the room, and by my side, she snickers, "Damn, that's one bitter man."

"Now," he speaks again. "I know this course is directed mostly to basic education, but you will have plenty of preparation for your teaching techniques in another subject, so after consulting with the other lecturers, I'll be focusing on what the regular Portuguese subject should be. That means we'll focus on literature instead."

I hear loud groans across the classroom, making me giggle quietly. I am glad since I used to love the literature side of the subject back then.

"I will pass a few sheets with the books I expect you to read and write a report about. Delivery dates are also on the sheets as well as the guidelines you should follow. In class, we will discuss five books—which are not on that list. I expect you to read those, too, and come to class with your comments about them. Your participation will make up thirty percent of your grades."

Everyone groans loudly—*again*—while I happily scribble notes about what the professor's saying. Reading those books won't be a problem. Not only do I like to read, but I also make it a habit to read to Dylan as often as I can for him to fall asleep. He quickly became fond of this habit, so much so that we ended up running out of books for him at home.

He has started asking me to read him my books, claiming he is grown up enough to listen to them. It's funny because while he is awake, he keeps interrupting me to know the meaning of words or about situations he doesn't quite understand. It's adorable!

A nudge to my ribs snaps me out of my thoughts. When I notice my surroundings, it's entirely quiet, and a few faces are looking at me, the professor included.

"Have you finally come back to us, Ms..." Professor Adell asks sarcastically.

"Hanlon," I finish for him. "I zoned out for a moment, yes. I am sorry, everyone." I smile apologetically.

My gaze travels back to the seats behind me for just a quick second, but all I see is Ethan's encouraging megawatt smile, followed by a quick nod. When I look back to the front, Professor Adell's expression is somber. "Well, Ms, if you prefer to daydream instead of paying attention to class, you can see yourself out. There's no point in being here."

I gasp at his rudeness, and for a moment, I feel the need to lash back at him. Sure, I just spent like five minutes scribbling with a smile on my face, thinking about my kid, but there's no need to overreact in this way. However, his taunting attitude won't make me lower mine to his level. I won't snap back.

That is not who I am.

"Of course, Professor Adell." I grit my teeth.

I am not one to believe in first impressions, but he certainly left a negative one on me. How can someone so beautiful *seem* to be so ugly on the inside?

Stealing a glance at him, our eyes lock. His gaze is intense and intimidating, making me look away. His jaw clenches when I do, the discomfort in his stance matching mine. After a long minute in silence, he clears his throat and continues, jumping straight into work.

The task is to write a page worth of information about one of our favourite books and hand it over by the end of class. Once I get to work, time flies by. I get so immersed in writing about *The Picture of*

Dorian Grey by Oscar Wilde that when I look at the clock, I notice how I only have five minutes left.

Once the clock hits eleven, marking the end of class, Professor Adell clears his throat and salutes everyone goodbye. Everyone stands, handing over the paper before leaving class. I am one of the last ones and when I get to his desk, I barely place the sheet on the table when he talks.

"I hope it doesn't happen again, Miss Hanlon. I'd hate to think my class is filled with spoiled brats."

Fighting the urge to react to his offensive statement, I answer, "Looks can be deceiving, sir; I certainly was hoodwinked at first. But rest assured because it won't happen again. *Never* again." Turning away before he can respond, I rush out of the classroom.

Outside, warm air hits me but does nothing to help my burning cheeks. I'm probably blushing like crazy as the adrenaline of answering him back slowly wears off. I don't know what got into me to answer him like that. I mean, he's a professor; he can very well make it his mission to fail me.

Damn, what have I done?

"Girl..." the girl who had been sitting by my side–who hasn't given me a name yet—*tsks* me when she gets outside. "I have never seen eyes burn with such fire like our professor's after your reply."

"Oh god. I don't know what's gotten into me. I don't snap back or anything like that. *At all*," I stress.

Ethan and Hazel appear by my other side. Her lips are tight, and her face blank, but Ethan chuckles, probably having heard everything—once again—and says, "Well, sometimes, there are people out there that bring a side of us that is usually buried deep, *deep* down."

His voice is slightly low and raspy, and his eyes glint with mischief, locking me in a brief trance. For a second, it's like I'm hypnotised, but I quickly snap out of it.

"No chance," I say with determination. "I don't want a war with him. He's the one calling the shots inside the classroom, and I can't afford to fail, or my scholarship is gone."

Oh god, now I'm stressed.

"Come on, then. I think some coffee and food will do you good to destress." The intimidating brunette laughs at my nervousness.

"I feel like I should know your name before we take the next level in our relationship," I joke lightly.

She chuckles and adds, "Friendship, you mean." Then with a mega smile, she answers, "I'm Johanna!"

"Nice to meet you, Johanna!" I nod with my own honest smile before following the three of them to the café for a well-deserved break.

THREE

Willow

IT'S BEEN TWO DAYS SINCE THAT DREADFUL CLASS. I USED TO LOVE literature and all that comes with reading and deciphering the books, but I don't think I'll enjoy it as much this time around. He is *terrifying*, and still, he hasn't left my mind. Even now at work, I keep replaying his petty actions in my head.

Why was he that awful? And why me? Sure, Johanna was loud, but there were a lot of other students whispering all around, and he didn't even care. He kept his focus on me the whole time.

Despite this, all other subjects have been amazing. It's everything I ever imagined. Every assignment that has been given has me eager to start it—even though I'm sure I'll be crying in around a month or so.

Shilah breaks me from my trance. "Willow? A few customers have arrived at my table area, but Xico needs my help. Can you cover them?"

The crowd's out and about tonight. All of the bright yellow booths are occupied, and new food plates keep coming out. Even the modern grey stools by the main counter are occupied with people eating. It doesn't even look like we're in the middle of the week. It's almost as bad as the weekends.

"Of course. I'm on it."

Secretly, the work is welcomed. Anything to keep my mind off these running thoughts. The couple is already seated in one of the booths, so I quickly attend to their drinks while letting them choose what to eat. Even though I'm fairly new here, this has been the kind of work I have been doing since before Dylan was born, so the agility to get things done is there.

When I got to Nana's, I was determined to still get a job—even if just a temporary one, while already pregnant. And then as soon as he was six months old, I went back to work. Only part time at the beginning, and then full time after I graduated.

Working and studying online while still taking care of a newborn was the hardest time of my life. Especially before even turning eighteen. It was exhausting, but looking back now...it has been rewarding.

After giving the couple their drinks, I make haste to clean one of the booths that just became free when the entrance's bell rings.

Once it's spotless, I straighten and turn around to allow the client to sit down, running into a hard chest. The impact robs me of my almost non-existent balance as I hit my hip on the table in the process. But then, strong hands steady me. Flinching at the foreigner's hold, I look up and...freeze.

Professor Adell.

"Uhm, I am s-sorry," I stutter, stepping out of his firm grasp.

With an ever-present frown on his face, he nods. Then he proceeds to walk past me and sit down at the closest table, completely dismissing me.

Shilah did an amazing job with the decoration. It's modern and sleek, but with such a pop of colour with the yellow items. The walls are a bright white and the floor just a shade darker in a light grey tone.

The chandeliers are disco balls instead, but the leather benches of the booths are yellow like the flowers decorating the tables. I love it.

A displeased grumble resonates next to me, bringing my attention back to the grumpy man sitting down on one of those booths. He's squinting at the disco balls with disgust before his eyes slide back to me.

Great, he still hates me.

Not letting my emotions get the best of me, I give him the food menu and ask, "While you choose, can I bring you something to drink?"

"Huh?" He looks up at me with furrowed eyebrows.

"What will you want to drink, sir?" I repeat.

His shoulders slump slightly, and his expression goes back to the expression I have seen most of the time during class.

"Just water," he breathes.

Not even losing another second, I turn around, scurrying off to bring him his water. My hands sweat, and my heart skyrockets as I look for the bottle of water. If he hates me at school, what will he say or do now that he knows where I work? Just the idea makes me anxious, not letting me focus completely on my task.

Where are the freaking water bottles?

Hopefully, he'll be more polite tonight than he was at school. Right? It's my job after all...He'll be considerate. Or not? What if it just makes him act worse? Ugh, what am I going to do?

"Hmm, that one's quite handsome, honey," Shilah whispers, making me jump at the unexpected sound of her voice from behind me.

"Yeah, and he's also my professor," I moan.

She whistles slowly before adding, "Damn, and here I thought I had found you some boyfriend material."

"Don't play matchmaker on me, Shilah. All I want from men is distance." She just shrugs her shoulders at me, probably meaning 'your choice', and I finally find the water bottle he has asked for.

"How long does it take to bring me some water?" Is the first thing that comes out of his mouth when I get to his table.

Certainly not nicer. Nope. Asshole it is, apparently.

Silently, I place it on the table, avoiding eye contact for as long as I can. When I finally give in, amusement whirls around his brown irises along with a mischievous smile.

"I-I apologise. I just started a few days ago and still get confused about where to find what." I do my best to keep a kind smile. "Have you chosen what to eat?"

"So, you're new at this job?" He completely ignores my previous question.

"Ahm, yes," I say quickly. "Actua—"

"I am curious now. What made a girl like you search for this kind of job?" He cuts me off, and my head reels back in shock.

"Excuse me?"

"You don't seem the type of girl who would spend her time working. As a waitress on top of that."

I feel the heat creep up my neck right onto my cheeks. *The embarrassment.* What's wrong with being a waitress? It's honest work and honest money. His eyes lower, noticing my reaction. The proof of his amusement is in his smirk. How can a person who's supposed to help his students improve and develop their intellectual capacities be this horrid?

I won't retort. At this moment, he's a client, not to mention he's also my teacher.

With shaking hands, I bring my notebook up and face him. "What can I get you, *sir*?"

His jaw clenches, and his eyes close before he grits out, "Just a burger with fries, please. Extra cheese."

I write down and nod as I prepare to leave. This man must be miserable to try and reassure himself of someone else's misery. This next semester will be hell, for sure. All his handsomely evil face promises are ruthlessness and loathing.

"Wait!" His hand hastily grabs my wrist, pulling me back. "Can you bring me another water?"

I flinch at the sudden touch, shadows from the past quickly creeping in and quickening my heart. He seems to realise with the way his eyes widen. Just as quickly as he grabbed me, he lets go.

"Sorry." He looks down, not meeting my eyes.

"Sure," I breathe out.

Keep your distance and it'll be okay, Willow.

The problem is, I always have. And look how that worked out for me. It brought me here, a teen mum starting college at twenty-two.

The memories that this thought brings make my heartbeat spike and my breath hitch.

Heading to where Shilah is, I hand her the paper and ask for my ten-minute break. She seems to notice—or read my mind—because she doesn't even hesitate to agree.

"Thank you," I squeak before heading to the back room, locking myself in.

Secluded from the rest of the world, in this bare grey room, my brain reproduces the one thing I dread the most. His voice.

Come on, Lo. You'll like it.

It's as if time stopped all of those years ago. Sometimes, it feels like I am still there, trapped. Not only do I hear him, but I can also see and smell him. More times than I'd like to admit.

"No, no," I whisper to myself. "Don't remember."

Shutting my eyes, my fingers start to massage my scalp in an attempt to relax and send the bad memories away.

Dylan. Think about Dylan. My baby boy, my treasure.

A couple of sobs escape my throat, making it difficult for me to forget. I will never forget it, not really. But by now, it wasn't supposed to be like this. So long has passed, you'd think the pain would have eased, but it hasn't.

It never goes away. I just need to learn how to live with it.

From the pocket in my apron, I take a napkin to blow my nose. Now unclogged, it allows me to focus on my breathing to calm down.

Breathe in. Breathe out.

I need to grow a thicker skin, once and for all.

A knock on the door startles me, and I run to unlock it.

"Everything okay, darling?" Shilah peeks through the door.

"Yeah, sorry. I am just nervous; you know, being new and all…" I give her a weak smile. "Are my ten minutes up?"

She nods and gives me a warm smile. "No need to be nervous; you're doing wonderful."

I thank her for her kind words before heading back to work. It's busier, and I end up running around the diner, serving the clients and refilling the drinks every time I notice the empty cups. Half an hour goes by, and I'm glad I'm able to avoid Professor Adell.

Unfortunately, that's as far as my good luck goes. With Shilah telling me she's going to the restrooms, I notice him finishing up his meal. The obnoxiously loud sound of the cutlery feels on purpose, but I try my best to ignore it. Right then, his hand raises, and I take a deep breath.

Here we go.

"How was everything?" My hands twist in each other, anxiety building up again.

"Good," he answers with a light shrug.

"Would you like some dessert?"

"I'd like the check, please."

"Sure." I nod and head to the register to close his tab. When I bring it back to him, I place it on the table. "Here." Thankfully, before he can say anything else, another couple calls me. "I'll be right back."

With a coffee request, I quickly serve them. From the corner of my eye, I see Professor Adell placing money inside the leather case and politely excusing himself. He stands to meet me when I've finished serving the couple.

"Never took you for the type of girl who would study and work at the same time." He presses on the work subject again.

"There's a lot of things you don't know about me, Professor Adell. It only shows that your assumptions about me are shallow... and well,wrong."

I give him a tight-lipped smile at the end. My voice might have come out softer than it was supposed to, but I mean...it's progress seeing that I am shaking like a leaf on the inside.

"I guess we'll see. Won't we?" He smirks before walking off abruptly.

What?

I just stand there dumbfounded. His expression this time around wasn't all about anger or distaste. It was more like amusement.

Huffing, I pick up the leather case and bring it to the register to put the money in. When I open it, I notice that from a twenty-euro meal, he just left a thirty-euro tip.

What in the...

"There's something seriously wrong with this man," I mumble to myself.

"Who, dear?" Shilah asks from the kitchen door, behind me.

"Just a rude customer. But look, he left us a thirty-euro tip." I wave the bill in front of her.

"No way. You know the rules. What's yours is yours. If he gave you that much, it is because you deserved it! You've been doing great!"

"Oh god. Thank you so, so much." I hug her tightly.

It might not be much, but all the money I can make will better help me with the bills... Uni, to help Nana, and especially care for Dylan.

Once my shift ends, I do my best to leave as much done as I can so they don't have too much work when it's closing time, then drive home to find Dylan asleep on my bed. I am so exhausted that I don't have the energy to carry him to his. Instead, I put my pyjamas on and snuggle in bed, bringing him close to me.

He automatically latches onto my body, and I sigh in relief at the feeling of his warmth on my chest. He might be young and little, but he holds such power over me. Dylan calms down my racing heart and gives peace to my restless soul.

He's the only place I feel truly safe.

FOUR
Willow

EXHAUSTING.

That is the only word possible to describe how this week felt. Juggling school, work, and a needy five-year-old—soon to be six—is hard. To help make things worse, I fell asleep in one of Professor Adell's classes this week after Johanna loudly asked me to go out with her sometime. If he had let it go the first time, he certainly didn't afterwards.

The only bright moments I currently have are hugs from my boy. This kid is the oxytocin source of my life, with his miraculous cuddles. And that is exactly why today is going to be all about him.

"Good morning, little devil," I whisper close to his serene face.

A small frown appears quickly, followed by a slight stir, but still, he doesn't wake from his sleep. He is spread out on his wooden bed, only half covered by the dinosaur sheets he chose—his favourite—and it takes me a few more calls and some nudges for him to groan and open one eye. "I'm tired, Mummy."

I can't help but snort. After twelve hours of sleep, he's still tired?

The window on the left side is completely open, as the bright rays from the early morning lights up his bedroom. The wooden furniture is not high-end or modern, but it's good quality and functional. A bed for him to sleep, a desk and chair to study and do his homework once he starts elementary school, and a closet. Other than that, there is a bookcase with some of the books I read to him at bedtime and a few drawers where I store his toys.

The bed's head is covering part of the light green wall, with a huge framed picture of Dylan, Nana, Jake, and me a few years ago at Christmas.

Sometimes, I wish I could give him more—better. But he has never once seemed bothered by his bedroom. In fact, he's very fond of it.

"Can you guess what day it is today?"

"What?" His voice is still groggy.

"It's Mummy's free day. We're going to the park!" I excitedly tell him.

For a moment, he doesn't react, but then...in slow motion, as if his brain just registered my words, his eyes widen, and he jumps into a sitting position.

"I forgot!"

Of course.

Muffling my chuckle, I shake my head in amusement. Dylan gets up, and I watch as he, in all of his clumsiness, notices the set of clothes I laid out for him on the desk and dashes for it.

Not wasting time, I see.

He starts getting dressed by himself, with that ever-present desire to be a grown-up. Just witnessing his antics puts a smile on my face. This boy is so genuine it hurts sometimes. Slightly more impulsive than I'd like him to be, but he makes up for it with how tender and loving his heart is. Not to mention he's got spunk and a lot of attitude on top of that.

Some kids love to be loved; my kid loves to show some love. Even if he goes about it the wrong way and has me running after him to correct it or downplay his dramatics once in a while.

He definitely got the dramatics from his uncle, though...

"Mummy, how do I look?" he asks, turning around to show me his outfit.

With practice, his dressing abilities have been improving. The only thing he can't do by himself yet is tying shoes and, depending on the day, he can struggle with the buttons of his jeans. Dylan has always been very independent from the beginning. Since holding the bottle on his own from as young as three and a half months to starting to walk even before being one year old.

It tugs at my heartstrings, though. He grows too fast.

"You look handsome, baby. Let's go brush your hair."

"But I did it last night after showering," he pouts.

With a slight glare from me, he gives in, groaning a "fine".

Fifteen minutes later, we're ready. Breakfast has been eaten, and Dylan and I wait for Nana to be ready. There's a basket of food hanging from my arm, so we can have some food while spending time in the park. As soon as she arrives, we head for my old car, and they get in as I place everything inside the trunk.

From the corner of my eyes, I notice a head of blonde hair approaching, knowing right away who it is.

"Good morning, Ms Hanlon." The little girl smiles sweetly at me before looking at Dylan. "Hey, Dylan."

"Hey, Abby." He waves back at her with a wide smile and a heavy blush on his cheeks.

She blushes back, looking away from him, suddenly acting all shy. Abby is such a cutie with long, curly blonde hair and bright blue eyes. Her light skin tone gives her this sweet porcelain doll look. *Adorable.*

"Are you leaving?" she asks me, hands behind her back and curious doe eyes.

All it takes is one look at Abby's unknowing begging eyes because five minutes later, as the sun shines bright, the four of us are driving together to the park, towards what I hope is a relaxing and fun day.

The drive is quick, and we're swiftly engulfed by the vibrant greens, deep blues, and dazzling yellows of the park. Dylan is quick to pull Abby with him to play football while Nana and I choose a place to spread a blanket over the grass, watching them.

It's the city's biggest green area, literally called the City's Park. Trees, flowers, and bushes surround us, as well as people strolling by. Once in a while, I see a squirrel running around, and the birds chirp happily while flying above us. The soft prickles of the grass tickle my feet, and the fresh air softens the warmth that the sun expels.

Sometimes, depending on how close to it you are, you can listen to the ocean's strong waves. It couldn't be more relaxing.

"How's school been, Lo?" Nana sparks a conversation after a few minutes of enjoying our surroundings.

"Tiring, for sure." I nod. "One of the classes has been harder than I expected but nothing I can't handle."

Well, that's one way of putting it.

"I noticed how tired you've been. Much more than usual," she sighs. "I know you always avoid asking for my help for fear of overworking me. I know I'm old, but I am not an invalid yet. Dylan's easy to take care of, feel free to ask for my help whenever you need it. Alright?"

With a resigning sigh, I nod.

"I know you're a strong woman, baby, but you're not Wonder Woman." She chuckles, patting my knee.

She's right, but she has done so much for me already. Dylan can be a handful sometimes, even if he behaves better with her than with me. He tends to test my limits while he's nothing but respectful and abiding with her. I don't know what she does, though. Maybe she bribes him...Who knows?. It makes sense sometimes, the knowing smile she gives him, leaving me out of the loop.

"Lo?" she calls me, apparently not for the first time by the look on her face.

"Yes, Nana?"

Her hand covers mine, squeezing it. "I know things can be hard, and sometimes, it feels like nothing will ever fall into place. Especially in a new place where you barely know anyone."

With a knowing smile, I nod. When this opportunity arose, Nana didn't even think twice about putting her home up for sale back in Évora, a small city in the south of the country, and buying one here to move in with Dylan and me. Truth be told, I don't know where I would be if it weren't for her. She stood by me when no one else did, and for that, I am forever indebted to her.

"But just know that if I believe there's anyone that will make it, it's you. I am so proud of you."

Her recognition is everything to me. She became my mother when my own parents didn't care to help me during the time I needed them the most. I will be forever grateful to her. Grateful for helping me fight and helping me keep my sanity so I can start a new chapter and make my dreams come true.

"You've managed to raise him on your own, and look how well he is turning out. Such a loving kid."

Unaware of the meaning of our words, Dylan waves at us with the biggest grin before focusing back on a running Abby. Many have told me I'd regret having a kid at sixteen—an unplanned kid that is.

I can't deny it was a shock, knowing a baby was growing inside me at such a young age. The pressure to get rid of him was real, from my parents first, and when that didn't work, my doctor did as well.

For a moment, I almost gave in. My parent's approval had always been everything, but in the end, how could the baby be the one to be punished when he didn't even ask to be made?

It's not that I fault those who do it. I think every woman has the right to do as they decide with their own body. Just as I did. I wouldn't be able to live with myself. Harming my baby was out of the question. It wasn't his fault; it isn't, and I couldn't do it.

It didn't make it any easier. The moment my parents knew that an abortion was out of the question, everything changed. That day, I cried myself to sleep on my brother's lap. He was the only one on my side, besides Nana, and even though he is a little crazy, he's the best uncle.

Many regrets are eating away inside my heart, weakening my soul with each passing day. But there is one thing I can't regret, and that was having my boy. Amid chaos and pain, he brought me joy, love, and strength.

My world shifted, and now everything revolves around him.

"Thank you," I whisper with a shaky voice.

A knot settles in my throat, not letting me speak further, but the pat on my knee lets me know no more words are needed.

As if sensing the shift in my mood, Dylan looks at us and beckons Abby to follow him before running towards me. He runs, not even slowing down, and like the impulsive brat he can be sometimes, he throws himself onto me, bringing us both down.

I groan in discomfort when my back hits the floor due to impact. "Ouch. You're too big to keep doing this."

Instead of letting me go, his arms squeeze around my neck as he mumbles against my hair, "Thank you for today, Mummy."

"We'll come back next weekend. Is that alright?" He nods eagerly, just as Abby sits down next to us. "You must be hungry. You've been running non-stop since we arrived."

Nana passes me the basket, and I take the food out, laying it in front of us. They both end up eating the most, preferring the sandwiches and chops, while Nana and I snack on some crackers, chorizo, and fruit.

Watching them both makes me thankful for the habit of packing more food than needed. Not so much because of Abby but more because as time goes by, Dylan's hunger increases greatly. But then again with the amount of energy he has, no wonder.

A little after the food and some relaxing time under the sun, Dylan has finally had enough of staying still. "Will you play with us this time around, Mum?"

With a grin, I ask, "Football?"

His answer is a barely visible nod, followed by him jumping on his feet and picking the ball up.

"Can I stay here a little longer?" Abby intervenes, with her head close to Nana's lap and half-closed eyes. "I am still a little bit tired."

"Of course!" I smile at her before getting up, too.

"You're such a girl." Dylan rolls his eyes, and Abby sticks her tongue out in response.

"Don't be mean." I tap him lightly on the shoulder in warning before beckoning him to the green field ahead of us so we can pass the ball around between us.

For half an hour, I run around with Dylan. The ball is passed back and forth for a while until he decides he wants it to be one against the other. The little rascal gets me to trip quite a few times with his newly learned tricks: the crossovers. He's skilled, I'll give him that.

Maybe signing him up for a local football team could be a good idea, especially to get all of that energy out. He loves sports, moving around, and he is becoming quite the athlete.

Just like him.

The sudden thought reminds me of easier times. Back when my best friend and I used to play like this. We were inseparable ever since we met for the first time, up until the moment I had to leave.

Even though, for a while, Jake had me caught up with everything that was happening in my absence, it became so unbearable that I eventually asked him to not talk about it—*or him*—anymore. It's a decision that will haunt me to the very last day of my life, but back then, I had no choice. Not in my eyes.

All other options were going to be messy and more painful than what it was. At least, that's what I hope. In the end, putting Dylan first was what made up my mind.

But I wonder—almost every single day—does he look the same or has he changed? Are those blazing blue eyes as soft as I remember?

How about his body frame? Taller and bulkier than he had been? Is he still caring, or was I the cause of a bitter side being brought to the surface?

For a long time, I believed firmly that he was my soulmate. But maybe we're more like those star-crossed lovers you read about in romances because I know...there's no going back from this now.

If there are relationships that ever get to a point beyond repair, this is it.

"Mummy, you're distracted," Dylan whines, bringing my attention back to him.

There's a frown on his face, showing how displeased he is with my mediocre performance. He's so expressive it hurts.

"I am tired, baby."

This boy never runs out of batteries. But I do. Not to mention I still have work tonight. By the time my body finally hits the bed tonight, I'll be exhausted, but just watching his smile and happiness today will make it worth it.

"I'll call Abby, then," he huffs, annoyed.

Laughing, I turn around, walking to the towel where Nana and Abby are. My feet take a couple of steps before a familiar voice stuns me in place.

"Willow? Is that you?"

FIVE
Willow

IT'S NOT LIKE I PURPOSEFULLY HIDE DYLAN OR THIS INTIMATE part of my life. But ever since everything happened, I've grown to appreciate my privacy more than ever. Especially when it comes to my son.

There's a protective side of me that was born at the same time he was. So, the fact that Johanna coincidentally just found me with him in the park brings some *unease.*

"Willow? Is that you?" I turn back to see Johanna and another girl in a set of workout clothes. Tight shorts and a sports bra barely cover her fit frame. Her friend, with long blonde hair and bright blue eyes, is dressed similarly.

Johanna is *drop-dead*-gorgeous with a hot body, and her friend is not far behind. If I didn't have too much to worry about in my life now, I'd be jealous. *So jealous.* Between juggling work, school, and Dylan, all the free time I have left is meant for my son or sleeping.

"Hey, Johanna." I try to smile at her. "I wasn't expecting to see you here."

She has been nothing but nice to me ever since we met, and yet, I just can't get completely comfortable around her. Not yet, at least. Once upon a time, there was a younger version of Willow Hanlon who would trust easily. Naïvely.

Not anymore.

"Yeah, I love to run, so I come to the park a lot. It's also a good way for me to cure hangovers." She chuckles. "This is my friend, Sofia. We always work out together."

"Hi," I greet, and so does she. She smiles at me, widening a white set of perfect teeth, putting me a little more at ease.

"How are you?" she asks, but before I can answer, Johanna cuts in.

"Oh my god!" Her hands flail chaotically around her, to match her excited reaction. "You're the perfect person for—"

As if fate knew I was getting off too easily with something—*anything*—Dylan interrupts us by abruptly stopping by my side, eyeing both girls curiously. They look back at him, Johanna with a visibly confused expression on her face.

Is she going to judge?

"Who's this little one?" Sofia is the first one to break the awkward silence, flashing him another megawatt smile. With an intrigued glance at me, she crouches down to his height, and Johanna weirdly follows.

"I'm Dylan," he announces, his chest puffing in pride.

As if listening to him talk just broke a spell, she unfreezes, smiling at him for the first time, and greets him back, "Hi, Dylan. I'm Johanna. Nice to meet you, young man."

Her hand extends to him with the obvious intention of shaking his hand, but my son, being the charmer he is, takes her hand and tugs it close to his face, kissing her knuckles. Johanna's eyes widen in shock for a moment before she cracks up laughing. Sofia copies Johanna's actions, laughing even harder when he does the same to her.

My cheeks set a flame, and I bury my face in my hand with a defeated shake of my head. This is what I get for letting my big brother be a bad influence on my son. Note to self: do not let Jacob Hanlon babysit Dylan. *Ever!*

"What a gentleman. Who taught you that?"

"My Uncle Jake," he proudly admits, confirming my suspicions. "He says this is how a gentleman should greet pretty ladies."

Seriously, what things has my brother been teaching my five-year-old kid? Jacob Hanlon is a man-child, that's what he is. A hazard to all children around the world, the kind who's not above using them as bait to seduce a pretty woman.

Jesus Christ.

Johanna clears her throat, catching my attention again. They're both now standing, even though Sofia is still focused on Dylan's cuteness. Johanna is looking at me instead with a curious glint in her eyes.

Then he, suddenly bored with the situation, says goodbye and happily runs back to where Nana and Abby are.

"Dylan is..." I pause, taking in a deep breath. "My son. I study, work, and raise a kid. There isn't much free time." I chuckle awkwardly.

Her mouth opens and shuts a few times, words evading her. Standing like a gaping fish, it's safe to say she looks shocked.

"I didn't know," she comments.

"No, I know..." I trail off. It's not something I like to talk about very often.

"He is so handsome, though," Sofia comments, unfazed by the rising tension.

"Thank you."

"Well," Johanna claps her hands together, a clear sign of how uncomfortable she is. "I was going to ask, are you working for the next few days?"

"Yes, why?"

"I am going on a date with this guy I really like, but I'm nervous. If you wouldn't mind, could we meet there? That way I'd be more at ease, with a friendly face around?"

"Sure." I smile tightly. "Let me know when it is so I can make sure I'm working. Yeah?"

"I'll text you." She beams. "Alright, we're going to continue our workout."

"Of course, girls." I nod. "Have fun."

They say their goodbyes and run off on the park's pathway, disappearing into the distance. It's only when they're out of my sight that my body finally starts to relax a little.

Just when you think the bad luck streak has ended, it comes back to bite you in the ass. Not literally, of course, but things *have* been running smoothly. Despite the professor that hates me for no apparent reason, things have been going rather great.

Of course, something had to give.

Dylan has been feeling sick for the last two days. And even though Shilah has given me two days off to take care of him, school is trickier.

My body protests against my brain with every step that I make. Or is it the other way around? In the end, I'm at war with myself. The thought of not being able to tend to my baby is making me sick. *Physically.* My hands are clammy and shaky with nervousness, and my stomach is funny, too, churning heavily more often than not.

Beads of sweat are profusely running down my forehead by the time I get to school. Even if Nana has promised me everything will be alright and that she'll call me right away if something changes, my head's not in it today.

Still, the phone stays with me today. Just in case.

Halfway through the day, Nana has already reassured me a ton of times that everything is still the same. I have been glued to the tiny screen all day, worried sick. In the end, it is my downfall. *Literally.*

My body is knocked down by a sturdy wall, making me fall flat on my ass.

"Is there gold on that screen, Ms Hanlon?" Professor Adell's voice rings loudly in my ears, warming them—and the rest of my body—with his words alone.

"I'm sorry," I mutter as I stumble on myself to stand up.

His strong hand grabs my elbow, helping me up. His hold is gone as fast as it was on me, grunting a "watch where you're going next time" and leaving me here, dumbfounded.

"Good morning, Willow." I hear Johanna's voice to my right and see her approaching me.

Right behind her, Ethan and Hazel are walking in my direction, too. Like every other day, Ethan seems happy and good-humoured while Hazel seems to be grunting something at him, an annoyed expression etched on her face. They're complete opposites but seem to understand and respect each other's differences.

"Hey, girl," he greets when the three of them reach me.

"Good morning, everyone," I greet them all.

Hazel grunts something before turning her attention to her phone, suddenly finding it more interesting than the world around her.

"How are you?" Johanna asks. "You look tired!"

I sigh. "Dylan spent the night with a tummy ache. I barely slept with worry that he would wake up, and we'd have to head to the hospital in the middle of the night. Thankfully, he was better this morning, but he still stayed at home with Nana. But yeah...tired." I chuckle and she winces.

"Who is Dylan?" Ethan asks, a curious glint in his eyes.

"M-my son," I stutter.

He breathes out, smiling softly. "Damn, that's rough. I hope he gets better soon."

He's always so kind. I quietly thank him just as Johanna's words take over the conversation.

"God, I can't imagine how hard it is. You work, study, and have a son to raise on top of that? Damn, girl, you're like Wonder Woman."

A shy smile appears on my face in response those words. As much as I appreciate her praise and admiration, I feel anything but that. Especially considering how everything came to be.

"I am not because if I was, I wouldn't be tired." I chuckle.

"Well, if you need anything, just let me know." She winks at me before extending her arm around my shoulders.

I'm a petite woman in comparison to others. Especially around her fit and taller frame. I'm only five-two and Johanna might be around five-six or more, but it's enough for her to use my shoulders for support. I don't mind, though; she might be becoming a good friend to me, or so I hope.

"I second that," Ethan adds while Hazel keeps ignoring us.

I laugh, thanking them, but Johanna speaks again before I can say more, "Wait! We could schedule a friend's dinner night at my apartment around next week. What do you guys think?"

"I'm in." Ethan shrugs, a lazy smile on his face. "Hazel, too."

"No, I'm not," she cuts in for the first time, not even glancing up.

"Shut up," he counters back.

"I'll have to work around my schedule at the diner, and I'll let you know. If that's alright with you guys."

"Of course!" she squeals, definitely excited. "Oh my god, it's going to be so fun!"

We walk together towards the classroom we share this morning. We arrive on time, and it goes smoothly. As well as the second one. Exhaustion starts to creep into my brain, and by the time we sit down to start Professor Adell's class, not even the two espressos I had before are enough to help me fight it.

When the bell rings, I am already sitting down in my usual spot with Johanna by my side. The classroom is already filled since everyone knows better than to get on Professor Adell's nerves.

He enters the room, and I sigh.

"Good morning," he grunts while crossing the classroom from the entrance to his desk.

Placing all of his backup material on the table, his gaze travels all around the class. I would swear he lingers a second longer on me, but I could be imagining it, right? Just then, he starts to teach.

Has he always been like this?

Probably not. No one has always been like that. Life does it, it changes us. I, of all people, should be familiar with that fact. And this man right here... Something turned him bitter; I just know it.

The lesson's rolling, and it's a struggle. My line of thought keeps steering away from what I should be focusing on, my eyelids feeling heavier by the second. It's a battle just to stay awake. His gaze sweeps over me a couple of times, but thankfully, he ignores me as I try to focus all of my energy on this class. But it's no use.

"And with that, I'll want you to..." I zone out of his voice again.

Half an hour later, when half the class has already gone by, the unthinkable happens. My phone rings loudly, and everything freezes. Literally.

I innocently look around and feel all eyes on me, as well as Professor Adell's. Then, I look at my phone and my heart pounds in my chest for a second before I spring into action. I collect my things and start to rush towards the door saying, "I am extremely sorry to interrupt your class, but it's a family emergency, and I really need to—"

"Miss Hanlon, if you leave through that door, don't bother coming back this semester."

"Wha—" I interrupt myself. "Can you even do that?" My voice comes out clipped, my patience slipping away.

I need to go. My motherly side is screaming at me to just leave him stranded, but my educated side keeps my feet planted on the ground.

"I won't tolerate students trying to bail my classes on whims," he retorts.

Whims? It's my son!

"You know what, Professor Adell?" I snark back, for the first time in my life. I've finally had enough. "Do what you want. I'll answer to whoever I have to for 'bailing' on your class as you put it. It just won't be to you, that's for sure. I'd say to have a nice day, but with that bitter heart, I doubt that's even possible for you!"

I hear a few gasps to my side, but I am beyond caring at this point. I turn on my heels and rush outside, finally calling Nana back while I rush to my car.

She fills me in on how the pain developed into vomiting and fever, and the only emotion I can feel is panic. It feels like electric shocks run through my body with every hasty step I take.

Just when I am arriving at the parking lot, my shoulder bumps into someone's arm, almost sending me flying to the ground. The person mutters a curse word, and I say sorry, not giving them the time of the day.

"Whatever," he speaks, a deep voice rushing to my ears.

I need to get to Dylan.

I barely get my balance together before continuing to walk back to my car at a fast pace. I can't be of use if I fall and break something, can I?

However, a familiar scent stops me in my tracks. My heartbeat races and my eyes widen as I turn around to look at the male figure walking away. He's already far, but his tall frame with broad shoulders is clearly defined. The sun shines on his short locks, making me stagger back.

It can't be him.

He is three hundred kilometres away from this city, probably already starting his work as a doctor, as he always wanted. It's just someone who looks and smells like him from the back...

Dylan.

Deep down, in my mother's heart, I knew something was going to happen. I've kept my worries at bay because I knew Nana has been watching over him, but still, a mother always worries.

My brain doesn't register the signs of the changing season. The yellowish-brown leaves fall over the ground, often covering parked cars, the slightly chilled air that blows once in a while, or the way the sun is not as high in the sky as it used to be during summer. It all fades into the background as my brain focuses on driving to my destination.

Arriving at the hospital, my mind is still a deep mess due to the poor attempts at understanding why it is that my life always has to be so problematic, alongside the rush of getting to my baby boy and meeting him at the ER with Nana, in hopes that it's nothing serious.

SIX

Willow

"HOW ARE YOU HOLDING UP, BABY?" I ASK DYLAN.

It has been five days since I ran out of class. He caught a bug that affected his stomach and gave him a fever. With the medicine he was prescribed, he is already much better.

Thankfully, the doctor gave me a credential to deliver to college and Shilah, to justify the days I've been absent, taking care of him. Tonight, though, I have to get back to work.

"Better, Mummy. I ate today," he informs me proudly as if I haven't been hounding his every move.

My heart has been on my sleeve ever since this little one was born. The worry never fades, like that ever-present feeling of being a constant failure as a parent. We all feel like we're messing up constantly. Terribly.

It's his genuine smile that eases those fears. That blinding smile melts my heart every time. Especially when it's paired with that tousled brown hair and puffy eyes from napping on top of me.

Despite everything, I felt connected to him from the moment I knew I was pregnant, but Nana was right. There isn't anything in this universe that can beat the feeling of when we get them in our arms for the first time.

There was a shift in the deepest parts of my soul. Which might be stupid for some, or maybe it doesn't happen to others. I didn't believe it either, but when those tiny eyes opened wide and his frail wails settled at the sound of my voice, the only thing I could do was cry.

The tears flowing were unstoppable. For everything that it was and especially for what *wasn't.*

"Mum?" His cold hand on my cheek catches my attention. "Can we watch another movie?"

We're still on the couch on the spacious living room. The walls are all stark white with two big windows on each side of the brown wooden doorway. On the opposite side of the room, in front of us, there's the obnoxiously huge TV that Jake gifted us last Christmas, claiming his godson needed a proper set-up to watch the Lion King.

Nana let me choose the design and placement of the shelves on that same wall, alongside the dark grey cabinet underneath the TV.

Dylan's leaning onto me, ready to keep on watching movies nonstop for the remainder of the night, but I am already dressed and ready to leave for work at any moment now. There's some relief in knowing he is doing better, even though I'll be worried all night.

"Not tonight, baby. I have to work."

"Ugh," he whines as his head falls back on the grey couch. "I wanted to watch a movie!"

"How about we do that during the weekend?"

"If we have to..." he sighs, still very annoyed.

"Will you be okay with Nana for a bit?"

"Yeah," he groans, fussing around the couch.

Dylan is not the kind of kid who is afraid to show how he is feeling. Whether it's through words or actions, he'll let everyone know. He's getting better at communicating, but there are still a few moments where it feels like he is going backwards. Just like right now, being unhappy about my departure.

"I promise that during the weekend, I'll let you watch whatever you want."

One eye opens, curious, then the other, and when I nod in reassurance, that million-dollar grin of his shows up.

This light shade of blue is my synonym for love, for different reasons. Surely because of this little boy, but also because they eerily look just the same as the ones I fell in love with all of those years ago.

The thought itself makes me sigh in nostalgia. The word "*Saudade*" comes to mind again because it's not translatable and it conveys exactly what I have been feeling for so long. This huge dark gaping hole in my heart can only be soothed by my son.

Still, it's not healable. Not without *him.*

"Okay." He gives in, bummed, and—thankfully—takes me out of my dark thoughts.

"Dylan!" Nana calls him from the kitchen.

"Yes, Nana," he screams back.

Jesus Christ. It's like this every time.

There's no use in scolding them about yelling around the house because they have gotten to the point where they ignore me. They probably do it on purpose just to get a rise out of me. The few times Nana hasn't ignored me, she waved me off by saying that she is old, almost deaf, and has every right to yell.

These two love to get on my nerves a little too much, that's for sure.

"The cookies are ready! I need my professional taster to certify the quality."

Dylan doesn't even answer; he simply runs to the kitchen like he's the Flash. The mention of food is enough to have him wherever. He'll fly if he needs to.

I chuckle before sighing. These two will be the death of me, but I love them. *A lot.*

Going back to my messy bedroom, I pick up my bag. The double bed is still unmade, with the rosewood-pink-coloured cover all twisted out from sleeping here with Dylan. Since he's been sick, I have been allowing him to sleep until late and getting lazy cuddles afterwards.

Looking into the full-body mirror, I remember Johanna's request. Last week, she begged me to not miss work today because it's her date, and she needs all the support she can get. I even received pictures wanting my opinion of which outfit she should wear.

How would I know what's appropriate? The only dates I've been on were with...*him.* Whenever I had issues with what to wear, he'd kiss my forehead and say I'd look beautiful in a trash bag. In the end, I tried my best, but as you can imagine, my sixteen-year-old closet was nothing like a twenty-two-year-old one. And obviously not like Johanna's.

"God, I miss him," I whisper to myself, my hand rubbing at the skin right over my heart.

People say the heart doesn't hurt, but it does. So much. In addition, my eyes sting from trying to keep the tears at bay.

No way, they're not coming out.

I manage to blink them away after a few deep breaths. I've shed plenty in the past, and it has changed nothing. In the end, I made my bed, and now I have to lie in it.

I was broken long before I left—especially in the head—but leaving him destroyed me beyond repair. Not only my heart but my soul.

I just hope he has moved on with an amazing girlfriend.

Ugh, girlfriend?

The mere thought of him having one feels like someone is stomping on the shattered cracks of my heart. Still, I wish nothing but happiness for him.

"Enough with the pity party, Willow," I scold myself in a whisper.

As soon as I'm ready, I leave for work after kissing Dylan on the forehead. The sun's setting and the traffic is mostly gone, allowing me a light drive to work. The streets are still quite packed, though; Porto is the second biggest city in the country, and at the end of the day, it seems to fill with people from everywhere, eager to go out or go home.

As I drive, I notice more of the artificial lights and the buzz created by moving people and cars. I spent six years in my nana's small town, after leaving Lisbon, and it made me forget how soothing this controlled chaos is. Sure, it's not my home town, the capital, but it's close enough. And just as beautiful!

When I arrive, things are still calm since it's Tuesday. It's also a good day for Johanna to have her date. With fewer people, there'll be a shorter waiting time for tables and less noise.

"How's the little guy?" Shilah asks as soon as I get out of the staff room while tying my apron around my waist.

"Much better. Thank you so much for asking."

"You have to bring him one of these days. I want to meet him." She winks at me.

"Sure, we'll set a day to eat here on my day off so you guys can meet him or something." I smile at her. "Now, what do you need me to do?"

"Tables three, four, and five are almost done. If you can keep an eye to get them cleaned as soon as the customers leave and that's it." She beams, and I nod, going into work mode.

The shift goes by quickly, and when the time for my break arrives, I take advantage to go outside and see how Dylan is feeling.

The rhythmic ringing is interrupted by a whiny voice, "Mummy, are you coming home already?"

"Not yet. I still have a couple of hours of work. How are you feeling? Are you feeling better?"

I hear shuffling and then Dylan's voice returns to the phone, "I am alright! Nana put the Lion King on for me to watch."

"Of course." I chuckle. It's his favourite. "Did you have dinner yet?"

"Nana tried to give me soup. I hate it." I can almost imagine the frown on his face. Dylan is not a fan of soup.

"I know, but you have to eat something so you can get better."

"I know, I know," he groans.

"Don't be stubborn, okay? I have to go back to work now."

"Okay, Mummy. I love you." I hear some background noise to my side but ignore it since I am already about to hang up.

"I love you, too."

Sighing, I lean my head back onto the wall. There's a little relief to the fact that he hasn't gotten worse, but if it's not going away too, I probably have to take him to the doctor tomorrow. The problem is that this kid has such a strong hate for hospitals, it's almost unreal.

He might very well punch or kick the doctor if he gets irked up just enough. It wouldn't be the first time.

"Shouldn't you be working?" The now-familiar and gruff voice startles me.

I clutch my hand to my chest and turn to my right-hand side to look at the person I've been dreading seeing since school started. Professor Adell. I swear this man's snarky comments and hostile behaviour are not what I need tonight. But, of course, life couldn't get too easy, could it?

"I work, Professor. I am using the time from my break to make an important call." I look at my watch, and even though I still have five minutes left, I feign surprise. "Would you look at that? My time is up."

"So, you use your work breaks to call on your poor little boyfriend? I heard he is sick, can't he stomach the flu without you? You surely can be apart for a few hours while you work...or not?"

I scoff at the ridiculous speculation. Of course, he'd think I was calling my perfect little boyfriend. When will this man stop making assumptions about me? He has this image in his head where I have the perfect world, where I never had to work for what I have or what I want. He's made-up a la-la-land where everything was given to me on a golden platter.

The creativity is there, in that dark brain of his, I'll give him that. But I won't give him what he wants and lay out my life or react to his provocative actions. Why is he doing this in the first place?

"This is not professional behaviour," he snickers.

Oh, because his behaviour is?

"Is that how you're going to act when you graduate and find a job? I mean, does your boss even know how attached you are to your phone?"

I fist my hands by my sides and clench my jaw. One can only take so much...right?

"My employer is very well aware of my behaviour and my phone calls. Let's not forget that I am free to spend my break time as I wish. And that, *Professor Adell*, is what she'll probably tell you if you want to make a complaint." With a final huff, I turn my back to him and head to the staff room, leaving him—hopefully—dumbfounded by the entrance.

When I come back out, I expect to see his grim face seated down by one of the booths, but he's nowhere to be seen. That knowledge itself is a relief because it means he won't be taunting me anymore tonight.

Maybe I was too harsh on him? I didn't mean to be, but he was pushing my buttons tonight, and with Dylan being unwell, I don't have the patience to deal with his tantrums.

The problem is that I'll have to face him tomorrow in his class.

Great. Just great.

A little later, I'm busier to the point that I don't even see Johanna come in and sit down. I'm finishing up a request from a couple when I see her wave like crazy to catch my attention.

A chuckle leaves my lips as I signal for her to give me a couple of minutes while I leave the request for the kitchen. Once I'm done, I head to her booth, sitting down since it's calm at the moment.

"You came alone? Where's your date?" I ask, looking around.

"He told me he'd probably be a bit late because he's coming directly from his shift at the hospital, so I told him to meet me here instead of picking me up," she huffs.

"That's what you get for fetching a doctor." I laugh at her.

The fact that her date is working at the hospital reminds me of him and how he wanted to do it, too. But I need to shut it down right away. There is no need to have a blast from the past in the middle of my shift.

"I know but he's so, so handsome, Willow; he has these amazing blue eyes. You can't even imagine."

I freeze. *Is this a sign to not forget my past?*

It's probably just destiny trying to remind me of how much I messed up. As if I didn't know already.

I want to tell her I can imagine it because I keep close and often recall the memories of the most amazing ones I've seen myself, too. But instead, I shake my thoughts away and focus back on her.

"Well, while you're waiting, tell me how you met him. I still have a little bit of time!"

"A party right before classes started." A dreamy look settles on her face as she looks up at the ceiling, most likely recalling the moments. "He was out on the back exit of the dance club. I was so sweaty after dancing and went there for some air, I had kept an eye on him so I knew I'd meet him there... And there he was. Alone, broody, and so damn hot."

My eyes widen. That seems...dangerous.

"I was sassy, and he was, too. One thing led to another and...well, he recently called to set us up for a date so, he must like me." She beams. "I am swooning. For real!"

I chuckle and am about to tease her for being head over heels when a lady calls me. I apologise to Johanna and promise to come back as soon as I can. After helping her, another client asks for me as well before I go inside to help Shilah bring the beer keg upfront.

When I'm finished, I see Johanna. Her eyes are sparkling and her smile is wide at the guy in front of her. His back is to me, so I can't see much but a mop of dark blond hair from the top of the booth. For a second, I hesitate, not really knowing why. Then I shake the funk away and grab my notebook, ready to get their order.

Not looking at them right away, I greet them, "Good evening, what can I get you?"

My focus is inside my apron's pocket, where my pen lies.

Once I finally find it and my eyes rise, I stop moving. And so does the world. Time and people cease to exist as I focus on the sight in front of me.

It can't be *him*. It shouldn't be him. This is supposed to be my fresh start, my final opportunity to have a semblance of normalcy. Only for fate to come and prove to me that I deserve no such thing.

My eyes blink in disbelief as my heart stops and restarts a few times. Am I hallucinating? Or is this real? His body goes rigid when his eyes lock on mine, my breath catching in my throat.

He's staring back at me, straight into my eyes. The most beautiful pair of blue eyes I've ever seen. The original ones I can't seem to forget, and they're angry.

SEVEN

Liam

MY BREATH HITCHES THE MOMENT MY EYES FOCUS ON THE FACE I thought I'd never see again. And the sight of her brings back memories I have been spending too long trying to bury in the deepest, darkest parts of my brain…and heart.

"Liam, I don't understand this," Willow whined, looking up at me with begging doe eyes, making me chuckle.

She was sitting on my bed, in between my legs with her back on my chest, while I explained some equations to her. This girl was amazing with our mother language, English, Literature, History, Geography, and even Science or Biology, but when it came to Maths, it was like her brain froze.

Ever since we met, as toddlers, we had been inseparable. Then, just at the start of high school, we began the tradition of studying together. It had been like this for years, where I helped her with numbers and she helped me with the rest.

It was crazy how well we seemed to fit most of the time. In school, our sense of humour, our personalities. Everything, honestly.

Even with how different we were—me being more outgoing and outspoken while she was shy and quiet—we got along so well…

It all felt so right.

After months of having tried to ignore this, trying to brush past all the butterflies and nervousness she created inside me, I couldn't anymore. It was way past a teenage crush because I knew she felt the same. I saw it in the way she looked at me, the way her touch lingered when we were holding hands or when we hugged. Hell, even just the fact that whenever she was uncomfortable, she would seek my touch to ease her mind.

I was her safe place, just like she was mine.

We were young, and although my brother used to tell me there was a whole ocean of girls out there, no one else made my heart beat this wildly. She was the only one to make me nervous enough to stutter my words when I was, otherwise, the most confident asshole around.

I didn't know what it meant—its depth or dimension—but I knew there wasn't anyone else. Not for me.

And at that moment, that day...I needed more. I wanted more. I wanted her to be my girlfriend.

"Come on, Lo. I'll explain one more time, and then you'll answer the question on your own, okay? I know you can do it, baby." I kissed her cheek and pretended not to notice how she blushed right after.

Slowly, I had been leaving hints here and there. Some endearing names that I wouldn't usually use and being touchier with her. Especially with kissing. I hadn't had the balls to kiss her on the mouth yet, but...maybe soon. Willow never shut me down or pushed me away and that helped my confidence grow.

Soon.

Barely focusing on the subject, I got through another fifteen minutes of explaining it to her. When she finally got it right, she squealed in happiness, and my heart warmed instantly.

"I did it! I did it. Thank you, Liam. I couldn't pass this subject if it wasn't for you!" She turned around and hugged me tightly.

I wrapped my arms around her tiny waist and pulled her up for a proper hug. Part of her shirt rode up, exposing some of her porcelain skin, and I couldn't help but press the pads of my fingers against the swell of her hip. Soft and warm.

With a tight squeeze, she giggled and tried to lean back a little in an attempt to look better at me. The way the bottom half of our bodies pressed together wasn't lost on me, and it didn't let her get much distance since I could still feel her breath hit my face.

"You know I'd do anything for you," I whispered while tucking a strand of her chocolate-coloured hair behind her ear.

She blushed again, and if I weren't hypnotised by her beauty and delicateness, I'd tease her.

The moment her shyness dissipated a little and she gained the courage to look me in the eyes, the entire world came to a halt. This happened every single time. It was as if Chronos had a soft spot for us, momentarily stopping his hourglass just so we could get lost in each other.

Her plump lips parted, bringing my attention back to her. Damn, I wanted to kiss her. When our eyes locked a second time, her pupils seemed larger and my fingers rose to her collarbone area, gently grazing her skin.

I leaned in closer, tentatively, giving her the chance to break the moment if she didn't want this.

My hand splayed, wrapping around the curve between her neck and shoulder, where it was warm and silky. My thumb kept rubbing the soft skin on her neck, feeling her frantic pulse underneath–just like mine. Always in sync.

Wild brown hair fell in wide waves over her collarbones and chest, framing her delicate face. It matched the colour of her eyes, the only contrast being her reddened lips. With the distance closing in, her scent filled my nostrils. Wildflowers and sun.

I couldn't get enough of her.

"Liam," she whispered before her eyes fluttered, and I took that as my cue. As her calling.

We kissed.

Her lips were soft and sweet like candy floss. It was overpowering. She always managed to overwhelm me. There was colour and light. There was warmth and comfort. There were fireworks blowing up all over my body, and I couldn't stop the shaking that overcame me when I pulled her closer to me by the waist, again.

It was like everything was crumbling around us while she kept building me up from the inside. Making me feel like all I needed was her.

If I was sure I liked this girl before, I surely knew I was crazy about her, then.

It can't be.

And yet, here she is...in the flesh, right in front of me.

At the worst time possible.

After so many years of trying to fill the void she left—*and failing.* After so long of succumbing to that self-sabotaging behaviour of fucking around with multiple girls and ignoring the wreckage she had caused, I finally found someone I am willing to give it a go with. A real chance.

Finally, the prospect of moving on and maybe—just maybe—finding something more and better with someone else was exciting. Johanna is the kind of girl I instantly felt attracted to. The moment we met at that party a couple of weeks ago, with her presence, unabashedly straightforward and funny. She was not shy at all and so certain of herself. I felt hopeful.

Johanna is the exact opposite of Willow. Not only personality-wise but also physically. A sign that it could finally be my chance at moving on.

Why couldn't I forget her after all of these years? I can't tell you. I mean, I can Love as deep as what we had doesn't just go away like that, even if we didn't know it back, then. Especially with it being unresolved—at least, in my mind.

But after all of these years, I had convinced myself she wasn't going to come back.

And the quest to find a "happy ever after" without her was *finally* on the cards. Why has she decided to appear now? *On my fucking date?*

W*hat kind of sick joke is this?*

Can life be this cruel?

Can fate be this much of a twisted fuck?

I would pinch myself to wake up from this nightmare, but I can't move. My body seems to have lost all connection with my brain to the point that I can't even speak.

We're both paralyzed, looking at each other.

Time has stopped running. The world has stopped turning, and everything else has faded away. Just like it used to happen all of those years ago when we looked at each other. Just like the first time we kissed. Just like when she told me she loved me, too, and we made love for the first time. And most certainly like when she disappeared off the face of the earth without an explanation or a goodbye.

She was my rock, my haven, and then she left me stranded. It was the final blow to my heart and brain. After all the promises we had made to each other, she broke them all when I needed her the most. Not being there for what came afterwards was the worst, and for years, I hated her for that.

I still do.

"Liam?" A feminine voice breaks me out of my trance, and I finally look at Johanna.

She's smiling, but it's visibly a forced one. She's probably thinking "why the hell would I be looking at the waitress during our first date?". I steal another glance from the corner of my eye before answering Johanna with an absentminded, *"Hmm?"*

She hasn't moved yet, besides her shaking hands plastered to her stomach.

"This is Willow, my friend from uni. She's in my class."

Willow.

I haven't heard her name out loud in such a long time. After everything, I refused to talk to anyone about her. It was a non-subject.

Wait...her friend? *Of-fucking-course!*

"I know who she is," I blurt before thinking.

Johanna gasps, and I can feel Willow tense, still frozen in place.

"How? She's just a freshman like me! Where do you know her from?"

"We grew up together," I spit the words, looking briefly at Johanna as I settle my glaring eyes back on Willow. Hers are pleading, but I ignore them. "We were best friends, but someone decided to just disappear off the face of the earth."

Mercy? Sorry, no can do.

"I—" Her voice is barely a whisper but it reaches my ears perfectly. Loud enough to reach my heart, making it skip a beat. Even my stomach flips.

Her voice is still soft, kind, and musical. Even better than I remembered. And it confuses the hell out of me.

How can my body react this way to someone I hate?

Fuck! Even after all this time?

"I can't do this. S-sorry." She bolts from our booth, and the last thing I can see is her hands tucking the notebook in her apron pocket, yet failing miserably as it tumbles to the ground.

But that doesn't keep her from leaving. Running away from me, once again.

I guess some habits are hard to break.

My hands start to shake in rage, and I clench them into fists while my jaw ticks. After all of this time, instead of being happy to see me, she bolts. I can feel my body tensing in that auto-pilot mode, wanting to go after her and find out what's wrong. It's so fucking tempting... but I won't.

She doesn't deserve it.

That black hole in my chest pours right open, and all of the anger I have been bottling up inside threatens to come out.

It reminds me that she's the one who owes me the truth and not the other way around. She's the one that has to come to me or just stay the fuck away once and for all.

Fuck. I can't stay here.

"Sorry, Jo. I need to leave. Can we do a rain check?" My voice is strained.

I am barely keeping myself together, and I know this amazing girl doesn't deserve to be discarded, but I seriously can't handle anything else tonight.

She nods and stands up at the same time as me.

"How did you arrive here? Do you want me to take you home?" I ask, just to save my conscience. Otherwise, the guilt would assault me later. I am just hoping she drove here.

I am one second away from snapping and breaking something.

"That's okay. I brought my car. Call me when you're free?" She gives me an apologetic smile while waving her hand, dismissing me.

"Thank you," I say in a low tone but strong enough for her to hear.

I bolt out of the diner as if the devil's on my tail, eager to get in my car.

I can't even control the shakiness in my body any longer. This dark cloud filling my brain is full of rage, grief, and...hurt.

Just when I was about to accept the fact that Willow is no longer part of my life, she barges right in. Once again leaving me in the eye of a hurricane, cornered with no way out. *Why?*

The fragile seams of my self-control break and one fist hits the driving wheel. From there it's a non-stop rage-filled assault on my car as I let it all out.

My hands hurt from the hits but not enough to ease the one raging on the inside. It's dark and consuming, destroying the rest of my decaying heart.

"*Fuck!*"

EIGHT

SEEING HER HAS BROKEN EVERY LITTLE PIECE THAT I WORKED SO hard to fix all of these years. Losing my brother was troublesome in itself, but it was something I knew was coming considering everything that was going on, then.

She had been the real problem for me. With time, things got slightly more bearable. The memory of her wasn't as strong. I couldn't smell her anymore nor remember the sound of her voice, and most importantly, the pain had become a dull nagging in my chest, giving me the illusion that I was on the right path.

Except, she showed up, sending all of that hard work out the window. And now, I am in this limbo with my brain trapped in the past, overwhelmed by the memories of when things started to crumble.

By the time I was sixteen, things had been awful at home for a while. My parents had always been very strict and set in their own prejudiced perspectives. And for quite some time, they had been extra harsh on my older brother, Mason. Particularly, my dad. Nothing he ever did was good enough or met his expectations.

The continuous pressure, the back-handed comments, and the indifference took a toll on us—on Mason especially. Even with my mother's futile attempts at diffusing the tension, he started spending less and less time at home to avoid confrontations. Except, that only worsened the short periods we all spent together.

In their eyes, there were only two paths for Mason: become a football player or go study law. When he told them he'd do neither and would take a gap year to figure it out, shit hit the fan.

First, my father cut him off, to force him to decide what he wanted, but instead, he got a job. *As a mechanic.* My mother almost had a heart attack because of it; I would have laughed if it wasn't so bad.

She tried everything to get him to quit and come back home, but my dad never gave in to her, telling her my brother needed to learn the hard way.

I was proud of him because it was his way of getting some independence and showing our dad that the emotional blackmail wouldn't work. However, things soured quickly. One morning, thinking they'd already be out, Mason came home to pick up some belongings of his, since he had been staying with some kind of friend for a few months. But my dad was still at home.

They immediately started arguing, with my dad following Mason around the house, throwing insults at him as he headed to his bedroom.

"Where do you think you're going?" my dad bellowed. "Answer me!"

"Out," Mason answered.

Alright, I need to step in before the situation gets worse, I thought, feeling the urgent need to de-escalate the situation.

"Mase," I called as I opened my bedroom door.

My brother stopped and looked to his right side, fixing his eyes on mine. Dark and sunken bags framed the bottom of his eyes, his stubble had grown, and his oily clothes gave him an unkept look. It worried me because I could see how tired he was and couldn't do anything to help.

Double shifts at the shop to save money for his apartment, he had said last week.

"Shouldn't you be in school, *kiddo*?" he rasped, sounding as tired as he looked.

"Just about to leave." I paused, looking at my dad's fuming face. He was holding it in because of my presence. Even within these four walls, appearances meant everything. But I wasn't going to stick around just to let my brother be a target again. "Do you need a ride?"

"Liam, go to school," Dad gritted. "Your brother and I need to have a conversation!"

"Actually," Mason started, completely ignoring him. "That'd be awesome, kiddo. Thank you!" His hand raised, landing on my shoulder. His movements were slow, and when he touched me, I noticed the tremors. They were light, barely there, but I could feel them.

Was he hungry?

"I'll meet you downstairs in five. Let me just get some things."

I didn't move, though. I knew better than that. Without another word, my brother walked up to his room at the end of the hall as my father followed closely. Once inside, they shut the door, and automatically, the yelling began.

Did he honestly think just because of the wall, I couldn't understand what was going on?

"I am not going to fucking law school!"

"Look at yourself! You're going nowhere with your fucking life. You're fixing cars when you could be studying at one of the top universities in the country!"

"I am not living off your money, am I? I thought the problem was me being lazy! But nothing is ever fucking good enough for you."

"You need to get your shit straight, come back home, and finish your education. What will people think of this? You look like a homeless person. An *addict*!"

Mason let out a sarcastic laugh. "That's all you care about, isn't it? Fucking appearances," he countered. "What will people think? I don't give a fuck about any of that! Why don't you care more about the fact that I could be struggling? How am I making ends meet? Do you even care about anything other than your own ass? This is just shitty parenting!"

A slow and deep thudding sound pierced my ear through the thin walls. *No.* It was more like a dry and dull echo, followed by a pained groan that made my skin crawl. Then silence. *Could it...*Instinctively, my feet took me closer to the door, and I pressed my ear to the cool wood, but all that could be heard were the harsh breaths inside.

"Look what you made me do!"

My heart sped up at the realisation of the possibilities–what it could mean. That was all that took for me to burst inside.

Mason was sitting on the edge of the bed, cradling his face with an enraged look. At his feet sat a black duffel back with a few clothes spilling out of it.

"Me?" He was still laughing sarcastically.

"Mase," I cut in, cautiously.

"Even if I did your bidding and went to law school, I'd be miserable trying to meet your unrealistic expectations! I'd rather be that homeless guy you say I look like rather than live under the roof of someone who *pretends* to care for me."

"Get out," Dad yelled. "Get the fuck out of my house, and don't you dare come back. You hear me?"

"Gladly," Mason growled in return.

It pained me to see my brother like that, struggling to make ends meet when my parents had more than enough to spare and refused to take care of him, just because he was not bending to their will.

He roughly grabbed the duffel back, swinging it over his shoulder and stalking out. With a last, disappointed look at my fuming father, I ran after my brother.

"Mase," I called him when we reached the driveway. "Come on, I'll give you a ride."

"It's fine, brother. I don't want you to be late for–"

I scoffed, "As if I care about that. Hop in!"

After a few minutes of consideration, Mason sighed and gave in, heading to my scooter. It was his–given by our parents–but he had decided to give it to me when he started working at the shop, knowing full well it would be taken from him, too. He told me back then, he would be working on a new ride for him at the shop, but...I didn't think it was true. Or at least, it hadn't happened yet.

I took the duffel bag from his shaky hand and put it in the compartment underneath my seat. At the time, I figured it was because of the adrenaline and anger of fighting because I didn't know better.

After getting in, we rode in silence through the city for a total of fifteen minutes. It was only when we got there and parked that I ventured a word out. I wanted Mason to know I understood him and had his back, but then again, how much could a sixteen-year-old do?

"They have a weird way to show it, but they want what's best for us."

Now, it was his time to scoff. "They want us to be the best to show off, otherwise, they'd know that what's best for us is to be happy and have loving and supportive parents."

"They don't know better." I sighed. "I am not excusing them but, Mase—"

"But what?" he gritted, eyes blazing on mine. "I need to lower my head and do what they say, is that what you mean?"

"No, but—"

"You know you're the lucky one, right? They dote on everything you do, everything you say!"

"That's not true, I was just fortunate to choose a degree they approve of. If I—"

"That's exactly why I am doing this!" he cut me off again, his words rushed and harsh. "If you were to choose something they wouldn't approve of, they wouldn't let you either. I am doing this to show you that you have other options, and they can't rule your life." He took a short pause for a deep breath. "*Our lives.*"

"I support you, brother," I told him. "I want you to figure out what you want, but I also see how miserable everyone is—"

"And how the fuck do you think I am, Liam?" His voice rose. His eyes were bloodshot and wide, almost popping out of his head. If he weren't my brother, he'd be scaring me, but I knew how fuming he was. "I was cut off, I had to find a job to survive and have been recently thrown out of my childhood house. Do you think you got it hard?"

"We *all* have it hard, Mason! One way or another!" For once, my voice boomed, matching his. "Do you think it's easy to see Mum and Dad fight every damn day? Ignoring each other right after. Not seeing you daily? Not knowing how you are, or knowing if you need anything? They're barely giving me any money, afraid I'll give it to you! Which I would, you know? All you'd need to do is call me. I'm just a fucking kid, thrown into the middle of this hurricane, and I am expected to go on as if my life was perfect. *When it isn't*!"

"Look at you," he spat, an unknown fire brewing in his eyes. "Acing every subject at school, being the golden boy at even more sports than I was. You are our parent's favourite, soon to be in med School. You even got your perfect little girlfriend, that innocent little thing that you prance around everywhere." The edge of his voice was eerie and terrifying. This was a side of my brother I had never seen before. "But poor little Liam has got it hard!"

It was at that moment that I should have known. It was the beginning of his downward spiral, but I was just too naïve to know. *To understand.*

"Mase—"

"You know what?" He pushed me aside and took the duffel bag out before continuing, "Thank you for the ride." His voice was final, not leaving any space for argument as he turned and left.

I followed him in a desperate attempt to get him to understand. I didn't want to lose my family. Especially not my brother.

"Come on, Mase. That's not what I meant."

"I know very well what you meant. Don't worry, brother."

"Mase!" I called but he ignored me, walking down the road to the shop entrance. "Mase!" I tried one last time only to be met with his middle finger.

That was the last time I saw him seemingly sober, at least. It fucking hurt after that but I still had my haven—*Willow.*

Until I didn't. And those events are just as ingrained in my brain. A couple of months later, my parents had been out for the weekend and weren't supposed to arrive until the next morning, so I had planned to have another romantic night with her.

But it was anything but a romantic night; it was the beginning of the shitstorm for me. It wasn't until it got close to the time we had planned to meet that I realised I still hadn't thrown away that old condom box that I had hidden in my bedroom, and it was empty.

After the almost heart attack we had when the condom broke once before, I *had* to go to the convenience store for a new pack—it was that important. However, since it was close, I made the mistake of walking instead of using the scooter. What was supposed to be a ten-minute walking errand, though, turned into an hour, and I was beyond livid.

The store was closed due to some technicality I didn't bother to check. At that moment, all I was thinking was getting it done quickly to go back in time to meet her. So, I rushed to the second closest one—a twenty-minute walk.

The fact I hadn't had a text or a call from her yet kept my mind at ease.

Maybe she's late, I had thought.

After a long line filled with restless sighs just to pay for a goddamn pack of new condoms, I rushed back, hoping to find her by the front door, waiting for me. Except, she wasn't.

What I found instead had my heart stomping aggressively inside my chest. The front door was ajar when I knew for a fact I had closed it before I left. Willow never had a key, so I knew it wasn't her right away

The lock wasn't forced which meant whoever had entered either had a key or knew how to get inside without forcing it. For a split second, my mind thought of Mason, but I shook it off. There was no way my brother would have left the front door open.

Especially if he was inside.

Placing the bag down, I silently walked a few steps ahead to try and peak in. My throat closed up as I pushed the door open. My eyes swept around the inside of the open space before me, and the sight of it made my gut churn. Some of my mom's precious porcelain vases weren't there, and the living room was turned upside down.

It was silent inside, and my main thought was if whoever was here heard me, I could be in real trouble. When I made it to my dad's office without making a single sound, I almost sighed in relief–if it weren't for the mess inside.

Even his safe, which was usually hidden behind a fake book shelf, was wide open and empty. That gave the perpetrator away. The only people who knew about it were my parents, myself, and my brother.

Dread flooded my veins as I rushed to my brother's bedroom, hoping to still find him there. *No luck.* His bedroom had his drawers and closet opened, with the few pieces of clothing left hanging from the wooden furniture.

Quickly, I sent Willow a text, telling her not to come because something had happened. I had to deal with the consequences of my brother's actions, after all. Calling my parents and the police was a priority, and by the time everything was wrapped up, it was well after midnight.

Willow's absence and lack of response were a small afterthought in the back of my brain due to exhaustion. I knew that come morning, I'd make it up to her. Grovelling in the morning and taking her to her favourite bakery in the afternoon would just be the first step.

I waited outside of school for a full hour in the morning, and her brother, Jake, never stopped at the usual spot to drop her off. Even after texting, she never answered. Calling was useless, too, as they went straight to voicemail. In the end, I gave up and went to class, arriving late. That whole day was torture.

Time had never gone by so slowly, and I had never realised how boring and annoying school was without her by my side. Some of my other friends made fun of me, saying I looked like a miserable lost puppy. And maybe I did because I was fucking worried. It wasn't like Willow to cut contact entirely. We were that disgusting kind of couple that talked all day long, even that one time she had the flu.

It was stressing me out. I couldn't focus on anything, my brain kept drifting away and there was this voice living rent-free inside my head, shouting at me to just get up and go check on her. And every time it happened, this gnawing feeling in my chest, this prickling sensation on my skin overwhelmed me.

Something was definitely *wrong.*

The afternoon classes were even worse. So right after school, I almost flew to Willow's house. The usual ten-minute drive only took five, and there was definitely some tire screeching as the scooter abruptly came to a halt close to her house.

Such was the eagerness, the rush, I didn't even turn it off before I ran up to her front door, knocking on it continuously. I probably looked like a madman to some. But I didn't fucking care.

It felt like forever until the lock finally clicked, and the door opened. I was ready to dash inside and look for her, but Jake appeared instantly, forming a barrier between me and the house.

"Where's Willow? Can you call her?"

"No," he'd answered. "She's sick."

Sick? She seemed just fine yesterday. The days were getting longer and temperatures were slowly rising. It was spring. The flu season was pretty much gone, and she had no allergies.

"Alright, I'll go check up on her."

"No," he repeated. Though the edge in his voice finally made me look up.

The Hanlons are fair-skinned, almost porcelain-like, but Jake, from spending too much time outside and on the beach, is the most tanned of them all. Yet, that day his skin looked like a vampire's. He was weirdly pale, and there were dark and deep circles around his eyes. If that wasn't enough, the scleras were reddened like he'd been crying, and his hair was tousled and oily, as if he had been running his hand through it far too much.

Jake looked like shit, and for a guy who loved looking good, this spoke volumes.

"What's wrong?"

"N-nothing," he stuttered. Then he looked around, avoiding my gaze before he continued, "Look, she barely slept with... fever and... I don't know. She's been sick. The doctor has been here and ran some tests. We're waiting for the results but she's sleeping right now—finally."

"Let me just peek into the room to make sure—"

"Are you telling me I can't take care of my sister?" he growled.

Shit. Jake was never that protective of Willow; not when it came to me. Probably because he knew I cared about her as much as him, but in a different way. He'd just leave a few playful hints here and there to let me know he had an eye on me, but I always shrugged it off. There was no way I'd ever do anything to hurt his sister.

"Shit, Jake. No! I'm worried," I sighed, trying to regain my composure. "She never answered me yesterday..." I trailed off, stopping when Jake's eyes and lips pressed together tightly, his jaw clenched.

A movement from underneath caught my attention, allowing me to see his fists clench and open a couple of times. When I finally looked up, shiny green irises were watching me intently, irritation burning in his eyes. He was upset but furious, too—I had never seen Jake so torn. He was always the life of the party.

"Jake, seriously..." I tried again. "This is scaring the hell out of me. Is she alright? Can I do something?"

"Sorry," he gritted out. "She'll answer you as soon as she can."

And with those final words, Willow's brother closed their front door in my face.

he touched. And while a part of me wants to break free, the other, tamed by trauma, is still keen on staying trapped in this loop.

"Do you want to be my girlfriend?" he questioned when our faces finally separated from a breath-taking kiss. Smiling widely, I eagerly nodded, saying yes. His face mirrored mine, and in the heat of the moment, he picked me up, swirling us around. Warmth filled my heart as both of our laughter spread into the peacefulness of the night.

Why does this keep happening? Why doesn't the pain just go away once and for all? Why do I let myself be a prisoner to my own pain? Why do I let it incapacitate me after so long?

"You see, Lo? We were made for each other, we fit so well." His slippery lips wandered all over my neck and shoulders, licking and biting, eliciting even more pain. I couldn't hold it in anymore, soft sobs broke from my lips and even more tears streamed down my face.

Dread slithers through my veins at the sound of every word told in his voice. Even if I know it's all in my head, it still steals all fight away from me.

"Are you sure?" His hesitation made me look back at him and nod. The sun hung low as we stared at each other intensely. The yellowish tone made his tanned skin glow, and his eyes shine more. We were a mess of tangled limbs and skin. It was hard to know where one ended and the other started, but all our sensations were heightened. "Lo, baby. We can wait." There was this bubbly feeling inside of me, being activated every time he touched me.

"I am one hundred percent sure.," I was, and there was no one I'd rather do this with. As he had said once, he was my forever.

It's a never-ending loop between the best and the worst memories. Both of which not letting me go, reminding me how fucked up I am.

His unfamiliar scent made me nauseous while his foreign and calloused hand squeezed my breast too tight, making me whimper in pain. My brain kept blaring alarming sounds in a final warning, and my past experiences let me know this was not what it should feel like. But at that moment, I was powerless, and all I could do was block my thoughts in a desperate attempt to prevent the gravity of this situation from sinking in. Because I knew, once it did, everything would be destroyed.

My body slumps further against the wall. These ghosts insist on dragging me to the depths of hell, scarring my soul even more. How much do I have to suffer before I can put it all behind me?

I was naïve to think a fresh start would solve all my problems. And having my past walk back into my present is proof enough. There's no escaping this torture.

I am unworthy of anything good. Dirty. Useless. A shell of what I should be, of what I used to be.

"Willow?" A faint muffled call finally reaches my ears, slowly bringing me back to consciousness.

I want to answer, but it's hard to free myself once the spiral starts.

"Willow, dear? Please open up."

My chest and scalp hurt, probably from fighting myself to make it stop. How I wish I could reset my brain from all the pain and hurt and be able to function properly again. After all of these years, I still can't.

Weak.

"Are you alright?" the same voice speaks but I pay no mind.

I can't.

"She's not responding."

"Willow? Darling?" the woman calls after a couple of knocks. "Deep breaths; do it with me. Focus on my breathing." The warm and familiar voice, Shilah's, finally reaches my ears.

Trying to follow her direction, I try to breathe in deeply, only to fail miserably and sob again.

"Keep trying! Don't stop, come on," she says, and I feel her grab my hand, placing it on her chest.

In. Out. In. Out.

In. Out.

In.

Out.

Slowly, my breathing slows down, and oxygen finally makes its way to my lungs. The surroundings become visible again, even if still blurry. When I can finally focus, I notice Shilah and Johanna crouched before me with deep frowns and sad eyes.

Oh, the pity...I hate it.

After two attempts of trying to stand up and failing, Johanna and Shilah help me up, sitting me down on the bench right next to the lockers.

"You're okay now, darling. No need to worry." Shilah coos, patting a humid towel down my forehead.

Johanna is completely silent with her intense gaze on me. With just one look at her face, I can see a million questions swirling in her eyes, even if she knows better than to ask at this moment. I am not sure if, after this panic attack, I will even be able to answer whatever it is she is curious about.

"Thank you, both of you. This hasn't happened in a few years. I am so embarrassed," I mutter between hiccups.

"Don't you dare apologise," Shilah fake-scolds. "Triggers happen when we least expect them." Her smile is kind but all I can focus on is Johanna's tight lips and sombre expression.

Even though Nana and Jake have an idea of what might have happened, no one ever pushed me to speak about it. Especially since I found a coping mechanism through Dylan. Shilah is not the kind to prod either, and Johanna and I aren't that close for her to have the courage to bluntly ask questions. I can see it in her eyes, she's drinking up as much information as possible.

Sooner or later, I might have to spill the beans, especially if I don't want her to think I'm going to steal her potential boyfriend.

My best friend. My first and only love.

The mere thought of them together makes me feel sick...Who would have thought that the only friend I've made so far in college would be falling in love with the man I first fell in love with?

"I'm sorry," I sigh, rubbing my face. "I just need a few more minutes to put myself back together, and I'll go back to work."

"Nonsense," my boss exclaims. "You're in no condition to go back to work tonight. Once you're ready, you can go home and have some rest." Her cold hand pats my back before she straightens. "It's calm tonight anyway; we'll manage just fine."

"But–"

"Not up for discussion! Will you keep her company until she's fit to leave?" she asks Johanna.

"Yes, of course." I hear her mutter.

Shilah exits the room, leaving Johanna and me alone in an awkward silence. A few minutes pass as I get rid of the last ragged breaths and stray tears. When I finally feel stable enough to face the rest of the world, I remember him.

Is he still waiting for me? Does he want to finish the conversation I owe him? Oh god...

"Is he—"

"He's gone," she cuts me off curtly, without even being able to look at me.

"I'm sorry." I sigh. "I ruined your date."

"Don't be. It's not your fault!" She finally smiles, but it's weak. "Maybe things happen for a reason. You clearly have an unresolved past. Maybe you finally have the opportunity to hash it all out and move on."

This girl makes me jealous of her, and not because she was just on a date with Liam—okay, maybe that, too—but because of her personality. The way she sees the world. She can still see the positive whereas I can only see the negative.

At this moment, it feels like the entire world is against me. But I've had enough of self-commiseration; it's time to put on my grown-up pants and suck it up. That's why, instead of letting myself fall back into that black hole or staying in here feeling sorry for myself, I try to smile back at her.

We stay in silence for a couple more minutes until Jo taps my knee, a clear message that she's had enough of being here with me. With an understanding nod, I take off the apron and grab my belongings from the locker before following her out to the parking lot.

The drive isn't long since the rush hour has long ended by now. In a matter of fifteen minutes, I am home, walking up to Dylan's room.

Instead of climbing up into my bed in my room, I manage to fit into his, cuddling him to my chest. He doesn't even stir as I accommodate the both of us in his tiny bed.

There's no way I'll be sleeping alone tonight. I need the comfort and warmth of the only good thing that life has given me. The only light created from the darkest period of my life.

Thankfully, his presence gives me a dreamless night, with his body close to my heart, and his touch on my skin, slowly healing the deep wounds that keep ripping at my heart. Tearing it open over and over again.

TEN
Willow

THIS PAST WEEK HAS BEEN ROUGH.

Sleep has been evading me, and schoolwork has been growing. With my heart a wreck and Professor Adell breathing down my neck, I don't know which way to turn anymore. The tiredness in my body and mind has been preventing me from focusing on what I should be—my school and work, besides Dylan, of course.

The only thing that has kept me from going completely crazy is that Johanna hasn't touched the L subject anymore. I can see the curiosity in her eyes every time she looks at me, the jerking moves or the opening of her mouth before she thinks better of it and stops herself. I know that sooner or later, she'll give in to temptation. I'm just grateful she is giving me enough time to...well, prepare myself.

Liam has always been on my mind, but now that I know how close he is, it's been impossible to not have all my thoughts consumed by him, the memory of him. Of course, it leads me to think about them together, if they're still getting to know each other, and to what point their relationship has developed. It hurts too much, realising he has moved on. Although it bothers me, I don't have that right. I lost all claims or rights when I decided to abandon him.

Even if it was my *only* option at the time.

Why did he have to show up? I had made my peace that he was out of reach a long time ago and that an *us* would never be in the picture again. But seeing him in the flesh, even more handsome than before, has moved something inside of me.

Liam is older. Long gone are the boyish features he had, even if he is still as handsome as he used to be. His bright blue eyes, even though they barely changed, are now filled with a weight he never had before. There's a maturity to the little lines etching onto his face that weren't there the last time I saw him. He is bigger, most likely taller and even though he has a different stance from the lively and naïve boy he was, he seems just as fiery and stubborn as he used to be.

It woke up feelings that had been dormant inside my heart. The dam broke, and all of it has been overflowing out of me ever since.

Love. Pain. Guilt. Regret.

"Hey, Willow. How are you doing?" Abby's mum greets me by the school's entrance, interrupting my self-wallowing.

At the end of the afternoon, we both wait outside for our kids to be back in our arms.

"Hi. Everything's alright," I lie. "And you guys?"

"We're fine. But you look upset. Are you sure you're okay?" she insists, concern lacing her eyes.

"Yeah, just tired, you know. With work, school, and Dylan, my days can be pretty draining." I give her a tight-lipped smile to try and ease her worry.

Since we moved here, she has never been a noisy neighbour, but since Dylan and Abby are so incredibly close, we've come to know each other more and more.

"If you say so..." She smiles back. "Look, here they come!"

Abby immediately runs to her mum, hugging her. Dylan walks a little bit behind, with slow-paced steps and slumped shoulders. The fact he is not running either, eager to go home—even if he now thinks he is too old and too cool to hug me—has me frowning. As soon as he reaches me and keeps still, quiet, and looking down at his feet, I crouch down to his height and poke his cheek.

"What's wrong, baby?" He just glances at me for a second, shrugging his shoulders and looking away.

"Nothing," he mumbles.

There's something wrong *alright*, but I won't make him talk in front of other people.

"Let's go home, then," I say, pretending I let it go. "Nana is waiting for us for the afternoon snack."

His eyes sparkle a little at the mention of food, but instead of hugging me, he directly heads to my car. I glance at Nina, and she's still watching me with concern in her eyes again, as well as Abby. With an awkward smile, I say my goodbyes and hold his hand, not letting him cross the road by himself.

When we reach the car, I open the door for him and let him hop in. After having him buckle up properly, I close his door and round the car to the other door. For the first couple of minutes, he's silent. It's really getting to me now because if there is one thing my son isn't, it's silent.

"Dylan, remember how Mummy always tells you to voice what you're feeling? What's wrong, baby?"

I'm watching him through the rear-view mirror, and he has his arms crossed over his chest with his serious expression looking out the window. At the sound of my voice, his eyes flicker to me before he gazes outside again.

Sighing, I patiently wait for his stubbornness to give in. Forcing would only make him uncomfortable and I want him to know he can talk to me about anything.

"Why don't I have a dad?" he asks out of the blue.

I freeze.

It's the one subject I have dreaded talking to him about my entire life, and it has come sooner than I'd ever expected. With a gulp, I think about what to answer because this is not the kind of subject I can give him the wrong information about.

"Why do you ask that, baby?" I try hesitantly.

He huffs.

"We had to talk about family today at school," he starts slowly. "I was the only one who didn't have a dad to talk about. Someone asked me why I didn't have a proper family, and..." His voice trembles, and he clamps his mouth shut.

Looking through the mirror, I see his eyes watering, and it feels as if a sword has just pierced through my chest. There's no worse pain than this one, that's for sure.

"Who did you talk about?" I ask, trying to lighten the mood.

"You, Nana, and Uncle Jake," he mumbles.

"Isn't that your family?"

"Yes, but they meant my dad. Even Abby has her dad! Then Brody laughed at me, saying I didn't have a family." With a shaky voice and watering eyes, I try to keep myself together because it's only making me want to throw driving to hell and just hold him.

"Well, that's not true," I sigh. "Families are complex and different, baby. Some families have a mum and dad, others only have the mum or only the dad, some have two mums or two dads, others even have none, just other family members taking care of them," I explain, noticing he's focused on me now. "You know that we can't control what happens around us, and sometimes we can't prevent the fact that someone who should be in our lives isn't."

He looks down at his hands with a frown, taking in what I am telling him.

"Is Uncle Jake my dad, then?" I'd laugh if this conversation wasn't this upsetting to me.

"No, baby. He is your uncle, my brother."

"But do I have a father or not?" he insists, and I press my lips together even tighter.

"Yes, baby."

"Then why is he not here with me, like you are?" His voice raises, and I can sense the frustration irradiating from him. "Doesn't he like me? Why doesn't he like me?"

He's getting anxious, and thank god that we're arriving home. I hastily drive into our driveway, push the hand break down, and turn off the car. As soon as it is secure, I unbuckle myself, twisting and leaning over my seat to unbuckle him. He easily clutches on to me as I clumsily pull him to the front and place him on my lap.

"Alright, can I tell you the story?" He nods eagerly, and I take a deep breath in before continuing, "I was really young when I discovered I was going to be your mum, and a lot of people were angry that I let that happen. My mum and dad—your grandparents—were really mad at me, baby, and I was afraid. Nana offered to help me, and I left even before your dad knew you were going to come." I try and simplify the story as much as I can. "So, he's not here, not because he doesn't love you, but because he doesn't know you exist."

He is still frowning, and I know what questions are brewing in his mind. The problem is that I can't tell him the truth—the complex and complete one. How the hell am I going to do this?

Before he can ask anything else, I add, "We were so young, baby, and it was a very complicated situation for both of us. I thought that by taking care of you by myself, I was protecting you both."

He doesn't answer me but keeps the side of his head supported on my chest, fidgeting.

"Well, I'm bigger, so he is too, right? Can't he meet me now?" he asks, and my heart aches at his request.

I had silently hoped he would never care about his father. I was sixteen and naïve, not thinking of moments like this one.

"I don't know, baby; I never saw him again. I don't know where he is." He looks up at me with shiny eyes.

Oh god, please don't cry.

"Mummy, I want to meet him. Can you find him?"

"I...I..."

My eyes sting, my throat burns, and my chest tightens.

I don't think I can.

It would uncover so much dirt and so many problems. But my son deserves the world, and he wants to meet his dad. The thought alone makes me crumble, and I hug him to my chest, crying silently onto his head. He hugs me back, without saying a word for a while. It's when I feel his hiccups that I realise he's crying, too, breaking my heart even further.

Then he leans away, looking at me with his pleading blue eyes and begs, "Please, Mummy."

How can I say no to him? I can't.

From the outside, one could call me a bad mum. What kind of mother robs her child of the right to meet their dad? A lot will decide that, and I think I get it. *I do.*

I would be fuming if my mum had kept me from my dad when I was Dylan's age. Growing up, I used to be a daddy's girl. My childhood would have been miserable without him. Even if, in the end, when I needed him the most, he didn't back me up.

I cherish my childhood memories and those shouldn't be taken away from a kid.

Even if my reasons for having fled are strong, they're not stronger than wanting to give my kid what he deserves. I am just afraid that what he wants is *not* what he deserves.

There is a lot I may need to face before he can meet his father, but if that is ultimately what he wants, I'll do it. There isn't any kind of hell I won't go through for him.

"Okay, baby. I will try and find him for you." I give in after exhaling a shaky breath.

His eyes light up, and he hugs me tight, repeatedly saying thank you while kissing all over my face. I'd laugh if I wasn't dreading the outcome of this.

ELEVEN

Willow

EVER SINCE THAT TALK, DYLAN HAS BEEN ASKING ME ALMOST EVERY day if I've found his dad. And every day, I feel ashamed to keep up with this lie. The truth is I haven't found the courage to deal with the problem that is his *father*. Every day, he gets sad and disappointed. It hurts so damn much But I need time, time to find the courage and strength to face this because as soon as the Davis family knows about Dylan's existence, I am in for one *hell* of a ride.

That's a given. *I know it.*

And maybe Dylan doesn't understand now why I did things the way I did, but I know that one day he will.

And to think, I thought life would be easier from here on out. *Ugh!*

I need to contact Liam; we both need closure. That's a fact.

In the end, he is right. No matter what happened back then, I should have told him I was leaving instead of blindsiding him. But the trauma had distorted my mind; all my brain was telling me was to leave, in a fight or flight kind of state, and to do what was best for me.

It all came crashing down when, weeks into my bedroom seclusion, my parents didn't stand by my decision to keep Dylan. Even with Nana's words and Jake's attempts to protect me, they were clear when they said that I either get rid of it or I had to get out.

At sixteen and pregnant, I made the decision that I thought was safest for us. How was I to trust Liam when the ones closest to me—supposed to protect and help me—let me down? Having to tell him the whole truth and going through the shame again? We were both kids, and putting a burden on him that was only mine to carry...it never felt right.

"Willow, darling, are you there?" My Nana's frantic voice takes my focus away from a sleeping Dylan.

I walk out to the corridor, careful not to wake him, and answer a weak, "I'm coming" before heading downstairs.

On the ground floor, I find her sitting down on the sofa. She's holding her cell phone tight in her hands and looking directly at the ground. Just the fact that she doesn't look up at me when I arrive is enough for me to know something's wrong.

"What's wrong?"

She looks up at me with a sad expression and shiny eyes—*are those tears?*

I rush up to her side and hold her hands, repeating my previous question.

"Uncle Todd has passed away, darling."

I gasp in shock. Uncle Todd was Nana's youngest brother. He was the funniest and most relaxed one of them all, a lot like Nana but in more of a hippie kind of style. Nana has five siblings in total, and she's the second oldest of them all. I can only imagine what she's feeling; I'd be devastated if something had happened to Jake.

I hug her tight, and she immediately lets the tears fall freely. Her body seems frail through her soft cries as I wait for her to let it all out. We stay like this for a few minutes as I wait for her to calm down. After a while, her sobs stop a little, and for a split second, I hope that the comfort of the hug might have helped. Hers surely have helped me a lot through my toughest times.

"Dear, I don't want to leave you unattended with Dylan, but I must go. I have to go say goodbye to my baby brother," she finally says.

"Of course, Nana." I don't even hesitate to agree. "Go. Don't worry about Dylan and me. I'll ask Abby's parents to take care of him while I go to work for the next few days." I smile weakly at her in reassurance.

"Are you sure?" she presses, and I nod. "Okay, I am preparing a bag to go back to Lisbon for a few days."

"Sure, Nana. I have to call Abby's parents, so go do what you have to do."

As she goes upstairs, I rush to call Abby's mum. Work will start in just a couple of hours, and I know this is probably awful to ask of them since I only leave work around ten p.m., but I have no one else.

"Hello, Willow! How are you?" Nina answers the phone in a cheery voice.

"Hi, Nina. I'm so sorry for disturbing you, but I have a huge favour to ask," I start. "My nana has to leave for a few days to help some family members, and I have no one to watch Dylan today or the next few days while I'm at work." I ramble like a mad person. "Would you guys be able to watch over him? Even if it's just for today; I'll try to find someone for the next few days."

Asking favours like these to otherwise strangers makes me uneasy, but it's not like I have a choice.

"Calm down, darling," she offers. "I don't mind looking after him for the next few days at all! But today is impossible, sweety. I'm sorry. We are already at my parents' for dinner, and it's an hour and a half drive. Even if we wanted, we couldn't make it there on time."

I am so done.

"Of course. I understand," I answer, defeated. "I am so sorry. Thank you so much."

"You're welcome, darling. We'll settle things tomorrow when we pick them up from school, alright?"

"Sure, have a nice evening." Hanging up in a hurry. Immediately, I call Shilah, explaining to her the situation and asking if I can make it up to them with extra hours next week. But like the amazing boss that she is, she suggests I bring Dylan along because it's a weekday and it'll be calm. The fact that her daughter is there helps because she can keep an eye on Dylan if we get too busy.

I swear that woman is an angel.

"Thank you, thank you, thank you!" I tightly hug Shilah as soon as I enter the diner with Dylan by the hand.

To say he is excited to come with me to work is an understatement. He is ecstatic. He's been jumping and thanking me for being able to come with me, and now, as I hug Shilah, he is thanking her, too.

We brought a couple of playing cars and colouring books to keep him busy for the next few hours. Shilah also insisted on us having dinner here, even though I usually eat before starting my shift.

"Nonsense!" She gently pried herself off of me. "Now, let me meet this handsome young man!"

"I'm Dylan." He happily extends his hand.

"I'm Shilah. Nice to meet you." He once again kisses her hand, and she puts her free hand to her chest, fake swooning.

Dear god, this kid will be nothing but trouble.

"Are you excited to spend time with us?" she asks, and he beams at her.

With a smile splitting his face, he exclaims, "*Yes!* Can I help?" His big blue eyes shine with curiosity, and I chuckle at his eagerness.

"Unfortunately, no, dear; you're still too young. But do you see that booth?" He nods his head eagerly, looking at the table she is pointing at. "It's everyone's favourite table, and you'll get that one tonight." She winks at him before continuing, "You'll even have dinner there. Are you up for a burger?" He nods while bouncing on the spot. "Good. Now, go sit up there. Hannah, my daughter, will be spending time with you for as long as she can, while Mummy and I start work, okay?"

"Yes, ma'am."

Hannah extends her hand to him, and he easily accepts it, twisting and kissing it. *The charm.* She giggles before telling me not to worry because she'll take care of him. Hand by hand, they go towards the booth and sit down across from one another. That kid has never been a timid one.

Quickly, I head to the staff room to get ready for work. There are still a couple of hours left until dinner time for Dylan, thank god I wasn't doing the last shift tonight.

As soon as I'm ready, I approach him and Hannah. He's sitting with his things spread across the table, talking to her animatedly.

"Baby," I call to get his attention and sit down next to him. "Mummy will be running around working. I will come to you whenever I can. Don't think that I have forgotten you, okay? Call only when you need something. In a little bit, I'll bring you dinner, and please don't forget: do not speak to strangers, yes?" He bobs his head and hugs me lightly, kissing me on the cheek at the same time.

"Now, little man, are we going to colour or what?" Hanna grins at him, and he promptly opens the book for them to share as I stand up and dive into work.

Just as Shilah predicted, the night goes smoothly, and in no time, I am giving Dylan his beloved burger.

Soon after he finishes his food, the place fills up a bit more, and as I get a little busier, my only solace is that when I look at the booth, Dylan is there with Hanna. She's nineteen and could easily be annoyed for having to babysit. Except, just like her mother, she's a total sweetheart, keeping him entertained. She's amazing.

It's easy to whine and complain about the problems we have in life, and even though things aren't perfect, I often seem to forget about the luck I have. Shilah and her family have been nothing but fantastic, supportive, and understanding since we arrived here. And that makes the work a whole lot easier.

I notice the beer kegs are empty, and since it's still not too busy, I take a bit of time to change them. I do it whenever I can to avoid having Shilah do it because of her back. She is not old but had an injury a few years back, so it's best if she doesn't carry anything heavy.

Not even ten minutes have passed since I last saw him but when I come outside and fail to see Dylan in his booth, my chest constricts.

Neither of them is there, and my first thought is to look in the restrooms. Failing to find them there either, panic sets in. Sweat starts to pour from me as I exit the women's toilets and search in the kitchen. Xico is there alone and looks at me with a frown. Ignoring his confusion, I head to the staff room and peek inside, but when I notice it's empty, too, I feel like pulling my hair out and throwing up at the same time.

"Shilah!" I call her franticly. "Have you seen Dylan?"

At that same time, Professor Prick decides to come into the diner, but I am too far gone to worry about his attitude. He can taunt me all he wants, today is not his day.

Or mine.

He strides toward me with confidence, but as I watch the door behind him, it occurs to me the one place I haven't searched for them yet: outside.

I scour the entire parking lot in a desperate hope of finding them playing together, only to find it empty. An eerie silence feeds the dread coursing through my veins. No rushing steps, not even hushed voices.

"Eleven-two," I mumble, repeating the Portuguese emergency number. "I have to call eleven-two."

The doorbell rings as I defeatedly rush back inside, tears brimming my eyes, threatening to fall at any moment. Giggles and a deep chuckle immediately catch my attention, and my eyes widen, only to be met with a worried Shilah hugging Dylan, and Hannah giggling side by side with my teacher.

Any other day, I'd be composed, but this battered heart can't take being scared like this, so I rush to them, ripping Dylan out of Shilah's arms and crushing him against my chest.

"Where were you? I was worried sick!" My voice comes out shaky as I keep him in my hold for just a little longer.

"*Stop,*" he whines and looks at me with an angry face. "I wanted to pee and Hannah took me to the toilet inside. She said the one out here stinks." He crinkles his little nose.

Ugh, I panicked for nothing. I checked the staff room, but I didn't enter to check its toilets, not thinking about them in my frantic state of mind.

"Dylan, please don't go anywhere without letting me know first. I thought you had disappeared." I hug him once again, and he groans a muffled agreement.

His face settles on top of my shoulder as he adjusts before asking, "Who is that man?"

And that's when I remember just who has been watching this whole show. My body tenses, and my brain spirals, going through the thousand ways he can taunt me from now on, having discovered Dylan.

But when I finally let go of my kid and turn around, facing him, he has an easy smile stretching his cheeks, the kind I have never seen before.

"Hey, buddy. I'm Arthur. What's your name?" His husky voice speaks first.

It's not the usual gruff dark voice he uses, no. While addressing Dylan, his tone is lighter, even playful.

"I'm Dylan." He puffs his chest and extends his hand to shake my professor's.

"I can see that." He chuckles. "You caused quite a commotion here, young man." He tuts, looking at me with a curious glint in his eyes. The cherry red of the blushing heat covers my cheeks under his intent gaze.

"My mummy worries too much. I was just at the loo." Dylan attaches himself to my leg, suddenly shy.

"Your *mum*?" Professor Adell glances quizzically at Dylan before he looks at me.

When our eyes lock gazes, his expression morphs into a shocking acknowledgement. Widened eyes and a slacked jaw tell me exactly what he's experiencing. What I don't understand is why. His mouth twitches as if he wants to stay something but can't utter a word.

Well, I guess that for once, I've left *Professor Prick* speechless.

TWELVE

Willow

THE COMMOTION OF SEARCHING FOR DYLAN STALLED THE SERVICE, causing many people to be waiting for their food or their bill.

Great, more stress.

"Hannah, I will need your help, at least until it calms down a little," Shilah tells her daughter. "I'm afraid you'll have to wait a couple of minutes, sir," she informs my professor. "All the booths are occupied and one is out of service, as you can see." She motions to Dylan's booth.

"Shilah, if you don't mind," I start. "I'll stick to this side of the restaurant so I am closer to him. Is that alright?"

"Sure, dear." She nods before turning back to Hannah while they agree on what to do and what to cover.

As I am about to go tend to a few clients, who are on the verge of finishing, Professor Adell finally speaks.

"I can look after him if you want." His words stun me in place.

"Ahm, there's no need," I answer way too fast. "I–I'll be around now. Thank you, though."

"It's not a problem at all," he admits, shrugging his shoulders. "Also, I need a table to eat, and he happens to have one. We can keep each other company." He scratches the back of his neck, clearly uncomfortable.

Is he even used to being with kids? I mean, he is a teacher, and I reckon that at some point, he has dealt with them...right? But his whole stance worries me. Is he being weird because he is uneasy with me, the kids, or the situation in general?

As his cheeks blush lightly and he looks away, I suppress a gasp. Is he...shy?

Surely, it *can't* be.

Stealing a glance at my kid to make sure he is still where he should be, I consider it real quick. I once believed this man only had bitterness in him, and yet today, I'm seeing a whole other persona in front of me. Still, having him watch over Dylan, as much as it'd help me, I don't know if I trust him enough.

"I mean, I can fix you a table in five minutes probably, if you don't mind waiting."

"There's no need. He seems like a laid-back kid; I don't mind it at all."

His words seem honest, making me feel torn, but as I look around and see the number of people still unattended, I give in. A nod is all he needs to head over to the booth and say something to Dylan. A second later, my son smiles, and Professor Adell sits down across from him.

With that thought still swimming in the back of my mind, praying that this won't come back to bite me in the ass later, I focus on work and tend to the customers that are waiting to pay. It's only when I am finally caught up that I realise I haven't asked the professor what he wants.

Turning in their direction, I stop once I catch a glance of them. It's so surprising that it has me blinking several times just to make sure it's true.

He's already eating a burger, but that's not what surprises me. He's talking animatedly with Dylan while feeding him fries once in a while. My kid is thoroughly entertained and munches whatever is given to him, despite having had dinner already.

They're both gesturing a whole lot and laughing alternately between themselves. It's the first time I've seen my son connect this easily with someone who isn't family or a kid his age. Though it isn't really surprising; my boy is the opposite of me. A social creature. But watching them warms my heart.

At least until my brain is invaded by his little weak voice, asking for his dad.

Is this what it would look like?

The two parallel images make me shudder. Neither of these possibilities are exactly welcome in my mind. In the end, both get him taken away from me. And that is something I wouldn't recover from.

Still, watching Dylan and my professor together feels like a slap on my face. It's an upfront show of how much I have robbed him. *Or them.*

But I *had* to.

And I can only hope that he'll understand, someday...

"Seems like he's good with kids," Shilah comments behind me, startling me.

With a defeated sigh, I turn to look at her. "I wouldn't know. He's never been nice to me, so I was reluctant to let him watch over him, but I guess..."

"Well, look how well that turned out. Sometimes, fate works in weird ways." She winks at me.

Automatically, the thought brings me back to Liam, and I visibly wince. It works weird alright. After leaving when I was young, the prospect of seeing him again was one chance in ten million. Still, we were able to choose the same city to study and live in without trying to. I mentally snort at the thought before a memory of when we were sixteen washes over me.

"Your dad will be fuming when he finds out," I muttered.

"Let him, Lo. You know damn well I don't need no private colleges; public ones are even more prestigious in our country, and you know it." He shrugged unaffectedly. "Besides, you're not getting rid of me that easily." He wrapped his arm around my shoulders, squeezing me into his side.

I loved the warmth of his voice and his dedication to staying with me through college as long as there was a medicine program. I didn't want to be away from him either, but this would have turned into a big problem. His parents only tolerated me because they were friends with mine, but deep down, I knew they didn't like me.

I could see it by the way they looked at me like I wasn't good enough. Sure, I was a quiet and shy girl with good grades, but I wasn't a genius nor the most beautiful girl around. And I struggled with numbers a lot; if it weren't for Liam, I would've failed math every time.

But Liam was adamant to stay close to me. Truthfully? That was all I wanted, too. I had been in love with him, my best friend, forever. I couldn't even remember when it started; it probably was love at first sight.

His parents were pushy with him about his studies and grades. They wanted him to be the best and go to the best college there was out there. They'd send him off to Oxford if they could, especially since Mason, Liam's older brother, refused to go to college and started working right away.

But every time I mentioned it to Liam, he shrugged me off.

"But still." I looked at our intertwined hands, avoiding eye contact. "You're giving up a dream college for me. I don't want you to miss out on anything."

"Lo," he called, and when I didn't look up, he gently pushed my chin up with his free hand, making me look up at him. "That's their dream, not mine. My dream is to be a fucking good doctor with you by my side. It doesn't matter where I decide to study."

I blushed at his words.

"And," he insisted. "I am not worried about that yet. We still have two years to decide and plan on which college we go to together." He squeezed my cheeks.

"If we go to the same one," I pressed.

"Well, if we can't go to the same one, we'll choose the ones that are closest." He grinned. "We'll make it work."

"Sure, Casanova. With all the girls falling at your feet, you'd forget me in less than a month."

I freed my face from his hands and tugged at one so we could start walking. Instead, his hand tightened the hold on me, pulling me back against his chest, awakening the dormant butterflies in my stomach.

"Baby, I could never forget you; not even if fifty years had passed by."

"It's safe for you to go home now." Shilah's words startle me out of my memories.

I stop cleaning the counter and look back at her quizzically. I had told her I'd stay until closing time to make it up to her.

"Look." She points at the booth where Dylan and Professor Adell are, and I gasp in shock.

Sure enough, he's sitting by Professor Adell's side, instead of across the table from him, with his head leaning on the side of his chest while one big bulky arm is wrapped around my kid's shoulders and the other holds a small pocketbook on the table. My professor's attention is focused on it, seemingly reading.

Are they reading together?

Without thinking, I approach them, only to be stopped by movement. The book is closed gently on top of the table, and Professor Adell rotates his head, looking at me and shushing me. My eyes widen, and I get even closer to confirm my suspicions.

Dylan is snoring softly, nestled into his side.

"When he learned I'm a Portuguese and Literature teacher, he asked me to help him with his reading," he whispers. "He told me he wants to start first grade knowing how to read, and after a few minutes of me reading to him, he fell asleep."

Oh my god.

"Thank you so much for looking after him. This won't happen again. I know he can be a handful sometimes," I mutter, embarrassed. "I'm done already, so I'm just going to change quickly, and I'll be back to pick him up. Is that okay?"

"Sure, don't worry." He nods before opening his book back up.

Without another word, I head to the staff room with a frown etched onto my face.

This man is giving me whiplash.

He was nothing but awful to me since the beginning, and now, he's being nice and helping me out?

All I can think about is...why?

When everything's properly folded inside my locker and I check I have everything in my purse, I head back outside, ready to pick up

Dylan and carry him to the car, but to my big surprise—once again tonight—Professor Adell is already standing up with a sleeping Dylan in his arms and his big jacket over his small body.

Dylan's chubby face is flushed and squashed against his left shoulder while my professor's arms hold him from under his bum. He is waiting casually close to the exit, talking softly with Shilah as if my kid weighs nothing. Something in my chest warms and my stomach flips.

For a second, the feeling has me hesitating. But not understanding why, I quickly shrug it off and walk toward them. All conversation ceases the moment I arrive next to them, and Shilah quickly kisses me on the cheek before going behind the counter again.

"Ahm, I–I can take him from here," I stutter.

Smooth, Willow, real smooth.

"Nonsense, I'll follow you and put him in the car if you're okay with it. He's a big guy." He gives me a small tight-lipped smile.

I freeze.

He smiled. *He smiles.*

The corners of his eyes crinkle just a tad, and it rejuvenates him for at least five years. The man is handsome, even more so with a tiny smile on his face. I can only imagine how much younger he'll look with a full laugh.

"Shall we?" He breaks me out of my trance.

"Yeah, sure," I answer and hold the door open for him, since, you know, he's carrying my kid.

We arrive at the car in no time, both in silence. There, I unlock the car, and he places him down on his chair, buckling him in and straightening his head up while I hold his jacket for him. All the while, Dylan doesn't even stir. That kid is a heavy sleeper.

When he straightens from bending inside the back seat, I give him his jacket back. He thanks me quietly before putting it on.

"Thank you, Professor, for everything. It was very kind of you." I smile weakly, trying to hide the discomfort of this favour that I now owe him.

"Please, call me Arthur," he requests quietly, and I nod absentmindedly. Knowing full well I won't do it anytime soon.

"I want to apologise, honestly," he starts, scratching the back of his neck. "I was nasty to you from the beginning, and I had no proper reason to be. I made all of these wrong assumptions based on a really bad experience I had in the past, just because you remind me of someone."

I open my mouth to speak, but he cuts me off.

"I was fucking awful to you, and every time you were nothing but polite and respectful, *even* when defending yourself." He sighs before continuing. "Then, when I saw that Dylan was your kid and not your boyfriend...and, em, it dawned on me that you're not who I assumed you to be. Fuck," he hisses quietly. "I'm rambling now." He rubs his forehead before looking back at me. "Anyway, I really am sorry."

His dark brown eyes are looking directly at me, unwavering, and it makes me feel weird. Even though what he did is not okay, it takes courage and self-introspection to recognise one's mistakes. And in reality, I'm not one to hold grudges.

"Of course, Professor. Let bygones be bygones," I say simply. "I have to go now, toddler to put to bed and all."

We smile back at each other before I slip inside the car and drive home with a sleeping kid in the back and a small smile on my face. I don't know why but a weight seems to have been lifted off my chest and I feel lighter.

THIRTEEN

Liam

"DAVIS, CAN YOU CHECK THE VITALS FOR ME?" DR SHAWN ASKS, AND I head to the machine right away, telling him the heart rate and oxygen levels, as well as everything else he needs to know to ensure the patient is stable.

At first, I had to be walked through the steps; now, I do it automatically. It comes naturally. The hospital is the only place over the past few years where I've felt completely relaxed and sane. Even through the roughest shifts.

"Good, we're almost done," he comments, screwing the last screw into the titanium plate that's stabilizing the patient's leg.

This man was in a terrible car accident, being admitted exactly a few minutes before my shift was finished. But as the workaholic I am, I couldn't pass the opportunity to stay behind and learn more while assisting Dr Shawn.

He sure can be a pain in the ass sometimes and quite demanding with me, but I've come to realise, over these last three months, that he's extra hard on those he sees potential in, and it makes me proud and even more dedicated.

We're past the point of talking about me staying extra hours when things like this happen; he wants me to stay, and he knows I won't let the opportunity pass. It's a non-spoken agreement between both of us.

After telling him the vitals, I rush to his side, trying not to miss much of what he's doing. He's already suturing up the patient's leg which had a nasty open fracture. Fortunately, this is the worst that the accident has given him besides a few broken ribs, bruises, and skin burns. But still, this has been a two-hour surgery.

And since my shift was a ten-hour one this time, it means I've been in this hospital for about twelve hours. I don't feel the exhaustion...yet. I'm sure the moment I shower when I get to my apartment, I'll fall on the bed and sleep through the day.

"And we're done!" Dr Shaw claims. "Deborah, Ella, can you prep the patient and take him to his recovery room?" The nurses nod, and Dr Shawn finally turns to me.

"That was awesome," I tell him. "It took you almost three hours, though, old man. Sure you're not losing your touch?"

"Don't push your luck, boy, or I'll have you do it the next time something like this comes up," he grumbles while we doff our garments and gloves and head to the small room outside of the surgical area to start washing our hands.

"Who says that's not what I want? I've seen how it's done now; I could do it with my eyes closed." I wink at him.

"You're one arrogant bastard, I'll give you that." His voice is low and steady, with a slightly disapproving tone to it, yet it's resigned.

It makes me laugh, and even though his lips tug up, he complains, "Pull a stunt like that again, Davis, and I'll put you in the cleaning services for a whole week."

I put my white coat as I answer him, "As if; you'd go crazy with all those dumb assholes running around like lost sheep when they don't understand what you want from them." I wink at him again before continuing, "Tomorrow's my day off, and since I've been here for an extra two hours already, I am going to go now. Don't miss me too much."

He mutters something under his breath that I can't quite catch, but I don't bother. He makes it seem like I am some obnoxious kid, but he knows damn well how dedicated I am to this shit, and he recognizes it, even though I enjoy riling him up.

Heading to the locker rooms so I can change, grab my backpack, and head off, I have to go through the paediatric department, which is my favourite, and the only speciality that made me waver on my decision to go through with choosing cardiology.

I am distracted by my work thoughts until something stops me in my tracks. From a small doctor's office, a wailing sound travels to the hallway.

As curiosity gets the best of me, I notice a paediatric doctor and a woman in her early thirties. She seems amused by something, and when I follow her line of sight, I see two kids. They both look like they're around five years old, and if it weren't for the extensive physical differences between them, I'd have thought they were siblings or something.

The girl is crying–hiccups and all–about something, and I deduce that she must be the one that needed the visit to the doctor while the boy, slightly taller than her with caramel brown hair and bright blue eyes, comforts her. A wave of foreign feelings overwhelms me, and I come a little bit closer to listen to what they're saying.

I don't know why this need is taking over, though. The need to listen and to take a better look. The boy looks oddly familiar–from where, I have no idea–but when I see better how he cares for the scared girl, I shrug it off knowingly. What's drawing me in is their closeness, how they interact, and their age.

The same age I was when Willow and I became friends.

"Thank god mum had work, and I could stay with you guys for the last days. Imagine having Abby here at the doctor by herself," he complains. "She's such a scaredy cat."

The doctor and the woman accompanying them chuckle at the same time. I can't stop the snort coming out of me.

Quite a pretentious kid, eh.

"She's not alone, Dylan. I am here with her. Her mother, you know?" The lady playfully narrows her eyes at the kid, who I now know is called Dylan.

But he doesn't seem fazed. Again, he looks so oddly familiar. I can't shake it away.

"Besides, she's only here to have her eyes checked because she might need glasses."

"I don't want to," the girl whines.

The kid, Dylan, turns to her and grabs her cheeks.

"Abby, I've done it before, too, when I came with my mum. It doesn't hurt; you'll only see some bright lights, and then try to see with glass in front of your eyes, I think to see if you need help or not," he explains, and I am surprised at how much older the kid seems by talking in this way. "Come on, you are so brave, Abby. Go do it," he encourages her.

She nods and stands up with her mother by her side. The boy follows closely behind as they walk to the room right next to the one they were in. This time around, the door is closed, but it doesn't take long until they are all returning to the original office.

"Thank you, Dylan. You're such a good friend to Abby," the mother whispers when they sit down.

He smiles, proudly, making me grin automatically as well.

"I am her best friend, and I will be forever," he claims, and my chest clenches at the sound of those words, giving me the push I need to walk away from this office and head to the locker room, while still taking my mind back in time to when we were fourteen...

"Get out of here, freak!!" a girl screamed, making me turn back to see Stacey yell at Willow.

I knew this would happen if I brought Willow along. But I had promised Willow we'd spend the day together, and Daniel was adamant that I had to come for a football game with the boys. In Willow-style, she just smiled and said it was fine, that she'd tag along and just sit by the fence to watch me play.

Daniel didn't seem to mind Willow; he was used to me bringing her along to pretty much everything, but other kids were not as understanding. Especially Stacey.

She had been quite clingy to me since school started that year. I tried to ignore her the best I could, but it seemed as if it wasn't enough because she hadn't gotten the memo. She also knew Willow was my best friend and we were always together. She should have known that to be my friend, she'd have to treat Willow kindly, and yet all she'd ever done was the opposite. If she thought I was going to be her friend when she treated Lo like shit, she was damn well wrong.

I quickly passed the ball to Daniel right then and there and motioned to him that I was going to leave the match. With a glance to where the girls were sitting, he seemed to understand and nodded, calling one of the kids that were on the bench waiting for a turn to enter our game here on the field by the park.

As I headed toward the fence separating us from the people watching our small game, I saw Stacey grabbing Willow's arm and pulling her out of her seat, pushing her forward before sitting down where she was, and red took over my vision as I stomped toward them.

Of course, Willow said nothing and straightened as if nothing had happened, leaving without standing up for herself. Except, one of Stacey's friends stuck her foot out, making Willow trip and fall on her face.

Oh, hell no!

I ran out, seething. By the time I got there, she was already on her knees, cleaning her hands the best she could while those vicious girls laughed like hideous hyenas.

"What the fuck is wrong with you?" I growled, helping her up.

The girls gasped in shock as if they weren't expecting me to catch them red-handed, bullying my best friend.

"I am so sorry, Liam; you know how clumsy she is." Stacey pouted, feigning innocence. "She fell on her own, and we couldn't hold the laughter."

"She fell my ass. I saw your minion sticking her foot out." She paled at the sound of my words. "Yeah, that's right, I saw the whole thing. Don't even bother talking to me again. Ever."

Her jaw slacked in shock, and I didn't hesitate to turn my back on them to check if Willow was alright. Besides a few scratches on her knees and jaw, she seemed to be fine. Still, I told her, "Hop on."

"I can walk, you know," her soft voice sounded.

She was always so serene and unaffected by others' lack of kindness; it often made me feel like I was overreacting, but if I didn't stand up for her, no one would. Especially since Jake didn't hang out with kids this young.

Ignoring her, I crouched down and motioned my head for her to climb onto my back. Up until last year, she had been taller than me, but as my mum kept telling me, puberty was finally hitting, and I had almost five inches on her now. That combined with her scrawny frame made her very easy to carry around.

With a resigned sigh, she did, and I started walking back home effortlessly.

"Thank you," she mumbled against my shoulder.

When I stole a glance back at her, her melted chocolate irises were peeking through her thick lashes. Brown eyes are underrated. People were often obsessed with mine because they are light blue and big, but hell...hers? They were enthralling. And they always awoke those tingling effects at the bottom of my stomach.

"Always," I managed, not choking on my saliva after swallowing the lump that formed in my throat.

When we got to my house, I put her down on the couch and started to examine her better. After moving both of her legs and confirming nothing was broken, I got the disinfectant for her wound and a few band aids.

"It's going to sting," I warned.

"Stop playing doctor; you're not one yet." Her voice sounded a little annoyed, making me chuckle. "It's just a few scratches. It'll be fine with a bit of water," she mumbled weakly.

She wouldn't tell me, but I knew how insecure she would have been feeling after being humiliated like that. What she didn't get was that no matter how much other girls tried to catch my attention, she'd be the only one getting it.

"But I will be one day, so I know better." I fake scolded. "Now, squeeze my shoulder if it hurts too much."

With a shy smile and nod, I got the confirmation I needed to patch her up.

We ended up watching a movie on the couch, snuggling, and eating popcorn. In the end, it was much more fun for me. There weren't mean kids bullying her or activities to distract us. We rarely argued, and things were just simple. Perfect.

There was nowhere I'd rather be than with my best friend because I knew that no matter what, we'd be best friends forever.

Well, it certainly wasn't forever.

The annoyingly loud sound of my ringing phone brings me back to the present. While being way over my head because of these stupid memories, I didn't even realise someone was calling me. As I am exiting the wide doors of the hospital, I look at my phone, only to see a number I've never seen before.

I frown at it, but—and I want to blame it on the daze of the memories—I accept the call without giving it much thought.

"H–hi, Liam."

My steps falter at the voice on the other side. Regret instantaneously washes over me as I realise who's talking to me. I shouldn't have answered. Because once again, the universe mocks me. I accepted the call of the only person on this Earth I'd rather forget everything about. The last voice I want to listen to—or so I want to believe.

If I knew this was going to happen, I wouldn't have fucking accepted the call.

"L–Liam?" My heart thumps faster and faster at the sound of her voice saying my name again.

Fucking hell.

Her voice is just as smooth, delicate, and innocent as it was all those years ago. It fills my ears and reaches my nerve endings, penetrating through my body silently and lodging itself in every cell like a bad disease that doesn't want to leave.

And it angers me. It angers me so much that I still love it, her voice and how my name sounds coming from those lips. It battles within me, tearing me in half, trying to cancel the side that misses her, us.

And every time I fail to make it happen, it enrages me. I'm not only furious at her but also at myself because despite everything, I still can't move the fuck on.

And that is the reason why I swallow the prideful part that wants to tell her to go fuck herself and answer, "What do you want, Willow?"

FOURTEEN

IN THE BEGINNING, THAT WAS ALL I HAD HOPED FOR: A PHONE CALL from her explaining everything, apologising to me, and telling me where she was so I could meet her. But as time went by, the flame that kept hope awake weakened.

For years, I had thought that this one phone call would be the solution to my broken heart, but after all of this time, all it does is stab at my chest with her sickly-sweet voice as the blade that pierces right through my heart.

And that is all it takes, just the sound of her voice, to bring unwarranted memories.

It was spring, but it seemed like one of those dark and cold winter days.

I guess the weather was mirroring exactly how I was feeling that day. The clouds were low and dark, threatening with one of those strong rainfalls. The wind was strong, bringing the storm closer and closer to me as if it had a magnet to my state of mind.

Which was a mess, for that matter.

I had undergone all the emotional states one can go through for four weeks by then. We were close to May, and two of my favourite people were missing from my life.

Since that night Mason had broken in, we never heard from him again, and I was fearing the worst. My parents tried their best to seem unaffected, but I wasn't falling for it. Their social events had reduced significantly, and my parent's marriage—which already was imperfect—was slowly crumbling to the ground.

Where could he be? Had he gotten himself into trouble? The fact that he stole so much from us meant that it was a high possibility. The worry and concern were leaving me restless. If only he had come to me for money, I would have fucking given it to him.

And as if that wasn't enough, there was Willow, too.

The morning after I met Jake at their house, she sent me a text saying she had Mononucleosis and had to endure at least a one-month quarantine until the doctor could see her again. The next morning, school confirmed it, and my parents even forced me to go to the hospital, too, even though I had no symptoms.

I'm not stupid, and since I wanted to be a doctor, I had a pretty good idea of several different conditions, illnesses, and viruses. Mono is the latter. Also known as the kissing disease because it's mostly spread through saliva.

And there is where it sounded suspicious to me.

If she had it, I had to have it, too, because exchanging saliva was something we had been doing a lot back then.

And no one else did, besides her and her family. Apparently.

The fact she was quarantining was not what was bothering me, though. What bothered me was the fact that it took her forty-eight hours to tell me herself, and despite my incessant calls and texts and "Get Well Soon" baskets, her answers were all scarce and curt.

It was pissing me off, feeling like talking to me was a chore, when all I wanted to know was how she was feeling, if she had a lot of fever or headaches...When I was just worried about her. It got worse when a week after she started her "quarantine", she stopped answering at all. Not only her but everyone in their house, too.

All of that was breaking me from the inside out.

The only comfort I had in my seemingly lavish life was blowing me off big time, with no apparent reason why. It didn't make sense at all, but mostly, it was shady. The math wasn't mathing.

With a knot in my stomach, a racing heartbeat and shaky hands, I drove that afternoon from school to her house. It was the supposed last day of quarantine, so there was no way she could avoid me any longer.

From what I had gathered, they were all in quarantine—which may have made sense, I guess—since I'd once seen a guy delivering groceries when I was "driving by" in hopes of catching a glimpse of her from the window.

And that day, knowing she was supposed to be finally free from that so-called quarantine, no one was going to stop me from finally seeing her. Different thoughts were racing through my mind as I drove there, mostly all of the different scenarios that could happen.

Would she open the door looking healthy and apologise for all of the radio-silent time?

Would she still be feeling ill, showing me why she hadn't answered? I knew the quarantine time for mono could be extended if the meds weren't helping fast enough. I just hoped that wasn't the case.

Would her parents not let me see her? Or even Jake? Too bad that it would force me to camp in front of their house because, this time around, I wouldn't leave their house until they let me see her, anyway.

Everything felt like it was dragging back then, school, the entire days...and that drive was no different.

What was different was the ruckus I saw in front of Willow's house when I turned onto her street. I couldn't detect what was going on, but there were two huge trucks in front of it, with a lot of furniture and boxes on the front lawn.

Dread settled right over my lungs, like a heavy weight depriving me of the oxygen it needed so much. Those moments before my feet hit the green grass of their property were a distant fog in my mind as it screamed at me to get there as fast I could.

What the hell was happening?

Willow's parents, Monica and Stephen, huffed as soon as they set their eyes on me, turning around to the boxes behind them and picking them up.

"Good afternoon, Mr and Mrs Hanlon," I greeted them, eager to get to the point. "Where's Willow?"

Monica scowled at me, and Stephen's jaw clicked, making my own lock, too, when they ignored me and headed to the back of the truck. What was with all of the hostility? Did they believe she fell ill because of me? And what was it with all of the boxes?

"What's going on?" I asked. "Are you guys remodelling?"

"Get out of here, boy," Stephen snapped. "Enough harm has been done. You're no longer welcome in our house."

My brain felt like a broken record at that point, asking, "What the fuck?" repeatedly inside my head. Surely, this couldn't be all because of one little virus. She was never in danger, otherwise, I'm sure Jake would have warned me.

Speaking of the devil, he showed up right then, exiting the house with a box in his arms, too. He only noticed me the moment he placed it down, his face blanching the moment our eyes met.

"Jake," I called right as he turned around to go back inside.

"You need to leave, Liam," he warned, sounding tired.

"What the hell is going on? Where is Willow?"

When he didn't stop, I tightly grabbed his arm. Jake stopped but only because he wanted to, I knew it. He was four years older, only one year and a half away from finishing his degree in architecture, and even though he was a geek, he was huge and muscular—way more than I or Mason ever could be. But he was also the soft and considerate one.

On the other hand, I was always one to act first and think later. Especially if it came to her. I wouldn't stand down to anyone. Not even him.

"Kid, this is too fucked up," he gritted. "There's nothing we can do; believe me, I tried. Please go home."

"Jake, all of this is way too weird," I answered, tightening my hold on him.

His jaw ticked, and he looked away, clearly uncomfortable with the situation, but I couldn't care less.

"She gets sick out of the blue, needing quarantine? Why did she even stop talking to me? Where is she?"

Jake shook his arm, freeing himself from my hold, and sighed. The silence stretched, and I turned to look around him, making it a statement that I was not going to leave until he answered me. All the while, my eyes were looking for her, scouring every corner that I could find from the opened door...and nothing.

"Liam, I tried." His voice was shaky, bringing my attention back to him properly.

Just like that morning I had come to check on her, he looked exhausted and pale. Jake looked like he was carrying the weight of the world on his shoulders and failing miserably. The proper sight of him made my heart thump violently against my ribcage as the black poisonous liquid of fear slid through my body.

The sudden sickness, the quarantine, and her sudden silence were an augur that I was blindly trying to ignore.

"What do you mean?" I choked out.

"They wouldn't budge," he admitted.

Even without knowing what the hell he was on about, it fed the panic growing within me. Because I had probably stood there for almost ten minutes, and she was nowhere to be seen.

"She left."

What? Not possible.

A nervous smile stretched on my lips, and soon, it developed into a chuckle. He was joking. He had to be.

"Cut the crap, Jake! Where is she?" I slapped his shoulder, still laughing anxiously while at the same time, my guts coiled.

"I'm sorry, man," he whispered.

For a moment, I froze, trying to make sense of it. But nothing did. So I followed my instinct and burst into their house, heading straight toward her bedroom. Jake's fading voice fell on deaf ears as I focused on finding her. It was the only thing I could think about as my legs burned from rushing up the stairs.

There was hope that I'd find her doing the same her parents and brother were, that she'd give me a proper explanation and things would end up being fine, eventually...but when I pushed the door open, my heart dropped.

The desk was clean, and the bed was naked. The shelves were empty, and if I dared open the drawers, I knew they'd be the same way, too. The only thing marking the bedroom as hers was the soft pastel green on the walls.

She wasn't there, extinguishing the little spark of hope that clung to me. That was when Jake's words started to resonate through my head.

She left.

She couldn't. She wouldn't.

My vision blurred as I picked my phone up from my pocket, a desperate last attempt to get a hold of her. But when the call didn't even go through, telling me the number was no longer registered, my legs buckled.

Willow left, and she didn't even dare to tell me what the fuck was wrong. She gave me no opportunity to choose if I wanted it or not—whatever the hell it was. It was right then and there that I finally realised just how strong my feelings for her were.

If they were only a teenage crush, there was no way it'd feel like a final stab right through my heart. The ultimate betrayal.

My world fell to the ground that day, at the realisation that the two people I loved the most had abandoned me, without even looking back.

FIFTEEN

Willow

IF THE EARTH OPENED TO SWALLOW ME WHOLE, I'D WILLINGLY GO. All because Liam answered the phone. Every prayer I made, all the requests I begged for were *not* answered. He was not working or sleeping. He wasn't even busy enough to let it go to voicemail.

Fate had to throw another punch and have him answer the call. My fear of having to face him is now a constant. Like a second shadow, following me everywhere.

Thankfully—or not—he had free time. And that is why I am currently getting ready to go meet him. I'm a walking nervous wreck, playing the conversation we had over and over again.

"You've kept my number all of this time?" he asked when I called.

"I would have if I had been allowed to keep my older phone. I had to beg Johanna for your number," I answered quietly.

"What do you want, then?" he questioned, his voice as sharp and hostile as the day in the diner.

After that, he stayed silent, waiting. Liam had always been the one to give me space to organise my thoughts and encouraged me to speak my mind.

But this was not that. He was forcing me to be the one to put in the effort, to take that step forward and give him what I owed him. A proper apology and an explanation.

Which one would it be, not even I knew then.

"Look, Liam..." I started hesitantly. "I am sorry about the way I bolted. It was hard to see you, but we should talk. If you want, of course. I—" I cut myself off mid-sentence.

God, this was so hard.

I was so afraid he would just hang up on me or tell me to piss off.

My body was trembling with anticipation, and I kept gnawing on my bottom lip, trying to find the courage to continue.

"I want to explain myself and..." Another deep breath. "Apologise to you. If there is someone in my life who's owed an apology, it's you." My voice was shaky by the time I finished.

"Fine," he said coolly.

He said yes, I repeated to myself. My breathing was shaky but relief washed over me momentarily. Then it dawned on me that I would have to face him again, and anxiety took over.

I was a mess.

There were a few moments of silence between us until he took the lead.

"We can go for coffee tomorrow; I have the day off. I'll text you the address and the hour."

"Sure. Work won't start until seven p.m. anyway," I informed him, hoping he wouldn't want to meet me during work hours.

With that, he hung up.

Sadness overwhelmed me in response to his cold demeanour, but I shouldn't even be bothered by that. He could have been way angrier, and I should just be glad that he agreed to hear me out.

"Let's just hope this isn't a disaster," I whisper to myself.

I'm still trapped in front of the mirror, looking at the foreign woman staring back into my eyes.

The woman on the other side of the mirror looks just like me, wearing my favourite beige summer dress. It's a straight neckline with off-the-shoulder short sleeves. It's tight from my chest down to my waist, where it flows freely. The petite pink flowers give it a splash of colour, and the split that comes up to my left thigh, just above my knee, makes it a less good-girl kind of dress.

All the right things are covered to avoid unwanted attention, though. She is presentable and composed on the outside. Me, however? I am crumbling on the inside.

It's the most effort I have made in years, and just standing here, looking at myself, is hard enough. It's been almost seven years since I've looked in the mirror and liked what I was seeing.

Now, the brown eyes on my face have lost the spark they had, haunted by the demons that live inside my brain. My skin no longer glows, and I often felt like it did, especially when Liam was around. Covering it has been a must over the years, and it's been a while since I've looked at myself without clothes. The last time, I was pregnant, admiring the unborn baby growing inside me.

But it's Liam I am about to see, and I can't not make an effort. Is it stupid that I don't want him to see how messed up my life is? How messed up I am?

With a resigned sigh, I grab my purse and head to the car. The café he chose is a twenty-minute drive and quite close to my university.

The drive is too fast, and the next thing I know, I've arrived. Ten minutes early. Trying to get my nerves under control, I stroll from where the car is parked down the street, gazing at the stores absent-mindedly.

My thoughts are consumed with all that is Liam. About how things ended up back then. How I left, and, consequently, how he must be feeling—how he felt then, too. There's a sliver of curiosity about his life, the fact that he is studying here instead, and possibly moving on—without me. But that part is completely shadowed by the worry about this encounter.

What if he doesn't want to listen? Worse, what if I can't talk? It's atrocious to live like this, but I think I fear the outcome of the truth more than the consequences of the question mark.

Then, too quickly, my feet bring me to the glass door I'm meant to open, and I freeze for a second. My biggest fear is right inside, and I was stupid enough to think I could face it.

To face Liam.

The café is quaint, small yet spacious to the eye, with blue and wooden details. It's the type of place I would choose to work on school projects while eating and drinking something. Taking it in, I look around one more time, noticing the slight hustle of people sitting in with their freshly requested food or some others preparing to leave. It's not crowded, but there's a decent number of full tables.

It doesn't take me long, though, to find the lone mop of dark blond hair that I was expecting to find. With his back facing me, he's seated in the corner booth of the café. His head is tilted down to the front, probably using his phone while waiting for me. The door is still open, my hand clutching the knob, and my resolve crumbling to the ground.

What am I going to say? I can't...I can't tell him everything; he'll hate me.

Worse, he won't believe me. Why would he?

My feet feel heavy as if they are made of cement, not letting me move. With my body still sideways, I am literally one foot in and one foot out—probably because of my brain's constant flight response.

And while there is a huge part of me wanting to flee, the rest has me rooted in place. Especially the part that keeps remembering my son's eager requests. This moment of hesitation, though, it's enough to make it look bad. Because that is exactly when Liam turns around, locking his eyes with mine. His once-neutral expression hardens the moment he notices me. It worsens when he realises how I was probably about to leave without even talking to him. Something that *I* asked him to do.

He stands, stalking in my direction with a wildfire burning in his eyes. My opportunity to escape is long gone—even if I wasn't going to use it, this time around—and I just wait, bracing for the truck of rage that is about to hit.

"Of course you were going to run away again," he scoffs. "That's all you know, isn't it?" he spits the words out as if he is disgusted by me.

Don't worry; I am, too.

It hurts, but it's valid. All I've done so far is run away, even if I think I had a good reason to do it. Even if I thought that by leaving, I was doing everyone a favour.

"Let's go," I sigh in defeat, following him to the booth he was just sitting down in. The table has an empty coffee cup on it with the menu at the far end. We keep quiet for a few moments, and it doesn't take long for the waiter to ask what I am going to order.

When I order a bottle of water, I decide to speak first, hoping for Liam to stop his glaring contest.

"I'm sorry; I panicked," I mumble, my eyes never leaving my hands.

I want to look up at him. The other day, I was far too shocked to notice his face properly, but now, my brain is itching and begging for me to do it, to just glance up at him. But I can't bring myself to.

"It seems to be turning into a pattern, isn't it?" The question is rhetoric, so I don't bother answering. "I can deduce what made you panic now to make you run, what I can't wrap my head around is why you did that almost seven years ago." His tone is cold and detached. Understandably so, but it still throws a spear right through my heart.

"Right to the point, as always," I say, flicking my eyes to his face...*finally*.

At the proper sight of him, I suck my breath in.

His dark blond hair seems even darker than it used to be. He always managed to have natural colour changes in his hair, making it much brighter in the summer and darker in the winter. I guess it makes sense, since autumn has arrived, and his hair is now a light brown colour. But his vibrant blue eyes are the same. The arctic-blue shade, which has always sucked me in, is a colour that every family member has, except for his mother who has green eyes.

The biggest difference I notice is his physique, of course. We were sixteen the last time I saw him, and even though he had always been bigger than me since we were like twelve, he is much taller and broader now. He's filled out. He doesn't have a face full of beard, but the light brown stubble is there, mainly around his mouth and chin. It's a style that doesn't flatter many men, but he rocks it so well.

Liam always rocked everything he did or wore; it's not a surprise it hasn't changed. He's even more handsome, and it makes my heart beat faster like it's ready to jump out my chest while my hands get clammy with sweat.

"And I'd appreciate you not wasting my time. You owe me this."

"You're right," I answer while fiddling with my fingers.

Just then, the young guy comes back with the bottle, and I make sure to pay him. After a quick swig of it and still not being able to look him in the eyes, I admit, "I wanted to apologize..."

"What for?" he presses, wanting for me to speak for myself.

"For everything," I whisper.

He scoffs and leans forward, a menacing look in his eyes. His words come out harsh, making me wince when he finally speaks, "That's all you called me for? To say sorry? How about a fucking explanation!" His voice rises, and I instantly jump at it, shutting my eyes tightly.

The proximity, the harshness in his voice, it's edging me. Triggering me. And in this situation, I can't panic.

Not now, not in front of him.

He wouldn't hurt me, too, would he?

My subconscious screams at me, telling me to flee right away, reminding me that no one is reliable. Especially men. My hands shake, and my eyes blur as I fight it.

It's Liam.

He wouldn't do anything. I know it, and I try to ground myself to it as my brain tries to bring those dreadful memories back.

"Please," I breathe to myself, trying to stay in control.

When I open them again, he is looking at me with a frown, confusion etching his expression lines. It only lasts a second until his demeanour goes back to detached and cold again.

"Why did you leave?" he presses in a low angry hiss.

I take a couple of deep breaths and look down at my lap. How do I go about this?

"My parents threw me out. Not even Jake could reason with them to help me. My only option was my Nana. She told me I could live with her. I–" I pause, mustering up the courage to say as much as I can without touching the subject I'll take with me to my grave. "I didn't know what to do; they didn't even let me bring clothes or my phone. The only thing I had was the money Jake gave me for the bus ticket."

It isn't the whole story but true, nonetheless. I'm not ready to bring Dylan into this or how he came to life. *Not yet.*

"That's bullshit. You could have come to me, and you know it. You could have stayed with me," he countered.

And I know it's true. He was the first person I thought I'd go to. Liam always made me feel like he would have gone through hell and back to take care of me if needed. I believed it then. But how fair was it to put such a burden on his shoulders?

He had–still has–his future ahead of him. I would have turned into an obstacle, a thorn in his parent's side.

And even without them in the equation, even if they accepted me. How could I, after everything that was done? Or everything he was already going through?

I remember it like it was yesterday, the relief in his eyes every time we spent time together. The way his eye bags would slightly disappear when he took naps, cuddling me. Life inside the four walls of his house wasn't as perfect as his parents made it out to be, and he was hurting. He hurt for them all, for...

Oh god.

He had told me time and time again, I was the only good thing in his life. And I ripped it right away from him.

But if I had stayed...if he had known the truth...

It was too much for me, by myself. It would be too much for him, too. That I am sure of.

"Your parents didn't even like me, do you really think they'd take in a disowned sixteen-year-old?" I ask in a shaky voice, all these memories taking a big toll on me. "I wasn't their responsibility, nor yours. What would you have done? Found a job to help me?"

"You know damn well I would have if it was needed," he growls before leaning in on the table, closer to me.

Too close.

A gasp leaves my lips without permission, and my body hits the back of the booth harder than I intend it to. It has been way too long since a man—other than my brother—was this close to me. Even if it is Liam.

He doesn't relent, though, staying put and not leaning back again. It's bittersweet because that old part of me is relishing in the proximity she never thought she'd experience again. While the current one, the broken one, is terrified.

"You know damn well I would have done everything for you back then," he whispers weakly with a broken expression.

One of his hands rises to the space between our faces. His eyes swirl with so much emotion that I can see the different shades swim around the irises as if he is having an inner battle. I am so lost in his eyes that it's almost too late when I realise what he is about to do.

To touch me. *I am not ready.*

When the tips of his fingers are just about to touch my cheek, I suck in a ragged breath and turn my head away, closing my eyes and whispering, "Please, don't." His hand freezes mid-air, and one second later, he distances himself from me.

"Are you afraid of me?" Shock and hurt lace his voice with the way it cracks when he speaks.

At the sound of his voice, I snap my eyes open, seeing the defeated expression on his face, and I can't deal with it. To see in front of me the extent of the damage I've done. How much I've ruined him breaks me even more, forcing a sob out of my mouth. I quickly press my hands over it before mumbling a quick, "I'm sorry."

The next thing I do is the only thing I know to do properly.

I run away from him, without looking back. Once again.

SIXTEEN

Willow

FIVE SECONDS. THAT WAS ALL IT TOOK FOR SHILAH TO UNDERSTAND something was wrong and to give me the night off when I called her. Without realising it, she took a huge weight off my shoulders because it was going to be a challenge to get there and endure the night.

My body and brain are overwhelmed. There are some demons which I have learned are better left dormant, and that's the main reason I ran away from him again. I'm not ready to face mine. *Not yet.*

With burning lungs and jelly legs, I flop down on the first bench I set eyes on. Thank god for Nina for taking Dylan for a few hours. At this point, I need some time to calm down.

Deep and slow breaths. I'm here, by myself, with nothing but the rushed sounds of the city lulling me to peace. The wind blows, and the cars drive by, creating the perfect frame. From high up here, the river sets the city's scenery, mixing with the street lamps that flicker on as the sun sets lower.

It's a beautiful view. A strong contrast to the ugly ones afflicting my mind. Seeing Liam and trying—failing—to talk to him about our past has brought memories back. And not the best kind.

Wondering how he would react to everything reminds me exactly of the moment that my parents realised I was pregnant.

"You will have an abortion," my mother stated icily.

As if it weren't enough, but I didn't blame them. Not when I hadn't been able to utter a word about that night. Everyone had realised that something had happened; I was so affected I got a fever the day after...If only my parents had been as understanding as Jake was when I refused to talk.

Refusing to talk or see the police or go to the hospital had not worked in my favour. Deep down, I knew it was frustrating on their part, wanting to help me and being unable to, but it led to ugly words that made it harder than it ever could be.

The cold shoulder, the disgust...

As if I didn't feel disgusted enough with myself.

"Mum, I will get a job. You won't have to spend a penny on it!" I countered.

"Are you crazy? You are sixteen. If you don't get one of your own volition, I will sign for you to have one. Don't forget, you're still a minor!" Her high-pitched voice reverberated through the living room, threatening to pierce my eardrums.

"I won't do it!"

My eyes slid to my father, silently seated next to where my mum was before she stood up, screaming. His face and neck were red, and the veins were popping out–the only sign of his anger. Regret hit me as soon as I looked at him.

For a long while, he was who I'd run off to for reassurance, for protection and now...the only person who had shown to be by my side was my brother.

He was the only one who saw the real state I was in when I got home that night. Who took care of my fever when I refused to go to the hospital, and the only one who had been sleeping on my bedroom floor just to wake me from my nightmares.

I wished I hadn't burdened him with this...it was visible in the weight he'd lost and the worry that looked back at me every day from his irises, not to mention the paler tone of his skin and the deep bags under his eyes. I was tearing them apart, ruining my family.

And still, from the moment I found out I was pregnant, two days before that conversation, he was nothing but supportive. There was a hidden pain in his eyes when he learned and a sad smile when I told him I wanted to keep it despite the...circumstances.

"Where have we failed, huh?" My mum's body slumped back down on the couch, a defeated tone etched on her voice.

"You didn't," I answered.

I did. But this baby wasn't at fault, and I couldn't bring myself to just get rid of it. Get rid of something–soon to be someone–who was going to be half mine. Even knowing that the procedure had always been a polemic subject worldwide, it was a no-brainer to me.

Each woman should have the right to decide what to do. Just like I did, and I chose to keep it. To keep him.

"Well," she started, swiping her tongue over her teeth in that obnoxious way she always did when things didn't go her way. "I won't sit here and watch you destroy your life. If you want to stick to that decision, you won't be living under my roof anymore."

Despite her harshness, I gasped in shock. I was expecting a severe grounding or being forced to work, but never to be thrown out of their house when I needed them the most.

"No way!" Jake, who had been silent until then, stood up in a flash, stepping in front of me. "She's sixteen. You can't do that!"

"If she is grown up enough to get pregnant and birth a kid at sixteen, she is old enough to find a roof, get a job, and raise it!" Without giving my brother time to answer, she turned to me and continued, "You have twenty-four hours to get out of my house."

The memories swirl in my brain, reminding me of some of the most painful moments, but a strong and gruff voice breaks me from my forced reverie.

"Willow?" It's familiar, and it makes me shiver as realisation settles.

Not again.

In a hasty attempt to wipe the tears away from my face, I rub my sleeve underneath my eyes. I was so deep in thought I never even noticed him getting closer to me.

"Professor Adell," I breathe out in panic. "Wha-what are you doing here?"

"I just left work." He points behind him, and sure enough, on the other side of the road, I can recognize a few of the university's buildings.

Oh.

It still makes me uneasy, though. The last thing I need right now is for him to mock me for catching me bawling my eyes out in the middle of a deserted street.

He moves to sit down next to me, and I can't help but jump to the opposite side of the bench, keeping as much distance between us as possible. My brain is still on shaky grounds, with one foot in the past and the other in the present. One little trigger and the dam will break.

If I'm uncomfortable with the touch of my childhood best friend and boyfriend, I sure as hell am not ready to be touched by anyone other than my son.

A moment of silence stretches, and my body heats up with the feeling of his eyes on me, though he does not attempt to get closer or touch me—thankfully.

"Are you alright?" His voice comes out in a soft tone.

Such a different one from what I am used to from him. This one is comforting and soothing, the exact opposite of his hostile demeanour from before.

"I am, thank you." I give him a weak smile, mentally holding my breath for his answer. He will call me out on my bullshit.

Instead, he surprises me by steering off the dreadful subject. "You're not working today?"

"Not today." I sigh. "But I have to go, though. I have to pick Dylan up soon." I sigh before standing up.

"Huh..." he hesitates, standing and slowly looking around us. "How are you going? Do you need a ride?"

"I–I don't want to be any hassle. It's just a short walk up to my car." Hopefully, he'll let it go.

"Well, I'll walk you to your car, then." His big hand scratches the back of his neck. "It's getting dark, and I'd be worried."

My mouth opens as I go to refuse his offer, and he shakes his head, cutting me off. "I'm not taking a no for an answer."

I nod. "Thank you." All that comes out is a broken whisper before we start walking side by side.

As we walk in silence, I start to regret accepting his offer because I obviously ran a longer distance than I realised.

"Sorry," I blurt out. "It's a little further than I thought."

"Good thing I offered to walk you, then." His lips turn up slightly in a subtle but obvious smile. A kind one.

Heat creeps up my neck, straight to my cheeks, and I look away almost immediately, focusing on something else.

The sky colours change from light to dark as the sun sets far away on the horizon. And as the streetlights start to take over the illumination, I understand what he meant by getting worried. With the twilight, the city feels emptier and more dangerous.

Even though Portugal is one of the safest countries in the world, awful things will always happen—even where you feel safe—and when you least expect them.

I would know.

"So..." his voice interrupts my wandering thoughts, and for once, I appreciate it.

I was about to go down a dark path. *Again.*

"Why did you decide on elementary teaching for your degree?" Professor Adell asks, glancing at me from the corner of his eyes.

It's a much-appreciated distraction. Can this man read minds?

"Well," I start, keeping my sight on the street ahead of us. "I've always wanted to be a biologist, but Dylan changed my mind." Sweet memories of baby Dylan swarm my mind, etching a smile to my lips.

"How so?" He cocks an eyebrow, making his curiosity obvious.

It's confusing, really. How is this man beside me the same one who used to taunt and pick on me? Surely, they can't be the same.

He used to be cold, rude, and arrogant, but now...his eyes seem pained, and his voice sounds soft. It's like the Dr Jekyll and Mr Hyde case—two personalities within one body.

"Willow?" his husky voice snaps me out of my thoughts *once again.*

"Ahm, sorry. I'm just a little bit in my head tonight." He nods, seemingly understanding. "What made me change my mind was my son. When he started walking and talking...I still can't explain the feeling. He was and still is the best part of my days. And teaching him everything, I just fell in love with it. Doing it with other kids means I am making a difference in their lives and in future generations. Makes me feel useful like I have a purpose."

Another silence stretches as I wait for his reaction, and when it doesn't come, I look at him, just to find him looking at me with a weird expression on his face. For the first time tonight, things turn awkward. His deep gaze makes it feel like he is looking right through me.

"Professor Adell?"

He shakes his head before letting out a barely there hum, and when he finally looks back at me, he seems to have recollected himself.

"Sorry," he apologises with a shy smile.

This man seems to have smiled more tonight than his whole life combined. Which is a shame because he has one hell of a smile.

"If that is how you feel about it, then you chose the right profession," he comments.

I know. In a parallel universe, I might still be a biologist, but in this one...I was meant for this. Even if it hurt too much to get to this point, everything was still worth it because I have Dylan.

Having him was the best choice I made amid all the chaos. He became my anchor, my reason to keep going.

"Thank you. And what about you? What made you want to be a literature teacher?" I prod in the same way he has.

"Well, believe it or not, I was this scrawny, shy nerd when I was a kid that had no friends, and reading books was my bonding time with the only friend I ever had. My sister."

His statement makes my jaw fall wide open. How could this tall and muscular guy have been scrawny? I find it hard to believe that a small, shy kid transformed into this...*monster!*

"I know it's hard to believe. I did grow up a lot," he chuckles. "But bookworm was—and still is—my middle name. Literature became a passion...so much so that I learned four languages just so I could read my favourite books in all of them. It's fascinating to see the differences the languages add or take from a book."

He avoids my eyes as he talks, but it's palpable. The little glint in his irises, and the subtle giddiness in his voice...he is exuding passion, and it's fascinating how someone I deemed as cold and robotic shows so much passion for books and literature.

Just then, we reach the parking lot where my car is. The café where I met with Liam earlier is now much emptier. The lamp lights are dim but strong enough to give a good view of the street surrounding us. The iconic grey of the stone used in the city's buildings makes it seem much darker than it really is, but it doesn't make it less beautiful.

"This is me," I say once I stop close to my car. "Thanks for walking me, Professor Adell." I give him a shy smile before taking my car keys from my bag.

"No problem." He smiles while putting his hands in his pockets. "Are you feeling better?"

"Surprisingly, I am!" *And partly because of you*–is what crosses my mind but I don't dare say it.

Then he smiles *widely* for the hundredth time tonight, and it's dazzling. It throws me off my game, hypnotising me to his handsome features.

"I'm glad," he admits. "I'll see you in class."

I start turning around when his voice stops me.

"Wait," he calls, and I turn around to face him again. "Just know that with college, work, and Dylan, I can help however you need. Don't hesitate and ask, please."

My eyes widen at his words. *What?*

"I–I don't think..."

"Think of it as me making up to you for treating you like shit at first," he answers quietly. "I won't take no for an answer."

Not wanting to argue, I robotically nod and mumble a thank you before getting in my car. Even after I rev the engine and drive off, I can still see him from the rearview mirror, standing in the same spot, waiting for me to leave.

This change in his demeanour gives me serious whiplash and knowing what to do or how to react is tricky. Although, I'd be lying if I said I don't like this change in attitude because I do.

I guess Professor Prick is not a prick after all...

SEVENTEEN

Willow

"ARE WE STILL ON FOR TONIGHT?" JOHANNA'S VOICE RINGS IN MY ears from the other side of my phone.

This dinner has been in the making for weeks now. She's been trying to organise it, juggling to try and find a day we all could fit it into our schedule, and she's finally done it.

We're all going. Ethan, Hazel, and her friend Sofia, as it seems. Hazel wasn't very interested at first, but Ethan convinced her to come, too. I've come to understand that it's just her nature and not to take it personally. Although Johanna seems intent on winning her over.

"Yeah, Jo. I'll meet you at six o'clock. Is that okay with you? I don't want to get home too late; I have to put Dylan to bed," I tell her.

Just then, I see him emerge from the school doors. A smile finds its way to my face just at the sight of him, and I wave excitedly.

"Good," she answers. "No need to bring anything. I've got it covered!" We say goodbye just as he brushes against my legs, hugging me tightly.

"Who was that, Mummy?" Dylan steals a shy glance at me from under his thick lashes, hope blooming in his gaze. "Did you find my father already?"

My heart cracks, dissolving the good day I was having into nothing. The shadow of disappointment hovers over us like a hound.

"No, baby," I answer defeatedly while picking him up.

He settles over my hip, my hack to better support his weight. A frown takes over his face, and it hurts me even more.

This is such a mess. How can I explain to a five-year-old that he probably is the outcome of non-consensual sex? That I ran away from the situation and never wanted to take a DNA test because of what that could mean to me, to my ex-boyfriend, and to who the real father is. I just...can't.

"I haven't found him yet," I tell him, grazing my finger over his reddened cheek. "As soon as I do, I'll contact him and ask him to meet you, yeah?"

Stalling isn't the solution, but I can't bear to truly break his heart.

"It's okay," he mumbles, wrapping his arms around my neck and placing his head on my shoulder as I walk us both to my car.

"So, what did you learn at school today?"

"Oh," he exclaims, raising his head and looking back at me. An exciting glint swirls in his irises. "We were taught to count even more numbers, Mummy! Like, they don't have an end." His hands wave and move in the air in rhythm to his speech, and it's so amusing to watch.

Just like that, he forgets about what was making him sad, easily getting distracted by what he enjoys, babbling and laughing throughout the entire car ride home. The afternoon passes quickly as I help him out with some educational games, and we play football in the backyard.

Nana came back yesterday, but she still looks pretty tired from the days away, probably taking care of everything for her little brother's funeral. So, before leaving for this friends' date, I'm cooking dinner for them.

This is my favourite part out of the entire house. It was already fully renovated when Nana bought it, with these beautiful wall-built cabinets in sage green covering two walls, making an L. The bottom row of cabinets is topped by a white counter and a built-in stove and oven.

It has tons of storage and a cooking area. It's divine. There is also a huge island in the middle and a little corner by the window with a rustic-style dining table—my favourite.

"Lo, dear?"

"In the kitchen, Nana," I yell just as I turn off the stove. "Do you want me to set the table?"

"No, dear. You've done more than enough. Go get dressed and have fun. I'll take it from here." She smiles at me and sits down beside Dylan who gives her a wide grin.

Upstairs, I put on some loose mum jeans and a tight white top, then brush my hair into a loose French braid. I head downstairs to head out, kissing them both on the head and picking a bottle of wine before walking to the car.

It's a quick drive to Jo's since she lives so close. When she opens the door, there's light chatter in the background, letting me know everyone else has already arrived.

"Willow! You're here," she squeals in delight as if it were a surprise to see me here.

With a small, shy smile, I side-hug her. She's always so radiant, happy, and full of energy. It's always as inspiring as it is intimidating.

"Hey, Jo. I brought some wine."

"I told you I've got it covered, silly!" She waves me off. "Oh, wow! That's a decent wine. I didn't expect you to bring a good one. Nice job!"

What?

My eyebrows twist in a frown, confusion hitting me. But before I can answer, she twirls around, heading inside, and I take the hint to move into the living room.

Ethan stands up right away, hugging me tightly. Sofia follows, kissing my cheek, and Hazel nods in acknowledgement. I guess that's as good as you can get, so I smile in return. She's hardened on the outside, but it looks more like a defence mechanism than anything else.

We all sit down at her white oval table, which is already set and prepared.

"Were you waiting for me long? Sorry—"

"We just got here," Ethan answers with a smile. "Like one minute before you."

"Oh, good," I exhale in relief.

I hate being late; it's not polite at all.

As we wait for Johanna to return, I look around a little. The decor really suits her vibe. The walls are stark white, the furniture a light grey with modern and straight lines. The decoration is kept to a minimum, but it has splashes of colour here and there with the pillows, the paintings and the chandeliers or lamps—giving it just enough personality.

Soon enough, she's back with a fuming tray of what seems to be lasagna. *Maybe cannelloni?* Once it's set down, she's adamant about serving everyone before herself and sits down between Hazel and Sofia. I am on the other side of Hazel, with Ethan between Sofia and me.

We all fall into easy conversation, getting to know Sofia a little better and talking about our college projects for the semester.

"Ugh, Professor Prick is such an asshole," Johanna groans after downing the last of the wine in her glass.

"He's not that bad," I answer before I can help myself.

All eyes turn to me—except for Sofia because she doesn't know what we're talking about—and I immediately regret my words.

"Excuse me," Ethan starts, an offended tone to his voice. "Are you living in this world? That guy is a Grinch, and by the looks of it, you're Christmas!"

Johanna and Sofia chuckle as Hazel nods, agreeing with her cousin. I join in awkwardly, too, choosing to keep silent.

Except, Johanna doesn't let me, "Speaking of, have you been in contact with Liam?"

Oh.

"Have you guys talked ever since?"

"Well, I–"

"Wait!" Sofia cuts in, interrupting me. "Isn't Liam the one you were going on a date with?"

Silence follows. A thick, heavy tension settles around the table as everyone's eyes jump between Johanna and me. Her attention is locked on mine, with an expression I've never seen on her before.

Determination.

So far, she's let it slide. And I was too hopeful that this moment would never come. But it seems that, once again, fate has other plans for me. Or, in this case, Johanna does.

"The very one," Johanna admits, opening the can of worms and perking everyone's curiosity.

It stings. Up until now, she's acted as a friend, a good and respectful one. And this is the best—worst—wake-up call there could ever be. Johanna was waiting, but not for me to open up and tell her everything. She was waiting for the opportunity to corner me into telling her everything.

"Ahm..." Anxiety prickles at my brain, sending my blood pumping and raising my body temperature.

Everyone is waiting for an answer, and no one is merciful enough to stop it. Their interest is more important than my pain, if they can even notice it.

"Girls," Ethan starts. "Maybe–"

"Let her talk," Johanna grits. "She can speak for herself."

Oh god.

Ethan clenches his jaw but keeps quiet, letting her win.

"Liam..." It hurts just to say his name aloud. "Was my childhood best friend for years."

Maybe there's no need to tell the entire story. Our story is just that, ours. And the only person I owe an explanation to is not sitting at this table.

That's until Johanna's body deflates, and she sighs in relief. That awakens the green monster I always try to ignore inside me. These foreign feelings are never welcome, but every time they show up, I lose this inevitable battle.

Knowing in my gut that his reason to move forward is right here in front of me. That sooner or later, I'll have to witness that happening with someone I see daily guts me—wrecks me.

And that's why the word vomit happens, the need to let her know that there's more. *There was more.*

"He was also my first boyfriend."

A couple of gasps are the only sounds. Just as I expected, in a matter of minutes, the dinner is ruined, reminding me how volatile friendships and other relationships are.

"The plot thickens," Hazel speaks up, finally showing interest in something. Of course, it has to be me squirming for a way out. "Don't leave us hanging! Tell the deets!"

"Yes!" Sofia agrees.

"As I had asked, have you talked ever since?" Johanna presses.

"We met yesterday—"

"Oh!" Sofia gasps. "Then he was probably the one I saw you walking with last night. Wow, he looked hot!"

What?

"He did seem a little older, though," she comments, deep in thought. "But then again, it was already dark, and I wasn't particularly close."

"That was Professor Adell," I blurt.

"*What?*" Ethan's voice comes out high-pitched, more than he probably intended.

Oh my, what have I gotten myself into? My cheeks burn with shame as all eyes stay locked on mine.

"Well...Things didn't go well with, ahm, Liam. I was trying to, uh, recompose myself when Professor Adell found me."

"He better not have been an asshole," Ethan sneers.

And thankfully, just like that...all attention shifted away from one precarious situation to the other. I'd rather spill the tea—even if there isn't any— about Professor Adell than my first and only love.

"No, actually..." I trail off, remembering how kind and attentive he was.

For someone who made sure to make my life hell at first, he never once tried to prod at my privacy, knowing I wouldn't want to talk about it. Much unlike Johanna has done in this dinner, putting me on the spot in front of everyone.

I end up settling with a simple, "He was nice."

"He was?" three voices ask in unison, surprise lacing all of their tones.

"Yes, he walked me to my car because it was late and dark. Didn't even ask questions about what had upset me. I reckon it's a development from the hostile behaviour from before..."

Ethan is the first to react, smiling kindly and commenting, "That's good. He finally got some sense into that thick skull."

From there, the conversation carries on, laughter erupting more often than not, and slowly, I feel my body relax as the comfort seeps back in. Johanna still locks gazes with me a few times but doesn't attempt to pull the subject back to Liam.

As it gets later, Sophia is the first one to leave, having to work early the next morning. And Ethan and Hazel go a few minutes after as well since he has to take her home. Awkwardly, I stay behind in the hopes of talking to Johanna.

"It's getting late; I have to go, too," I say as I help her carry the empty plates to the kitchen.

"Yeah, sure." She smiles tightly, walking me to the front door.

Putting on my thick coat, I take a deep breath as I brace myself for the words I'm about to force out. "Look, Johanna," I start. "Just know it's not my goal to meddle with your relationship with Liam."

"It's not that easy, Willow," she sighs. "You two obviously have history but not closure."

I wince. Just as my mouth opens to answer her, a loud knock on the front door startles the both of us.

"I'm so sorry," I mumble. "I'll get out of your way."

My hand finds the doorknob, twisting it open, but instead of finding my escape home, I come face to face with Liam's blue eyes.

Again.

EIGHTEEN

Liam

LIKE A DEER CAUGHT IN THE HEADLIGHTS, THAT'S HOW WILLOW IS currently looking at me.

My body awakens in the worst way possible as mayhem rises in my blood. I've been warring internally for the past few days, and these unplanned encounters mess up my brain more than I'd like to admit.

"What are you doing here?" I bite out as, once again, my impulsiveness talks louder than my rational side.

Willow visibly flinches at the harshness of my voice, and for a second, forgetting all of the hurt, remorse gnaws at my chest, constricting it. The urge to hold her, protect her, and apologise is still inherently part of me, but all of the bad memories she left quickly decimate any shred of empathy I still harbour for her. It's truly fucked up how dissonant my body is.

As she quickly dashes right past me, avoiding any kind of physical touch, disappointment washes over me. My words were more an attempt to get a reaction out of her than wanting her to leave.

But who am I kidding? It's Willow. She is *not* confrontational.

"I thought things had been solved between the two of you?" Johanna's words finally bring my attention to her.

"Yeah, right," I scoff. "No way."

"Then why did she say so?"

"To avoid talking about it," I tell her. "That's Willow, constantly running away from her problems."

Johanna stares off into the now-empty common hall, a pensive expression on her face. Then, with a heavy sigh, her head tilts to the side, beckoning me to come in.

"Are you ready?"" I ask, following her in.

"Give me five minutes to freshen up." She disappears into the corridor, leaving me alone in her apartment.

It's the second time I've been here. The first was when we hooked up on the night we met at the club. It's been a few weeks already, but with starting residency and everything, my time has been scarce.

And the ruined first date didn't help either. Today, though, I am finally taking her on a second date. Making it up to her for that disaster at you-know-where.

I need to move on for my sake and to prove to myself that Willow is part of my past. Johanna could very well be my future for all I know.

"I'm ready," Johanna's confident voice catches my attention as she emerges.

Dressed in a short dress that hugs her figure and high heels, she's seductively stunning.

"Let's go, then." I hold my arm up so she can loop hers around mine.

When we get downstairs and step out into the street, Johanna freezes.

"What's wrong?"

"She's still here," she whispers.

My eyes follow the direction she's looking, and there, in the middle of the almost-empty parking lot, is a small old car. The car isn't working, and the lights are off, so for Johanna to recognise it... it's because she's probably still inside.

"What the hell is going on between you, Liam?"

"Nothing," I grit out.

"Doesn't look like it. You're always so on edge whenever she is around, and she...well, she has too many secrets for me to understand what the hell she is on about."

Secrets? What secrets?

I glare at the car as if it will magically tell me everything I need to know when I know damn well it won't happen. With a side glance at Johanna, her worried expression guilts me into the present.

This beautiful woman wants to be with me, and here I am, letting my world be turned upside down by someone who doesn't even deserve it. There's some hesitancy in her body language, enough to tell me how threatened she feels by Willow's presence.

I can't let that happen. This needs to work, so I can move on. I need to show her she has nothing to worry about.

"Too bad for her," I grumble. "You harvest what you sow."

Tugging on her, I turn us around and head to my car. There, I make a point of unlocking it and opening the passenger door for Johanna before entering the driving side. Still, her car's not working. There's no sign she's driving away anytime soon, and with a sigh, I rev mine and slowly head off.

Our last encounter has been eating away at my brain and heart. She doesn't look much different physically, but that's all there is. It felt like I was looking at a another person who resembled her. Like a long-lost twin no one ever knew existed.

The way she talked, moved, and behaved was certainly not like the Willow I once knew. The continuously shaking hands or the constant check over her shoulder, the sunken and dull eyes over her pale skin were an obvious tell that life has not been easy on her. It was heightened by the way her eyes widened in panic and how she flinched at the prospect of my touch. It broke parts of me I thought were already dead.

It was her broken whisper and the fat tears rolling down her cheeks that put the last nail in the coffin. It stole all the fight from my body at the sight of this broken version of her, and as much as I want to stay mad at her, I wonder so fucking much if…

If she had a valid reason to leave.

"Are you okay?" Johanna asks.

I can't go soft.

"Sorry, yeah. Just focusing on driving," I lie.

When we get to the bar, the host directs us to the booth in the VIP area that I booked for us. It's close enough to the dancefloor that we can join if we feel like it but private enough that we can just enjoy each other's company. The gold and black of the decorations clash with the bright and blinding lights that are in sync with the music's beat.

"This is awesome!" Her eyes sweep over the place. "I've never been here before. It's such an exclusive place!"

So it's said, but luckily, one of my closest friends is the owner's little brother, and he had told me that to impress a girl, this would be the place to come. I felt stupid at the time because in what world do people live in to be impressed by a bar?

It was never in my mind as a first choice, but when Johanna mentioned it through text last week, well, it was enough to make up my mind.

"Yeah, if Sean wasn't my friend, I couldn't have put us in here either," I admit.

"You didn't have to go through such trouble." Her eyelashes flutter as she slides significantly closer to me on the couch.

I wave it off. "It wasn't. And for you, only the best."

Her body leans in, and the anticipation makes my heart pump faster, warming up my body. Beautiful. Stunning. Sexy. All a man could wish for. Then why is it when her lips graze mine, images of Willow flash before my eyes? The instant guilt leads me to tilt my face automatically, letting her only kiss the corner of my lips.

It's not wrong. Almost a month ago, I never cared about kissing her or hooking up. We're both single, and yet...*it is.*

"Let's go dance," I whisper in her ear as my hand slides to her lower back in a desperate attempt to save this date.

Maybe—*just maybe*—if, by dancing, a moment starts and we get lost in each other, I'll be able to focus on the right woman for me. This one, right here.

"Yes." She beams, jumping off the couch and grabbing my hand, leading us to the dancing area.

After weaving our bodies through the sea of people, we find a spot where we fit, flush against the other's body and moving to the beat. Dancing isn't one of my favourite hobbies, but I do alright. Johanna's hands lock around my shoulders, and her hips swaying snuggly against mine helps.

We dance for a while as I hopelessly try to keep myself in the moment, in the woman attached to me. I try to convince myself of how beautiful and intelligent she is, of how understanding she has been with this cluster fuck, stepping aside, knowing Willow and I need to solve certain things on our own. But nothing works.

As the club's lights flash around us, they seem to pierce right through my eyeballs. And as they reach my brain, memories of Willow flash through them. There is no space between Johanna's body and mine, but my brain feels like it's a thousand miles away. And that's when realisation settles in my chest like a heavy weight I can't get off.

I need to let her go.

In a hopeless attempt to get my mind off her, I bury my face in Johanna's neck while my left arm snakes around her back, pulling her closer to me.

Her perfume invades my nostrils. The warm spicy note hits me hard as the soft hues of wood clash with it. It's strong and surprisingly enticing. A strong perfume for a strong woman just like her. It fits her, but it still doesn't compare to what my brain craves.

My hold loosens up as disappointment spreads. Being with Johanna here is wrong. Not because of Willow's existence but because...I'm still not over her, and leading this outstanding woman on while there's a past I can't get over is not acceptable.

Ugh. I need to set this straight.

My head rises, and Johanna tilts hers, looking straight into my soul with loving, warm brown irises. It pains me to know that I have brought her to a date that is just going to end early...

"Johanna," I call. My voice comes out strained as if I'm in pain at the anticipation of how hard shit is about to hit the fan.

Her eyes widen before a smirk slips through, letting me know she's got the wrong idea.

"Look–" I am cut off with the slam of her lips against mine.

For a moment, I freeze and consequently let her think I am into it. But when my brain finally catches up with my body, I grab her by the shoulders and slowly pull her away. The moment I do, her face slightly twists into a confused frown, and I take a deep breath, preparing myself for impact.

As if two broken hearts weren't enough in the middle of this shitstorm, I'm about to break a third.

NINETEEN

Willow

TODAY IS ONE OF THOSE DAYS.

One of those where you're sad, angry, and tired.

What was going on in my head to make me stay there for that long? I'd hoped they'd be out instead of staying in. My breath of relief got caught up in my throat the moment I saw them leaving the building with Johanna perched over Liam's body.

I can't be mad at them either. Johanna met him before she knew who he was to me, or what he meant. And after all of this time, I couldn't possibly think he hadn't been living his best life, moving on. I know.

But the *thought* of him moving on is less hurtful than *seeing* it with my own eyes. And my brain seems to hate me, too, replaying the image of them together more times than I can count. To worsen things, I forcefully have to stay back at the library to finish up a project until my shift starts at the diner, meaning I won't be seeing Dylan until late at night when he's already sleeping.

These kinds of days are the days I never wanted to have and I'll fight my best to keep them to a minimum. I don't want to be the kind of mum who leaves early in the morning and only comes back late in the evening. *No.* I want to be there for my boy.

But I know sometimes, these kinds of days are inevitable.

"Hey," Johanna's voice catches my attention. "How's it going?"

Her voice sounds off–flat, a contrast from her usually chirpy self. As I turn around, she's standing behind me with a stack of books in her arms. Her expression seems slightly cold and detached, leaving me to wonder what happened.

However, I don't have the courage to ask. It's not like it is my business so, shuffling to the side, I make room for her to sit down next to me.

"I'm hanging on. Days like today when I barely see Dylan are the hardest," I mumble. "And you?"

"It's going." Then she sighs and keeps quiet for a little.

But it's not like a usual silent moment. There's some kind of tension rolling off of her, and I can't pinpoint why. We were fine a few days ago, during dinner.

"Can I ask you something?" Looking back at her, I notice how her back straightens as she tries to appear surer of herself.

Weird. I have never seen Johanna not be sure of herself.

"Is he Liam's?"

I splutter. *What?*

Johanna's eyes blaze towards my own, a different kind of fierceness burning in them. The kind I have never seen before.

Meekly, I ask, "Why do you ask that?"

"Well, besides the obvious unfinished business?" Her voice comes out pointed, defensive. "They look alike. *A lot.*"

"I–" Words fail me from the blind-sighting move she played on me. This is not a subject I'm ready to speak about. I never have with anyone, not even my own brother, let alone a girl I just met a few weeks ago. "It's complicated."

"It's not. He either is or he isn't."

I sigh, defeated. *I wish I knew.*

Keeping silent, I train my eyes on the book page in front of me. Reading is impossible, but it helps if I pretend. Maybe she'll let it go?

"You're not going to tell me," she confirms her suspicions. "Got it. But I am leaving you a warning. That man does not deserve this. He is hurting so bad he can't let himself move on." Her voice wavers, finally bringing my attention to her. "I'll give you some time to think this over and do the right thing. If you don't talk to him and tell him, just know that I will."

Her words hit me hard like a slap to the face. I never considered myself to be selfish before what happened, but her words call me out on it. It is selfish, and from what she said, it seems Liam is hurting more than I'd ever imagined.

For Johanna to know all of this—and I know how much she likes him—is because something happened. And it wasn't good.

He is hurting so bad he can't let himself move on.

And so am I.

Once again, I'm at war with myself. This bittersweet feeling is overwhelming and wrong. On one side, I know he is hurting, but a deep part of me, the one that never got over him, is ecstatic he still hasn't moved on. Which is stupid because that tiny ember of hope is just nonsense. After everything, Liam wouldn't forgive me. He won't.

A rustling sound catches my attention, and I turn just in time to see Johanna stand with her belongings. With a glance at my watch, I notice it's time to head out, too, so I gather my things and head out as well.

The walk to the car is silent. We are both tired and on edge after that awkward conversation. Just as we get outside. heading towards the parking lot, Johanna's voice brings my attention to her.

"I didn't know Professor Adell smoked?" She looks at me quizzically.

"Neither did I," I admit while looking around, trying to find him in the sea of people still walking around campus.

Sure enough, there he is on the opposite side, leaning onto one of the university's buildings, smoking a cigarette. He has these dark jeans on with a white button-up that clings to his body. It is already slightly unbuttoned at the top while his face is adorned with a pair of sunglasses that hide his eyes from everyone around him.

But I can see the frown on his forehead along with the messy hair. It's slightly longer at the top while shorter on the sides, but it seems like he's been running his hand through it a lot today. This man is the epitome of a private, brooding, moody guy, even if it suits him well.

"Ahm, I have to go to work," I break the awkward moment.

She only nods before saying her curt goodbyes. I silently walk to my car, more than ready to drive to work. It's quick, and in no time, I already have the apron tied to my waist while running from booth to booth to keep up with the number of people who decided to come in today.

By the time my break time comes up, I'm breathing heavily from the cardio of waitressing. Still, deciding I need to talk to my brother, I walk outside to the parking lot, calling him.

"Hey, baby girl!" Jake's voice echoes through the Facetime call. "Calling me during work?"

I haven't been talking to him enough lately, especially since school started. But with Dylan's birthday coming up, I want to make sure he can make it. Though, with how much of a dedicated uncle he is...I almost know for sure he wouldn't miss it for the world.

"Hey, Jay. Yeah, it's been busy, and I wanted to take advantage of my break to check up on you."

"Everything's the same. Working and hanging around with friends." His tone isn't suggestive, but his wink gives away the type of company he is referring to.

My brother seems to be a playboy through and through. Not that I care. What he lacks in romantic relationship commitment, he sure compensates with his dedication to his family.

"Well, you do you, brother." I clear my throat, changing the subject. "I called mainly to know if you can come to Dylan's birthday. It's less than a month away, and I wanted to throw him a little party since he's turning six."

"As if I'd miss it; it's only my godson's birthday!" Jake feigns offence, and I roll my eyes at him. "I'd turn the world upside down for that little shit!"

"I know, I know." I chuckle tiredly, my batteries already running low from the full day I've had. And even from the phone, Jake notices.

"You seem tired. Have you been overworking again? Lo, I can send money if you need it."

I hastily shake my head. "No, Jay. It's not workload. Sleep has been evading me lately. A few things have happened, and I've been feeling kind of off, but I'm trying to pull it together."

"Are you sure?" His frown deepens. God, he worries so much. What did I do to deserve such good people? "Anything I can help with?"

"No—not really, no."

Even through the screen, I can feel the heat creeping up my skin from his intense stare.

"What happened?"

For a second, I hesitate but I feel like I'm going to burst into a thousand pieces at any moment. I might as well talk about it to someone. Who better than my only brother? He is the only one that, without knowing it all, has the understanding to some extent of what happened.

"I saw Liam," I admit.

"What? How?"

"He works here apparently? I'm not sure. He was on a date at my workplace. It's safe to say it hasn't gone well," I sigh, feeling defeated. "This is a mess. He hates me, Jay. It's one thing to imagine the consequences of your actions, but it's so damn different to experience them. To feel the extent of the damage I caused, it's so much bigger than I anticipated."

"Lo, I know, rationally, you could have gone about everything in a better way...but—" He stops himself by taking a deep breath. The following words come out laced with pain, one I never thought my brother had experienced. "I saw what it did to you, too. From the outside, I saw you being torn to pieces, an empty shell of the happy, shy, little girl you were. Don't fool yourself into thinking it was—or is—your fault. Out of all of us, you were the one who was hurt and wronged the most. In the midst of all of that pain, you made the best out of it. As well as you could."

My heart swells in appreciation, and my eyes water. This man—my older brother—is the only constant in my life.

He was there when I got home that night. It was the last thing I wanted—for someone to see me like that, but he did. Dishevelled hair, puffy face, and ripped clothes. Right away, he knew something was wrong. But nothing prepared him for my reaction to his touch. The shrilling sound that flew out of my throat was otherworldly, and any other day, I would have cared how horrified my brother looked. But at that moment? All I could think about was getting rid of that moment. Of *his* touch.

From there on out, he knew not to get too close, not to touch me. For a long while, I couldn't stand it. Even now, I still have trouble with it, especially if it's unexpected.

Jake spent the night on my bedroom floor, against the door, with the light on, one of his desperate attempts to make me feel safe. He woke me up from every single nightmare, and every time my eyes shot open, I was met with his tear-flooded cheeks and reddened eyes.

With all of the pain that was around me besides my own—how much my parents struggled to accept or understand—I felt like I was making everyone's life a living hell.

In these situations, it's easy to forget who the true victim was. *Me.* And despite this being hard for him as well, Jake never once let me forget that. It makes me wish I could speak about it properly and tell him everything. The two people who deserve to know everything are Jake and Liam.

"Has he met Dylan?" Jake's voice breaks me away from my thoughts.

"God, no," I exclaim. "Things are bad as it is. It would be disastrous, Jay." My voice cracks as the words leave my mouth. Trying to keep my emotions at bay, I take a deep breath.

"Lo, you'll have to tell him everything at some point," he warns. "If you live in the same city, it's only a matter of time until he runs into you with Dylan." His voice comes out cautious, knowing how sensitive this subject is to me is moulding his words.

I don't think I can do it, though. It's taken me a long time to come to terms with how things turned out. Opening the wound will be excruciating...

"I'll think about it," I say, not committing.

Jake keeps silent, his signature way of telling me he disapproves of the situation. He has always been a "head-on" type of guy, liking to face things properly and solve them as fast as possible, but I'm not like that. I'm not him.

And while some would call me a pushover, I don't care. Confrontation terrifies me to the point I become a nervous mess. So, the solution is avoiding them.

"I have to go back to work, Jay. I'll call you in a few days, yeah?"

"Call me, sis. You know I'm here for whatever you need."

His words make me smile. I know he is.

Until I left to live with Nana, he was always there, despite everything I threw his way. For a whole month, he became more than my own parents and those times were *hard.* Touching was a hard no, and while I could see in his eyes how much it pained him to not be able to comfort me, he managed.

He was ever present at arm's length. Jake endured my hours-long cries, outbursts, nightmares, apathy and lack of hygiene. Even when everything I wanted was for it all to stop. To disappear. To die...he never left.

The first step was forcing me to get out of bed. Then to eat, and finally to shower. And even if I wasn't really speaking, he did. Telling me about his days and avoiding the subjects he knew I wouldn't touch, doing his best to make me feel normal again.

When we said our goodbyes before moving away, I managed to bear a kiss on the forehead without freaking out.

And one thing is for sure, Jacob Hanlon is the most dedicated man you'll find. For five whole years, he travelled almost two hours every weekend to visit. That man never missed an important day either. And with time, as the pregnancy evolved, it got easier because I had better things to focus on.

His constant presence eased the pain, too. And as if knowing it, Dylan always got calmer with him around. Whether still inside my belly and relaxing when his uncle touched my belly, or after he was born, having crying fits that would only stop with his favourite uncle's rocking.

It was a long and slow process, and I bet with my whole heart that my brother is not even aware of how much he has done for me. How much he helped me improve and heal.

After saying my goodbyes, I go back inside. Shilah's busy so I just jump on the first things I see that need my attention. People come in and out faster than I can keep up with.

Even my professor shows up, but I'm so busy I only have time to treat him as a customer, all possible small-talk forgotten. Hours go by at a fast pace, but the intensity has me exhausted.

Once the shift ends and I get changed, I head out. The cold air hits my warm face as the autumn nights steadily get colder. The parking lot is almost empty as the last clients filter out into their cars, ready to go back home.

By the time I get to my car, it's almost empty, and before I can unlock it, a movement catches my attention, scaring the living hell out of me.

I freeze, raising my eyes only to see a shape—a *person.*

It's moving, walking towards me confidently while I stand still like a cornered prey, watching him as my heart speeds up, anxiety filling my bloodstream.

Then he leans against my car, crossing his ankles like he has no intention of moving from there anytime soon.

As the surprise turns into acknowledgement, I gulp.

"What are you doing here?"

TWENTY

Willow

"I HAD A LONG CALL FOR WORK WHEN I WAS ABOUT TO LEAVE, AND by the time I finished, I realised you were already clocking out. So, I just waited for a couple of minutes to see how you're doing."

My insides turn as a wave of foreign excitement courses through me.

What is happening?

In a weak attempt to ignore my body, I exhale those sensations, breathing once before answering, "Professor Adell—"

"Arthur," he cuts me off. "Call me Arthur."

"I-it's hard. You're my professor." My words come out weak as I try to remind him—*and myself*—and the reality we find ourselves in.

There's a solid, thick barrier around what a student and teacher relationship should be. And it's clear it should never be disrespected.

"Calling me Arthur isn't wrong. I am extra strict on a daily basis because—and I don't mean this in a smug way—it's very common to have students flirt or try to have something with me. Drawing that line from the beginning is imperative."

"I understand." He is a handsome man. I reckon it would be frustrating after a while.

"And now that I know you're not going to disrespect those boundaries, I can relax with a student for the first time in...years."

"I'm glad, then." I smile, and he returns it.

It's awkward but at the same time, peaceful. We've found common ground. One where he doesn't hate my guts, and I'm not constantly in fear of his next move. It almost seems like instead of just tolerating my presence, he enjoys it... like friends.

I resist the urge to laugh at the irony. Friends with my professor? Professor Prick out of all of them? Who would have thought?

It's weird. Too weird.

"I–" Stammering, not knowing what to say, I decide on a silent departure. My body moves on its own accord, stepping away from the car so I can start looking for the keys to unlock it.

This is too much and too confusing. It's also late, and I need to get going.

Except, my bag falls to the floor, and just when I am about to crouch down to pick it up, a firm hold on my arm startles me. I jump at the same time my heart does, almost escaping through my mouth.

My brain fogs, too, as the darkest part of it opens unwanted memories.

"Shit," I whisper-yell, clutching at the knot in my chest.

"Sorry," he hastily says, walking closer and stopping when I take a step away.

Rationally, I know I'm not in danger. There are a few cameras in the parking lot, and he's my professor. He has looked out for Dylan, too. I am ninety per cent sure he wouldn't hurt me, but...ever since that night, there will always be a part of me that is permanently alert. The constant flight or fight mode is exhausting, but there's no turning it off. Not anymore.

Breathe in. Breathe out.

When my heart rate finally slows down and I will myself to open my eyes, Professor Adell is looking at me with a deep frown and concern shadowing his face.

"I didn't mean to scare you. I–" Professor Adell stutters.

"It's fine," I cut him off with a weak smile. "I just wasn't expecting it."

He bends down and picks up my bag, giving it to me right away.

"Are you alright?" Professor Adell's voice brings me back to the real world.

"Yes, um, just a little tired. Today was a full day." I smile at him. "But um, did you need something from me?"

"I—" He stutters again. "You looked tired during work. I wanted to check in on you, to see if you needed something."

"That's kind of you, Professor A—" His sudden glare has me hesitating, and I correct myself. "*Arthur.* Thank you, but you didn't have to wait for me. It's already late."

"It's fine. How's school? Besides my subject, of course." He scratches the back of his neck. "With Dylan and work, I bet it can be overwhelming sometimes. I just wanted to make sure you're alright, and if there's anything I can do to help, let me know."

What? Why?

Is it still the guilt? I don't get it...

"Pro—*Arthur,* just because you weren't nice in the beginning, doesn't mean you should feel obliged to be nice all the time. I can manage on my own."

"That's no—" He stops himself and takes a deep breath. "That's not why I am checking in on you. I just..." He trails off, not finishing what he was about to say.

"You what?" I press, confused.

"I just worry." He blurts out, stunning me.

He worries. He...*worries?*

My mouth opens and closes like a gaping fish.

"It's just..." he continues after another deep breath. "Look, I feel like you need a friend," he states, shocking me even more. "Hell, *I* need a friend, too, and I...I don't know! You're the first person I've felt comfortable with in years."

"What?"

"Yep." He nods, assuring me—or himself? I don't know anymore. "Friends."

The déjà vu hits me unannounced. Late at night and alone with him, with the word friends ringing in my ears, it certainly takes me back in time.

"Come on. We're friends, Lo," he whispers in my ear. "It's meant to be."

Bile rises in my throat as the memory invades my brain. Not again. I don't need or want male attention. I just...*oh god, I can't do this.* I have to find a way to go, to leave.

"You're my professor." That's all I can say. "This isn't...I'm not..."

"No, no, no!" he defends, fear consuming his expression. "That's not what I meant, Willow. I meant it in a platonic way. I just..." His humourless laugh stops his words. "Look, I don't know what I am doing, really. I was completely wrong about you from the beginning and ever since I met Dylan...I feel comfortable, like you're trustworthy, and I liked getting to know you a little more. That's all—" Another sigh. "It's nothing beyond regular friendship, I swear!" He puts his palms up, the universal sign of surrender.

The clarification calms me down a bit. *But just slightly.*

"I don't know if we should," I whisper. "It's still wrong. It still goes beyond what a student and teacher should be."

I see his shoulders sag and dejection overcome his features. My mouth opens but before words can come out, he speaks, "It's fine. I understand, Miss Hanlon. Just let me know if I can help with something, I'd be happy to help out."

The cold type of stare he used to give me, in the beginning, is back, and it makes me shrink back into myself. Guilt stabs into my skin like those nagging splinters you can't get rid of. What if he is telling the truth and all he wants is an innocent friendship? It wouldn't be wrong.

Still, the whiplash from how quickly he changes from nice and warm to cold and detached is real. It confuses the hell out of me, more often than not leaving me lost on how to act around him.

"Y-yes. Thank you." God, it feels like I am back to my teenage years of stuttering around like a goddamn fool.

"Good." He nods before continuing, "I'm sorry for taking up your time, you must be exhausted. Go rest. I'll see you in class, Miss Hanlon."

With a curt nod, he turns on his heels and disappears into the night, leaving me dumbfounded next to my car.

Oh god, what am I doing?

This man is my professor for goodness' sake. I shouldn't be feeding into these walks and talks and whatnot. The fact I enjoy his company and attention only makes it worse, it makes me feel guilty and disgusting.

Unlocking my car, I get in with a trembling hand, immediately locking it once I'm inside. While the statistics claim the country isn't that dangerous, my brain tells me otherwise. In my experience, *everywhere* is dangerous for a woman.

I surely, know that.

After ten minutes of driving, I get home and eagerly get in a hot shower, one I wish could wash away the exhaustion, stress, and most of what happened tonight. Arthur seemed full of good intentions, but it doesn't mean the memories weren't there, trying to come back in full force to remind me of the constant dangers that exist out there.

I've worked so hard to overcome these fears and to make my peace with the past, but it doesn't make it any less painful. Every time they come back, they hit me like a train. And here, alone in the safety of my shower, I allow myself to let it all out. A few sobs come out but the sound of the water running swallows any noise I make.

I don't know how long I stay here, but by the time I get a grip on my emotions, my fingers are wrinkled. Getting out, I dry myself and dress in my pyjamas before taking a peek in Dylan's room.

He's lying on his stomach on the bed with his arms and legs spread wide, snoring lightly. He's too cute and too important to me. He's my anchor. Without thinking twice, I enter the room and pick him up. He stirs a little but sleeps the whole way from his bedroom to mine, on the other end of the corridor.

When we get to my bed, I place him carefully on it and get under the sheets, pulling him to my chest and cuddling with him. He immediately latches himself onto me, like it's natural. Relief reaches me, and my body relaxes into the mattress. In no time, slumber takes over, and I dive into a deep sense of calmness.

He's my calm. My calm in the middle of the storm.

TWENTY-ONE

Willow

"I LOVE YOU," HE ADMITS WITH FINALITY.

Every time he says these three little words, it's like my body gains new life. My weak heart resurrects, beating faster than ever. My stomach flutters as if I had butterflies trapped inside, frantic for a way out. These three little words are enough to make me light-headed and dizzy, almost like when you're floating in the calm ocean.

He doesn't understand the effect he has on me, and neither did I before we kissed for the first time.

We've said these three words to each other many times before, but it never felt as loaded as it does now. It giddies me up as much as it hurts me because I don't think he understands their true meaning. I'm not sure I do either.

This first time we kissed, it was magical. But I was brought back to Earth pretty quickly. For a few weeks now, Liam has been weird and oddly distant. Being the stupid shy girl I am, I've let it continue.

Today, though, he is back to normal—almost. His gaze seems more intense, and his words sound certain and calculated, but I don't understand why. Since he is acting how he did before, he must want me to understand we're only going to be friends.

Which I understand. He probably regretted it the moment it happened. I mean, why would he be interested in me? Plain old Willow, the shy little girl who can't even talk without stuttering.

There are prettier and hotter girls at school pining after him. He probably understood what he was missing.

With a sigh, I say, "Me, too. I'll see you tomorrow."

I am trying to dismiss those words the best I can. I don't want him to understand how sad I get every time he says it without meaning it the way I do. Hoping to avoid dragging the awkwardness of the moment even more, I climb off his scooter, giving him the helmet back.

But instead of being able to turn around and walk up to my front door, his hand grabs mine right before he climbs off of it as well. In a swift and assured movement, he takes his helmet off, placing it right next to mine on top of the scooter's seat.

He pulls me against his chest with force, stealing a gasp out of me.

"We're having some communication problems it seems, Lo." He hums my name at the end, tilting my chin up to look at him.

My lashes part, giving me the best view ever. His bright blue eyes are darker than normal, and the shine seems stronger than usual. It sears through me, straight into the deepest parts of my soul, warming it.

"You silly girl." He laughs. "When I say I love you, I mean it. I love you and only you." His words raise the hairs on my skin, causing shivers to run through it. They only grow into persistent tingles the moment his nose bumps into mine.

Like a fish out of water, my mouth opens up, but no sounds come out. Spring is just shy of starting, with the temperature carrying a chilly wind and the last remnants of humidity too stubborn to disappear, but I feel warm. I'm blazing hot, more so than the temperature outside.

It's the blood being pumped frantically through my veins; I know it. Because that is what Liam Davis does to my body. He overworks and heats me up, almost causing it to break down.

It feels like he has the power to break me apart. And something inside me tells me it isn't just a feeling.

His hand comes around my waist, pulling me even closer to him, almost as if he knows I am about to lose my strength. Then, he takes me by surprise, pushing his lips against mine.

He's gentle at first, the soft grazing of his lips against mine, but he quickly gains momentum. His hold tightens just as his tongue peeks out, asking for permission, and I melt. Letting my body fit against his, I bring my hands to the nape of his head, tangling my fingers in his dark blond hair, opening my mouth.

Everything else but him disappears as we get lost in the sensations of each other.

Trust and safety envelop my heart in the same way his arms envelop me, ruining me for anyone else in this world. This is it. This is all I need.

When we finally separate, panting for air, he whispers, "Do you want to be my girlfriend?"

My heart swells, feeling too big for my chest, but I can't help the smile that stretches on my face. It's all I want.

I nod eagerly, repeating the word yes a few times. He laughs and hugs me tight. For a few moments, rapture robs the both of us of common sense as he picks me up and starts swirling me around in the middle of the street.

Just as quickly, our loud and happy laughter ceases to exist, being replaced by a groggy and slurred voice. One I never wish to hear, ever again in my life. And yet, it's still around, lurking from the deepest corners of my mind, ready to taunt me for eternity.

"Shit. What have I done?"

In any other situation, I'd care that he sobered up and realised the mistake he just made, but this time around, it's too late. Some things can't be undone. The rustling and stumbling echo throughout the large living room, but my brain has drowned out all noises.

Tears stream down my face aggressively, but I don't dare move a finger. If I remain still, he won't come back. He won't remember I'm still here.

It's only when I hear a door shut in the far distance, on the first floor of this three-storey house, do I dare breathe.

I can't stay here a minute longer. Safety. I need safety.

So, I run. I run until that damned house turns into the safety of my bedroom, of my bathroom. I ignore the banging on the other side of the door, turning on the faucet. There's a tiny sliver of hope that the scorching water that runs out of the tap will clean my dirty body.

It doesn't, but I welcome the burn. It helps ease the physical and emotional pain. My knees hit my chest, and I circle my arms around my head, crying into the small cocoon I've made.

Everything and everywhere hurts.

But nothing hurts more than realising what this means. To me. To him and everyone around us...I can't be the reason for so much pain. And that's enough to make me realise this is my cross to carry. Alone and in secret, no matter how much it'll cost me.

A sharp sting in my chest startles me, waking me up from my sleep. The safety of consciousness doesn't seem much of a relief from the nightmare—there's no difference in the kind of pain that consumes me.

I may be miles—and years—from what happened, but my body and brain seem to remember it as if it happened just yesterday.

"Mummy?" Dylan's voice grounds me back to the present, away from the torments that my brain seems to find to torture me.

"I'm here, baby. Did I wake you up?" I whisper so he doesn't witness the shakiness in my voice.

He nods and comes closer to me as I take a shaky breath.

"Sorry, my love." I kiss his forehead before lying back down, closer to him.

Then his little hands start to wander through my shoulders until he finds my face. It may be weird to a lot of people, but he likes to do this sometimes in the middle of the night. To touch my face and make sure I am here with him, a kind of reassurance habit he gained over the years.

When he touches my cheeks, his hands freeze, and I can already imagine his frown upon realising I have a tear-stained face.

"Are you crying, Mummy? Did you have a dream-mare?" His words make me chuckle lightly.

When Dylan started talking, and I started teaching him words, this was one of the words he struggled the most in learning: nightmare. I don't even know why but because he couldn't say it, he started to say dream-mare.

Even though he can already say it properly now, it's stuck.

I find it so cute. My baby is so cute.

"Yes, baby, but it's gone now. You made it better." I cuddle him. "You make everything better," I whisper.

"You too, Mummy. I love you."

"I love you, baby. Now, go back to sleep. We have a big day ahead of us." I chuckle slightly and hold him close to me as he slowly falls back asleep.

As for me, sleep has evaded me. It always happens when I have nightmares—or memories, rather. They always start with good or happy moments that somehow transform into that dreadful night. Everything I went through wasn't bad enough, my self-sabotaging brain is still trying to find ways to stain all the good memories I still hold dear.

Staying awake, fighting off unwanted thoughts and watching my angel sleep is the best way to keep some of my memories safe. As well as what's left of my sanity.

"Mum, look!" Dylan shrieks in excitement. "It's a lion!"

He lets go of my hand to try and run to the glass wall, but I hold him tighter, not letting him go far. The zoo is crowded, and the last thing I need is to lose sight of him.

"Dylan, we'll get there. What have I told you? Do not let go of my hand," I repeat for the thousandth time today.

This kid is impulsive and rash. A true hurricane that I find exhausting sometimes. Saturdays have been a day that I try to focus on him and quality time with him. So, this time around, we came to the zoo.

Last night left me exhausted, but nothing beats the sheer happiness on Dylan's face. Seeing him so excited and happy makes up for everything else. He makes all of the sacrifices and efforts worth it.

"Come on, Mum. You're too slow! They'll run away by the time we get there," he whines, and I chuckle, keeping my slow pace.

"Where will they run away to? Not the city I hope," I joke, and he gives me a glare.

He still likes to think the animals are in the wilderness, and we just have a special ticket that takes us directly there—as though we'd teleported. Before him, I'd forgotten how much our imaginations run wild when we're kids. It brings back a few pleasant memories from the treehouse that I imagined being my "prison room" at the top of the highest tower of the palace.

I used to force Liam to pretend to be my prince charming and to come up there and save me. He hated it, but he did it nonetheless. It brings a smile to my face.

"Look, Mummy. They are so big! If they get mad, they will be angry and-and..." He puffs his chest and arches his arms towards his belly making this ugly, angry face before continuing, "They will roar like this: *roawaar*!"

"Oh, yeah?" I ask, making him think he is teaching me something. "What will they do if they are hungry?"

"Eat insects!" he says as a matter of fact, and I burst out laughing.

This kid has watched *The Lion King* one too many times. I think I need to make him watch proper wilderness documentaries one of these days, otherwise he'll think lions only eat insects, like Simba.

"Alright lion whisperer, let's go see the zebras!"

After a few minutes of walking, we arrive, and he is in love with them.

"Mummy, they're just like horses." I nod in acknowledgement. "But they just have stripes!"

"Something like that, I guess." I chuckle. "Want to see something else?"

"Not yet. I like the zebras. Can I have one for my birthday?" He makes these manipulative puppy eyes that make me give in ninety percent of the time.

Well, the ten percent apply to situations like this, when getting a zebra is as impossible as it is illegal.

"Unfortunately no, baby. Zebras need space to run, and our backyard is really small," I tell him.

"I will walk her every day, Mum. I promise." I burst out laughing again.

"Dylan, a zebra is not the same as a dog. They grow a lot, eat a lot, and need to run hundreds of miles sometimes. I promise that when you get a little bit older, we'll get a dog. Okay, baby?"

"Fine," he huffs, crossing his arms over his chest.

"What else would you like for your birthday? It's only one week away!"

October has gone by, and since it's the fourth of November, we are exactly one week away from his birthday, next Saturday on the eleventh. Jake told me he'd get here by Friday and spend the weekend with us.

I was hoping he'd get some more time, but I understand that he can't take days away from work now, so three days is better than none.

"You won't be angry if I tell you?" he asks hesitantly.

"Of course not, baby," I assure him.

Dread replaces the blood inside my veins, freezing my body momentarily. There's a bit of hope he won't ask for what I know I can't give him, but the way he keeps looking down, refusing to meet my eyes, playing with the hem of his T-shirt, tells me everything I need to know.

"I would like to meet my dad," he whispers so only I can hear.

Every time I think my heart can't break anymore, I'm taught a lesson. Not really knowing what to do, I hug him.

"Oh, honey. I'm sorry!"

"Can you do it?" His lips move against my shoulder, and I take a moment to think about what to say as my hand rubs his back in circular motions.

Tears sting my eyes, threatening to fall at any moment. This is not the way I was expecting the day to go. He hasn't touched the subject of his dad for a few weeks, and I thought—stupidly—that he had forgotten about it. For a while, at least.

How could he forget? He's at the age to learn and understand the world around him better and better. And I owe him the truth—not only him—but I thought I'd have more time to figure this out...to know how to deal with it.

How I'll do it, I don't know yet, but I need to. Whatever it takes—for Dylan—I need to muster up the courage for it.

"I honestly don't know, baby. But I will try, I promise."

TWENTY-TWO

Willow

THE OBNOXIOUSLY LOUD AND CONTINUOUS SOUND OF THE doorbell wakes me up.

"Who the hell is ringing this aggressively at six a.m. on a bloody Sunday?" I hear Nana's angry voice walking down the corridor as I groan.

"I'll go, Nana. Go back to bed," I say as I open my bedroom door and step out into the corridor.

"No, no! I'll go get my fake gun just in case," she mutters, shocking me in place.

"Nana, are you out of your mind? There's no need," I whisper-shout. "I will look through the peephole, and if it's some weirdo, we'll call the police."

Going down the stairs, I close my robe tighter to my body and knot the ribbon around my waist. Perching myself on my toes, I peek through the peephole to see who is on our porch at this ungodly hour—on a bloody Sunday.

My eyes zero on a mop of messy brown hair first since the figure is looking down. When it moves, the light sensor snaps and the light turns on, showing better the big, bulky man on the other side. When he raises his head and looks right into the peephole, even though he can't see me, I can, and I am met with the warmest green eyes and the goofiest smile I've ever had in my life.

"*Ahhh*!" I shriek, opening the door right away.

On the other side stands my big brother with the widest smile on his face. He's wearing a plain white T-shirt with his signature dark jeans. I barely give him time to open his arms before I jump into his embrace, wrapping both my arms and legs around him.

"Aren't you a little too old for this kind of hug by now, Lo?" Jake chuckles.

He always complained about my clinginess but never really did anything to stop it. So, I counter with a shrug. "I'll never get too old for some sibling love!"

With me not really moving, he decides to enter the house with me still wrapped around his torso.

"Jakey, my boy. What a lovely surprise!" Nana exclaims, finally putting down that ridiculous artifact.

He bends down, and I begrudgingly let go of him, letting him greet Nana. He kisses her cheek and gives her a light side hug. When she turns around to go store the gun, he lip-syncs the words "crazy old woman", making me chuckle.

As always, Jake is unpredictable. Even though we are opposites, we always got along perfectly. He was never too protective until that night, especially because I spent ninety-five percent of my time with Liam, and he knew I was safe. But after everything went down, a lot changed, and his protectiveness only grew.

Even with the distance still existing between us, he comes around so often to spend time with Dylan and me. Always has, since I left to live with Nana. Besides the quality time, he also took it upon himself to do all the things that normally the father of the child would. The appointments, the ultrasounds, the shopping sprees...

I know he always felt responsible and obliged to help me every time he could. The distance didn't allow him to be present on a daily basis, so he compensated however he could. And even though I told him—and still do—time and time again that he doesn't have to do all of this, there is no deterring him.

It's hard and tiring sometimes, not only physically but emotionally. I noticed the ever-present sadness swirling around his eyes whenever my bump got bigger, the unusually long periods of time he'd just hold Dylan against his chest or the way he'd watch him so closely or trace his tiny nose, chin, and hands. It was hard on him, too, even if I don't understand the real reason.

I never dared ask, but he knew he could tell me if he wanted or needed to. Still, he never said no to us. He still doesn't say no and there's no way I can stop him. There's no going against Jacob Hanlon.

"Can I go wake up our little champ?" he asks, breaking my little reverie.

"Go ahead," I tell him. "It's almost time for him to wake up anyway. I'll set up breakfast for us." I smile as he excitedly kisses my forehead. Then he disappears into the hallway towards the stairs.

For whatever reason, he—or the gods—have decided, he's still single. Ever since that nasty break-up he had a few weeks before I left, he has never settled down again. His only focus was his goal after college—becoming an architect.

And he did. Now, he comfortably lives in his penthouse in the capital, making good money. Thankfully, he can't be around every day now, otherwise, he'd be spoiling all three of us instead.

Not even five minutes after I start preparing the food for breakfast, I hear loud laughter from upstairs followed by Jake's signature chuckle. Just hearing them makes me smile.

After that slump at the zoo, this is a good surprise for Dylan. The best distraction to give me some time. Hopefully, enough so I can figure out how to solve this.

Just as I am about to finish everything, Jake shows up carrying my kid by the legs, upside down.

"Jay, what the hell are you doing to my child?" I exclaim, horrified.

"This monkey asked for it. He just mocked his uncle." Jake scoffs while manhandling him from one hand to the other, and Dylan all but giggles at the action.

Eventually, everyone settles to eat breakfast. Dylan is hyper about having Jake with us for the entire week until his birthday—instead of just the predicted weekend. He's telling Jake everything from when we got here to meeting Abby and his new friends at school. And even though, by the end of his speech, everyone surely feels tired of listening to him, no one shows it—especially not my brother.

We spend the morning in the park. Jake keeps busy with us the whole time, not even checking his phone which keeps ringing.

When we are getting ready to leave, I can't help but blurt, curious, "How come you are this good with kids and don't have your own yet? You're older than me for god's sake. You're almost twenty-seven!"

For a split second, his expression falls. Anyone else wouldn't notice, but I do.

Pain. It has been silently present ever since he and Daniela broke up, more so at first. And even though I tried to coax it out of him, he always refused, probably not wanting me to worry about him while my life was a hurricane in itself.

The period following their split was the wildest—one-night stands and casual encounters. There hasn't been a stable girlfriend ever since. While I used to think it must have been a phase, I am starting to realise now...

My brother's heart has been bruised far deeper than I ever thought, and it pains me that I haven't been there for him as he has been for me. This is the look of a man who has been carrying the weight of the world on his shoulders. *For years.*

Surprisingly, he recovers, smiling widely and answering me, "Well, sis, I have too much love to share for now. And kids are for when you settle down. I'm still too young for that." He laughs but it doesn't reach his eyes.

If it were any other person saying those words, I would have been offended, but I get what he means. The commitment phobia is palpable in his voice, the desperate need to be as free as a bird and taste as many fish as the ocean has to offer so he doesn't get burned again.

There's no need for more words, knowing he will only open up when he's ready. That's why I squeeze his hand in silent comfort and understanding. In return, he raises our hands, kissing my knuckles.

"I'm hungry," he mutters, breaking the moment.

Dylan overhears, turning his attention to us and nodding eagerly in agreement. So, we walk to Shilah's dinner, just short of ten minutes away from the park. The moment we enter and Shilah's eyes lands on us, my son rushes to the counter in excitement, telling her all about Jake.

"He's staying until my birthday!" he exclaims, making her chuckle.

"When is that buddy?"

"Next weekend," he answers her. "At least, that's what Mummy says."

She hums, with a focused frown on her eyebrows before asking, "What are you going to do for your birthday, then?"

Instead of answering, he looks at me with an expectant gaze. I've thought about doing a small party for his friends at the house, but I haven't told him anything yet. I wanted to speak with the parents and invite them first–to make sure I'll have some guests.

"I'll probably throw him a party back at home for his school friends," I give in to his puppy eyes, answering. His eyes sparkle with happiness, and I can't help but add, "*If* Dylan behaves until then."

The megawatt smile falters, and we can't help but chuckle.

After that, we all sit down in a booth, and Shilah quickly brings us some food. Jake and Dylan spend the entire time in their typical banter, lifting my mood. In their presence, I forget all of the troubles and problems that plague my mind. They make it seem easier, even if just for a little while.

"Hey, kiddo!" Hannah calls from the counter. "I have a surprise for you back here. Do you want some dessert?"

He nods eagerly and looks at me in question, but as soon as I nod in agreement, he jumps out of the booth and runs towards Hannah. Is he a toddler or a starved dog? Sometimes, I can't find the difference.

As soon as he's out of earshot, Jake nudges me with his shoulder, bringing my attention to him.

"So what's new, sis?" he asks with curiosity oozing out of him.

"Nothing much, uh–" I pause to collect my thoughts. "After that encounter I told you about, I have tried to talk to him but couldn't. And ran away...again."

"Lo," he sighs, shaking his head negatively. "You not telling me or Nana, I understand. But sis, think about Dylan. Liam deserves to know."

"I can't talk about what truly happened; I'm not ready."

"Have you thought about going to a therapist? It might help..."

Jake's right. He's always right, but the mere thought of talking about it makes my throat clog up. The panic always rises so high my brain gets foggy and my heartbeat skyrockets. I get enough of these as it is. Diving into them willingly? No, thank you.

I just want to forget.

As if my brother just read my mind, he mutters, "There's no forgetting it, Lo. You just learn to live with it."

I nod but don't answer, and Jake keeps quiet for a bit. At the far end of the diner, Hannah is giving Dylan a chocolate mousse, helping him eat it without getting it on his shirt. We both watch them in silence for a few seconds, the heaviness of the previous conversation still hanging around us.

Talking about Liam and all of this is the last thing I want to do today. The goal is to enjoy the little time I get to spend with my only brother before he has to go back home. But apparently, he has other plans.

"You need to tell Liam," he mutters, pain lacing his rough voice.

"About what?" I ask, playing dumb.

He scoffs. "About Dylan; what else?"

"Jake..." I sigh, not really knowing what to say anymore.

Rationally, I know what I need to do. But my heart has been so battered before that I don't know if it could take any more pain.

"He deserves to know, Lo. The sooner the better, otherwise, he won't forgive you," he says with a soft tone.

"The worse has been done. He won't forgive me either way..."

"You don't know that." He shakes his head. "Look, sometimes love is strong enough to overlook all of that and forgive. If he loved you the way I know he—"

"Stop." My voice comes out shaky, cracking right at the end. "Please, Jay. I don't—"

"What if he sees you around town with Dylan, huh? What then? That boy is the carbon copy of Liam. He'll put two and two together, and—"

"Mummy?" My shoulders sag at the sounds of Dylan's voice, interrupting us.

Thank goodness.

"Yes, baby?" I pull him onto my lap.

"Your friend just left."

What? What friend? Is he talking about Johanna?

"Johanna? Why didn't she come to say hello?"

"No, Mummy. The one that stayed with me while you were working here," he clarifies.

That's...Arthur?

"Oh." I am at loss for words.

"Yeah, he said hello, and then he left. I think he was sad, Mummy."

My jaw slacks open, and I look at Jake. He has a brow cocked upwards, and I know I'll have to answer his questions in the future. He will be all about who the hell is the person Dylan was talking about, and that is one conversation—well, another one—I don't want to have.

"I don't know, baby; maybe something happened to him. I'll ask him when I see him. Have you finished your dessert?" He nods in response. "Good. We can go home now."

We both pay for lunch and thank Shilah for having us. When we exit the diner, I see my professor leaning against a car and smoking. His face is hunched down and shaking from side to side. From afar, I can't be sure, but it looks like he is muttering something to himself.

Just as I'm about to look away, he lifts his head, and we lock gazes. He seems pained, but I can't understand properly why. This man is the most mysterious and confusing one I've ever met. Why is he here? And why does it seem like he is waging a war with himself?

Seeing him like this reminds me of the night we talked to each other out here after my shift. How he showed his intentions for us to become...friends?

Maybe I was a fool to refuse it, to refuse him because now it looks like he needs one.

TWENTY-THREE

Liam

"WHEN WILL YOU COME HOME, BABY? WE MISS YOU SO MUCH," MY mum coos, hoping I'll visit soon.

"Probably around Christmas or the New Year. I've been working a lot."

Well, I've been willingly drowning in work so I don't think about other things. So I don't think about *her.*

And yet, she's still living there rent-free.

Fuck!

"That's still two months away from now. If you're not coming over, we'll visit you."

"Now's not a good time, Mother. I would barely have time to be with you guys. I promise if I have a weekend or something, I'll visit." A blatant lie.

I love my parents. I honestly do.

But ever since Mason left, spending time with them has been overbearing. Insufferable. If we both used to be scrutinized, now, I am the sole target. I am hit with it double.

All hell breaks loose when they mention my brother. He left because of them—because of their self-centred egos and their constant pursuit of proper appearances. For the perfect life.

The irony, huh? That wanting everything to be—to look—perfect is what broke us all apart. Just thinking about it angers me, knowing that I was the lucky one because of a degree choice. Ultimately, I lost my brother.

"Liam? Are you listening to me?" My mother's voice sounds from the other side of the phone. My thoughts got so loud—as usual—that I missed everything she has been telling me for the last few minutes.

"I was telling you that your father finally gave in."

"Gave in on what?" Even if deep down, I knew.

"We're going to look for your brother, honey. We're going to bring him home."

I keep silent for a bit, digesting this new information. I love my brother, and it gutted me when he disappeared but after what I seen he chose for his life, I can't say I am thrilled. Not even by offering him help, asking him to come with me and living together here was enough. He was already far too deep.

Fuck, this is one conversation I don't want to have.

"Hey, Ma. I have to go," I cut her off, not even listening anymore.

"What? Why?"

"I have to go to the grocery store. If I don't go now, I won't be able to in the next couple of days because I'll be doing double shifts. I'll call soon. Tell Dad I said hi. Love you."

As soon as she says her goodbyes, I hang up. In a flash, I put my shoes on and take the car to the supermarket.

This is the only part of caring for a house that I hate. The effort of not forgetting what I need to cook is too much, and there's always something that's left behind. It forces me to come back after a couple of days, and it drives me crazy.

Adulthood. We've got to do what we've got to do.

Ten minutes in, and I'm already regretting being in here. The aisles are filled with people who keep on bumping into each other or pushing them out of their way to get what they want. And man, do I hate that. Is it so hard to be polite and ask people permission or something? I mean, fucking hell.

Ugh...I'm in a mood.

Thankfully, I get what I need quickly, eager to head back home. But the sight of a familiar face freezes me on the spot.

Sure enough, right down the hall, stands Jacob fucking Hanlon. In the same fucking supermarket as I am with a kid perched on his hip. The young boy looks to be around five or six years old, and while I can't see his face, he obviously inherited the Hanlons' dark brown hair.

They seem deep in a heated discussion in front of the chocolate shelves with Jacob consistently shaking his head, and the kid's arms flailing around them.

Can't I fucking escape any of them? I moved up here for a reason, after all.

As the anger gets the best of me, I walk up to them and blurt, "Have you all moved up here or what?"

They both shut up and look at me startled. I focus on Jacob's face, not really wanting to drag the kid more into the middle of this more than I have to. It's enough that he's witnessing my outburst. Just then, Jake's face changes from shock to acknowledgement.

With a slight sway on his step, he turns to face me and answers, "As a matter of fact, no; I'm just visiting."

"Look–"

"I still want the chocolate!" the little boy whines, interrupting us.

As our attention is brought to him, I freeze again.

Mixed feelings overtake me as I study his appearance. He is familiar–*too familiar*–but I can't pinpoint the reason. Besides the hair, the kid looks nothing like his father, their skin a striking contrast. While Jacob and Willow have a paler skin tone, the kid has a golden, slightly darker tone to it as if he spent long hours out in the sun, but what strikes me the most is the eyes.

He has shiny and clear blue eyes. Very similar to mine.

Weird.

As curiosity gets the best of me, I ask, "You a father already?"

Imagining Jake married with kids was never on the top five positions of my list for possible future outcomes. Hell, it wasn't even in the last position. If anything, I imagined I'd be married to his sister and having kids with her long before he ever did. Jake would have been the cool single uncle.

Would ours look like Jake's kid looks like?

Fucking hell, I need to get a grip.

Looking back at the kid, he's finally quiet, his eyes intently locked on mine, now. A shiver runs down my spine so strong I have to shake my head and look away.

Wait, I remember him!

"You were at the hospital," I say a little too loud, pointing at the kid, not giving Jake the time to answer.

His eyes widen and he nods, "With my best friend."

"Right," I hum. "She needed glasses?"

"Yeah..." the boy trails off, looking at me slightly suspicious.

"Em..." Jacob hesitates, glancing at the kid before looking back at me.

He places the kid down on the floor and crouches down to his height before muttering something in his ear. The boy nods and runs towards the opposite end of the aisle, right where the other sweets are located.

He finally answers, "Look, it's complicated–"

He's being so awkward that I chuckle. "Alright, dude. No need to panic. You know having kids is not something to be ashamed of."

He smiles in appreciation, still looking highly uncomfortable. That's my hint to change the subject. It's not my place to meddle in his private life. Nor do I care enough to do it.

"Look, I wanted to ask if this time around, you'll tell me why she left. Because after the three times I've met her, she's adamant to run away from me."

Jake sighs, lines that didn't seem to be there before appearing on his forehead and between his eyebrows. His eyes glaze over, all emotion fleeting temporarily.

With a shake of his head, he answers, "Liam, you know it's not my place to meddle. You both need to have a serious talk."

I scoff, "Don't you think I've tried? She keeps running away from me like a coward. At this rate, I'll never fucking know. The least you could do is lay it out for me."

My voice rises slightly as the anger slithers into my veins once again. But his stance doesn't falter, not until his eyes focus on something behind me. His shoulders seem to sag, then I turn around, looking in the direction he is looking at.

A wave of nausea hits me as I watch the kid holding a bunch of different sweets and chocolates in his arms, his face moving quickly as he looks from one to the other, visibly torn. It makes me wish that was the hardest choice I had on my mind now. Life is way simpler when you're young.

"You need to understand..." The assertiveness in Jake's voice makes me look back at him. "That's my baby sister you're talking about. Would I have done things the way she did? Probably not, but I can't know for sure because I'm not in her shoes." He sighs, lowering his voice. "There's one thing I can assure you, though. Out of all of us, she's the one who's had it the hardest. You included."

I laugh, but he adds, "It might not be fair to ask this of you, but could you be a little more patient? If there is one person she'll tell everything to, it'll be you."

For a few moments, the darkest scenarios run through my head, squeezing the strength out of my heart. For years, I've wondered what could have happened that justified making her leave. For a long time, I was sure it had to be something serious, otherwise, she wouldn't just abandon me.

But as the years went by and the resentment made a home out of my heart, I stopped thinking about whatever explanation she could have, fiercely believing they could only be excuses.

But what could fucking explain all of this?

"Well, it's hard to be patient when she refuses to talk and leaves me hanging mid-conversation."

Jake sighs. "Just...don't give up on her," he asks with a sad smile. "Otherwise, there might not be hope. For any of us."

"What do—"

"Dylan's almost done," he cuts me off. "I have to go. Sorry."

"But—" I interject.

"Just talk to her, Liam," he hollers from the other end of the aisle, picking the kid up and placing him back on his shoulders before disappearing into the crowd of shoppers.

"Fuck!" I yell to no one in particular.

A rustling sound startles me, and I turn around, coming face to face with an old lady. She's eyeing me with one of those disapproving looks on her face with narrowed eyes, tightened lips and a negative shake of her head. Ignoring the judgement, I walk away, continuing to pick up the last needed items and heading home.

The whole time, Jake's words reverberate through my brain, giving me a headache. In a matter of minutes, my head is throbbing the way it usually is after a fifteen-hour shift in the ER.

In times like this, there's a slight nagging feeling, asking me—no, begging me—to make it stop. To just make it all stop.

And I am embarrassed to admit that I've considered it more times than I can count, just to be hit by guilt. The guilt of knowing that there are people out there having it harder than me and still pushing through, being resilient. And here I am, constantly breaking down because of a woman.

The rest of my day is spent trying—and failing—to regulate my emotions and balance my mindset. Life really is a bitch.

But there is one thing Jake said that sticks with me. Imprinted on my head.

Don't give up on her. Otherwise, there might not be hope.

It makes me question, where the hell is he seeing hope because it feels like hope has abandoned me a long time ago. Is it worth the try? Probably not, but knowing myself, these words are all I needed to keep trying.

Just one more time.

TWENTY-FOUR

Willow

DYLAN'S ALREADY IN SCHOOL—JAKE'S COURTESY TO LET ME SLEEP until later. After a good night's sleep, as I slowly get closer to the kitchen, I hear Nana and Jake's hushed voices. I know it's not polite to eavesdrop, but for them to be talking like this, I'm guessing I'm the subject.

"Do you believe that boy is the father?" Nana asks.

"It's the only option. I mean they do look alike. *A lot,*" he mumbles.

Oh god. If he knew...

"But something's not adding up, Nana. I can't figure out how the hell it happened." He sighs. "That night, it was excruciating for me. I can only imagine for her. She ran home in such a state that when I tried to touch her, she screamed. It was so loud, from the deepest depths of her lungs, that I had no reaction. Letting her go was the only option, and she went straight to the bathroom."

I barely hold down a gasp. This is the first time I've heard Jake talk about it in detail. With me, he is always careful with his words.

"After an hour and a half of pacing outside the bathroom, I made the decision to go in. Nana, to this day, I don't know if I am grateful or not because...all of those bruises and bite marks were slicing through me like a knife. And there she was, rocking herself underneath the scalding water with bright red skin." My heart squeezes at the memory. "I lost it. I thought it had been him. I was going to kill *him for it*, but when I finally mentioned his name, she broke down crying, and begging me not to tell him, that he couldn't know..."

"Oh god," Nana cries. "Our little girl. Life is so unfair."

"That's when I realised it wasn't him. I brought her a towel and helped her to bed–without touching her. The morning after only confirmed my suspicions. He knew less than I did."

My eyes squeeze shut, and I try to breathe in through my nose and out through my mouth as Jake taught me back then–a weak attempt to keep the bad memories away.

"From what you've told me back then, the boy's persistence in finding her for so long...he must really have loved her. They probably still love each other, and I can only see this as fate working up to solve this mess."

Not being in the room deprives me of seeing their expressions, but their soft voices tell me all I need to know. The love and worry they carry are huge, and it only makes me feel guilty about not being able to open up. I wish it were as easy as fate being able to make things right. What they don't realise is that there are forces so much stronger than that.

What happened back then made it impossible for whatever there was between Liam and me to be mendable. He wouldn't believe me. He'd hate me.

Hell, I hate myself.

Liam has been hurt enough by my abandonment. I saw it in his eyes when we talked. The pain and the despair were swirling in those blue irises like wildfire. They always turn darker when he's emotional. It's uncanny how long has passed by, and I can still pinpoint every emotion crossing him, even after all of these years.

Maybe because Dylan's do the exact same. The irony of having my baby looking like him grows more and more every day.

The hurt that will come out of knowing the entire truth is not worth it, honestly. To everyone; not just me. Including my baby.

Especially my baby.

Trying to snap out of this mindset, I leave them to their talk and go back upstairs to get dressed. Tomorrow is Dylan's birthday, and I have a lot to do. All of his school friends, Abby included, have been invited and have confirmed their attendance. I extended the invitation to my college friends, and all of them were excited to meet Dylan. Even Hazel, which was surprising.

It'll be a day to celebrate. To be *happy*.

When I'm finally ready, I head back down, finding both of them still in the kitchen.

"Hey, Lolo!" Jake greets when he sees me. "What are we doing today?"

"Preparing everything for tomorrow. First, we make a list, then we go buy and then hide it, so Dylan doesn't find out."

He chuckles but stands up to grab a pen and a sheet of paper so we can get down to business. The day goes by in a rush, the three of us busy getting everything we need for the party. By the time we're done shopping, Jake insists we need to take a break to eat, and what place is better than Shilah's?

"I'm starving," he whines, following Shilah to our booth.

"Oh, don't be such a big baby. I only agreed because it'll be faster to hide everything before we have to pick Dylan up."

"Hide what, darling?" Shilah asks, handing us the menus.

"Oh, the set-up for his party. That kid is like a hound. He always finds out whatever I hide. All kinds of surprises."

"Where are you going to do it? The party, I mean."

"The only place I can do it, at home, why?" I ask when I see that expression she does every time she's deep in thought.

"I was just thinking that tomorrow is one of those days where we'll barely have any movement, and we still have the back room vacant. When we opened, we didn't have enough time to renovate the other one, and we just kind of left it as a second plan," she hums a little at the end of the sentence. "You could use the room, hide everything there, set them up there, and surprise the hell out of him." She beams.

"No, Shilah. I don't want to abuse your goodwill. You've already given me an extra day off to be able to prepare this, now using the diner as well? No."

"Nonsense, girl! I won't even accept a no for an answer. Let me just wrap up a few clients, and I'll bring you the key to the other back door so you can bring everything inside!"

Since Shilah is adamant, I end up giving in. It is, in fact, handy to not bring everything home. As she goes back to get our food, Nana excuses herself, going to the restroom.

"Lo?" Jake calls.

"Hmm?"

"I saw Liam at the supermarket yesterday."

Automatically, my attention snaps to him.

"Oh no, he met Dylan?"

"I mean, he saw him, but he assumed he was mine. I didn't correct him because it's not my place to tell but, sis...he kept looking at him weirdly, and he asked about you. About why you left since you haven't been honest yet."

"You told him?" I whisper-yell, panic lurking underneath my skin, heading right towards my heart.

"Lo, who do you think I am?" He glares. "I only told him you need to figure it out and keep me out of it."

Oh. Oh god. Why am I panicking? I never even told my brother. I told no one. Am I going crazy?

"Sis, what the hell happened back then?" His soft hand covers mine, and all I can do is shut my eyes tight and try to contain a sob.

I feel like I'm suffocating as if my lungs were being filled with stinging water. Everything is just catching up to me, pulling me deeper underwater into this bottomless black void.

Why can't I just get out of this spiralling black hole? *Why?*

When his arms wrap around me, holding me tightly, I finally break down. "Why, Jake? Why me?"

He squeezes me closer. "Oh, my sweet girl...I hate that you're carrying this weight by yourself, Lo. Let us help you."

I shake my head in his chest, telling him no. *I can't.*

With a resigned sigh, he mutters, "You know I am here for you, right?" I can only nod against his chest. "I'll be here when you find the courage to open up. I will always be here for you."

"I'm sorry, Jay." He shushes me before squeezing me tight again. "One day. I promise."

I barely manage to get myself together before Nana comes back, but if she notices, she doesn't call us out on it. Instead, she quickly monopolises the conversation, reminding us about Jake's antics today.

How he got jealous by me saying Nana was the best after reminding me we still had to go look for drinks.

"I was *not* jealous," he counters. "But how is she the best if I'm the one who has come a week earlier to help set everything up? She just reminded us we had to buy sugar-based drinks—AKA fuel for the spawns of the devil."

I can't help the loud laughter that bubbles from inside my chest. This full-grown man sometimes—more often than not—can act like a kid but still be adorable.

After we're done eating and preparing some stuff in advance in Shilah's back room, he isn't done with the bad jokes yet, "Com'on Lolo, we're driving in your Polo."

"Jake, no! No crazy rhyming game."

"Oh, come on!" he whines. "You used to love it."

"Yeah, when I was ten. I am twenty-two now. I grew tired of it and your same old childish rhymes."

"Too bad because Lolo is stuck with this loco." He smirks, pointing at himself before closing the car door on me and entering the driver's side.

"That doesn't even rhyme!" I cackle and he shrugs, unbothered. "If you're going to rhyme, I am going to sing," I warn him, and his eyes widen.

I suck at singing. A lot.

Jake makes it much easier, the way he can easily take my mind off of things is magical, and I will always be grateful for the blessing that is my big brother. Forever.

It's finally his birthday and even though I'm exhausted, I am relieved that everything's nearly done.

Thankfully, Abby's mother volunteered to take both of them to the park while Jake, Nana, and I finish everything. All his school friends are due to arrive in the next thirty minutes. Once Dylan arrives, everyone that's coming will be able to celebrate with him.

This irrational fear that something can go wrong doesn't let go of me, but I push through for my boy. Since I can't give him what he wants the most in this world yet, I need to make sure I give him the second-best thing.

This is becoming so messy and complicated that I know it'll end up blowing up right in my face. I can feel it in my bones. Hopefully, it'll just be later rather than sooner.

"I'm done," Jake exclaims exactly when Nana and I finish the last details as well. Doing a quick once-over and confirming everything is in place, I head out of the diner. A few people are already waiting outside, and after greeting everyone, I see Abby's parents' car driving down the road.

"Everyone needs to get inside," I yell as Jake quickly guides them towards the door.

Just shy of the door closing, their car pulls up, right in front of the building. The back door opens, and an overexcited Dylan rushes to me, jumping into my arms.

"Mummy! We played football, and we went for ice cream. I—" he stops himself and frowns. "Why are we here? Are you going to work today?" His face contorts into a big pouty expression and I can't help to chuckle at the sadness that is trying to force its way through at the simple thought of my working.

"No, baby. I thought you could be hungry after all that exercise. What do you think?"

"Just us?" He frowns. "I wanted more time with Abby."

"Come on, silly. We're all going inside." I put him down and grab his hand before greeting little Abby and her mother.

The few steps up to the back door are enough to have Dylan frowning. Of course, he thought we'd enter the main room and sit at one of the booths and eat so when we don't, he's confused.

I slowly open the door and push him forward. At the same time that he appears, everyone inside screams, "Surprise!"

He shrieks for a few seconds before laughing loudly.

In a flash, he starts running towards Jake, then Nana, greeting and talking to everyone at the party. He even introduces himself shamelessly to Ethan and Hazel. Unlike Johanna's weird behaviour, the rest of my friends are all over him, giving him their presents and doting on him. Watching them interact with him so well warms my heart.

And just like that, my kid spends the entire afternoon running around, playing, laughing, and yelling. Happy and crazy just as he usually is, softening my heart even more. I keep the conversation going with some other parents, but the constant company are Ethan, Hazel, Sofia, and Johanna. She still seems detached but keeps up with her nice, easy-going ways. All along, everyone else seems to be delighted with Dylan and his eccentric and bubbly personality.

Jake keeps Nana entertained, and Shilah and her husband even pop in twice to see the birthday boy and chat a little. I bet they would have loved to stay longer if they weren't working.

"Well, it turns out the party is a success," my older brother chimes in next to me while the kids run like crazy in front of us.

I am about to answer him when Dylan's shout interrupts me. "Mummy!" Dylan beams when I reach him, jumping straight into my arms. "I love the party. Thank you so, so much!"

"Are you having fun, then?" I ask, moving a tendril of his hair from over his eyes.

He's a sweaty mess but is having so much fun, it brings a wide smile to my face.

"*Yes*! A lot. Thank you, Mummy!" He hugs me tight.

"How about we sing you happy birthday so you can blow out the candles and play a little bit more? Before it gets too late." He nods eagerly and I wave for Jake to bring the cake. "Come on, kids. It's cake time!"

Everyone hollers and some follow me to the table. I set Dylan on the chair, and he sits on his knees, bouncing up and down with excitement. When Jake appears with a huge Avengers cake, he starts hollering *yes* after *yes* while clapping excitedly.

With lit-up candles, we all sing him the happy birthday song, and sure enough, Dylan sings along before blowing out the candles.

"I want the first piece!" he demands, stealing the show and making everyone laugh.

If he already eats this much at six-years-old, I can only imagine how it will be by the age of fifteen or seventeen. The thought has me shuddering. I will have a twenty-year-old by the age of thirty-six.

Damn.

"Mwom, you know I wove chocolate cake," he says with a full mouth.

"Dylan, eat first, speak after," I scold.

"He sure looks like..." Jake starts, but I elbow him when Johanna's head swivels in our direction. "Like me. I was going to say he looks like me," he whines while rubbing his ribs.

"Sure, you were," I mumble while I glare at him.

I jump in surprise at a sudden movement right next to me, noticing how Dylan has already eaten his piece of cake and is running towards the playing area. Looking around, I notice most kids have eaten their cake, too, and are busy playing together again.

"Be careful, children. No fighting!" I urge before sitting down for a bit with closed eyes.

Damn, I'm tired. One kid is tiring as hell, imagine a dozen. On top of that, entertaining the adults as well.

"If you need a break, I can take over for a little bit," Jake whispers next to me.

"It's okay."

"Sis, don't be stubborn. I can look over them. Go take a breather." He gives me a side-eyed warning, and I huff in defeat.

With a last look at Dylan and the other kids, I slip out of the room and cross the diner. Shilah gives me a wave, which I answer back before stepping outside.

The nights are cold by now, and even though I am using a long-sleeve shirt, it still makes me shudder with the temperature drop when I step outside. Taking a deep breath, I lean back on the diner's wall. It's particularly calm today, and I bask in it because it means there's no one outside.

It's not even six in the afternoon, but the sun has already set, so the party is bound to finish soon. My thoughts go back to Liam and what to do. Because I *have* to do something; Jake is right. I can't keep dragging this on. If we had never met again, I could have gone the rest of my life with this part of my life behind me, in the past where it belongs. I guess I need to reopen these wounds just once more so they can finally heal properly.

"How am I going to solve this?" I mumble to myself while rubbing my eyes. I'm exhausted.

"I wonder the same, too," an all-too familiar but unexpected voice answers.

I look up to face the person next to me.

The first thing my eyes notice are his. The bright blue irises focused solely on me are soul-stirring. With the blatant heaviness of all of our story perched in the front row of the circus. And yet, I know might be mirroring the same.

Sadness, hurt, longing...

"Liam..." I whisper.

TWENTY-FIVE

Liam

"LIAM..." THE STRAINED WHISPER WRAPS AROUND MY LUNGS IN A tight squeeze, stealing the breath out of me.

Her dark brown eyes widen in shock at the sight of me. Admittedly, one glance is enough to lock me in chains, effectively rooting me in place as the heavy silence that follows settles around us, thickening the air with tension.

It's just the two of us in this darkened street, but the yellow light of the lamps allows me to memorise the tiny differences in her face.

Some fine lines decorate the edges of her eyes, the only ageing visible in her face. To my amazement, it only makes her more beautiful, more mature. She looks the same and yet so different from the innocent girl I used to date.

No, in front of me stands a woman. A woman who cloaks the kind of wisdom many avoid at all costs. Willow no longer has that lightness and innocence etched in her eyes; she looks like the person who has been carrying the weight of the world for seven long years. As she should.

And still, one second, one glance is all it takes to bring me to my knees. At least, metaphorically.

The Pandora's box where all of the feelings have been kept under lock and key is open. They all bubble up to the surface as if she never left me. Not even all the time in the world would be enough to make me get over her. It is as familiar as it is foreign because these old feelings are not alone anymore. Anger, hurt, and the need to know the truth are riding in the same carriage.

"Will you finally talk now?" Defeat weaves my voice like a spinning-wheel weaves yarn.

I am so tired of this avoidance. If she doesn't want anything to do with me, fine, but I need those answers.

Was I not enough?

Didn't she love me?

Why did she leave like that after ignoring me for weeks?

"I was trying to find a way to solve this. I was going to contact you soon, but please," she begs with a shaky voice. "Not tonight. I can't, I—you need to leave, please."

Nervousness and despair flow out of her mouth so strongly I can almost taste it. But after all of these years, all of this agony, I can't just turn around and leave. No. I won't budge.

She's probably working, so her break should be enough to set everything straight. That way we can both move on with our lives. Separately.

Fuck, it stings.

Do I want to move on?

"No," I counter in a decisive tone, answering her request to leave but most importantly, myself.

"Oh god," she murmurs before looking around, scared.

What the fuck is going on?

"What are you nervous about?"

Willow looks like a deer caught in headlights.

"I—I—" she stutters, taking a step back. "Please, I have to go. We can talk tomorrow or whenever you can. I—my brother is here, and I—"

"I know he's here," I cut her off, automatically taking one step closer to her. "Look, just tell me what I need to know. Five minutes is all I need. Then, I'll leave you the hell alone for good. I promise, I won't...bother you again." This last part comes out forceful because, despite everything, the mere thought of losing her all over again seems unfathomable to me.

I am starting to wonder, though, if knowing is going to make it easier. I have a feeling I am dead wrong. That it surely won't.

"Five minutes are not enough for me, Liam. I—back then, things were...oh my god." Her hand flies out to her chest, clutching tight as her breaths get ragged. "I can't–I can't do this." Fat tears start to stream down her face, and my resolve crumbles.

Like muscle memory, I gently grab her face and wipe those tears away. I've always been a sucker for her, and apparently, that hasn't changed. A couple of tears are enough to tear through my heart all over again. Watching her hands clutch my T-shirt in her fists and her forehead digging into my chest to hide the loud sobs hurts more than my own pain.

Willow has always been sensitive, but she was never a crier. Maybe Jake was right. What happened? Was it bad enough to justify her sudden departure? Has she been the one who has indeed hurt more than all of us?

My arms wrap around her tightly as she lets it all out.

"I am so, so sorry," she says between sobs, and I squeeze her to let her know I am listening.

I have dreamt of hearing these words from her mouth for almost seven years now. But I never thought they'd be as healing as they are. I needed these words. More so, I needed her. Because even though she is the source of my pain, she is also the cure for my illness.

"I didn't—I didn't want to leave you." She cries harder into my chest. "Never you. That is my biggest regret."

Her words cut deep, making me shiver. It takes me a few breaths to be able to reopen my eyes without giving in to the urge of crying. Never in a million years would I think we'd be so broken beyond repair because back then, I would have walked through fire for this girl.

The problem is that even today, after everything, I still would.

Without thinking, I tilt her head up, forcing her to look at me. We're much closer now, so much so that her warm breath burns my skin upon contact. The tingling I hadn't felt in years comes back, just to prove me wrong. If I thought I'd ever get this kind of feeling with someone else, now I know, it only happens with her.

My body and soul yearn for her while my brain is still waging an internal war.

She has barely grown up in height since we were sixteen, whereas I'm almost thirty centimetres taller. My hands, with a life of their own, slide down until they settle on her hips, confirming my suspicions. While still on the skinnier side, she has filled out and has become a lot curvier than she used to be.

The proximity intoxicates me enough to focus only on the good. The familiar scent of wildflowers invades my nostrils, while I admire the way her porcelain skin contrasts with my golden as her body moulds into mine. We still fit perfectly.

Everything changed, and yet, so much still remains the same.

Would her lips still feel and taste the same?

My heart takes the lead, bringing my head down until our lips meet. My mind blanks, all of the background noise disappearing into thin air. Her soft plump lips feel the same, taste the same. Like cotton candy, it's everything I expected and remembered. And more. So much more.

For a split second, Willow freezes, and underneath my hands, I feel her stiffen. If I didn't know her so well, I would have missed it because right afterwards, she melts into me with a relieved sigh, kissing me back.

Her fists tighten their hold on my T-shirt, and my hand moves to her waist, pulling her closer to me. It's like the past, present, and future are clashing together in this one moment, setting the rest of the world apart.

As they say, lost for ten, lost for a thousand, and I've lost the battle. All of the hurt, sadness, and the grudge. None of it matters anymore. Especially when my tongue sweeps at her lip, asking for permission to enter.

When they finally touch, it's like a strike of lightning going through my body. Willow lets out a little whimper, and it intensifies this hunger for her, making my hands slide down towards the swell of her ass.

Home.

No one ever feels as good and right as she does. Nothing can compare.

When I give in to the urge to squeeze her butt-cheek, she gasps, pushing me off her. Confused, my fingers cover my swollen lips as I ask, "What's wrong?"

With closed eyes and her hands raised in front of her, she steps back, against the wall.

"Don't! Please, don't!"

As I'm about to take a step forward, she slides down to the ground, shaking and sobbing uncontrollably.

"Don't do this," she begs, her eyes still closed.

Agony rips at my chest as I crouch down to meet her face. "Lo," I call. "I am not doing anything. I would never–"

"St-Stop! Please!"

What is happening?

A knot forms in my throat and tears burn my eyes as I watch her. It's agonizing. This is not *my* Willow. She was sensitive, yeah, but happy, fun, and trusting. But right now, all I see is someone who has been bent until she broke. A shell of the joyous girl she once was.

"What the fuck happened?" I growl to myself.

I regret it instantly as it makes her cry harder, her face now tucked between her knees.

"Lo, baby," I try again. "It's Liam. Please, look at me." My voice cracks at the end.

Seemingly trying to get her control back, I listen to her loud attempts at breathing. And I try to help her out with it. A few minutes later, her lashes finally flutter open through the sea of tears. Shiny dark eyes finally gaze up at me.

"Hey." I awkwardly smile. "Welcome back."

"I'm sorry," she whispers.

"We can go somewhere we can calmly talk. Would that help?" A sob racks through her chest as her head shakes aggressively. "I can't understand..."

"I can't talk about it." She shakes her head some more. "Please don't make me."

"Did someone hurt you?"

She nods, and the blood in my veins turns cold. My heart skips a beat, opening the gates of guilt. Letting my knees hit the ground, I shuffle closer to her, placing my forehead on her temple.

"I need to know, baby. I–we can't continue like this."

"You won't believe me." She hiccups. "You'll hate me."

"If I can't hate you after all of these years..." I admit. "I could never."

"Oh, Liam!" She drops her head back on my chest. "This–how–"

One of my hands gently caresses her back while the other plays with her hair in a weak attempt to stop her crying. I have always hated seeing her upset. "Slowly," I encourage her. "I've got time."

I am about to give her lips a light peck when the collar of my shirt is abruptly pulled back. I grunt with the force of the collar, almost choking me, falling on my ass. A big and bulky shadow moves in my periphery and I turn to see a man crouching down right by Willow's side.

"What the fuck?" I growl.

"Oh god–"

"Are you alright?" the man asks her, completely ignoring me.

"She's fine."

"She can speak for herself," he counters as I notice him helping her stand.

I do the same, noticing we're about the same height, though he has dark hair and eyes. He looks older, too.

"I'm alright," Willow mutters, cleaning the back of her jeans.

"Look, we're having a private conversation–"

"Ha, that's a good one," he cuts me off, laughing sarcastically. "Private conversation? I saw you forcing yourself on a crying woman. You should be ashamed, man."

"Who the f–" I push forward but Willow's hands and voice stop me.

"Stop it!" Her voice still quivering. "Liam isn't dangerous; he wasn't hurting me, Arthur."

"You know this dipshit?" I spit the words, jealousy burning inside me.

"Watch it, punk," he sneers.

But I ignore him, unfazed, and keep my attention on her.

"Arthur's a friend." Her hesitancy doesn't make it convincing. "Can we meet tomorrow to finish this conversation?"

"And him?" I can't help but ask.

The silence stretches to an uncomfortable length, and it dawns on me. She was by herself here in the parking lot. Waiting for him. Noted.

"Right," I scoff. "I'll leave. I only came here to pick Johanna up, anyway."

An eye for an eye. And the hurt is visible as her eyes widen, and she takes a staggering step back. Douchebag shakes his head disapprovingly while her eyes get shiny again as the new tears form, and I mentally curse myself. My impulsiveness has always gotten the best of me.

"Shit, Lo–"

The building's door slams open, catching all of our attention. A kid rushes outside, and I immediately recognize him as Jake's son. A tiny smile finds its way to my face as I watch him latch onto his aunt's leg.

"Jake says it's time to say goodbye to the guests," he informs her while looking at me curiously. He looks up, and his mouth opens to speak, but he freezes at the sight of her crying.

It only makes me feel guiltier.

Just then, Jake comes running towards us, stopping right beside his sister. "Shit, Lo. The sneaky little shit slipped away wi–" He pauses midsentence when he notices me, eyes widening.

Then the young boy–Dylan, I think–speaks again, "Are you crying, Mummy?"

I stiffen. Surely, I didn't hear it right.

But then, he repeats the word.

"Don't be sad, Mummy. I loved the party!" his voice cracks. "Please don't cry."

Mummy?

Rendered motionless and stunned, I rack my brain for an explanation, but none comes to mind. At least not one that doesn't burn my heart to ashes.

My brain spirals into a black hole of hurt at the realisation of what it implies. "Mummy?" I whisper.

TWENTY-SIX

Willow

THERE ARE MOMENTS I REGRET IN MY LIFE—DEEPLY—BUT NONE LIKE this one.

My brain is a jumbled mess, incapacitating my body from the action it should have. With Dylan crying from watching me cry, attached to me, and Arthur's warm chest grazing my back, the last thing I can do is think—or act.

I can't even look at him.

My knees almost give away from the panic. Powering through, I pick Dylan up, and he automatically latches onto me, wrapping his arms around my neck. My baby's tiny fists grip the back of my shirt, holding me as tight as I am holding him. *My haven.*

The comfort of his hold is the only thing I can manage to focus on in the midst of such stress. I can't even look around me to see how many people are outside, witnessing this. Because if I do, I'll surely break down.

Instead, I let my brother take over, believing he'll have my back.

"Okay, let's calm down. Look at her state, mate," Jake's voice sounds out. "I think you better finish this conversation some other day."

"Calm down? Jake, she's had a kid this whole time!" he shouts, surely bringing more attention to the scene outside.

A sob breaks free, and Dylan's shaky whisper is the only thing grounding me.

"I love you, Mummy," he keeps repeating.

"I thought he was yours?" Liam presses, and the long silence that follows seems to give him the answer he dreads. "How old is he?"

More silence.

"Is he mine?" his low and angry growl brings goosebumps to my skin.

He is *furious.*

However, my biggest concern is Dylan. He's right here and might not be watching it all unfold, but he is certainly listening. This kid is quick-witted and will understand what this is about in no time. About him.

"I understand you have questions," my brother counters. "She'll answer them. I'm sure." I visibly flinch. "Just not tonight. Look at her, man. She *can't* talk."

Ignoring my brother, Liam repeats his question through gritted teeth, "What age is he?"

"Lo?" Jake calls me, asking for permission.

We know each other well enough to talk through half-words sometimes. That's why I meekly nod, and he promptly answers, "He just turned six today."

With every silent moment, my heart drops with dread. I can almost listen to the gears turning in his brain as it processes the information.

"That's...seven or eight months after you left?"

After I left. Memories try to break free from the little drawer I keep them in, and the only thing keeping my head afloat are Dylan's gentle caresses and low whispers.

That good-girl vibe you have is surely a turn-on.

"No," I mutter to myself.

Oh, don't act like you don't know what you're doing.

"Is that why you left?" Liam's voice clashes with the demons trying to break free.

Thankfully, I keep them in check for a while longer. Probably because of the way his voice cracks at the last word.

"Alright," Jake steps in again. "Enough!"

"If he was born in November, then..."

Please, no. Don't say it.

Please, stop.

You don't want me to stop.

My lungs close in, and airflow stops, blinding me. Even Dylan's voice sounds far away. Too far away.

"Fuck...she's...attack." I don't know who is saying what, or if there is a commotion at all. My eyes are wide open, but they are seeing events from a long time ago. The ones I fiercely try to keep locked away.

The pungent scent of his breath hit my nostrils at the same time the exhale reached my cheek, making my eyes shut tightly in discomfort.

His unfamiliar scent gave me nausea while his foreign and calloused hand squeezed my breast too tight, making me whimper in pain.

I said no, over and over again, to no avail. I cried, screamed, and trashed against him, and still, he easily manoeuvred me, pinning me to the couch with his body. He undressed me despite my crying. He kept going despite my begging him to stop.

It plays in a loop. The memory of how a few minutes can feel like hours. A few minutes can be more than enough to destroy one's life. More than enough to kill someone. In this case, the person I used to be.

And now, I'll have to face all of it again.

"Mummy, wake up. Look at me, please."

My haven. Once again, he takes me out of the darkest place inside, finally bringing me back to the present. As I roll out of the trance, I startle with my surroundings. I'm in an unfamiliar car, sitting in the back seat with Dylan still glued to me.

"Hey, baby," I answer him, my voice hoarse.

My first thought is to at least sit him straight and put on the seatbelt but he refuses to let go.

"Baby, safety first." A strong head shake and a tighter embrace are enough to make me sigh in defeat.

"It won't work." A male voice sounds, unsettling me for a second. "Believe me, I tried."

Arthur.

"Just hold him. I'm driving slowly." His eyes look at me through the rearview mirror. "We're almost there."

"My brother?"

"He took that guy to his car," the harshness in his voice tells me he isn't fond of Liam after this chaotic encounter. "He stayed behind to send everyone else home. Thankfully, Ethan and Hazel vouched for me, saying you'd be safe enough. I just thought you'd need a change of scenery and some fresh air."

"Thank you," I whisper, and he nods, letting me know he heard.

By watching me finally be functional, Dylan places his head on my shoulder, hiding his face in my neck, still holding me tight. With a few threading movements through his hair, he quickly falls asleep on my lap.

I busy myself watching the view outside. The city lights seem unusually annoying, and the occasional cars passing by us are extremely loud. Even the scarce people walking down the streets seem to be walking funny. It's probably my puffy eyes making me see things.

There's no going back after this. Now, I surely have to tell him and come clean. Having the truth out will shatter me all over again.

What if he doesn't believe me?

What if? He won't. There were many reasons why I left, but this possibility was one of the biggest ones.

The car comes to a halt, and Arthur finally turns around, looking directly at me. "Are you alright?"

"No," I blurt truthfully, keeping my eyes on the sleeping toddler.

How could I even look into his eyes after the show he just witnessed?

"Want to talk about it? It can help."

"I don't think I can."

"You don't need to." He nods. "Just know you can."

"Thank you."

My eyes keep sweeping through our surroundings, avoiding him. At this moment, looking at everything but him is easier. The embarrassment has now replaced most of the fear, and at this point, I'll break down again if our gazes meet.

"You'll need to make a decision soon, though. From what I've seen, he won't stop until you tell him whatever truth he is looking for. Will you manage? I've noticed how much inside your mind you get. It has to be bad."

This man has pulled a one-eighty. He is now the day compared to the darkness of the night he used to be and so much more kind and understanding than I've ever thought. Not to mention that the concern in his eyes is evident.

Maybe telling someone will help ...

"I need some fresh air," I admit.

"Of course." Exiting the driver's seat, he comes around the car to the back and opens the door, picking Dylan up and helping me place him in the back seat. After covering him with his jacket, he opens a tiny bit of the window before closing the door and locking the car.

"We can't go far—"

"I was thinking we could sit on the hood of the car." He jerks his chin towards the front of the car.

I follow, and we sit, side by side, facing the dark landscape ahead of us. The faint sound of ocean waves tells me we're close to the beach, instantly reminding me of the times Liam took me stargazing, knowing how much I loved it. How I miss those days.

The silence stretches for a bit as we both stare into the nothingness ahead. For once, it's a comfortable silence. I no longer expect him to be rude at any given moment, and that makes me more comfortable than ever. Oddly enough, I feel safe.

"When I first saw you, I hated you," Arthur speaks, startling me with his sudden bluntness.

He doesn't look away from the spot he's trained on, though.

"Way to break the ice." I chuckle nervously. "I noticed you weren't a fan."

"I'm sorry, though," he apologises. "You reminded me of someone I hate, at first sight, and I couldn't help myself."

"Oh."

"Nothing particular against you. It's just...looking at you made all of that pain resurface and I didn't know how to deal."

His words make me look down at my hands in awkwardness. I mean, I'm relieved he's giving me an explanation for his erratic behaviour, but I didn't think it'd be this uncomfortable.

"But as I got to know you more, I understood that despite the physical resemblances, you aren't the same person, and the way I was treating you was unfair. Sorry about that."

"What did that woman do to you?" I can't help but ask. When his shoulders tense, I quickly add, "You don't need to tell me."

Instead–and surprising me completely– he smiles. It's contained and sad but honest.

"Talking about it might help so, why not?" With a shrug, he starts, "My sister, Alexa, who was two years younger than me, was my best friend. We were so close and still, she never felt comfortable telling me everything–something I deeply regret not having guessed because the signs were all there..."

Were?

"We had a strict upbringing with our parents being the conservative kind of Catholics. In a way, I understand why she felt like she couldn't say. But she didn't have to hide it from me, too. She loved women."

That's when his head finally turns in my direction, dark eyes meeting mine. With an assured nod, I urge him to keep going, letting him know I'm listening.

"With time, I started to see within the cracks of the front she put up to our parents. All the lies were taking a toll on her, and no matter how much I tried to let her know I was there, how I'd support her no matter what, she never gave in."

"She must have felt lonely, even if in reality, she wasn't alone," I comment.

"She ended up alone soon enough. I had to leave for college, and that's when our parents found out. They shunned her completely."

"I know the feeling," I admit. "My parents shunned me, too, when they learned of my teenage pregnancy."

"I'm sorry. No one should go through that."

"This isn't about me, though. What happened next?"

His soft gaze tells me otherwise, but he holds back, knowing full well I'm not ready to talk yet.

"I was fuming. I took her in to live with me. They shunned me, too, but by then, I was close to graduating and already had a part-time job so it allowed me to pay for most of the bills. Alexa found a job as well, and even though she was still extremely depressed, little by little, we got the hang of it, and she was better. Happier."

"That's so nice," I say. "You both deserved it."

"But short-lived," he grumbles with his fists curled tight on top of his thighs, showing how hard this is for him.

"Soon enough, she found a girlfriend, and I let her move in with us. I did everything to keep my sister happy, even if I didn't really like the girl." A short pause makes me look at him. This time around, he's looking down at his hands, picking at his nails, and looking almost embarrassed. "My sister was a part-time bartender while studying in college, so there were many nights when she was out working. Jennifer, her girlfriend, often stayed in and made breakfast. It didn't matter I kept to myself in my bedroom-slash-office, at meal times, we'd eat and spend some time together until it was time for Alexa to go to work. That night, I immediately got tired after dinner, making it only to the couch. I didn't even notice when she left for work."

"Isn't that normal?" I question. "You must have been tired after work."

"I'm a light sleeper." He smiles darkly. "I would have heard the front door, and I didn't. Not when she left and especially not when she came back. I only woke up with her screams. By then, it was too late."

Anxiety creeps in. *What happened?* Did she relapse and try to...did the girlfriend do something to her? *Oh god.*

"What do you mean?"

"Both Jennifer and I were fully naked on the couch." He chokes on the last words, his eyes shining with unshed tears. "I was so out of it I couldn't understand at first. Only then did I notice that they were arguing, and Jennifer was telling her all of this crap about how we secretly fell in love and couldn't hold it in anymore."

"Oh my god, the *bitch,*" I blurt, covering my mouth right after.

Arthur chuckles. "Why is it weird to hear you curse?"

"Because I rarely do." I smile awkwardly. "Sorry."

With a dismissive shake of his head, he looks back into the darkness, the gloomy mood taking over him again. "Of course, Alexa was naïve and believed her. She bolted out of the house, and I called the police to have Jennifer out of the house and arrested for SA. Of course, it took a shit ton of time and a trip to the hospital before I could get out to track my sister. For two torturous days, I couldn't find her, I feared the worst..."

"Please tell me you found her well and safe?"

A deep and dark sound rises from his chest, a mix between a sob and a choke before he finally breaks down in front of me. Unrestrained and completely transparent, Arthur Adell is crying in front of me, bringing my own tears to the surface and making me fear the worst.

"I found her an hour away from this town in another hospital. In a coma after being raped and beaten."

The pain that poor girl must have been in. After feeling betrayed by her brother, the only one she had left, to be attacked in such an inhuman way. The world can be so cruel.

"After two weeks of my crying and begging her to wake up, she finally did." He sighs. "We had a heart to heart, and she seemed to believe me. It was like a heavy weight had finally been lifted off my chest."

"How is she doing now?"

"She...she killed herself as soon as she got permission to go back home," he chokes.

"What?" I almost screech, flabbergasted. "But you made up, and she knew you wouldn't hurt her like that."

"She left the hospital two hours earlier, before I could pick her up, and left a letter on her bed. By the time I ran out to search for her, it was too late. She said she was glad she had me, but that she wasn't sure she could bear more pain in this horrible world."

"I am so sorry. No one should go through that. Not her and certainly not you."

"Unfortunately, you look like Jennifer, and I understood too late that you are nothing like her. I know the way I acted is unforgivable, but just know that I deeply regret it."

This poor man. I know it doesn't justify his cruel ways, but I do understand the desperate need to keep people at arm's length. If they're not too close, they can't hurt you. *Right?*

At the end of the day, we'll do whatever we can to prevent our hearts from hurting.

"It's water under the bridge." I wave him off. "We keep learning from our mistakes. I sure have a ton to learn still. Look how messy my life is." The chuckle is fake and meant to lift the heavy mood, but it's not that effective. Especially since what he just shared with me is giving me a sudden wave of courage. The sudden confidence to tell him what I've never told anyone.

Seemingly aware of my thoughts, Arthur's hand finds mine, giving it a comforting squeeze.

It's the propulsor for my bravery.

"Seven years ago, I was raped."

TWENTY-SEVEN

Willow

AS I LOOK AT MYSELF IN THE MIRROR, AFTER GETTING DRESSED THIS morning, I barely recognize the person looking back at me from the other side of the glass.

I did it. I finally found the courage to tell someone everything that happened.

Just like I had done, Arthur listened to everything without interrupting me once—not even when I cried. Every fear that had been simmering inside of me about his ulterior motives vanished last night.

Not once did he try to touch me inappropriately or take advantage of my vulnerability, even after telling him something so personal that no one else knows, showing me that he was being truthful about a platonic and harmless friendship.

In the midst of all of this, and how Johanna proved to be incapable of respecting boundaries and not meddling with what doesn't concern her, having Arthur being the exact opposite has made me feel less lonely. Like I truly have a friend.

And even after barely sleeping, I feel lighter this morning with renewed energy and slightly more confidence that I can solve this.

Last night also made me realise that I need therapy. In the end, I needed the bomb to blow up in my face to understand that sweeping my problems under the rug won't make them disappear. Not to mention the fact that it is completely unfair to everyone, especially Dylan *and* Liam.

Climbing down the stairs turns out to be a funny experience due to the extreme bickering coming from inside the kitchen.

"Good morning," I muse to the sight of Jake and Dylan completely covered in a white powder—probably flour.

"Ahhh!" they both screech in a high-pitched tone, immediately placing my almost-thirty-year-old brother in the same emotional intelligence bracket as my six-year-old son.

"No, Mummy!" He rushes to me, pushing me out of the kitchen. "You're ruining the surprise. Go wait outside!"

"Is this the way to greet your mother in the morning?" I complain in a fake scold but still comply with his demands.

"Look." He stops for drama, placing his tiny palms on his hips, cocking it to the side while raising his eyebrow. *What the hell?* How did this kid turn so sassy? "This a surprise. Uncle Jake told me you need to behave and wait in the living room until we call you!"

Look at that attitude! This boy will give me a lot of headaches when he grows up, that *I'm sure.* Hopefully, he'll keep this kind and affectionate side and spare me a few troubles.

Chuckling, I concede. "Alright, boss."

With a triumphant smile on his face, he goes back inside, and I plop my butt down on the couch, watching some random TV channel, waiting for this surprise.

"Come on! Come on," he yells, dragging me after him, back to the kitchen.

Inside, Nana's already sitting down, next to Jake with a breakfast banquet on the table. On one side, there's scrambled eggs, bacon, cheese, ham, and some oats. The other side has a plate with toast alongside some pancakes, butter, jams, and Nutella. And in the middle there is a variety of beverages like milk, tea, and freshly made orange juice.

My throat clogs up at the tender eyes trained on me; the love I feel for these three people is immense and I am beyond grateful.

"Thank you so much, to all of you." It's only loud enough for them to hear and smile at me.

"You deserve this and so much more, Lo," Jake comments, a white spot of flour on his cheek, drawing my attention. "We just wanted to remind you how loved you are."

"Now, get over here," Nana orders, a playful tone in her voice.

That's permission enough for Jake to go back to his silly self, immersing himself in intense bickering with his nephew. Nana asks me about school, purposefully avoiding last night's subject. I try to engage as much as possible, and the two silly males in the kitchen manage to force out a few laughs, but deep down, my mind is still stuck thinking about something. Specifically, someone.

He was raging. How will I even be capable of diffusing such anger?

"Sis," Jake breaks me out of my reverie. "Nana and I planned to take Dylan to the park today."

"Sure. Let me just grab my bag."

As soon as my foot touches the first step, the bell door rings. Chills cover my body as I turn around and look at Jake questioningly.

"Well," he quips, rubbing the back of his head. A rare sight for Jacob Hanlon, since he rarely gets embarrassed. "Liam told me he'd be here early today to talk to you. And Nana told me it was a good idea to let you guys talk properly without...distractions."

"Please, tell me you didn't give him our address," I beg.

"Nana did," he confesses.

"Couldn't you have given me just one more day off?" I whine just before the bell rings again. "I had already made up my mind about solving this the best I could."

"Then we just created the opportunity," Nana quips, heading towards the door.

"I'm ready!" Dylan calls from the staircase. "Mum? Why aren't you ready?"

"Mummy's tired," Jake answers before I can. "Give her a kiss, and let's meet Nana up front."

I follow them to the front door, coming directly face to face with a stoic Liam. He is focused on Dylan the entire time while my son initially ignores him. It's only when they step outside that he sticks his tongue out at him. If the urge to cry wasn't so strong, I'd be laughing at his vigorous personality at such a young age.

The silence and thick tension stretch for the entire time it takes for Jake to pull him to his car. Only when they drive off, does Liam look at me. His lips are whiteish and thinned from being pressed together, and his light brown eyebrows are twisted in a deep frown. All the while, his cobalt irises are piercing right through my soul. It's exactly the expression I expected.

Taking a deep breath, I open the door wider, letting him come in. He follows, quietly shutting the door after him. The clicking sounds of the door, the wood creaks from our steps, and our breathing are the only audible sounds, seemingly louder than usual.

I stop by the couch, motioning for him to sit down. We'll both need to be sitting down for this. Surprisingly, he does, not even uttering a word. The both of us, sitting down at opposite ends of the couch, keep silent.

A strong contrast from the raging emotions from last night, today, we're both contained. Under control. Let's just hope we can keep it that way.

"Let's—"

"Will you–"

We cut each other off by speaking at the same time.

"You first." Liam's voice is even, confirming he's keeping it together today.

"I just need you to let me talk at my own pace, without interruptions. Please, be a little patient with me," I beg.

"I–" he stops mid-sentence to sigh before running one hand through his messy dark blond locks. "Go on then..."

Lying back on the couch, he crosses his arms over his chest.

"I never had mononucleosis, I—"

"No shit!" he cuts me off, and I can't help but glare. *He didn't even last one minute.* "I'm sorry. Please, continue."

"I'll get to it, but first, I need you to understand that when I found out I was pregnant, I went to my parents. They were the ones who were supposed to help me, guide me. Protect me, even. Instead, they gave me an ultimatum. Either I terminated the pregnancy or I was out."

"But–"

"Liam," I plead, and he clamps his mouth shut. "Of course, I refused. I wasn't allowed to take anything with me, not even clothes or a phone. I've never seen them again, and they have never called me since. The only thing I had was the money Jake lent me so I could get to my grandmother's house. She took me in and helped me as much as she could. I was sixteen, pregnant, confused, scared, and alone. I know I should have told you, but I didn't know *how*."

How does one say to her boyfriend, *I'm pregnant and it's not yours?*

"But that doesn't mean I–" Raising my hand, I cut him off.

"How could a teenager, who had just turned to her parents for help, only for them to get rid of her, think someone else would even want to help? I am a mother *now*. There is nothing in this world that could have made me turn my back on my son. But they did. If my own blood doesn't care for me, how could others? In my sixteen-year-old brain, I had no one."

"That's where you're wrong, Willow," he tries to reason.

"I can't expect you to understand. But my mental health was really bad, and I did what I thought was best for everyone. Even if, by now, I realised it might not have been."

"I would have done anything you asked me," he mutters, looking straight into my eyes, piercing my soul. If there is someone who can shake me to the core, it's Liam Davis.

Would he have?

"How would that be fair to you?" I counter. "It wasn't your responsibility in the first place! I couldn't have asked that of you." I pause for a few seconds to prevent my eyes from getting blurry. "I could never."

"What do you mean not my responsibility? Do you think I'd abandon my girlfriend and my son?" he asks offended.

In my mind, back then, all I could think was that it wasn't fair to make him raise a baby that wasn't his. How do I explain that? How am I going to tell him that I was...

Instead, I settle with, "This kind of burden was never yours to carry, anyway."

"What does that even mean? Stop with the charades. All of this doesn't explain anything, Willow." Maybe it happens unconsciously, but we're much closer than we were when we started talking.

It always happens with us. This invisible force keeps bringing us closer together, even when there's a huge rift keeping us apart.

"What could possibly explain shutting me out for four weeks? What could warrant you to hide your pregnancy from me and leave without even giving me an explanation?"

"Let me talk," I snap, shutting him up. "I will get there. *Eventually.*"

"Tell me, then." He motions his hand, trying to get me to talk. "What could legitimise the fact that you took a kid from his father?"

"I did what I had to do. You need to understand this."

"What the fuck does that even mean?"

"It means that in the midst of a really fucked-up situation, I did the best I could. Even if it hurt all of us. It also hurt me. I never wanted to leave in the first place!"

"Are you going to carry on with the cryptic answers? Because it's not helping you in the forgiving field," he snarks back, visibly annoyed.

He's right, but how can I explain this without hurting him? Do I just rip the band-aid off?

Maybe.

"If by the forgiving field you mean by taking a kid from his father, then I don't need forgiving."

"What the hell?"

I close my eyes and take a deep inhale, filling my lungs with oxygen. My heart is beating like crazy, threatening to jump out of my chest at any moment. My shaking hands can't stop fidgeting with the hem of my T-shirt, and when I finally exhale and lock eyes with Liam, I prepare myself.

I prepare for the other shoe to drop. I prepare for the bomb that's about to explode.

"I haven't taken your kid from you because you're not his father."

TWENTY-EIGHT

Liam

MY BRAIN IS A JUMBLED MESS.

After years of anger for being just left behind by the girl I was willing to give my all to, I come to learn—by Johanna's invitation—that she has a kid.

A kid. A six-year-old boy who called her "Mummy" and stayed glued to her as if he was a part of her. A toddler who could very well be my son, too—that did me in, pushing me over the edge.

In seconds, the temperature rose, and I swear everything blended into shades of red. The moment realisation was slowly settling that the betrayal I had left had gone far beyond what I could have ever imagined. With a frantic heart pumping the boiling blood away, I was one second away from blowing up like a ticking time bomb. Honestly, if it hadn't been for Jake and that other guy getting me out of there, I have no idea how nasty things would have gotten.

After a lot of convincing from him, I agreed to be here today. Expecting—*hoping*—she'd finally tell me the whole story. Only to be hit with a bucket of fucking frozen water, freezing me to the bone.

Because you're not his father.

What the actual fuck?

"What do you even mean I am not the father? November minus nine months places the conception between February and March." I growl. "We were already sexually active by then. Remember?"

It's impossible to mask my angry tone.

After spending the whole fucking night thinking about this—about Dylan—by sunrise, there was this little part of me tingling. Excitement was growing with the prospects of understanding the whole scenery and getting confirmation. Of being a father.

The term itself still feels weird, even after repeating it a few dozen times this morning in front of the mirror—but fuck if I don't like it. Since last night, I had strong suspicions he is mine, and that explains exactly why he struck me the first I saw him in the hospital and that time in the supermarket with Jake. It wasn't because I thought Jake had a kid, it was because, without knowing, it felt like looking into a mirror. Looking at my own son—my body knew before my brain did.

My certainties only got stronger this morning when I saw him this morning. A mini-Liam, for sure. From the physical similarities—the skin tone and eyes—to his attitude earlier this morning, sticking the tongue out at me.

How can she claim the boy isn't mine?

He has to be. Similarities to the side, I was never a guy to care about intuition, but this time around? There is a nagging feeling coming from within, the deepest parts of my soul telling me—yelling—that Dylan is in fact mine.

There can't be any other possibilities in this universe. *Right?*

Willow purses her lips into a thin line, avoiding my eyes. This is one of her automatic actions when she feels shame. It always has been. The knowledge is enough to wake up a nagging feeling inside of me. Why would she be feeling shame? For me not to be the father. Did she cheat?

"Did you cheat on me?"

"I remember that we always used condoms," she trails off, avoiding the answer.

It works because immediately, I remember one event. We did always use condoms, but I remember well those times it broke.

"Except for those two times that it broke. Remember?"

"Yes," she sighs. "But we always were careful. Even with the condom, you always pulled out."

"You're fucking with me," I spit the words out. "Even with pulling out, Willow, we had sex for god knows how long in those goddamn broken condoms. We–" I pause as her words keep repeating in my brain. *Because you're not his father.* He's not mine. "You cheated, didn't you?" Hastily, I grab her arm, pulling her closer to me so she can look me in the eyes when she answers. "Is that why you left? To run away with him?" The blood in my veins boils, travelling throughout my body like lightning.

I can feel it reddening my face and neck as they warm. When her eyes raise to my forehead and widen, I am sure it is because of that vein that always pops out when I get mad.

I am so fucking livid.

All of this time, I thought she had gone through something traumatic. The way she responded to sudden and unexpected movements or touches told me so. I never in a million years would have thought she could–

Fucking hell, we were crazy about each other! We–

"L-Liam..." she pleas. She's shaky and frail, a stark difference from the confident voice that was speaking to me in the beginning. *She's afraid.*

Letting go of her, I stand and pace around, fighting the urge to ask if I hurt her. *I need to distance myself from her.* All the while, I keep opening and clenching my fists repeatedly in an attempt to control myself, I ask, "Just fucking tell me!"

The words are harsher than I intended, and it's only when a sob breaks free from her mouth that I understand the consequences of my lack of control. She tries to speak but chokes on a sob, and instead, stands up and races out of the living room.

Shit.

"Willow?" I call, going after her. "I'm sorry, I–" I pause when I walk past a door and hear her crying.

All the angry thoughts and feelings vanish from my body, being replaced with guilt. "I didn't mean to–" *Fuck.* "I'm sorry. I promise I'll keep myself in check."

She doesn't answer, still crying on the inside. I wait for a bit, hopefully giving her time to calm down before knocking again.

"Can you let me in?"

She's no longer sobbing but still doesn't answer. Here I thought that this time around we wouldn't leave space for loose ends. When the silence stretches for too long, hope that we'll finish this conversation leaves right through the front door.

"I'll leave then," I inform her.

"Wait," she calls, rooting me in place. "It's easier without you looking at me. Just listen to it all." She seems to take a breath. "That night we were supposed to hang out because your parents were away, you weren't there."

What?

"What do you mean? I went to the grocery stores, but you never showed up. You–"

"I showed up." Her voice rises to a high-pitched tone. "You weren't there!" she yells. "I called you, but it was going straight to voicemail and–"

"No one was home," I whisper, trying to make sense of her words. "It was already late. Did you go back home by yourself?"

A moment goes by before she answers in a soft cry, "Yes."

It feels like a punch to the chest. *No.* It feels like being run over by a truck several times.

Whenever I thought my world couldn't be turned upside down again, I'm proved wrong. In the end, we're nothing. Just a silly and insignificant puppet in the hands of this cruel universe.

Still, hearing these words hurt, tearing through me. Because never–ever–not even for a moment, did I consider she might have not have been safe.

Which is ridiculous, right? My parents have money, and that area of town is wealthy, but that doesn't mean there aren't sickos lurking around in the darkness. *No, please.*

"You were...attacked?" I can't even say the word.

She doesn't answer, and it makes it obvious because no answer is an answer.

Urgency takes over as my protective side kicks in. I'm late, too late. But my brain is screaming at me to get inside that fucking bathroom and just hold her. Hold her close and take all the pain away. "Fuck, Lo. Let me in." *But I can't. Can I?*

"No."

"Please, let me in," I beg.

For a few moments, the silence stretches, but then I hear the door unlocking, revealing what I now know to be the bathroom. She's sitting on the toilet lid with a piece of toilet paper scrunched up in her hand. Her body and head are slightly shaking from her cries.

Crouching down in front of her, I look up, trying to gauge her face. Her otherwise porcelain-toned skin is reddened, as are her eyes. Her pink lips are swollen as is her nose—probably from blowing it on the toilet paper. Her cheeks are also shiny from all the tears streaming down. Even with the ugly crying, she looks *perfect.*

My eyes burn, too, as tears threaten to break free. But I can't cry; this isn't about me.

"I'm sorry," I whisper. "I shouldn't have pushed you so hard to tell me. I didn't know and I—" *Hell, I am a moron.* "I was hurting, too. But fuck, this is nothing compared to the pain of what you—" I pause when she just cries harder.

"I'm sorry," she whispers between sobs.

"Don't you dare apologise! Fuck, baby." I wrap my arms around her waist, placing my chin on her knees and looking up at her. "It's my fucking fault, Willow. I should have been there! If I had been—"

"Stop," she cuts me off. "It's not your fault; you didn't do it." A brief pause to blow her nose. "There's no point in trying to think of what could have been done differently. There's no changing it now."

"But it is," I insist. "If I had been there, you wouldn't have gone back home alone and wouldn't have been attacked."

Her eyes flicker to mine for a second before they glance away, again with the embarrassment and the shame, only now, I know the reason. It breaks my heart because she has no reason to be ashamed.

"Tell me what happened." I need to know. "Because I wasn't there, you went back home and—"

"I don't want to talk about that." She shakes her head. "Please don't make me remember it again." Her pleading undoes my resolve.

Of course, she doesn't want to remember a traumatic experience.

Man, I am so stupid.

All of this time, I blamed her for my pain. For ignoring me right when my brother got worse with the drugs, leaving me to deal with the aftermath of his disappearance. I blamed her for abandoning me at a time when I needed her. And all the while she was hurting, too, *she needed me, too.*

I failed her.

And here I was, being a pretentious asshole and accusing her of taking my son—

"So does that mean that Dylan is—"

"That's what I always thought..." she trails off.

Well, not necessarily.

"There is still a possibility that Dylan is mine. Remember the broken condom?" I ask, scratching the back of my neck in embarrassment.

"The possibility of that having happened is like one percent, Liam."

"It's still a possibility," I insist.

"Okay. Let's not get ahead of ourselves here."

"We're not. He has my eyes and looks a lot like me." One of her eyes twitches, but I ignore it, the enthusiasm taking over me. "And I feel it in my bones. He is mine. I want to meet him, Lo."

"I—no. Liam, we need to think things through. Dylan's not a toy; he has feelings, and he wants to meet his dad. If you're not—"

"I don't care." I shut her down.

I want this.

"At this point, and knowing what I know...even if I end up not being his biological father, I want to be his father figure for all it's worth."

"I didn't put the responsibility on your shoulders back then and I sure as hell will not be doing it now. Liam, raising a kid is no joke. This is not like playing dolls. It's a commitment for life, and you're still single in your twenties—or you have a girlfriend, and I won't intrude or ruin your—"

"Just shut up, Willow," I snap, annoyed.

I get her. *I do.*

She's probably afraid that if he ends up not being mine, I'll want out, but...if that happens, would I love him less? Would I want a way out? The answer is *no.*

Because even if he isn't mine, he is hers. And that would be enough for me to love him.

"I won't change my mind. I want this."

"I–can you let me think about it first?"

"Yeah, sure," I answer. "I–" I stop myself, not knowing where to go from here.

All this time I've held onto the anger that everything was her fault, but it wasn't. Sure, she could have told me, and I would have been by her side every step of the way, but I understand where she was coming from.

"You need to go. Jake will be back with Dylan any minute now," she informs me, looking at her phone to check the time. "I need time to explain to him what happened yesterday and who you are." Her typical dark brown eyes are closer to a shiny golden shadow now from her crying.

I missed her eyes. I missed her so much.

Knowing all of this is heartbreaking and it makes me insanely mad. If there is someone who never deserved this kind of pain, it's Willow.

"Yeah, sure," I agree. "Just text or call me so we can talk it out and plan how we'll do it. That is if you want this..." With a last nod, I stand up after swiping one last stray tear that was on her cheek.

I help her up, too, before we slowly walk to the front door, side by side. There, she opens it so we can step outside.

Unlike the past few days, today is cloudy with a crisp gush of air flowing around. It's not enough to make me cold, but I notice how Willow hugs herself. We stand there for a bit, facing each other in silence.

It's weird to be here, looking at her with so much respect and worry when just half an hour ago, I'd easily have said I hated her.

"I truly am sorry." She finally speaks. "For the pain I caused you. It's no excuse, but I was lost. I felt abandoned and didn't know which was the right choice. In the end, I thought: what is best for my kid? And the only thing that I kept replaying in my mind was how I didn't want him to know he was the result of rape." Her eyes drop down, just like before.

We've been tiptoeing around this word, but now, she finally said it. It's real. Willow—*my Willow*—was raped by some miserable motherfucker.

It pains me, and impulsive Liam takes over, hugging her immediately. Knowing that she went through all of this, alone, and that I failed to protect her creates a whole different breed of anger inside of me. It feels like it's my fault that she was attacked.

This time though, she hugs me back right away, easing a little of that weight off my chest. I give her a peck on the top of her head before burying my head in her hair.

"Don't apologise," I mutter. "I understand now."

My nostrils finally get their fill with her scent. Last night, it wasn't enough, after so many years apart. Wildflowers. Who would have said they smell so good?

It feels like home.

"I was so unfair," I admit. "The pain and the grudge were consuming me. Things were hard at home back then, too. You leaving felt like the last nail in the coffin. The ultimate betrayal. But fuck, if I had been there that night, I—" I take a deep breath. "It wouldn't have happened."

"There's no point in crying over spilt milk. All of those *what ifs* mean nothing because we can't change them. We can only work to make better decisions from now on."

I squeeze her closer to me. She's right. We can only make the best out of the present and work towards a good future. With her back in my arms, it finally feels like a possibility again.

"Look at you all grown up." I chuckle, trying to lighten the mood.

"Right, Dr Davis. You're one to talk."

The stark contrast between her sweet voice and the sarcastic comment force a smile out of me. It's the oddest combination, but I love it.

"Well, not yet," I admit. "There's five more months of internship before my admission exam. After that, I'll have to choose a speciality and study for a couple more years."

"You have always been an overachiever." She beams a proud smile. "I have no doubt you'll ace all of that and rule that hospital in no time."

Leaning back a little, to take a better look at her face, I raise an eyebrow. "You know there's no such thing as 'ruling a hospital', right?"

The corners of her mouth curl up in a shy smile as her left shoulder shrugs. "Not yet."

A deep rumble forms in my chest. Willow has always been shy and quiet with everyone else but with me; I always get her funny and snarky side. The fact she could unabashedly be herself with me only made me fall for her harder, back then.

It's good to know she hasn't lost that side of her, not completely, at least. Because just like that, it feels like we've just travelled back in time. Like nothing changed and we're the same sixteen-year-old teenagers trying to figure out the balance between dating and being friends. As if there hasn't even been time apart between us up to now.

When our laughter finally quiets down and our eyes meet again, tension rises. A completely different one. That invisible force is back, like a magnet that brings us back together again and again.

It's weird how sometimes it feels like the Moirai keep entwining the threads of our lives, bringing us back together—even when we try to keep our distance. As if to teach us a lesson, to let us know that no matter how much we want to do something, they are stronger than us. They know better, and they *will* decide what we need instead.

And if by chance they do fucking exist, they know better because this is exactly what I needed to heal, to move on. I just didn't know it.

"Okie dokie," Willow speaks, cutting off my thoughts.

The combination of her weird choice of words and the awkward look on her face makes me raise a brow again, finding the moment amusing. She rolls her eyes and says, "It's mum vocabulary."

"Alright, alright," I pretend to agree. She always found the weirdest words.

It hasn't changed.

"You probably have stuff to do," she offers. "I won't keep you here any more than needed."

"Yeah," I lie. "I'll head off."

Turning around, expecting to see the empty driveway, I'm faced with three walking bodies. The shortest in the middle—Dylan—stops for a second, sizing us up, and then starts to run towards us. It's only when he stops in front of us that I understand the expression on his face is twisted into a frown. He's angry.

Sure, the plan wasn't to see him like this, again. I meant it when I said I'd let her talk to him first, but then again, what we want is not what we get.

"Hey, buddy," I greet him, trying to make the best out of the situation. "I'm Liam."

"I know who you are," he snaps back. "You're the bad man who made my mummy cry."

Jake and his grandmother's light chatter dies down at the kid's loud words, and my mouth gapes open. *That's pretty to the point for a six-year-old.* Looking to my side, I watch as Willow's face is mirroring my own. *Shock.*

"Dylan," she hisses. "That's no way to talk to adults. Apologise."

"No," he answers right away, not even an ounce of remorse in his voice.

Then he stomps up the steps, placing himself between his mother and me, forcing us further apart.

"I—" Whatever words were going to leave my mouth die in my throat as he pulls his mother inside the house with him. Everyone is speechless, watching the determination in this kid's eyes as he directs his rage at me.

Talk about being protective.

"Get away from my house," he snarls, shutting the door in my face.

TWENTY-NINE

Willow

"DYLAN! YOU CAN'T TREAT PEOPLE LIKE THAT. YOU EVEN CLOSED the door on Uncle Jake and Nana's faces!"

My cheeks are burning with embarrassment—most likely red, too—and if this moment was being drawn in cartoons, I'd have steam coming out of my ears. I am *not* raising my son to be rude.

"They have a key. They can come in," he huffs.

This was not supposed to happen. They shouldn't have met this soon. Knowing Dylan, he is still very much affected by how hard he saw me crying last night. He's only ever seen me that way after a panic attack, a couple of times. So, he knows it's a bad thing. Now he has linked that sadness to Liam as well—which honestly, is not ideal. I needed more time to be able to explain who Liam is and what he means to me. But I should have guessed. Fate is never on my side, and this is no exception.

"That is not the point, young man," I scold. "Liam is a friend. You can't treat him like that."

"He made you cry!"

"And? What have I told you about meddling in adult conversations?"

"To not stick my nose where it doesn't belong."

"Exactly! Now, Liam's a friend, and it's not your place to be rude."

"A friend?" he enquires, tilting his head.

Oh?

"What do you mean?"

"I heard Uncle Jake and Nana at the park. He is your boyfriend, and you didn't tell me!"

Oh god, those two forget that Dylan understands a lot more than they realise.

"What did I tell you that Liam was?" I press, crossing my arms over my chest.

"A friend," he grumbles.

"And have I lied to you before?"

"No." He looks down, suddenly interested in pressing the tip of his foot against the wooden floor.

"Then there you have it," I answer him. His shoulders sag with the finality in my voice. "Now, let's go apologise."

"What? No," he exclaims when I motion for him to reopen the door. "He...he made you cry!"

"Baby," I call before crouching to his height. He immediately comes to me, grabbing my face as he usually does. "We used to be best friends, just like you are with Abby. But I hadn't seen him in years. There was a lot we needed to talk about–we still do." *Because I still haven't told him the whole story.* "I was emotional, but it wasn't his fault."

"You promise?" I nod with a soft smile. "Alright, then."

The determined look on his face makes me chuckle before I stand and bring him with me to the front door. Outside, the three of them, who seem to have been talking in a hushed tone, stop completely upon seeing us. Jake looks proud while Nana seems amused. The only one who is as nervous as me is Liam.

"Go on," I tell Dylan, slightly pushing him forward.

He stumbles on his feet before looking back at me with widened eyes. When I nod in encouragement, he takes a few steps forward and starts, "Well, sorry."

Dylan's head is turned to the side, letting me know he is not even looking at Liam. He doesn't mean it. Liam's mouth opens, and I raise my hand, cutting him off.

"Dylan," I warn.

"I'm sorry for being rude, I guess," he mumbles, an ounce of annoyance palpable in his voice.

This boy.

"Jake," I reprimand when I notice him covering his mouth and poorly hiding his chuckle. "Do not encourage this behaviour. You're worse than him!"

"What did I do? I kept quiet," he whines.

"I already apologised," Dylan whines, looking at me expectantly.

Everyone else just seems amused, even Liam. But still, I don't give up the fight. He needs to understand he can't be rude.

"Not properly, I–"

"It's alright," Liam chimes in, cutting me off. Then he crouches down and talks directly to Dylan. "I'm sorry too, buddy. I didn't mean to make your mother cry, but we both got emotional."

"She told me," he answers, still with a cold demeanour. "She even told me you were best friends."

"She did?" he asks, clearly surprised. When he nods, Liam questions, "So, am I forgiven?"

"Yes."

"Then, how about a handshake to make the truce official?"

They shake hands, with this boy still giving him the side eye now and then. It's so natural and spontaneous that it's entertaining. It's a good restart for them to be friends. It makes me wish they are father and son when they clearly look so much alike. Not only physically but also personality-wise.

The reminder of those times the condom broke sparked a tiny bit of hope inside my heart. I just hope it doesn't come back to bite me in the ass because apparently, that is what life enjoys doing to me.

But as I look at both of them, in the same space, knowing about each other's existence. It takes such a heavy weight off my shoulders because this was what I dreaded the most. And the world didn't fall apart in the end, even if it felt like it for one night.

"Do you want to stay for lunch, Liam?" Nana asks, catching my attention.

"Uhm." He looks at me with panic in his eyes. It's too early. "I can't actually. I have a shift starting in a few hours, so I need to rest. Maybe some other day, if Willow and Dylan don't mind," he answers with an easy smile.

Dylan hums in approval at the fact the he was included, and I suppress a snort. This is exactly how one conquers my son, and Liam has just gained his one positive point.

Is my kid six years old or sixteen?

"I have to go now," Liam warns, looking at his watch. "Thank you for giving me a second chance, buddy. I promise we will be great friends." He winks at Dylan and ruffles his hair.

Then he proceeds to hug Nana and shake Jake's hand before turning to face me. He caresses my cheek before giving it a lingering kiss. Then, he murmurs, "Sorry for everything and thank you for this."

A sudden movement rips Liam's body from mine, making me gasp.

"Don't you have to go?" Dylan grunts, a frown marking the spot between his eyebrows.

Instead of being able to keep serious, Jake snorts, and Nana starts laughing loudly, immediately cancelling any kind of authority I could try to invoke.

I am about to apologise to Liam for my son's rudeness when he starts laughing out loud. Then he nods and ruffles Dylan's hair again before walking back to his car. He laughs all the way.

"Let's go have lunch," Nana decides after a few moments.

They chuckle and taunt Dylan as we go inside, completely ignoring the rising curiosity they have about how the conversation with Liam went. I know they want to give me space and not overwhelm me, but it's visible in their eyes every time they glance at me.

"How about you watch a movie while we make lunch?" I ask my boy.

He nods, and we walk inside the kitchen. Nana and I start the food while Jake sets the table.

"Ask away," I give in, letting them harass me with whatever questions they are keeping inside.

"Did you finally tell him everything?" Jake is the first to ask. "Can you finally tell us?"

I've talked about it twice by now. A third won't kill me, right?

So that's what I do. I spend the next hour preparing lunch, telling Jake and Nana everything. Even more than I told Liam.

I tell them everything carefully and make sure Dylan doesn't hear. Nana cries with me while Jake goes into shock before hugging us tight against him. He too blames himself, just like Liam did, thinking about how he could have prevented it when he couldn't. No one could.

And no one did.

And that's fine; I've accepted it by now.

It's my life, my pain, and my burden to carry. No one else's.

"My baby, I am so proud of you," Nana murmurs as I help her serve lunch after finishing the food.

Jake has gone to call Dylan, and as usual, it takes them a few minutes to come back.

"Thank you, Nana. I couldn't have done it without you." I press my forehead down to hers.

We haven't been spending a lot of time together because of my busy schedule, but I love this woman so much it hurts. And since I can't show her that, I try to do it most of the time by not making her worry and not tiring her.

At this age, she should be spending her life savings on futile things like vacations and luxuries that she probably couldn't afford when she was my age and yet, here she is, taking us in and helping out as much as she can when my parents didn't.

This woman is gold, and I don't intend to let her go ever.

"I love you, Nana," I whisper.

"My princess, you'll have everything you deserve. You'll be with your soulmate, and you'll be a happy family." Her soft breath fans my face while her frail hands grip my cheeks. "You are the best mother I've seen. Better than I was and so much better than your shitty mum," she grumbles.

"Nana!" I scold.

"What? She may be my daughter, but I can recognise a pretentious bitch when I see one!"

"What's a predentius bich?" Dylan's voice chimes from the other side of the kitchen, and I jump, surprised.

Oh, bollocks. He heard that.

"It's a bad person who thinks she's more important than others when in reality they're not," Jake answers smoothly.

"Oh, like Jaden's mum?" His excited voice worries me.

"What do you mean, Dylan?" I take him from my brother's arms and sit him in his seat at the table.

"The other day when Abby's mum was picking us up, I saw Jaden pick on one of my friends, Marcel. He was saying he was different and ugly, and when I got there, I told him he was dumb because he isn't different, and his mum heard. She said it was obvious Marcel was different and shouldn't be mixed with normal kids like Jaden." He frowns in confusion, looking at his friends. "But, Mum, Marcel isn't different from us."

"I know," I answer. "He was at your party, remember?"

Why would she say that? It can't be because of his skin colour... could it?

"She said that black kids need to have another classroom," he confirms my fear, while Nana and Jake gasp. But he continues, ignoring us, "She's wrong. So, she's a predentius bich!" His unfamiliarity with the words forces him to say them funny, making all of us chuckle.

"You're right, baby. That she is." This time around, I'm not even going to correct him. Because he is right, so I just kiss his forehead and sit down next to him.

We all happily dig in, conversing and chuckling at Jake and Dylan's antics. All the while, I keep going back to this lingering thought of how proud I am of this kid and how expectant I am about the man he will become one day. Just this small moment has told me that even though I might be struggling, I'm doing something right, and that puts my heart to rest.

Because I can do it.

I *am* doing it.

THIRTY

Willow

COMING TO COLLEGE WITHOUT HAVING TO TAKE DYLAN TO HIS school first feels as weird as it does good, courtesy of my dear brother, who decided to stick around for a few more days.

I have my suspicions as to why, though. He was concerned for me after everything that went down on Saturday.

"Good morning," Ethan's soft greeting startles me, cutting my thread of thought.

Right next to him, as usual, is Hazel. For the first time since I met her, she's looking at me.

"Oh, hey. Hi—" I stammer when I look into his eyes. He looks concerned. "Good morning."

Do they know? Were they outside? I can't remember anything after my panic attack, but surely they didn't notice.

"How are you feeling after everything?" he asks, confirming my fear.

They witnessed it. Taking a staggering step back, I cover my mouth. The embarrassment is intense as I look at Ethan and Hazel's concerned faces.

"Hey," he coos. "We don't need you to tell us the whole story. From what we figured out, that is between you and that...guy. We just want to know how you are feeling."

"Of course, she's in bad shape," Hazel tuts. "Johanna's move was dirty and fucking low if you ask me."

My head snaps up at the same time Ethan hisses, "Hazel!"

"What do you mean?"

"Look, it's not our place–"

"Like hell it isn't." Hazel snaps. "She started by meddling. We're only doing what's right."

"Still," he insists. "You are causing unnecessary drama."

What the hell are they talking about?

Then, Hazel's expression changes from her usually angry to a sad one. "That's what I would want if it was me in her place, anyway. I'd want to know."

Ethan's throat bobs as a guilty expression takes over. "Fine," he concedes.

"She seems kind of obsessed with Liam, to be honest," she comments with a roll of her eyes. "Whenever you aren't there, it's all she talks about, and as soon as she discovered you had a past with Liam, it got worse. When it came to your son, since they look alike so much, she's been more determined than ever to put you on the spot, claiming he deserves to know the truth."

"Which he does," I sigh, agreeing.

"Well, she isn't doing it for the right reasons. She's doing it with the hopes that he'll hate you so much she'll have a chance because the poor man is still head over heels for you."

"That's–"

"Don't even try to deny it," she cuts me off. "You guys seem to have a shitload to solve, but can I tell you a secret?" She giggles when I nod. "That bitch doesn't stand a chance!"

"Hazel!" I gasp, and Ethan chuckles.

"Who doesn't stand a chance?" Johanna's voice startles us, stunning everyone into silence.

My eyes widen when I notice Hazel's mischievous expression, only to be pushed back by Ethan. "My sister," he blurts.

"And you let her call your sister a bitch?" Johanna's perfectly plucked eyebrow rises.

"Johanna," I call before they can dig a deeper grave. "You called Liam to be there on Saturday?"

Our other two friends take a couple of steps back while I fully turn to face Johanna. Confronting people is not my thing, but she touched a part of me I will never let anyone mess with. *My son.*

After a long and awkward silence, watching her mouth gape, she admits, "Yes. I told you, he deserved to know."

"And I told you I was working on it," I grit. "It wasn't your place."

"*Are you kidding me*?" she snaps. "He is still so hung up on you, it's ridiculous. For what? You've been lying and hiding your son from him this whole time. It's obvious how much you've hurt him!"

"I don't care what you think. It was my son's birthday. Did you even think of him? How it would ruin his day? The impact it would have on him?"

When she fails to answer, I continue, "Of course, you didn't. But I did. Because of that and many other reasons that are not your business, I was taking my time, yes. I was figuring out how to go about it because it's not as easy as you think!"

"Tell her, girl," Hazel hollers.

"Did *you* think about him? Growing up without his dad?"

The words fly out of her mouth, strong and heavy, feeling like a punch to the gut.

I messed up really badly. I know that, but if there is one thing I think about all the time, it's my son. I make every decision based on him. What is best for *him.*

"I did. I always do. And that's exactly why I left. You don't know what happened nor what my reasons were. I hope you're happy now. I need you to stop meddling with my life."

"Alright, I'll admit it." She throws her hands up. "I hoped that by knowing the truth, I'd get the upper hand. To finally get him to get over you, close that door once and for all."

"Well, I hope that ruining my son's birthday and getting him to cry was worth it." Johanna looks away, a sliver of guilt creeping in on her face. "I'll be polite to you, but don't expect me to act as a friend or hang out."

Without sparing her a second glance, I turn around. "I'll see you guys later," I say to Ethan and Hazel.

"What? We're going with you," she exclaims, grabbing Ethan's hand and following me.

Inside, there's a little smile growing, but I act unaffected. I would never tell them who to hang around with or not, but knowing they are on my side gives me some sense of peace. While I'm now fully aware of how much I hurt Liam—and Dylan, too—no one else has the right to meddle, especially with how wrong her reasons for interfering were.

The rest of the day is tiring, with all of the projects piling up, Ethan, Hazel, and I end up spending the rest of the afternoon in the library. One late afternoon turns into five, and I'm not able to pick up Dylan from school on any of these days. god bless Jake.

By Friday afternoon, it feels like I've been dragging myself around with just enough energy to get things done. The only thought on my mind, as I walk up to the car, is cuddling with my tiny person on the couch until he falls asleep on me.

That is until the blaring ringing of my phone startles me. My eyebrows crease at the sight of an unknown number, but I still accept it.

"Hello?"

"Willow," the familiar voice on the other end of the call sounds, sending my heart into a frenzy.

I thought I'd saved his number.

"Liam," I sigh, anxiety creeping in.

"Are you free on Sunday?"

"Yes," I answer. "Why?"

"Can we, uhm, spend the day together?"

"Oh," I exclaim. "I—"

"With Dylan, I mean. I want to spend time with both of you. I want to catch up with you and get to know him...Uh..."

"I—yes?" Why does he always makes me this nervous? "I hope you don't mind being just his—*our*—friend. Until we figure everything out and tell him. When we're sure of things..."

"Yeah," he rushes out. "Sure, sure. I'll pick you up before lunch, yeah?"

"Yeah."

"Alright, I'm starting a double shift now. Well...see you on Sunday." He hangs up even before I can answer.

The cold wind ruffles my hair, hitting my hot neck. It's halfway into November, and it's way colder than it was just two months ago, as autumn slowly is turning into winter. From the starry sky above, you wouldn't guess we're getting closer to the time of year when it rains the most.

A deep shiver erases the warmth that speaking to Liam had just created inside, reminding me that my car is across the parking lot, waiting for me. I rush to it, grabbing my key in the meantime to open the driver's door.

The relief is instant when I get into the car, safe from the cold breeze outside. Sliding the key in the ignition, I twist it, revving the motor. Except, the motor's sound starts with a weak grumble before stopping altogether.

"That's not supposed to happen." My eyebrows furrow while I try a second time.

Nothing.

What the...

After the fifth try, I let my forehead fall onto the wheel in frustration.

Like, really? From all the days this freaking car could break down, it had to be today? When I am the most exhausted?

It's late and dark so trying to look under the hood is out of the question. Not that I would know what to look for anyway. A cab it is. There is no way I'll stay here for another hour just to wait for the Insurance's Assistance.

Just my luck.

Knock-knock.

The sound of someone knocking on the side window catches my attention. Dark eyes on a hard-featured face stare back at me.

Manually rolling the window down, I greet him, "Hey, Professor Adell."

His expression hardens for a second but then relaxes. It's probably because I keep addressing him by his surname, but I mean, habits can be hard to change.

"Hey, I was just leaving and noticed your car didn't start. Do you know what's wrong?"

I exhale, "I-I don't know what happened. It's not working."

"Can you try it once more? Maybe by the sound, I can understand what it is?"

When I nod, he distances himself from the window and keeps a focused expression as I try to start the car again. Unsuccessfully.

He hums quizzically before motioning for me to do it again. I do so, but again, no luck. When he comes back, he perches himself at my window and looks behind the wheel where all the sticks for the lights and such are.

Oh. *Oh*!

Looking at him with widened and panicked eyes, Arthur twists one of the sticks, turning off the light I forgot about this morning.

With a chuckle, he says, "My guess is your battery died since you left the lights on."

Like Liam likes to say: *no shit, Sherlock.*

But I pride myself in avoiding curse words—most of the time.

"Ah, damn. This has never happened to me," I mumble, pinching the bridge of my nose. "I don't have any cables to boost my battery. Would you have them, by any chance?"

"No, sorry."

"It's fine." I wave it off. "I'll scout the battery prices tomorrow. Thank you, Profe—"

"*Arthur*," he grits out, cutting me off.

"Thank you, Arthur." I give him a small appreciative smile.

"How are you going to get home, then?"

"I-I'm probably calling a cab."

He frowns at my words and seems to ponder something before offering, "I could give you a ride."

Oh.

"Oh, no. I don't want to force you out of your way. You must be tired."

"And you aren't? You're probably dying to get home as fast as I am." His eyes crinkle with little lines as he smiles softly. "Let's go."

My hands get clammy and I start to rub them on my jeans, looking away in thought. It's not that he makes me uncomfortable—he doesn't. But he's still my professor, and as much as I don't see any ill intentions on his side, he knows so much now...

It's embarrassing, honestly.

Does he pity me? Is he disgusted?

"Willow," he calls. "It's just a ride; it's no hassle. Come on, you can take care of the car tomorrow. It's getting late."

"Yes, I—okay. Thank you."

Gathering all my stuff, I get out of the car and follow him to his. While doing it, I look around. Other than a couple of cars, the parking lot is empty by now, and thank god it's dark because even though this is just an innocent ride, I wouldn't want anyone to see me getting in his car.

People can be cruel. I've seen it first-hand more times than I'd like to admit, and rumours about being involved with my professor are the last problem I need to add to my long list of existing ones.

Still, Arthur is slowly becoming a friend, I reckon. Everything I didn't expect but surely appreciate. He is kind and understanding, much more than I could ever imagine. He's respectful—well, since he stopped being an asshole anyway. And knowing the reason makes such a difference now. He was doing it to keep his distance, to protect his heart.

The passenger door opens, and I smile shyly before entering the car. It only takes him a few seconds to close my door and circle the vehicle onto his side. He starts driving right away, already knowing my address.

"How have you been since that night?" he asks after a few minutes of silence.

"Oh, uh..." I stutter. "We worked things out. Well, most of it."

"Was he mad that Dylan wasn't his?"

Right.

"Well, I forgot to mention because it seriously hadn't crossed my mind before but, he could be...though, I think it's very unlikely," I admit, avoiding his gaze.

"But you said—"

"Yeah, but there were these two times that the condom broke, and—" I cut myself short. There is no way I am telling him about this. That's *way* too intimate. "Nevermind."

"Still," he presses. "It's not fair. You got pregnant at sixteen. You went through something traumatic and had to raise him by yourself while he was partying his way through college."

"Life isn't fair," I comment. "And it's not his fault. We both were irresponsible, and well, I thought Dylan wasn't his to begin with. But now, I have hope," I whisper the last word, afraid that if I hold on to it, it will break me all over again.

"Hope?"

"Yeah, that Dylan is Liam's. That my beautiful, smart, and loving kid is not a rapist's son." I choke out the last part and jump when his big rough hand engulfs mine.

"Even if he is, Willow, he is yours more than anyone else's." He gives me a fleeting smile before focusing back on the road. "Now, this might sound inappropriate, but I am saying this as a friend. Of course, he had to be beautiful, smart, and loving. It's because he's yours."

My breath hitches, barely managing a thank you. He smiles, patting my hand before retreating his back to the wheel. We stay silent for the remainder of the drive to my house, taking only a few more minutes.

"Thank you so much, Arthur," I tell him when we arrive. "For all of the help and understanding. For everything."

"Any time, Willow."

THIRTY-ONE

Willow

"BABY, WAKE UP," I WHISPER.

"Hmm, no." His chest vibrates from the groan he lets out.

"I have a surprise for you." One of his eyes sneakily opens, looking at me expectantly. "We're visiting the aquarium today."

And just like that, he jumps out of his bed, running towards the dresser. I follow close behind, chuckling at his enthusiasm.

"Mummy, hurry up. Help me find what to wear."

"So the sharks can admire how stylish you are?"

Dylan side-eyes me, a slightly confused glint swirling, but doesn't comment on my sarcasm, digging through the drawers. We take a few minutes but decide on some jean shorts and a dark blue polo that matches his sneakers.

"I look good, Mummy," he gloats.

"Yes, you do, baby. Let's go eat now." Hand in hand, we go down the stairs and find Jake already preparing breakfast with Nana as the supervisor.

"Morning, guys," I greet them.

We both kiss their cheeks and sit down at the table while they wrap everything up. Honestly, having Jake here for an extra week has been bliss. Today, he heads home, and all I can think about is how much I'll miss him.

The food's ready in a couple of minutes, and we eat, with Dylan being unable to stop talking throughout the entire meal. I try to hide the anxiety of knowing that in a few minutes, the doorbell will be ringing, and Liam will be here, waiting for the both of us.

Trying to keep my mind off of it, I pout. "I wish you could stay longer."

Jake chuckles lightly, but I can see it doesn't really reach his eyes either. Being apart hurts us all.

"I'll be back soon," he tuts as we start to clear our plates.

Dylan keeps on eating, unaware of our little parallel conversation.

"Will you be alright?" my brother asks.

"I think so," I answer honestly. "I've started looking for a therapist to see at least once a week. I need to learn how to cope with this. And I'm sure they'll advise me on how to deal with this the best. I want to tell Liam everything." I sigh. "I just don't know how."

"I've got a client whose wife runs a chain of clinics. If I'm not mistaken there is one here. I can text you the name if you want," he suggests.

"That would be awesome. Thank you."

He hugs me, the goodbyes already in motion. "If you ever need anything, you call me. Yeah?" I nod. "And if Liam gives you a hard time, I won't mind coming back here just to threaten him, or *shake* some sense into him."

"Don't be stupid," I chastise, chuckling.

"No, but really...I am afraid that once he knows the whole story—"

Fisting my hand tightly around his shirt, I try not to give away my discomfort. "Let me deal with it. I am working on it. Once I figure out a way to tell him, I will."

"I don't think you're giving him enough credit." My brother shakes his head. "He has always been crazy about you. There is no way he'll doubt you."

I'm torn. There is a tiny part of me that keeps whispering to tell him, that he'll understand. That he'll believe me. But the other...the part that was bent and broken, made to believe that it was worthless, is very hesitant to do so.

It's a tricky situation, where my brain keeps me running in circles. If this huge part of myself still blames me for what happened, for being there when I probably shouldn't have been, for not being strong enough to stop it, for allowing him to do it, then, how could I not?

"I'll figure it out," I answer.

Jake's expression morphs into a disapproving glare. I know he's trying not to scowl at what I said, but that's the truth.

"Whatever you decide," he gives in, kissing my forehead.

It shows he's taking what I want into consideration. It makes me wish we lived closer because we were always joined at the hip when we were kids. He even used to be jealous of Liam growing up.

"Thank you, Jay, for everything. You're the best brother I could ever ask for."

"I know." He smirks and I feign an offended gasp. *So full of himself.* "But you are the best sister as well."

Dylan finishes his food up, jumping straight in the middle of us, killing the sibling-love vibes—like he usually does. While Nana cleans his plate off, the dreaded bell rings, announcing Liam's arrival.

"I'll open it," Dylan exclaims and rushes out of the kitchen before I can stop him.

I can only stumble on myself while trying to follow him.

Liam stands at the front door with a nervous smile on his face and a bouquet in one of his hands. Dylan has his back facing me so, I can't see his reaction, but he's standing still.

"Oh, hey, Liam," I greet him shyly.

"What is he doing here?" Dylan asks me but keeps looking at him.

"Liam is taking us to the aquarium," I say as I crouch down to his height.

Upon seeing his confused face, I continue, "It was his idea from the beginning because he wants to get to know you better."

Dylan scoffs and crosses his arms in front of his chest. From the corner of my eyes, I see a proud Jake closing the distance, watching from the front door.

"Are you trying to get to know me or get my mum to like you?" His serious expression with narrowed eyes surprises me.

I splutter, shocked at the words. *What the hell is going on with my kid?*

"Dylan!" I scold while Jake laughs wholeheartedly. "What are you on about? Liam is my friend, and you are a part of me so, it makes sense that he wants to get to know you. Don't be rude!"

"That's my boy," Jake hollers.

To my big surprise, Liam chuckles and crouches down just as I did.

"Hey, buddy. I am here to see you and get to meet you." He smiles kindly.

Gosh, his smile is still as perfect.

I had almost forgotten how breathtaking it is.

"Yeah, then why did you bring flowers?" Dylan doesn't even budge.

"Right?" Jake chimes in, a raised eyebrow and a cocky smirk, showing how much he's enjoying it. "You hitting on my sister?"

"Jake," I hiss.

Liam chuckles but ignores my brother, keeping his focus on the young boy in front of him. "Because she is your mother. And it would be rude to be here empty-handed. Don't you think?" Dylan weakly nods, but Liam doesn't give up.

He motions for him to get closer to him, to which my kid begrudgingly obeys, allowing him to cup his hand around his ear and fake a whisper, "I wanted it to be a boys' day only, but she wouldn't let me. This is my way of winning her over so we can spend some quality time in the future. What do you think?" Dylan's eyebrows raise, and he glances at me before looking back at Liam with curiosity exuding from him. "You know how much better it is to play a football match with just boys...right?" He nods eagerly. "Then shhh, don't tell her our plan."

My boy's face softens. He nods and takes the flowers himself and takes them inside, probably to give them to Nana.

"That kid is such a turncoat," Jake grumbles, and we both chuckle. *He's jealous.* "I'm out of here, guys." And he up and leaves, heading for his car and driving off.

"He is so clever," Liam remarks, talking about the six-year-old currently walking down the driveway, to meet us by his car.

"Yeah, I think Jake's been a bad influence the last week. He was never that protective of me; I don't know what's gotten into him. Sorry about that." My cheeks are aflame, but Liam doesn't comment on it.

"I like it. He's cheeky and has no shame, and he's also protective of you, which I appreciate."

"Yeah, well, I don't like it. He's six years old, not twenty. I hope it doesn't get worse as he ages; being possessive is not healthy," I mumble.

"You're right."

"Let me just get his seat from inside," I warn him. Since Jake stayed for way longer than predicted, I've been leaving Dylan's car seat at home instead. It proved useful since my brother has been his nephew's private chauffeur for almost two weeks now.

When I come back outside, both boys are waiting, with my sassy kid narrowing his eyes at my childhood best friend—and first love—every once in a while. I guess he still isn't fully convinced.

Once I have it placed in the back seat of the car, I call Dylan. "Come on! Let's go see the sharks, shall we?"

With an eager jump, he sits down on the kid's chair, and I secure him before closing the door. Liam owns a nice—and probably expensive—dark blue Mercedes-Benz that I couldn't even dream of affording.

Throughout the drive, my son finds ways to continue being a brat, constantly testing my limits. Still, Liam takes it like a champ, never being bummed about his bad attitude or snarky remarks. Part of me is worried that things won't get better, and the other is simmering just above the surface, excited about the meaning of this day.

We look like a regular family, about to spend the Sunday out for some quality time. The kind I've only ever dreamed about having but haven't dared to even think about in the last few years...

"That's a giant manta ray," I inform them.

Both of them know as much about animals as I know about maths, and it's been fun to teach them a bit about sea creatures for the last hour.

"Why won't the shark eat it? They eat everything on TV," Dylan mutters, visibly bummed by the lack of violence.

"Baby, what kind of movies have you been watching? They are not out in the wild hunting for food, not to mention those movies are fake. In here, they are all fed, so they don't need to fight other animals."

Liam is sitting on the floor with his ankles crossed in front of him and Dylan on his lap. Both of them are close to the big glass window that separates us from all of the sea creatures. It sends conflicting feelings through me.

Warmth spreads over my chest at the sight of how well they are getting along, but deep inside, it stings with regret as the realisation of what I have been robbing them both of sinks in.

They've been intently listening to my explanations like it's the most interesting thing in the world. It gives me that teacher-moment vibe, and I'll admit I'm enjoying it way too much. I am a little animal geek; biology used to be my college choice. But after having Dylan, I found another passion in teaching.

And who knows? Maybe I can teach a bit about animals and nature to kids as well.

"What's that ugly fish over there, Lo?" Before looking at me, Dylan looks at Liam with an odd expression, but Liam ignores it and keeps waiting for me to answer, and when I do, I catch both of their attention.

"That's the ocean sunfish. They can get bigger than us and weigh more than a car. The name is because of their odd round shape, and funny enough, their behaviour matches their name because they love sunbathing."

"You still amaze me with all of that knowledge about animals. Did you end up choosing that course?" Liam asks, and my face falls.

"No. I'm studying to be a teacher." His face contorts into a frown before asking me why. "Because life got in the way. I'm a freshman, not a senior like you are. And with Dylan, I found a new passion. To teach."

"Oh, of course. It's just that I've always imagined you as this marine biologist going around and saving the oceans. I'd never thought you'd change your mind," he mumbles while playing with Dylan's brown hair.

He's oblivious to our side conversation now, with his eyes glued to the glass wall, looking in awe at all the fish and sharks that roam around in the water.

"I'm happy with my choice. Dylan made me realise that there's still good and purity in this world. And I'll do what I can to be surrounded by that."

After what I went through, I need that beauty in my life. Dylan showed me that it is worth it to go through pain and hurt. Just seeing his smile—every kid's smile—and happiness is enough. And it is a little step towards my healing.

"Of course. Yeah, you're right," he mumbles, deep in thought and probably not knowing what to say.

I get that reminding him of what I went through is still weird. He used to see me as this innocent and happy little girl, and now, I'm a damaged woman with a kid that might not even be his.

"But what about you? Have you finally decided which speciality you're choosing?" Changing subjects will only help us now.

"I have just started practising. I'm still a newbie and do as I'm told, so I haven't fully decided yet."

"Well, that's still amazing. Are you enjoying it? Is it what you thought it was?"

"It's even better. I'll have to admit though, I do tend to find myself in the paediatric department more often than not."

"Really?" I prod.

"I was thin—"

"Mummy!" Dylan interrupts us. "Why are you two talking with each other instead of me?" He frowns. "You said he came to get to know me, but he doesn't ask me as many questions as he does to you."

I blush, and Liam cackles at his antics.

"We were just catching up, buddy," Liam answers him. "Tell me, which one is your favourite?"

"The dolphins," he exclaims. "Mummy told me they love their mummies, that they are clever and fast, just like me," he gloats, and we both laugh.

"He loves all animals. He wanted to get a zebra when we went to the zoo last time. And he went crazy when we saw the lions," I comment.

"They are cute. I still want one," Dylan mumbles.

"If it were up to you, I'd have the entire zoo at home, Dylan. I'll let you have a dog when you are old enough to take care of them," I tell him.

"I am old enough to take care of them." I roll my eyes at his whining.

"Why don't you have a dog? That house has a good space for one," Liam chimes in, and I glare at him in return.

He smiles sheepishly but stays put while Dylan gets excited.

"See? See? He agrees with me!"

"Sure, will you clean his poop? Take him at ungodly hours of the night for a walk? Remember to feed him and not give him our food?" With every word, his face falls with the realisation that having a puppy is not only playing around.

"I definitely don't have the time to do that with work, school, and taking care of you. Just wait a few more years, baby." He nods, and I ruffle his head.

"Look, the shark is coming closer." Liam's voice brings Dylan's attention back to him, and he enthusiastically sits back down on his lap.

I notice how shiny his eyes get when Dylan doesn't hesitate to get close to him, even if he's doing it absentmindedly. I know the proximity affects him, and it tugs at his heart as much as mine.

I get that confirmation when he looks at me with an expectant expression. Then he smiles widely before directing his attention back to him.

The soft blue hues of the aquarium's water cast upon their shadowed faces, highlighting their smiles. My heart beats louder under my ribcage at the sight before me. This is the family I used to dream about, and it's bittersweet to think that there is a fifty-fifty chance of it being like this—my teenage dream or the worst-case scenario.

Dylan's shrieks bring me back to the present, only to squeeze my heart even further. Liam is carrying Dylan around, closer to the glass wall and back, threatening to feed him to the sharks, probably because of something cheeky he told him.

They're bonding.

THIRTY-TWO

Willow

I AM STILL ON CLOUD NINE OVER THAT DAY WE SPENT TOGETHER. Dylan got accustomed to Liam pretty easily and even asked him when he was coming back to see him again. After that first tough kid act he had going on, he warmed up to him.

It could have been because Liam bought him everything he asked for and did everything he wanted. He carried him on his shoulders, bought him a giant dolphin, and even took us for some ice cream before taking us back home.

In a matter of a day, he has spoiled the kid I have been trying hard to teach how much life costs. But in all honesty, I didn't mind it. My son needed it, and from the looks of it, Liam did, too.

Hell, even I did.

On Monday, the battery I had ordered finally arrived, and Liam offered to install it. Which I didn't even know he could, but in the end, I was so thankful because it saved me a lot of money and time. This means that today—Tuesday—I drove to school.

The car door unlocks as soon as I pull the button on the manual lock. That's when a slight movement from the outside catches my attention.

Arthur.

"Good morning."

"Hey," he greets back. "How are you doing?"

"Fine. You?

"Yeah," he answers. "Just wanted to make sure you finally took care of that battery."

"Yes," I breathe out before getting out of the car and shutting the door. "I got it changed yesterday."

"Ah good," he hums before scratching the back of his neck.

Steps sound, catching both of our attention, and Johanna emerges, looking pointedly at the both of us.

"Morning," she grumbles in acknowledgement before shaking her head.

Right after her, other students pass by as the campus starts to pack with people. A few look at us but say nothing, keeping on their way. We're hardly the centre of attention in broad daylight, but apparently, the little attention makes the situation weird.

"Well, if you don't need anything else, I better go."

I understand, though; the last thing we need are rumours about us being too close for a student and professor. That's why I nod and stay behind as he walks toward the class building. The day goes by quickly, with so many projects to finish and notes to organise.

At the end of the day, as I park the car in the driveway, I'm surprised to see Liam's car parked a couple of spots down the road.

What is he doing here?

"Hey." I wave at him after knocking on his driver's window. He rolls it down, sporting one of his signature smiles. The one he used back in the day whenever he had done something he shouldn't have. "Something wrong?"

"No, I—" He stops himself for a moment. "I did an all-nighter, and after waking up this afternoon, I couldn't just sit around the house when I had this...urge to come and see you both."

His cheeks turn a darker shade of pink at the admission, and I'd laugh if I wasn't turning beet-red myself.

"I can go if you have plans or some—"

"No." I cut him off too quickly. "Come in. He'll be happy to see you."

I take a step back to let him get out of the car. We both walk in a half-awkward, half-comfortable silence to my front door. The keys jingle when I place them in the lock, unlocking the door. When I twist the knob and open the door, I'm tackled before I have a second to know what's happening.

My back hits Liam's chest, and thankfully, his arms are strong enough to stop me from falling flat on my ass. Still, Dylan's weight is enough to make him waver. Who would have known that a running six-year-old would feel similar to a speeding truck?

"Jesus Christ," I grumble when I am finally able to find my footing. "You're too old to be doing this."

Nonetheless, I pick Dylan up. Now, completely glued to me with his legs around my torso, arms surrounding my neck, and a megawatt smile right in front of my eyes. Still, what's distracting me is Liam's big hand plastered across my lower abdomen, burning right through my clothes. As if that wasn't enough, the warmth coming from his chest is still hovering over my back, as well as his chuckle right next to my ear.

Sensory overload.

It takes all my strength not to melt into his hold. My body begs for it, craves it.

"I just missed you," Dylan whines, bringing my attention back to him. Then he buries his head in my neck, mumbling, "You have school and work so much..."

"Well," I try to avert a crisis by not dwelling on the bad, "I managed to come earlier than I anticipated today. And apparently, someone else wanted to spend some time with you, too."

"I saw him." His words come out muffled from my shirt.

"Then why are you being rude?" I ask, tilting him in a failed attempt to get him off my neck.

He side-eyes Liam then looks back at me and shrugs.

"He missed you, baby. He wanted to spend some time with you."

"Yeah?" he asks, glancing back at Liam.

"Of course," Liam speaks for the first time. "You still doubt me?"

Dylan's cheeks start to redden, making him look awfully like the man behind me—except for the hair that he got from me.

Sweet Jesus.

Watching these two together often makes me forget that...how can I take care of this? How can I be honest about something as serious as this?

"No," Dylan grumbles.

"Are you hungry?" I ask.

"Yes," the both of them answer in unison, and I giggle.

"Alright." I set Dylan down. It's only when I move, bending forward, that Liam is forced to let go of me. "How about some pancakes?"

"Yes," my son yells, fist-pumping the air, then whispers, "They're fluffier than Nana's."

"I heard that, little rascal!" Nana shouts from the kitchen, earning a widening of Dylan's eyes like a deer caught in headlights.

"Let's go, then." I laugh, walking up to the kitchen where Nana is probably waiting for us. "Both of you will help me, then."

There, while I make the batter and light up the stove, Nana cuts the fruit, and the boys prepare the table. It takes about half an hour to get everything done.

"Hmmm." A double moan.

Looking to my right, I watch as both Liam and Dylan moan at the taste of the food. Their movements are completely synchronised as their left hands grip the forks in the exact same way, and their heads tilt back, too. It's like watching the same person—from past and present—in the same room. So creepy.

Nana glances at me, amusement written all over her face. They dive in for a second bite, still moving equally as if we're watching it all from the TV or a mirror.

"Lo," Liam groans, seemingly oblivious. "Just as delicious as I remember."

"What?" Dylan's head snaps up, faster than lightning.

"Remember we were friends?" I remind him. "I used to make them for the both of us, growing up."

"They are the best I've ever tasted," Liam compliments.

"Oh." A tiny twist in Dylan's eyebrows shows his inner conflict, but it only makes him more adorable. He looks like he is pouting.

"You were very friends?" he asks, probably asking if we were close.

"Yes, baby," I answer. "Like you and Abby, we met young and were inseparable until we were around...sixteen. Then Mummy had to move, and we—" I look at Liam uncomfortably, but he just nods, encouraging me. "We lost touch."

"We were always together," Liam concludes what I was hesitant to say, afraid to anger him.

The nostalgic smile on his face tells me he's—just as I am—reminding himself of the so-called "good old times". There are so many memories and moments that it's hard to focus, but ultimately, there is one that specifically sticks in my mind.

The first time that I felt fully loved and loved back. *Our first time.*

It was New Year's night, and his parents were away for some fancy party, so we had the huge house just to ourselves. It wasn't planned; after all, he had told me he wanted to make it special on Valentine's Day. He wanted to do it all, the romantic meal, the rose petals in the bedroom. And while that is all very pretty and romantic, it wouldn't have felt natural.

And with the both of us, things always happened naturally. They always had, and this time was no exception. It felt right then. And like everything else, he did my bidding.

I knew that the first time wouldn't be perfect or pleasurable because we were both virgins, inexperienced, and somewhat ignorant. But we were also hormonal teenagers who were in love and wanted to take their relationship to the next step, to show how strong and beautiful that feeling was.

"Is it still hurting, baby?" His voice was a low, shaky whisper, showing me how affected he was.

There was stinging at the beginning, and the first few times he moved, I whimpered in pain, even with all the lubrification from getting me off with his fingers and the condom.

But he knew what to do to ease that pain. His hungry kisses kept me busy, and his wandering hands travelled from my jaw to my chest, caressing and pinching my nipples to gripping my hip and groping my butt. It was odd, a wave of new sensations that I was sharing with him by being this full with him.

But besides that little stinging, that uncomfortable feeling, it felt good. It felt empowering and...epic.

I was giving a part of myself that no one else had access to. Something that was just his and mine. Ours.

"No," I whispered before leaning up for another kiss.

His tongue swept against my bottom lip, asking for access, and I opened it, letting him deepen it. Along with it, he thrust himself back in, filling me once more. That time around, instead of that lingering pain, it felt like a soothing stroke, more pleasurable than not.

It only heightened when his thumb pressed against my clit, making me moan loud. He was good with his hands; I had known way before our first time, but feeling it combined with him inside me was a completely different feeling. So full and complete.

His movements were slow and circular at first, gradually speeding up. I moved to meet his hips. Consequently, I was writhing underneath him, arching my back and widening my legs to give him more access. So good.

"Liam," I called for him, needing more but not knowing what.

"That's it, my love," he cooed, before burying his face in my neck.

"More," I groaned, scratching his back. He abided, changing the angle and hitting slightly deeper and forcing a foreign garbling sound out of me.

He chuckled. "Like this?"

"Yes! Oh my—" I couldn't even form words.

A strong tug on my lower stomach kept creeping down while my spine tingled. We were both slick with sweat, our torsos completely glued to each other, not knowing where one finished and the other started. But it felt right.

It felt like it was meant to be.

"Come for me, baby," he begged, grabbing my jaw with one hand, and forcing me to look at him.

With his piercing cerulean eyes staring straight through me, right into my soul, I shattered into a million pieces. He jumped over the edge and took me right along with him.

We clung onto each other as the climax took over, momentarily bringing us into a new dimension. It was only after a few minutes that we came down from the high, still panting, only to confess at the same time, "I love you."

"Willow?" Nana's voice rings through my ears, bringing me back from my memories.

I look around, only to find Dylan and Nana looking at me with confused expressions. "Yeah?"

"Back from la-la-land?" she asks, a teasing tone clinging to her.

Stealing a glance at Liam only makes it worse. He's sporting the smuggest smirk, making my cheeks burn with embarrassment. Could he know?

No. I shake my head, getting rid of the ridiculous idea. *He couldn't.*

Still, it's embarrassing enough for me to be thinking about sex in front of my grandmother and son.

However, it's also the first time I can think of it without... freaking out.

"Sorry." I smile shyly. "I got distracted for a bit."

"Oh, we saw it," Liam comments, shamelessly wiggling his eyebrows.

"Oh, shut up, will you?" I snark back, standing up to clean the empty dishes.

Hopefully, if I keep busy, he won't have the chance to tease me, or try to figure out which moment I was absorbed in. Imagine how appalling it would be to confess I was thinking of our first time. Terrible.

"Can we watch a movie, Mummy?" Dylan chimes in. "Pretty please!"

Yes. Anything to get out of this predicament.

"Of course, but be aware that Liam may not be able to stay until the end," I warn. "He might have to go home soon." It's important to manage his expectations. Liam still has a life and is not expected to change all his plans for us.

"I've got nowhere to be," he admits.

Oh.

"Okay, then," I answer, trying to sound nonchalant about it while on the inside, my heart is making an acrobatic choreography. "Go choose a movie with Liam and Nana while I clean up."

"I'll help you," Liam insists. Then he turns to Dylan and says, "We'll meet the both of you in five minutes."

Not giving a damn, Dylan shrugs and runs off to the living room with a chuckling Nana walking shortly behind him.

The moment we're both alone inside the kitchen the temperature rises and the oxygen in the air seems to lower, making it harder to breathe. I try turning my back to him while scraping the rest of the food off the plates but it's useless.

"So," he trails off. "What were you thinking of?"

Liam's voice is awfully close, more than I anticipated it to be, making me take a deep breath with my eyes shut tight. Though, this time around, when his hand touches my neck while putting my hair behind my ear, I can't suppress the shiver that takes over my spine.

It takes me longer than I'd like to admit, but I finally manage to choke out an answer, "Nothing important."

"I call bullshit."

"Language," I hiss. Maybe a scolding will lower the temperature in this room. "I have a six-year-old that can hear everything and retain a load of unwanted information."

"Your eyes glazed over and your breath quickened when you zoned out." Holy Cow. Not only did he pay attention to me zoning out, but he also read my body language. "What were you thinking about?" His nose nudges my ear. "Were you remembering something about us?"

Yes. "No."

"I don't believe you," he counters. I swear I can hear the smugness in his voice.

"Well," I insist. "It's true."

"I know you," he taunts, coming closer. His chest is now pressed to my back, both his hands gripping the edge of the counter, caging me between him and the sink. "And to be brutally honest, I was remembering, too."

That familiar coil at the bottom of my belly forms for the first time in years, making me gasp. His scent fills my nostrils, just like his hot breath fans over the back of my neck, travelling through my thick hair. My skin is buzzing all over, and my brain is easily getting drunk on endorphins as light-headedness takes over, robbing me of all common sense.

It's desire. It's as familiar as it is foreign, by now.

His presence and proximity are reminding me of things I had locked far away. Things I thought I could never recover. Now, he's here. Reminding me of how magical it was...how great it can still be.

"Lo," he whispers.

A gentle press of his hips shows me how much he is affected, too. The hard shape of his erection presses against the top of my butt while the cold marble from the counter digs into my hips. I may be physically caged, but I feel desired. Wanted.

"I want to kiss you so bad," he whispers, voicing my thoughts.

We're so close. I can give in. All I need to do is turn around and–

"We're watching the Lion King," Dylan shrieks as he comes running into the kitchen.

We both startle, and Liam jumps away from me just in time for him to round the island and not see us hogging each other's space. My hands grip the counter for dear life as my legs almost give in from the tension release.

With a knowing hum, Liam swoops Dylan into his arms and turns to me with a fake pout.

"Let's go watch Simba, Mummy!"

It takes me a few moments to put myself together before I follow them to the couch. There, Nana is sitting on her single chair, purposely leaving the couch for the three of us. Liam is on one end of the couch, with Dylan attached to him. He also left enough space in case I want to keep my distance.

It feels good to be given the choice.

That's why I sit down next to Dylan and him. The movie starts and with it, we all relax as the story starts to envelop us. It turns out to be an amazing night. Liam stays until Dylan falls asleep after dinner and helps me carry him to bed and tuck him in before leaving.

He doesn't attempt any other moves throughout the night, making me feel half-thankful and half-disappointed. He was always impulsive when we were younger, but now it's not just the two of us, I have to think about.

There's Dylan, and there's the giant elephant in the room that I don't know how to get rid of.

The fact I didn't panic was a victory in itself, one I didn't think I could have. Not so soon, anyway. But my heart aches because sooner rather than later I'll have to tell him the last shard of my secret.

This will be the last straw. The one which will send him running to the hills and make him realise that he deserves much more than all of these problems.

Just thinking about it wipes out my good mood. It's that cruel reality check that brings you down from cloud nine, straight into the dirt. It reminds me that dreams are fleeting and pain is real. Constant.

I am better living in the cruel reality that this has no solution. To live with everything that broke me.

THIRTY-THREE

AS I FINISH GETTING READY FOR TODAY'S SHIFT, MY BRAIN WORKS non-stop, thinking about Willow and Dylan. I want to keep my distance and not blur lines, but it's hard.

It's so damn hard.

That day that I spent with both of them was such blissful torture, a glimpse of what my dream used to be—what it still may be, and I just couldn't admit it out loud.

A life by her side.

However, it feels like I'm walking on thin ice. Every second that goes by is critical in the sense that if I say or do the wrong thing, it will all slip away out my hands—once again.

All I could think about was being close to her, smelling her, and kissing her.

The proximity is still as intoxicating as it was. Having Dylan, though, makes it all different. New. Brighter. On a few occasions, he's left me speechless with his cheekiness and impulsive moments—reminding me so much of myself when I was his age.

Quickly, it feels like the gaping hole that has been weighing on my chest for a while is finally being filled. It's closing, healing. So much so that my heart feels like it's going to burst sometimes.

And while I understand her hesitancy and doubts, not wanting to grow a lot of hope only for it to be shattered, I can't help but think—would dare say feel it, too—that he is mine. There is no way he isn't.

Despite the personality traits he is already developing, the physical similarities are striking. The eye colour, the skin tone...In my brain, there isn't any other alternative.

And oh my, is that possibility amazing. Sure, it will probably mean a lot of changes. Priorities would change and routines, too. The hospital would no longer be my number one concern, but my third.

My cell phone rings just as I finish putting my shoes on, cutting off my happy train of thought. When I pick it up, I groan at the sight of the name on the screen.

"Hey, Mum," I greet after accepting the call.

"My boy," she coos. "How are you?"

"Great." It's true.

She just doesn't need to know why I have been so great; my parents have a tendency to kill all happiness around them.

"Good, good," she comments. "I have such great news for you!"

"What's up?"

"Your brother is back," she squeals from the other side of the line, almost bursting my eardrum.

I can't help but sigh. This is a rabbit hole we're going down. *I know.* I've been there.

After everything went down with Willow, I was a wreck. When it became clear she wasn't coming back and wasn't going to be in contact, I had to find other ways to cope.

One of them was studying, which is why I managed to finish high school one year earlier. I'm no genius, but I worked too fucking hard.

The other was knowing that once I finished high school and started college, my parents would pay whatever they needed to ensure I was well off while studying. That meant an apartment, and of course, I saw it as the perfect excuse to help Mason without them knowing.

While settling here, I tried to find the areas he spent his time in and the people he met with to try and grow a pattern of which areas to look for him. When I couldn't, I paid for some help.

Still, it was too late.

Addiction is like a bottomless pit, where no matter how much you feed it to try and fill it, it's never satisfied. It's a sick disease that only takes. And it takes, not only from the person who has it but everyone else around them, too.

And my brother was so deep into his drug addiction that my offer of a place to live for free in a new city with new opportunities wasn't as alluring as offering him a line. He barely talked to me or even looked me in the eye the last time I saw him.

And it broke my heart, too, to think that he was so hopeless and misguided to turn to this as his only way out. My parents and I had failed him, and by then, if he didn't want help, there was nothing I could do. Or so I tell myself.

And that's why I wonder what his reason to be back is. What happened? Has he reached that low that he finally woke up? Or is he just pretending to get money?

"Is he hogging you guys for money?" I blurt out.

There's got to be something to it.

"Liam!" Her tone is harsh. "He says he's clean and yet, just to prove it, he's wanting to do a second month of rehab. It will be good to cement his improvement."

I keep quiet because her words surprise me. Has he finally realised he needs help?

"He wants to make amends with all of us."

This is all too sudden.

They never got along. My parent's pressure and unrealistic expectations suffocated Mason into rebellion, into bad company and bad decisions. And now, they're all turning a blind eye to all of these years of hurt and pretending like nothing happened? Like they aren't part of the problem?

They made Mason find a job to survive, couch-surf acquaintances, and take drugs to forget. He stole, disappeared, and never looked back. My parents never looked for him either.

Where is all of this coming from?

"Are you sure?" I ask after a while.

"Yes." She doesn't hesitate in answering. "He's put on weight, he has clear skin, and he's sober. He looks so good, Liam, and he regrets all he's put us through."

Her words make me sigh, partially in relief that he is in fact alright. The other half, though, is still quite reluctant.

But he's my brother anyway; I'll have to forgive him someday. And if he's trying, then I am willing to give him a chance.

"I'm glad, then. I hope he stays on track," I answer.

"We're going to visit you soon," my mum coos. "Mason wants to see you. And we miss you so much. You never visit anymore."

I barely do, ever since I moved here. Of course, this is the perfect excuse for them to come here without me being able to tell them I'm busy.

"Mum, I'll be pretty much swamped until after Christmas..." There's no harm in trying. Right? "Why don't you come for New Year's instead? It's only a month away."

"If you insist," she whines. "I'd rather go for Christmas, but there's no point in being there if you are working. I want us to have some family time. We haven't had it in so, so long."

No shit.

The mention of family time automatically reminds me of Willow and Dylan. Willow and Dylan. Shit. My parents will not take this well; I know it.

Maybe I should tell them right away?

"Mum..." I trail off. "There's someone tha—"

"Oh, my!" she cuts me off. "You finally got yourself a girlfriend? It's about time!" I can hear the excitement in her voice. "Is she from your class? Who are her parents? Is she from a good family?"

"Mum," I sigh. "Maybe we can arrange for you guys to meet them, someday. How's that?"

"Yes! That'd be—wait a minute!" If this weren't real life, I swear I could listen to the gears turning inside her brain. "Them?"

"Yes," I admit, excited. It's impossible to not get attached to Dylan. "She has a son, a little kid, his na—"

"Oh, no. No, no." She shrieks with a high-pitched voice, and I can hear shuffling around.

Probably scurrying to get my father. Ah, fucking hell....

"*John*!" she yells. "Your son has gone crazy, for real this time! He's been the victim of a scammer. Some skank has been brainwashing him!"

Fuck me. For once, I thought they'd be happy for me. For once, I thought my parents would genuinely be excited for me, for my happiness. Of course, they wouldn't. The Davises and their life of appearances.

Way to kill my cloud-nine mood. Fate really is a cold-hearted bitch. One has to be truly evil to pull me headfirst down to earth, after all of the rollercoasters these past few weeks have been.

For the first time in years, when I can almost say I feel close to being happy, my parents had to fucking ruin it.

"Mum, she doesn't want any money, and she didn't even want me to meet him." That's actually true, as well. "Give her a chance before you start throwing all kinds of insults."

"Liam, son," my father's calm and cold voice sounds from the speaker. "I will not allow you to date this...gold digger."

"Alright, that's it," I grumble before hanging up on them and shutting off my phone.

I'm not taking this bullshit any longer. I'm a grown-ass man, and their approval can fuck off for all I care.

After the shift from hell, my body is begging me to go to sleep for a day and a half, but I had promised Saul and the guys to catch up over some drinks. Especially because we haven't seen each other since that night out in early September.

Residency really takes social life away from you. And while I'm tired as fuck on a Friday night, I'm still excited to meet my friends tonight.

"Hey, man. You finally made it!" Saul greets me with open arms and a grin on his face, and I can't help but grin back while hugging him.

"I told you I'd come, didn't I?" We all laugh.

I greet both Paul and Victor next before sitting down next to them. The wooden surface, between the three of us, already has three half-drank glasses of beer; they've probably been waiting for me for a while.

"How have you been? We've barely been able to see each other," Paul chimes in.

"Between residency and finishing up my master's..." I trail off. "It's been hell."

There's this gnawing urgency inside me to tell them about Willow and Dylan, but I kind of don't want to, too. Nor do I feel like I should. To make them understand everything, I'd have to tell parts of the story that are not mine to tell—even if I want to shout to the world that we've reconnected.

To them, she's just the girl who got away, who disappeared from my life, and I'm not sure if that should change or not.

I love these guys to death. They put up with my wild days in college and saved my ass from a ton of problems and angry boyfriends, but this is different. Having Willow back and Dylan as an extension of her feels too personal to be sharing tonight. Is that because there's a part of me who wants to keep them all to myself? Maybe.

"Nah..." Saul snarks. "I don't believe that. There's this thoughtful look on your face. The last time I saw it was when we met back in freshman year."

"That's right!" Victor agrees. "Some chick finally got your attention?"

These assholes see right through me. Is there any point in denying it? *No.* But I can keep the details to myself.

"You could say that." A smirk finds its way onto my lips.

"Ohh," they all exclaim in unison.

Right at that moment, the bartender passes by, and I ask him for a beer. The guys down the rest of theirs, too, before asking for seconds.

"Right, now spill!" Saul exclaims. "Is this the goddess you met in the club a couple of months ago?"

My hand, which has been drawing circles on the table so far, freezes at the mention of Johanna. She is gorgeous and hot, I can't deny it. And I can't help but be sad that I had to put an end to it. But thinking back to every moment we spent together, it can't come close to what Willow and I share.

Could never.

"No," I answer. "And it's not just some girl. It's *the* girl."

"*What?*"

I can't help but grin as all of them look at me wide-eyed.

"The one who had you spiral back in freshman year?" Victor asks.

"Yeah," I agree.

"Fucking hell," Saul curses. "Tell us everything, man."

"All you guys need to know," I tell them pointedly, "is that we met a few weeks ago and have been talking. You know…" I trail off. "We've been clearing things out. All the questions and misunderstandings."

"Ugh, party-pooper," Paul whines when their third—my first—round of beer arrives.

"Fuck off." I laugh. "And you guys? News?"

One by one, they all tell me their news. Saul is a physiotherapist. We just shared a couple of subjects back in our first year of college, but we got along right off the bat. Paul and Victor followed, a few weeks later at some random party. They're from different areas, but the friendship we developed is solid.

It's a shame that we can't spend as much time together as we used to. Time flies by as we catch up. So much so, it's close to three in the morning when I finally look down at my watch.

"Guys, I have to go." They boo me. "I have a double shift tomorrow. I need to get some sleep."

"Workaholic," Saul coughs up the word, teasing me.

"Shut up, asshole," I counter, standing from my chair and saying goodbye to all of them.

Twisting my arms, I put my jacket on, covering my body from the chilly temperatures that will surely hit outside. Thankfully, it's not a dancing kind of place, so the walk outside is easy.

Just as I expected, the freezing air blows against my face, and all I can think about as I walk to my car is the warmth from my fluffy bed. A loud curse roots me in place, directing my attention to the stumbling woman right next to a very familiar car.

Johanna. She holds onto the side of the car, to bend down and pick up what I reckon to be her car keys, only to fall to the ground. Without thinking twice, I rush over to her, helping her up.

"Hey, Johanna?" I call slowly to try and have her look at me. "It's me. It's Liam."

With hooded eyes, she smiles lazily, her hand patting my cheek. With the exhale of her weak smile, the stench of alcohol reaches my nostrils.

"Am I dreaming?" she slurs, looking up at the sky before looking back at me.

"No–"

"I was asking for you to come and save me, and you've appeared. My knight in a shining armour."

"How much did you have to drink, Jo?"

"Enough." With a high giggle, she tries–and fails–to stand up on her own.

Bringing both of us to the ground, I sigh. There's no way I'll let her drive in such a state. My hand reaches forward, picking her keys up before I help her up–again.

"Come on," I urge. "I'll take you home."

"Pffft, I can take care of myself," she counters.

"Right. Let's go."

"Aren't you back with your little girlfriend?" When I don't answer, she continues, "Go back to her. I don't want your help."

"You don't need to want it. You'll get it either way," I answer, gently pulling her with me. Surprisingly, she doesn't put up a fight. At least, not with her body.

"You can't do this," she whines.

"What?" I ask, confused.

"Be nice. You broke up with me before we even had a chance to be good. You don't get to be nice and make me like you even more."

Her eyes well up, teardrops starting to stream down her face, bringing with it some of her mascara. *Fuck.* I really played a fucking number on her. Even if I didn't mean to.

"You're right," I agree. "I am not trying to be nice. You're in a vulnerable situation, right now. You're drunk and not thinking straight, and I couldn't live with myself if I let you drive like this or left you by yourself. It's dangerous!"

We reach my car, and she grumbles in agreement. I take the win before she changes her mind, helping her inside the back seat and driving her home. After a quick ten-minute ride, I park right in front of her building.

"We're here. Want me to walk you to the door?"

"Please." Her weak whisper breaks my heart. "Liam?"

"Yes, coming." With that, I quickly leave the car, round it and open the door for her.

This time, she initiates the physical contact, her body no longer shaky as it was before. My body relaxes a bit, knowing she's slowly getting a grasp of herself.

"Do you have someone you want to call to come and stay with you?" I ask her.

"Ahm, no," she mumbles, rummaging through her bag for her keys. "My parents are on vacation for the week."

"A friend or someone?" I press.

I'd be less worried if I knew she wasn't going to spend the night by herself after this.

"No. It's fine," she answers. "I'll be fine."

"Are you sure?"

She smiles weakly, her eyes jumping down from my eyes to my lips for a second before locking her gaze with mine.

"I knew I liked you for a reason," she confesses, bringing her hand to my cheek.

I can't help but smile lightly, tenderly cupping her hand with mine. A couple of months ago, my mind slowly filled with thoughts of her. Funny how quickly it changed, and she is just a fleeting memory I'm fond of. A good friend.

Oh, so different.

Nonetheless, she's an amazing woman and is deserving of a man who can fall head over heels for her. Someone who only has eyes for her. I am just *not* that guy.

Yet, the words get stuck in my throat as I watch her lean closer to me in slow motion.

"I was trying to forget you," she whispers as her hot breath hits my face. "But I can't."

There's a sliver of hope that she's not about to try to do what I think she is, not after I told her we couldn't pursue a relationship.

But when her tongue comes out, licking at her own lips, my common sense returns in full force as one specific face crowds my brain.

Willow.

My chest tightens right at the moment our noses bump into each other. *No.*

My hands grip her shoulders, slowly pushing her away from me.

"Johanna," I call weakly. "You're a stunning woman, and you don't need to beg anyone for attention from no one. Especially not from me."

"I thought that by having closure, you'd finally see me..."

"I see you," I admit. "But you aren't seeing me. I don't expect anyone else to understand, but to me, there's no one else. My heart only has space for Willow. I'm sorry." Not answering, she searches my eyes for something. Maybe to gauge if I'm telling the truth. When she finally seems pleased with my answer, she nods, and I add, "Please, call someone; otherwise, I'll worry about you."

She repeats the movement, sliding her key into the lock of the building before mumbling a "Sorry."

"Goodnight," I tell her, right before the door closes with her disappearing behind it.

With the lone company of my thoughts, I go back home, eager for some rest that never comes as I think about tonight's events. Being drunk and alone was such a reckless move for Johanna, but I also get that she's hurting.

How many times have I drank myself into a stupor while wallowing in my sorrows?

Way too many times.

The difference is that I don't automatically turn into a target when hammered drunk. She was lucky I was the one who found her tonight...other women aren't that lucky.

And that thought automatically brings me to one person. Willow.

Even though the scenarios and circumstances were really different, tonight, I was there to help Johanna. But Willow, she had no one.

All of the hurt and betrayal I once felt for her are now entirely replaced by guilt and respect. Because this woman, that truly, I never stopped caring about, still managed to go on and rebuild her life. Completely by herself.

THIRTY-FOUR
Willow

DECEMBER IS FINALLY HERE, AND WITH IT, PROPER COLD, TOO.

It doesn't snow here, since we are so close to the ocean. But it's humid and windy—not that nice either. And the rain. Ugh, it's been raining almost nonstop for the past week.

Thank god it's Friday. That way, I can spend the weekend cuddling with Dylan if it keeps raining. We can make movie days out of it. Warm sofa, blankets, hot cocoa, popcorn, and movies are my favourites.

Since Nana just left to go on a weekend trip to southern Spain—where the temperature is more welcoming at this moment—with some of her friends, I decided to do a few extra hours during the week so I could have the weekend off. I am thankful that Shilah is this flexible; I guess she understands me a lot.

Hannah was young when they opened the place, and she always complains about the time they lost. She told me it went as bad as Hannah not recognizing her as a mother, and that is one of my biggest fears.

The fact that Dylan is very mature for his age and understanding helps me so much more, but nothing beats the ecstatic glow in his eyes this morning when I told him it would be just us for the weekend.

It's well into the afternoon as I drive home from picking Dylan up from school. Just as I park, my phone rings, with Shilah's name shining in the middle of the screen.

"Hey!" I put her on speaker as I put everything inside my backpack. "Everything alright?"

"Sweety," she calls with a frantic voice, making me still. "I–Hannah is in the hospital, I–I need to go check up on her, but my husband can't take care of the diner by himself."

"I'll go. I don't have anyone to leave Dylan with, though. I'll just have to bring him with me again," I say sheepishly.

"Of course, darling. I am so, so sorry for this, but I–"

"No, no. Don't worry...just go. I'll be fifteen minutes, tops."

Turning around, I look at a curious Dylan.

"Em, baby. Do you remember Shilah from Mummy's work?" I ask, and he nods. "She had an emergency, and I need to go to work. You're coming with me. Is that alright?"

He pouts slightly but nods without complaining, and I sigh in relief.

When I get to work, Shilah rushes out with a frantic wave, and I place Dylan in a little booth close to the counter and away from the exit so I can keep eyes on him while walking around. Xico is on edge, but with the amount of food he has to send out, I bet it will keep his mind off of it.

Until dinner time, the diner isn't too busy. I can balance between taking people's orders, serving them, and wrapping up, and then giving Dylan some attention. He mostly draws at first but then remembers some exercises he was given by the teacher. I pop in once in a while and help him with whichever question he might have.

Then, around seven in the evening, just as I am wrapping up a couple's check, the bell chimes. The sound diverts my attention to the entrance, showing me no other than my professor walking in.

He gives me a shy smile, one I give back before pointing out a free booth for him.

"I'll be right over," I shout before heading to another calling customer.

It's busy but not overwhelming.

Thank goodness, otherwise, today would be a complete mess.

After leaving Xico another couple's order, I head to the counter to prepare their beer, just to notice it's empty.

"Dylan, do not leave your table! Mum's going to the kitchen for two minutes just to grab the beer keg," I tell him.

He looks up at me from his papers and nods. A lot of the clients are regular customers, and there's a lady right behind Dylan's booth that already knows him, and I know she's keeping an eye on him every time I get busier. She told me so when I placed her food in front of her.

It does help ease the worry that someone won't just barge in and take my kid with them.

"Arthur," Dylan screeches just as I finish placing the keg in place, making me pop my head up fast enough to see him wave over to Professor Adell.

Does he remember him still? It's been, what? A month?

My teacher gives me a quizzical look, and I just shrug in return. I'm not going to force him to put up with my six-year-old if he doesn't want to. He smiles, flashing me his pearly white teeth, before heading to Dylan's table. What a surprise. Still, I sigh in relief, knowing that someone is now fully paying attention to him.

Walking over to them, I ask, trying to sound as professional as I can, "Good evening, what can I get you?"

Arthur chuckles at my awkwardness while Dylan beams at me before saying, "Mummy, Arthur helped me with my homework. I did my letters and my numbers correctly. Look!"

"Wow, baby! They're so good," I tell him. "Thank you, Arthur; you didn't have to. I've been helping him here and there every time I have a bit of time."

"Oh, it was nothing. He's really intelligent and did almost everything on his own. I just gave him a few tips." He smirks at my son.

It's still weird to see him smile so much, even if they are just small ones. It suits him so much more than he could ever imagine.

"Have you decided what I can get you?"

"Yes, the usual, please. And bring something for Dylan—it's on me." Dylan's eyes shine at Arthur's words, making me laugh before answering him.

"Oh, no. Don't worry. Shilah and Xico don't charge me for his food, which is already being cooked by the way. But thank you, anyway. I'll be back with your food soon." He nods, and I turn to Dylan. "And, you, behave. Okay, baby?"

After Dylan's enthusiastic nod, I go back to taking requests, serving people and cleaning tables after they're done paying.

Another hour passes, with lots to do everywhere. The door rings so many times I lose count of all of the people coming in and leaving. One of them, though, freezes me to the spot for a few moments.

Walking in are Johanna and Liam. He opens the door for her, letting her in first before stepping into her side. When they settle by the entrance, looking around and locking eyes with me, they freeze. I can see the shock seep onto both of their faces.

Trying not to react in any specific way, I point out a free booth. Liam nods before extending his arm, signalling for Johanna to walk. They're walking side by side, not holding hands or anything like that, but they're close enough that their arms keep touching.

Liam and Johanna both knew I wasn't supposed to be working tonight—nor this weekend.

He knows because he asked, trying to schedule something with Dylan and me this weekend. So, of course, I informed him that I was completely work-free this weekend. Johanna knows because I was adamant with Ethan and Hazel to not leave her out, despite everything. So, she was there when I told them about my plans to have some quality time with my son.

Neither of them told me about the other, so my knowledge of their plans was lacking. *Until now.* This has to be a date.

They could have chosen somewhere else to go, though.

God, my brain is a mess. *I am a mess.*

After a few awkward moments, I force a smile, hoping it doesn't look like a grimace.

Doing the same thing I did with Arthur, I tell them, "I'll be with you guys in a minute."

I bring the bill to another table and clean one that had just cleared out when Dylan comes running to me.

"Mummy," he whines, tugging on my leg. A clear request for me to crouch down, and I do. "I need to go potty," he whispers to my ear.

Oh, man. The diner is still in full swing right now. Oh god.

Don't panic.

"Can you wait a couple of minutes?" He nods. "Let me settle things here, and I'll take you, okay?"

"Dylan?" Liam calls from behind me, making me turn to look at them both.

"*Liam*!" Dylan screeches, running up to him and jumping straight onto his chest.

With a "*humpf*" muttered on impact, Liam closes his arms around him, a content smile on his face with his eyes shut tight.

I decide to approach them slowly, to try and not let Dylan take too much of their time, but I slow my pace to a stop when I notice Johanna's adoring expression while looking at Liam.

I put myself between them.

It hurts. I don't know why, but it does...

Still, I shouldn't have and I need to correct this.

"Dylan, let Liam and Jo eat in peace, baby. Go back to your table. I'll help you back in a minute, please," I plead.

This is already beyond awkward, having everyone here, it's affecting me.

I'm on edge.

To help with the circus, Liam looks at me with a big frown, accentuating, even more, his confused expression.

"He can stay here with me. You're working, who's taking care of him?" Liam asks.

"Arthur!" Dylan chirps animatedly.

Great.

"My, uh, professor happened to stop by for dinner and saw me struggling. He, uh, offered to look out for him," I stutter throughout the entire speech, even though it's not necessarily a lie.

"Professor Prick?" Johanna asks, surprised.

Yeah, I had the same reaction back then...

"Why didn't you call me? I would've taken him." Liam's frown deepens.

He thinks I don't trust him.

I do.

If there was someone in my life I'd trust unconditionally besides my brother, it's him.

"I didn't have time. I was already picking him up from school when Shilah asked me to come here right away. And it's not his first rodeo, so I just came here. Em, it's a force of habit."

My explanation softens his expression, helping him understand that it wasn't anything against him, but still, it feels like I'm walking on thin ice.

Realising the amount of time I'm spending here with them I snap out of my panic and turn my attention to Dylan.

"Baby, go back to Arthur. Let me just hurry up so I can go and help you," I mutter to him.

"He can stay here with me. I'll help him with whatever he needs, and you can go back to working and not worry," he fires out.

I appreciate his willingness to take him and help. Especially since—and despite the possibility of him being the father—they've bonded over these last couple of weeks. They've become oddly attached. Liam is very protective and defensive when it comes to Dylan, and while it's been warming my heart so far, today, it troubles me.

It leaves me uneasy because, from the corner of my eye, I can see Jo's face deflate. Whatever she was hoping to get from this dinner, it won't be achieved with Dylan here, that's for sure.

That's why I assertively answer, "There's no need. I already have someone to take care of him for the time being, and I don't think my son interrupting your dinner would be the right thing to do. Come on, Dylan."

Liam winces at my tone at the same time Dylan begrudgingly obeys what I said. When I look back at them, I ask, "What can I get you to drink?"

They order their drinks first, and then their food. In a matter of five minutes, I take care of the chaotic madness that was forming in the diner and ask Arthur to keep an eye while I help Dylan in the toilet.

It's not that he needs a lot of help since he does most of it by himself by now, but I like to ensure he at least cleans his hands properly.

The last couple of hours drag slowly. A lot of glances are exchanged. Arthur sends me a few with a questioning glint in his eyes. He's probably curious about Liam and Johanna, and Liam's presence in Dylan's life. While on the other hand, Liam sends me a lot of regretful ones.

I don't know why, though. It's not like he owes me an explanation.

I don't even deserve one after what I did to him. But it still hurts, to see him possibly moving on, right in front of me.

They end up leaving not long after, and it's only when they leave the diner that my body finally relaxes and time seems to go faster. When Xico and I successfully close the place, Dylan is fast asleep on Arthur's chest, his cheek squashed over his shoulder, the sight making me chuckle.

For a sombre man with a troubled past, parenthood would suit him. And to see him not afraid to engage with children is attractive. *Especially with mine.*

What am I even thinking?

I snap out of the ridiculous thoughts and thank him for his invaluable help once again before saying goodnight and driving home.

As soon as I park in my driveway, though, my mood, which had lifted slightly at the sight of Arthur and Dylan, falls at the sight of a familiar figure waiting by my front door.

THIRTY-FIVE

Willow

LIAM.

He's here.

I step out of the car, and he comes closer to me, stopping only when he sees me taking a sleeping Dylan out of the car.

"Lo," he whispers. "Can we talk?"

"About what?" I sigh. "Dylan's sleeping, and I'm tired." Annoyance laces my voice.

I shouldn't provoke him. God, I know I shouldn't, but I can't help it. He's always brought out the bravest side of me. I've never been afraid to speak my mind, not with him.

"About what you saw at the diner and everything else."

The last thing I want to do now is talk. But as always, his eyes burn with determination. He's one of the most stubborn people I know. There's no point in arguing.

"Fine. Let me just get him to bed first." I try to look for my keys with the only hand I have available, while the other is under Dylan's butt, holding him onto me. His head snuggles against my neck, limiting my range of movement. When I fail to find the keys, Liam swiftly and softly takes Dylan out of my hold. He squirms a little in his arms until he's comfortable again and stills, snoring even louder.

I swear this kid can sleep through a freaking hurricane.

"Thank you," I mumble while opening the door and letting us both inside.

When I try to get Dylan into my arms, Liam says he's got him, nodding for me to lead him upstairs. With a resigned sigh, I comply. The silence between us is deafening, over the low padding of our bare feet. In Dylan's room, Liam helps me with changing him and tucking him in.

It is all so natural that one would doubt it's the first time it's happening.

"He's a heavy sleeper," he hums, smiling, his eyes locked on the sleeping boy. "He didn't even flinch while we manoeuvred him."

"He is," I agree. "And it's a struggle to wake him up in the morning. He's very passionate about his bed, to the point of kicking."

Liam's head snaps to mine with wide eyes. I probably just reminded him of that one time we fell asleep on the couch one afternoon and the way he pushed me off it when I tried to wake him up.

"Too good to be just a coincidence. Don't you think?"

Yes. Either way, it isn't a coincidence.

It's been easier to forget the other half of the possibility when things go this smoothly. It always feels like a punch to the gut whenever I remember.

"Don't get your hopes up," I snap.

It's not his fault. I know! But this is the best defence mechanism I can come up with. My brain keeps chanting that if I keep my distance, it'll hurt less. A stupid illusion.

His face falls, and I have to turn away, heading back downstairs. The way his expression contorts makes my heart tug, and not in a good way. I can see from it how much he wants this, and that alone makes me afraid.

More than I've felt in a long time because if he isn't, he'll question everything, and having him know everything that happened will destroy him. *Almost as much as it destroyed me.*

"Don't you think that was uncalled for?" he growls when we get downstairs.

"It was, but I know you. You're impulsive and emotional. I can see the way you look at him. You believe unconditionally that he is yours. I was just reminding you, keeping you grounded."

"No, you're being cruel. I understand that you're upset about seeing me with Johanna at the diner, but it wasn't what you're thinking it was."

Of course, he'd think that's what made me say that. It wasn't. *Right?* I have no right to be upset or jealous. We haven't been together for years now.

"I don't think anything, Liam. You're single, remember? You can see and date whoever you want, and I can't be mad at you." His mouth opens to counter but I cut him off, continuing, "Plus, you are dating her. It's not your fault I came barrelling down like a tsunami and ruined your life. If there's someone who's not right in this situation, it's me for stepping in between the both of you."

When I finish my speech, Liam doesn't answer me for a while. *A good while.*

He spends the entire time in silence, looking intently at me, his eyes roaming my face. They jump from the crease between my eyebrows to my eyes, cheeks, and then to my lips, only to go back up and do it again. *And again.*

"I am *not* dating Johanna," he answers. My heart roars in satisfaction, but I try to keep a poker face. It's still not my business. "I finished whatever it could turn into when I saw you at her apartment. We met earlier because the other night, when I went out with some friends, I found her outside completely intoxicated. After taking her home, I got worried and wanted to check in on her."

"Oh...is she okay?"

He nods. "Yes. I think so."

"You still don't have to explain yourself to me. It's fine, Liam."

It does lift some of the worrying feelings that were brewing inside me, but that fact only brings another load. The ability he has to reassure me shouldn't be there. And I shouldn't be bothered by any of this.

But I am. And I don't know what the hell that means. What it can mean scares the hell out of me.

I came to this city to have a fresh start, and so far, I've had anything but. I've barely been keeping myself afloat between school, work, and the emotional distress of having Liam back in my life.

"You don't look fine."

Damn him and his ability to see right through me.

"I am exhausted today," I answer. "I was supposed to stay at home with Dylan and had to go to work after a day of school. It's been a long day..."

"You could have called me," he comments, and I look away.

It's the same thing he said earlier when I was working and he saw Dylan. And while I understand where he is coming from, he also needs to realise that I have been doing this by myself–mostly–ever since he was born. My automatic response is to solve it by myself, not ask for help.

"I didn't have time," I explain truthfully. "This is new. I'm used to doing everything by myself; I just acted on it."

He frowns. "But you had your professor do it instead of me? Like what the fuck? He's the guy from that night. Should you even be that close to him?"

I freeze. His words are harsh, and while I understand what he means, I know there is nothing inappropriate going on. Arthur has been nothing but a gentleman and respectful of my boundaries.

He has helped me more than anyone else could, in such a short period. Without him, I wonder if I would have been able to tell Liam most of the truth. Probably not.

And yes, the man is sinfully attractive, but no other man has ever–ever–made me feel like Liam has. Like he still does.

This man right in front of me will always hold the biggest part of my heart. Whether I acknowledge it or not.

"He realised how much I was struggling as a single parent, working and studying, and has helped out a couple of times," I reiterate, my hands clenching into fists.

Why am I even trying to defend myself?

"Oh?" He tilts his head. "That's weird...Johanna mentioned he was horrible to you at first. He just up and stopped all of the sudden? Why?" His bright blue eyes are dark, an angry storm forming in them.

It only irks me.

"What are you trying to get at?" I grit out.

"Don't act so innocent, Willow! You know exactly what I'm asking!"

What?

I feel my face contort in confusion until it clicks.

My eyes widen in realisation. And I feel an uncomfortable heat rise through my chest straight to my face. Bile threatens to come out at the same time my eyes sting and tears fight their way out of my eyes.

My body starts to shake uncontrollably with mixed emotions. Anger. Revolt. Hurt. Sadness. If there is someone on this earth who could truly shatter me with these kinds of words, it's him.

"Get out," I hiss through clenched teeth.

"Not until you answer me," he barks back, closing in on me.

"Answer what?" I counter, my hands shaking with rage. "What the hell do you want to hear from me? That I fucked my professor?" My voice raises a considerable notch, getting a slight high-pitchedness to it. "Are you even listening to yourself? I was bloody raped. Sex hasn't been on my mind ever since!"

His mouth opens but no sounds come out, so I continue, "Not until you came the hell back!" My pointer finger pokes at his chest angrily. "So don't you dare stand in here and accuse me of something impossible. Not after everything!"

At this point, I can feel how the heat irradiating from my skin warms my cold tears. I can barely feel them anymore, but my blurry vision is a firm indicator of my crying. In front of me, Liam stands still, watching me.

"You think it's easy to recover from this? I still wake up drenched in sweat from recurrent nightmares; a single hand on my shoulder is enough to startle me; I get nauseous just from thinking of someone else that isn't you kissing me or any part of me. What gives you any right to say this bullshit to me, huh?"

His hands straighten towards me, and I take a staggering step away from him.

"Lo–"

"No," I scream. "Do you know how much I prayed that night? I prayed for you to show up and stop it." A sob breaks free from my throat, but I push through it. "Then, I cried. I yelled—begged even—for him to stop, for him to leave me alone. He didn't stop, and you didn't show up. Nor did my brother or my dad or anyone else. So, if you are coming to my house to accuse me of ridiculous acts then please, do the both of us a favour and get the hell out!"

He regrets his words now. I can see it in his face, in his eyes.

I don't think he had realised the extent of my trauma until now. People always say beautiful words and claim to understand. But, how could they understand if they haven't been through it?

They're not the ones who cry themselves to sleep and wake up yelling from nightmares. They're not the ones who break mirrors after taking a look at their reflection or scrub their skin until it bleeds with fake hopes of getting rid of that feeling of being dirty. They're not the ones who blame themselves for letting it happen. This is a constant cycle, just like a snowball that keeps on rolling and growing.

The true pain goes way beyond the physical one. It's like ivy. It sticks to your bones and essence, the same way ivy sticks to a wall, turning into part of the structure. The pain becomes part of us, and it never goes away.

The helplessness. The despair. It's incapacitating at times—and it takes the little control we manage to have over our bodies, over our lives.

"Shit!" He rubs his forehead. "Lo, I forgot...I—"

"Get out," I ask quietly.

"I was jealous," he admits. "Fuck, baby. I'm so sorry."

The words come out a little too late. I'm inside that cycle again, and nothing he can say will make me feel better about myself right now.

"Leave."

"Lo," he calls, coming closer. I take a step back again. "Please," he begs.

"Leave me alone." His body sags, dejected.

I don't care. I don't have the emotional or the physical energy for anything else. I feel defeated. All my brain keeps asking for is the fluffiness of my warm pyjamas and for my body to slide inside the bed and black out until tomorrow.

With a resigned sigh, he finally seems to understand that this is not getting solved. At least, not today. With an ashamed lowering of his eyes, he finally nods.

"For what it's worth," he tells me, while already gripping the door knob. "I *am* fucking sorry."

Then he turns around, slowly walking down the porch. I slam the door shut behind him before I crumble to the ground in an ugly wail.

This is too much to handle.

THIRTY-SIX

Liam

"MUMMY'S NOT COMING WITH US?" DYLAN ASKS AS I PLACE THE CAR seat in the back of my car.

He's on my side, intently watching me as I struggle to put this stupid thing in correctly. Willow finally agreed to let me take him for a day without any kind of supervision.

And while it stings that I had to hound her for it for almost two weeks, I understand that it is a lot to adapt to. She's been on her own for so long, and now, I just parachute myself into their lives, demanding changes in their routine.

A person with two brain cells knows that's not how it works. Thus, I should just be thankful for this leap of faith.

It doesn't help that I fucked up and she's barely talking to me. Those words have been living in my brain rent-free, even though I regretted them as soon as they flew out of my mouth. I can't change the past now. All I can do is prove myself to her.

Let's just hope I can turn this day around already. It's already started poorly. The initial plan was to stop at Willow's place so she could give me the car seat to pick Dylan up. But one hour before my shift ended, an emergency came in, and Dr Shawn pointedly told me not to bother coming back if I didn't stay for the surgery it entailed.

Apparently, I've not been working as many hours as I was in the beginning, and he's disappointed. The asshole gave me five minutes to get my shit together and show up in the surgery room.

Thankfully, there is one thing that hasn't changed about Willow after all of these years. She is not the kind to sabotage something just because she's hurt or angry. And in full Willow fashion, she understood right away, telling me not to worry about picking Dylan up from school; she did it instead.

I'm relieved she didn't try to raincheck because today is the day I'm taking him to enrol him in the local football team.

Everything is set, and we need to head out soon if we want to make it on time. If only the fucking car seat would secure properly. *Fucking hell.*

"It's just us today, buddy," I answer with a grunt, still struggling with the seatbelt. "It's a boys' day."

How on Earth can I be sure he is securely attached? Last time, Willow walked me through it, and I got too cocky.

The joke's on me.

Shaking the seat to make sure it's good, it swivels too much to the side, and I frown. What the fuck am I missing?

"It goes underneath," Dylan tuts with a bored tone.

"Huh?"

"The seatbelt. There is a thingy underneath to slide the seatbelt in. Then it should be done. At least that's how Mummy does."

I take it off and restart from the beginning, doing as he directed before I click the seatbelt into the buckle. When I try to shake it again, it barely moves, and I sigh in relief.

If my tanned complexion would allow it, I'd be blushing from embarrassment. Dylan knows how to secure a car seat better than I do. Bloody hell, and here I was last night, asking what could go wrong...Nothing like a six-year-old to humble you a little—*or a lot.*

There's no time to wallow in misery. I can bitch about not being fit to be a parent later.

"Alright, bud. Let's go."

"*Yes*!" He jumps straight inside, sitting on the car seat. After closing his door and rounding the car, I get into the driver's seat to rev the engine.

"Where are we going?"

Peeling off Willow's driveway, we slowly head toward Porto's junior team practice stadium. It's on the opposite side of the city, and with traffic, a good thirty-minute drive.

"A little bird told me you like football..." I trail off. "I reckon it's time to sign you up to play in a team. What do you think?"

"Porto?" The giddiness in his voice is audible, and I have to make a big effort to not groan. It's definitely is not my favourite team.

"Unfortunately," I grumble in distaste. "Hopefully, soon, I'll be able to convince you Benfica is best."

"Uncle Jake says they bribe referees."

"That's a load of—" I splutter, stopping myself before I curse. It is, though. "Do you even know what bribe means?"

"I asked Mum," he answers proudly.

"Of course, you did. Anyway, how do you feel about going for a try-out?"

"Oh." He looks down at his hands, picking at the seat's buckle. "Good."

I frown. "You don't want to? We can do something else..."

"No," he exclaims, eyes widening. "I just..."

"What's wrong, bud?"

"All of my school friends play football, too. They told me their dads always takes them to the practices, and..." he stops, looking outside, and my heart twists in pain.

Bloody hell.

The way his voice is weak and low alongside his deep frown feels like a punch to my gut. My throat clogs up with unsaid words. The ones I want to say ever since I've known the whole truth.

And while there is a small chance that takes away from the certainty of me being his dad...watching him like this makes me want to blurt those words more than ever.

I'm your dad.

It's what I want to say. But Willow and I have an agreement.

We can't tell him until we're sure, and I understand. His well-being matters more than our—*my*—feelings. I may be new to this, but I understand that perspective very well. After not being a priority to my own family growing up—not in the way that it matters—I have vowed to do better. To break the cycle.

And that means putting him above everything else.

"And..." I prompt him to continue, swallowing the forbidden words.

"I always thought by now," he side-eyes me with a sad expression before looking back outside and continuing, "that mummy would have found my dad, and he'd be the one doing this with me..."

Fucking hell! How do I go about this without fucking it up?

"Bud." I wait until he looks at me. "I'm sorry things aren't going as you expected." He huffs, looking away again, and I swallow as panic grips my throat. The words are ready to be spewed out and give him exactly what he wants. *Your dad is right here.* "You're too young to understand, but sometimes, things are harder and more difficult to solve than we realise."

"That's what Mum keeps saying," he snickers.

"If so, then she probably has a good reason for it. I'm sure that when the time is right, she'll introduce you to him or at least let you know who he is," I try, not knowing if my words are right. "Until then, you can't stop doing what you love. But if you don't want to enrol–"

"No," he cuts me off. "I do."

"And are you willing to be going with me instead?"

"I guess," he shrugs. "I just hope my dad doesn't get mad that I did it without him."

"Oh, believe me." I smile. "He'll understand just fine."

"That was awesome, bud," I holler to Dylan as he runs down the field after scoring a goal.

My whole body is simmering with the pride travelling through my nerve endings. He's pretty good and has excellent control over the ball. He still needs to learn when to pass it on or take the shot, but he's barely six years old. I reckon he has time to improve.

He could very well be the next Ronaldo. I feel the smile on my face as the fleeting thought crosses my mind.

The try-out goes on for ten more minutes, and right afterwards, I meet the coach as he's inside, getting ready to head back out.

"The kid's good," he comments nonchalantly.

They never like to sound too enthusiastic.

"And has great potential," I add. "I hope he can join the team?"

"He sure should. Here," he says, handing me a bunch of paperwork. "Bring this back by Tuesday at the latest, right before the next practice."

"No problem." I nod, eyeing the papers.

It requires the parent's permission signature, as well as a monthly payment of fifty euros. It's not much, but I know that amount doesn't have the same meaning to me as it has for Willow.

Even though she didn't seem concerned about it being an extra expense, it's not lost on me that she needs to work on top of studying. I'll pay for this myself—let's just hope she's okay with it.

"I hope to see you both next week." The coach waves as he heads back out to the field.

Just then, I see Dylan emerging from the gate, excitedly waving at me. He runs up as I walk in his direction, and as soon as he's within reach, he hugs me. My hand finds his head, gently threading my long fingers through the brown mop of wild, wet hair.

"You showered? By yourself?" I ask.

"No," he grunts. "I just put some water on my head; I was hot."

I nod. "You play way better than I could've ever imagined!" The praise rolls off my mouth naturally.

With a massive smile, he pushes away, holding my hand instead. "You think they will let me play more?"

We start to walk out. Our pace is slow as the little energy I had is slowly slipping away from me—from him, too, it seems. The tiredness is now taking a new kind of control over my body, making it feel slightly heavier.

"They'd be crazy not to. And besides..." He peers up at me. "I got the papers to enrol you right here. All we need is Mum's approval."

"*Yes*!" He jumps in excitement. "We need to go home and ask her to agree!"

Just then, my stomach growls, stopping the both of us in our tracks. It's been hours since the meal break I had in my shift, and it's taking a toll on me. We burst out laughing at the exact moment his stomach growls, too, as if in tune with mine.

"She'll agree for sure." I chuckle. "How about we go eat something and buy her a gift? I'm sure she'll love that we thought of her today."

That and it will hopefully gain me a couple of points with her.

With an eager nod, he pulls my hand in my car's direction before walking towards it.

Thankfully, it's only a ten-minute drive, and his non-stop excited chatter is enough to keep my low batteries running until we reach McDonald's. It's not like it's the best place to go, but it's what he begs me for, and I can't refuse him.

Once our bellies are full of food, we stop by the florist to make her a personalised bouquet. Dylan chooses a whole rainbow of colours, and I make sure to add as many baby's breaths as possible. Of all of the flowers in here, it's the one that fits her the most.

"Should we add perfume to the gift?"

"Perfume?" His head tilts to the side in thought.

"Yeah," I answer, pulling him with me this time around. "Come on; she'll love it."

The food was enough to keep Dylan's mood afloat—no tantrums or even spunkiness has peeked out. It's slowly giving me confidence. While I know an evening is way easier than having him for a night or two or even full-time, the time lets us get used to and know each other.

I've got this.

By the time we get to the store, I'm in automatic mode. I head to the shelves where I know the brand of perfume she used back in high school.

"Does she even use the same perfume?" I ask myself.

"Can I smell it?" Dylan pipes in, reminding me of his existence.

Fuck, I really am tired.

Spraying it on one of those white papers, I flail it to diffuse the scent before giving it to him. The slight crease between his eyebrows smooths down as he smiles and looks at me with a broad smile.

"That's how Mum smells," he assures me.

Somehow, I feel like I should know this. I've been around plenty by now, enough to know her scent by heart.

When I bring the paper to my nose, nostalgia hits me full force. It is Willow, for sure. And all of the memories of us together in school and after school quickly take over my brain.

"Alright, let's pay," I mutter, my shoulders sagging from the lack of energy.

My eyes feel heavy again, and the thought of sleep starts to ring through my brain like an alarm. Through the payment, the cashier flirts a little, noticing the flowers while Dylan is still walking around full of energy. Who does he get it from, anyway?

The numbers from the payment machine blur before my eyes–a clear sign that my body's exhausted. It's barely past eight, and I have around half an hour to get Dylan home before his bedtime. Somehow, it feels like I've been up for forty-eight hours.

"Thank you," the girl chirps as she gives me the receipt.

When I finally have the wallet inside my jeans pocket and the perfume bag in my hand, I turn to the exit. Ready to walk to my car and drive to Willow's. I'm five meters down the shopping mall's corridor when I notice something's wrong like I'm forgetting something I shouldn't be.

I rack my brain for what it could be as I look at the flowers and perfume in front of me. Willow's presents, they're here. Everything's good.

Now, I just have to get Dylan home, and–

"Fuck! Dylan!"

"Sir," a female voice calls just as I turn around to get back in the store.

She's holding Dylan by the hand, a panicked look on her face as I rush to them.

"Fuck, I'm sorry," I rush out, hugging him to me and not even caring how I am crushing half of the bouquet.

I almost forgot my kid in the fucking store.

"Mum says those words are bad," he chimes in, some sass in his voice.

"Fuck, you're right." The girl clears her throat, and I look at her as she widens her eyes in warning. "Shit–I mean…ugh!" Rubbing my face with the hand that's holding the perfume bag, I stop to take a breather. "I'm sorry, bud. I, uh…I thought you were right behind me."

The girl snickers and gives me a disapproving look, definitely judging me for forgetting Dylan inside. He just shrugs, unaffected, and adds, "Uncle Jake has done worse."

The worker gulps and speaks before I even have the chance to ask what the hell Jake did that's worse than leaving a kid behind, "Well, now he's back with his father, I'm going back to work. Have a nice evening, sir."

Crouching down to his height, I ask, "You good, bud?" My hands cradle his cheek for a moment to take a good look at his face. He nods with a smug smirk, and I sigh in relief, trying to expel the guilt that's biting at me from within.

How could I have forgotten about him?

He is relaxed–too relaxed–and the smile he draws out has me on edge, even if it makes him look cuter with those chubby cheeks filled out. "Don't worry," he tells me, unbothered. "I won't tell Mum if you don't."

With that, he holds my hand tight and starts walking, forcing me to follow him, slightly dazed.

I'm so fucked. Because being a responsible adult and a parent is harder than I was convincing myself it is. One thing I know for sure is I don't "got this". Not at all.

Not even close.

THIRTY-SEVEN

Willow

TODAY'S THE LAST DAY OF CLASSES. ALL EXAMS AND PROJECTS ARE officially over until early February, and it feels like a huge weight has been lifted off my shoulders. Now, I can focus on work, Dylan, and myself for a month and a half. *I need this.*

That argument with Liam two weeks ago was a turning point for me. I'd realised before that I needed therapy, but that night made me finally act on it. The following morning, I found a therapist close by, and scheduled an appointment.

I've been going twice a week ever since. Today, I have another session, the fourth one.

It's been way more helpful than I thought.

"Hello, Willow," my therapist, Dr Helen, greets as I open her office door.

"Hey," I breathe. "How are you?"

"Good. And you?" She cocks her head. "Please, sit down."

I do as she asks, sitting down on the bulky beige couch while she's in her big chair, right across from me. Dr Hellen is platinum-blonde with wild curls framing her high-cheeks. From the looks of it, she seems to be in her mid-thirties, her light green eyes make her seem younger, but the lines on the corners of her eyes are telling.

The hair and glasses give her that air-head, philosophy-teacher look, but her eyes are warm and homey. Like she could be someone's safety net...

"So, tell me what's new this week," she asks.

"School is officially over and Christmas is in a week or so," I tell her.

"That's wonderful. You'll have more free time on your hands. How's Dylan?"

"He's been great. Every day he comes home with something new he's learned in school." A smile finds its way onto my lips. "He's with Liam at the moment. He's been spending a lot of time with him lately. He's been taking him to football since he joined the team."

"That's good." She hums, scribbling something down on her notepad. And to my surprise, she changes the subject, asking, "And how do you feel about Christmas being around the corner?"

Here I thought she was going to ask about Liam *again.*

"Um, excited?" I shrug my shoulders with a small smile. "As Dylan gets older and understands things better, it becomes more and more fun."

It's true. Last year, he still believed in Santa Claus. Having him prepare the cookies and milk was so fun because he kept eyeing them like he was starving."

"And how does Liam fit into all of that?"

There it is.

My expression falls. "I have no idea."

And I really don't.

"Have you talked to him yet?"

It's safe to say she knows everything by now. And being able to talk to someone without having to watch what I say has been liberating, but Dr Helen has also been giving me exercises to do at home and has been teaching me better tools to use whenever I have panic attacks or when the past seems to take over my brain.

"No," I answer quickly. "I'm not ready for that yet."

"You should," she tells me. "While what he said was cruel and unwarranted, you have things you need to talk about."

"Can't I postpone it? Like after the holidays?"

"What if he wants to spend Christmas with Dylan and you?"

Oh. It had crossed my mind. I just hoped...it wouldn't be a possibility yet.

"We agreed during the last session that telling him the whole truth about Dylan's paternity should be done sooner rather than later. Right?"

"Yeah," I sigh. "But it's easier said than done."

"What's troubling you?"

"Everything," I admit. "What if he hates me when I tell him the rest? Worse, what if he doesn't believe me?"

"From what you've told me about him, I reckon he'll believe you."

"And then what? If he does believe me, it will destroy him. And on top of all of that, if he isn't the father...I—"

"You?" she presses.

I gulp, trying to swallow the knot forming in my throat. "I have hope again," I confess. "If he isn't the father, it'll break me all over again."

"Willow, if that were to happen, would it change anything?"

"Not for me. But for Liam—"

"If that changes something for him, then it's his loss. Not yours, not Dylan's." Her words make me look away.

She's right—to some extent. The real question is, will I be able to power through the pain of losing him again?

"Promise me you'll talk to him. Yes?"

"Yes," I give in.

"Alright." She slaps her thighs, bringing my attention back to her.

We talk for another forty minutes. There are some more questions about my parents—a side she is constantly trying to explore and that I keep shutting down—and some more about the different exercises I can do if I feel an oncoming panic attack.

We go over those quite a lot since mine tend to be strong.

Then, when it's just short of ten minutes to finish the session, she surprises me by asking, "How have you been sleeping? Do you still have nightmares?"

"On bad days," I confess. "Or when I'm too stressed."

It's never easy. Sometimes, I go weeks with regular sleep, and everything goes smoothly. Then sometimes, all it takes is a tiny trigger— a sudden touch, a familiar scent—to send me down the rabbit hole. Other times, it's just an exhausting day after an exam or a longer shift.

I never know what kind of night I'll have until I fall asleep.

For some people, it could be hell on earth. To me? It's just one more day.

The fact I can sleep a few nights out of a week is already a victory because there was a time when I didn't sleep until my body shut down from exhaustion.

"Have you tried anything I suggested for those?"

"I haven't had nightmares since after our first and second sessions. So, not yet."

"You can do them even if you don't have nightmares. Meditation, for example, is good for all kinds of anxiety. Or yoga."

"I'll try it now that I have more time. I have been reducing the TV screen and bright lights from eight o'clock until I go to bed."

"That's good. That helps a lot, too." I nod, agreeing. "You can also listen to some music if you feel anxious; it often helps you relax as well."

"Will do," I answer, noticing the clock striking five-thirty in the afternoon.

One hour has passed, and our time has finished.

"I'll see you next week," she concludes, standing up from her chair and shaking my hand. "Merry Christmas, Willow."

"Merry Christmas, Dr Hellen."

"Mummy, where have you been?" Dylan jumps into my arms as soon as I enter the house.

"Sorry, baby. There was a lot of traffic on the way here." I pout at him, feeling guilty for leaving him waiting.

"I kept him entertained," Liam pipes in from behind him, making me look at him.

Every time we lock gazes, the same thing happens: my heart feels like it's flying out of my chest and my hands get clammy with the nerves that overtake me. I'd hoped that after all of this time, I wouldn't feel this nervous in his presence, but I guess, given the circumstances, it's justified.

There was a sliver of hope that he wouldn't be here anymore. Ridiculous, since he has been waiting for me every single time in hopes of apologising and getting me to talk to him.

He's even bought me a bouquet of flowers and perfume another time he spent the afternoon with Dylan. It surprised me big time, and it was hard to keep my composure of indifference. Especially since he was so tired and still powered through the day. I almost gave in that day.

Nana has continuously been allowing him to come in and wait for me. I swear that woman is always up to no good.

"Thank you for picking him up from school," I mumble.

"Don't thank me," he groans. "We had a lot of fun, didn't we?"

Dylan nods eagerly, looking at me with begging eyes. *What now?*

"Are you hungry?" I ask him. He nods again, and I bristle, "Alright, let me cook dinner."

"Can Liam stay for dinner, Mum?" There it is. The real reason for his puppy eyes. They're still wide and shiny accompanied by his irresistible pout.

"Of course," I give in, huffing.

"Finally," he exclaims. "Why are you mad at him?"

"I'm not," I counter.

"You are," he whispers with a frown on his face. "You never talk to him. I thought he was your friend, too."

Jesus, can this kid let something go? I settle with, "Mom's just been busy."

"No," he tuts, shaking his head. Is this a six-year-old or a thirty-year-old? "You're angry."

"No, I'm not."

"You are. You do the same when I do something bad." His eyes turn down, looking at his hands. "Why?"

"Are you saying I ignore you when I'm angry at you?" I gasp, feigning offence.

I do when he's acting out. It normally just lasts a few minutes. Usually, it's enough to make him feel guilty and stop.

"You do," he exclaims. "I always have to whine to Nana for you to talk back to me."

"Kiddo, you're too smart for your own good," I say, placing him down on the seat by the counter.

It's only then that I remember Liam is right next to us, listening to the whole ordeal. As the red from my embarrassment tries to settle on my cheeks, I turn around to avoid letting him see it.

"Where's Nana?" I ask.

"I'm here," she calls out, coming in from the back door.

We start cooking dinner right away, and Liam stays silent most of the time, watching over Dylan. He's not usually quiet, but I guess that after two weeks of trying to get me to talk to him, he's finally given up.

Remorse gnaws at my chest at the thought. While he was ridiculous and cruel, I know it came from a place of pain. He didn't mean most of it—at least, I hope.

That argument feels so insignificant in comparison now. It's the thought of telling him everything that has been keeping me distant. I don't know how to do this, how to make it right without doing it the wrong way.

It's visibly taking a toll on both of us: there are bags under our eyes, and while I've been feeling exhausted, he seems deflated.

After an awkward dinner, we settle on the couch to watch a movie—Dylan's demand. There, he forces us to sit side by side, just so he can snuggle in the middle. His head digs into my chest a couple of times until he finds a comfortable position with his bum between both of us.

Nana says goodnight before going back to her bedroom, a smug smirk on her face. It's so annoying how easily she can read into everything. *Ugh.*

I fight a gasp when I feel something grazing my ribs. It's one of Liam's hands, being tightly held by Dylan's small ones, against his chest.

Oh my god. My heart somersaults inside while the guilt eats away at my brain cells. I feel like going crazy.

Dylan sighs in contentment, probably very comfortable and warm in the middle of us. So much so that not even ten minutes into the movie, he starts to softly snore.

A light nudge to my shoulder makes me look at Liam.

"Lo, can we talk?"

I nod. "Let me just take him to bed."

"I'll help."

Liam effortlessly picks Dylan up and climbs the stairs, with me following close behind. He no longer needs directions towards his room, walking with assured steps. There, he helps me put his PJs on before tucking him in.

"Thank you," I whisper when we're back downstairs again. "For helping out with him."

"No need to thank me. He's as much my responsibility as he is yours."

His words make me look away, and with that, he stops talking.

We don't know that yet. And this heavy feeling in my chest keeps telling me that something's about to blow up. I can't deny my biggest fear is that Dylan isn't his, especially since they've gotten so attached.

"Lo," he calls me, grabbing my chin with his index finger and thumb. "I regret what I said so much. I know you like the back of my hand. I should've known better. I truly am sorry."

He's sorry. *I know he is.* The looks he's been giving me for the past few weeks show it, and I want to forgive him so much. But something's holding me back.

Maybe it's the fear that if we get on good terms again, something will happen to take that away from us once more. Or it's the fear of his reaction when learning who else could be Dylan's father.

"I know," I breathe.

He rests his forehead on mine, and we both automatically close our eyes. There's warm and soft energy flowing between our skin, the comfort of having him close beating any other negative feeling away. "Then why don't you forgive me?"

"I–there's so much you don't know yet. And you need to know it all, but I–" A breath stops me for a moment. "Every time I get the courage to speak, it vanishes. I get physically ill just from thinking about it."

"I don't care," he counters, looking me in the eyes and holding my cheeks. "Whatever it is, it won't change the fact that I'm all in. You've told me the most important piece of information." *You won't think so when I tell you.* "And I know you'll tell me when you're ready. I'll respect your time."

"And what about the fact that Dylan might not–"

"No." He cuts me off. "I don't care about that. Even if he isn't biologically mine, I don't care at this point. He's mine," he breathes in, deeply and adds, "He's ours."

His eyes hold so much emotion. They're shiny and the brightest they've ever been, his sapphire blue locked on my plain brown ones.

Liam Davis is my weakness. No resolve can make me resist him and his charm.

"Are you sure?" I insist.

"I'm so damn sure." He steps forward, forcing me to stumble back. We stop only when my back hits the wall. "I've never been surer in my life. I can't sleep if we're not on good terms. I haven't been this sleep deprived since you left me. I can't go through it again." His breath feathers my skin, bringing back so many memories.

Memories that I hold dear in my heart, that I miss so damn much.

"Liam..."

"Let me," he asks, his nose bumping against mine. "Let me kiss you again." His voice cracks at the same time he presses me tighter to the wall.

"Liam...we shouldn't–"

"Please," he begs, cutting me off.

What the hell am I thinking?

I want this as much as he does. I want to give in.

He'll hate me once he knows the truth. And I know it's incredibly selfish of me to want to take advantage of this for as long as I can, but it's stronger than me.

The need for him to be right here, close to me. It's overwhelmingly irresistible. Irreplaceable.

With a sigh, I give in, nodding for him to do it, and he doesn't waste time crashing his mouth onto mine.

The kiss is not aggressive but it's desperate and emotional. It's what we've wanted ever since that talk in my bathroom and have been deprived of.

And like it used to be, the moment we get lost in each other, everything else ceases to exist. No more time. No more world. No more people. No more problems. It's just him and me like it used to be, all those years ago.

After all this time, the fire burning within should've been extinguished. It isn't. It was just dormant. And with every word, touch, and kiss that we share, it's slowly lighting up again, getting stronger and stronger.

It's making me fall in love with him all over again. But just like Frank Ocean said, "Feelings that come back are feelings that never left."

THIRTY-EIGHT

Willow

"HEY," LIAM WHISPERS WHEN I OPEN THE DOOR FOR HIM TO COME IN.

He leans on the door frame, looking at me so intensely that it feels like he's burning me alive from the inside out. That kiss kicked up the tension *a lot.* So much that I haven't been able to stop thinking about it, and from the looks of it, he hasn't either.

"*Liam*!" Dylan shrieks, cutting the moment off while pushing past me, before jumping into his arms.

He's no longer the "bad man who made Mummy cry". He's done a one-eighty, and my boy loves him, thoroughly.

"Hey, bud. How are you today?" He ruffles his hair with one hand, while the other is holding him close to his chest, half-hugging him.

"You almost missed us making the Christmas tree!" Dylan answers, excited.

"What?" Liam frowns, confused. "It's the eighteenth, how isn't it done yet?" Then he steals a heated glance at me and whispers, "Worse, how didn't I notice that yesterday?"

It makes me blush. My whole body heats up, especially in all of the places he touched last night. The curve of my bum, my lips...all of my front while it was trapped against his chiselled one. For the first time in years, I felt alive again. *Completely.*

I hadn't felt this...burning hot from desire—without panicking—for a long, long time.

Dormant feelings and emotions are back, hitting me full force and undoing years' worth of work.

"There's only one week left until Christmas," he tuts, looking around the half-decorated living room. "You're only decorating now?"

Looking at him, I can see the amusement on his face. A sly smirk and a cocked eyebrow are enough to give him away.

"Yes," I answer. "Nana refuses to do it earlier, saying it's a waste of money to have the Christmas lights skyrocketing the bill for a whole month."

"Damn right," she hollers from the top of the staircase before coming down. "I don't care if it was Mandela or Jesus that was born on the 25th of December, I won't pay more than I have to!"

We all laugh at her words, and I beckon Liam to come inside so I can close the door behind him. It's freezing outside.

"Well, thanks for including me." My stomach flutters violently upon seeing his charming smile.

With a deep breath, I try my best to keep my heart rate stable, only nodding in response.

"You do that damn tree," Nana orders, halfway through the hallway, walking towards the kitchen. "I'll make some hot chocolate and French toast!" Nana beams at us with an excited Dylan following her.

She loves every excuse to cook those at this time of the year. And like the gluttonous kids we are, we always shut up and let her do it because we love eating it.

"Are those the ones she used to cook us when we were kids?" Liam's eyes light up at the memory.

Back when she came over to my parents for the holidays, she'd cook us some after school. Those were easy and happy times with a happy and united family. Liam was around for some of those afternoons, eating away like a starved person.

"Yes." I giggle with the happy memories overflowing in my brain.

"God," he groans wistfully. "I missed that a lot."

"A lot, huh?" There's a tinge of taunting in my voice as I arch an eyebrow.

Liam's expression sobers when he looks at me, a smirk plastering itself on his face as he moves closer to me. He stops only when his body is barely an inch from mine. The heat that irradiates from his body warms mine, and the moment his lips graze my ear, I can't help but close my eyes in contentment.

"I didn't miss anything as much as I missed you," he whispers, his hot breath fanning my ear, making me shiver.

The slight tremble in the words coming out of his mouth is the only clue of how much he's effected by the moment. Just like I am. And my suspicions are confirmed when I open my eyes to look at him and see how heated his gaze is. The black pupils are blown wide to the point the bright blue shade of his irises is almost invisible.

"Liam..." I whisper in a plea for him to stop, but it comes out more as a moan because let's be real...I don't want him to stop.

Nana and Dylan are separated from us by a mere wall, yet we're both acting as if no one is here. I can't help it. That's exactly how he makes me feel—like nothing else exists or matters in the world.

"Yes?" he says with a nonchalant tilt of his head while his right hand finds its way to my cup my cheek.

"We-we're not alone," I stutter, looking around, afraid that Nana or Dylan will barge in at any moment now.

"Lo..." Liam brings my attention back to him. "I can't—" He takes a deep breath. "I can't take this anymore." *What?* What is he talking about? But before I can ask what he means, he resumes his speech, "Every time we're together, all I want to do is touch you, hold onto you, and never let go. Every time I go, I'm afraid you won't be here when I come back."

The pain in his voice tugs at my heart, knowing the extent of the damage caused by my actions and how much I hurt him.

"I won't leave," I whisper back, trying to reassure him. "You'll be the one who wants to leave at some point. I'm sure," I mumble, remembering the words still left unsaid.

But he shakes his head, "No. I could never, Lo. I love—"

"Okay," A loud, little boy barges in, cutting Liam off. "I want to do the tree now."

The intense tension that was surrounding us is immediately cut off. Liam's forehead falls onto my shoulder with a chuckle while Dylan wedges his body between the both of us, latching onto my leg.

Liam swoops him into his arms and carries him over to where the boxes are. I follow, and slowly, we start unpacking all the decorations and lights while Liam assembles the fake tree.

My boy is a goofball, and so is Liam. The both of them quickly get into this mood of picking and pranking each other. They continuously make me laugh with their antics, easily looking like two best friends who have known each other for a long time.

This...this is all I've ever wanted.

The dream I had of a happy family with my then-boyfriend. This is everything I planned on having until that horrendous night.

And it pains me to think that'll be ripped away from me, with this sour feeling lurking from the depths of my heart, telling me it's not meant to last.

"Mummy?" Dylan's voice brings me back to the present.

"Yes, baby?"

"How does the tree look?"

I assess their work. It's good–great even–but instead, I decide to tease them a little in hopes of pushing my thoughts to the back of my mind. I need to learn how to enjoy these moments.

"I don't know..." I trail off with my middle finger tapping on my chin, frowning as I walk around the tree. "I think you've missed a few here." I point to an area that is filled with decorations.

"I see what you're doing," Liam says with narrowed eyes.

"What is she doing?" Dylan asks, confused, before looking at me, horrified. "But, Mummy, there are decorations there!"

"You have to redo it, guys; it's not good enough," I taunt, and they both gasp, offended.

"That's it, buddy." Liam claps his hands, determination resonating in his voice. "She's mocking our perfect work. She's got to pay for this. May I?"

Dylan's eyes glimmer with mischief, nodding eagerly. I look at Liam, bemused until it dawns on me. He's rubbing his hands together while approaching me slowly, wicked eyes looking straight at me, and subconsciously, I start walking backwards just as he comes closer.

"Oh, no you won't," I warn, but he just smirks.

The nerve!

He launches his body forward to try and grab me. I squeal and barely dodge him, running away from both of them. Dylan and I giggle like crazy while Liam chases me around the living room.

He still hasn't caught me on purpose. I can see in his expression that he's doing this just to amuse us. It's working, though.

"You're supposed to help me catch her," Liam scolds my boy. "She offended our beautiful work; whose side are you on?"

That's enough to have Dylan run after me as well. They both reach me at the same time, Dylan latching onto my leg while Liam grabs my waist and drags the three of us to the couch.

Placing me gently there, he straddles my legs while Dylan climbs to the couch, settling on my side, and they lock a mischievous gaze. Their expressions are mirrored, and when they look back at me, it's like watching the same person.

"Ready?" he asks Dylan but still smirks at me. "Set!" They both raise their hands and lean closer to me. "Go!"

The tickles come before my brain can register them. I squirm underneath both of them, laughing non-stop, but Liam's weight prevents me from moving too much. They're everywhere, my waist, neck, and armpits.

Their laughter mixes with mine, and soon, that's all that can be heard throughout the house. The Christmas tree is long forgotten by now.

"Guys..." I pant in-between laughter. "I...can't...breathe!"

They stop but keep on laughing, probably mocking me, and I can't help but join in.

"You devils!"

My heart is racing, but not from anxiety or fear this time. It's complete happiness. Unrestrained joy.

Creating these happy memories is healing my soul faster than I could ever think possible. And being able to engrave into my brain the wide smiles on their faces, or the blooming bond that is weaving them together.

It's everything I've ever wished for.

"Kiddos," Nana calls from the kitchen door. "Food is ready."

"Oh, hot chocolate time." Liam beams.

He gets up—finally freeing me—before extending an arm to help me up. When I take it, he tugs me against his chest, and with my cheek pressed against it, his rapid heartbeat fills my ear.

Looking up, Liam smirks at the same time my cheeks blush furiously. Clearing my throat and stepping away, I grab Dylan's hand before walking to the kitchen.

There, I come face to face with a peculiar look on Nana's face. She looks amused but also like she's in on a secret no one else knows. Still, she doesn't mention anything, letting all of us settle down at the table to eat.

Dylan and Liam both serve right on the men's stereotype of munching down food like Neanderthals, barely stopping to breathe. It's not the most beautiful sight, but it's somewhat endearing.

"What?" Liam questions once he catches me looking at them intently.

"Nothing. I just love having you around."

It slips from my mouth before I can think about what I'm saying. But it's the honest smile and the twinkle in his eyes that make it worth it.

He's worth everything.

Sure, he can be hard-headed and hot-blooded, but those traits also add to the way he acts on love because he is so loyal and dedicated. He loves so fiercely and intensely.

He leans in closer, whispering, "I love being around. It feels like things have finally fallen into place."

I nod shyly, trying not to get Dylan's attention. It's already bad enough that Nana is awfully aware of everything.

"I want you guys to spend Christmas with me," he blurts, and I freeze, not expecting it.

Dylan abruptly stops eating, snapping his head towards us.

Oh god.

"I—"

"Please," he cuts me off, "I want you guys there with me."

"I can't leave Nana alone for Christmas."

"You can all come and spend it with me. Nana's your and Dylan's family thus, she's my family."

Dylan's silent but intently listening, his eyes frantically jumping between Liam, Nana, and me.

Ugh, this is not fair.

I look at Nana, asking for her input, and she says, "I was thinking of paying my daughter a haunting visit for the holidays, anyway." She smirks. "Why don't you spend it together this time around, just the three of you?"

"But–"

"No buts," he interrupts me again. "That's a deal, Nana."

I sigh in defeat. Like I can say no to this guy.

"Fine." I give in.

"*Yes!*" Dylan's tiny fist pumps the air as he yells in excitement. There's a wide smile on his face and a new gleam in his bright blue eyes. It's the happiest I've ever seen him.

Right next to him, Liam is sporting the same smile–just as wide.

What have I gotten myself into?

We eat the rest of the food, speaking about random subjects–Dylan's excitement monopolizing most of it. Nana keeps quiet for the majority of the remaining time, her eyes often swiping over the three of us. Automatically, I do the same in an attempt to engrave this moment into my brain.

"I'm done." Dylan jumps off his seat. "Let's go finish the tree." We all chuckle but finish up and follow him nonetheless. He rules the house, it seems.

When Liam reaches Dylan, both standing by the tree, he crouches down and puts him on his shoulders. I hold the star and hand it to my son, giving him the honour of putting the final touch on the tree.

After that, Dylan refuses to get off his shoulders, and the dummy is happy to oblige, carrying him around until he gets tired and slouches onto his head. I can't get enough of this day.

"Thank you for this," I tell Liam.

"No, *thank you,*" he counters. "I'm loving today." With that, he tries to look up at a sleepy Dylan.

"Let's get him to bed; it's been a hectic day, and he's tired."

He nods, following me up the stairs. Dylan doesn't even fight us on going to bed, that's how tired he is. If the sun hadn't set by now, I wouldn't even have felt that time had passed by today.

"Hey," Liam whispers when I close Dylan's bedroom door behind me. His arm wraps around my waist, bringing me closer to him. "Alone at last."

"It was a busy day," I whisper back.

"It was amazing." His hands grab my cheeks gently, and his thumbs caress the skin underneath my eyes.

It feels wonderful—so good I have to suppress a sigh. His touch has always ignited something in me, and this time is no different.

His mouth opens with his eyes locked on mine. He wants to say something, but I can see the internal war going on in his brain. What does he want to say?

But then he surprises me. "Fuck it! I can't wait anymore," he mumbles before crashing his mouth on mine.

His hands slide to the back of my neck while mine wrap around his shoulders. He keeps me in place while his lips mould to mine, reviving all of my nerve endings. The bliss takes over like a hurricane, warming up every crevice on my body.

This overwhelming wave happens every time, somehow still surprising me. Every new kiss feels like the first one.

"I need to be around you all the time," he mumbles in-between kisses. "Touch you." One kiss. "Kiss you." Another kiss. "It's torture to have to control myself at all times."

"Liam..." I trail off, pushing him away. "There's still so much to fix yet."

"I don't care. I'll wait." He nods his head, trying to reassure me. "I want to have everything—not just Dylan— you, too. The two of us together, with our son."

My chest constricts as the panic slithers into my body. "I—you don't know what you're saying, Liam."

"Let's try, please."

"What about Johanna?" I can't help but ask.

He frowns. "What about her? We're friends. Just that."

"Well, she wants more." He deadpans but I continue, ignoring him, "She does. I can see it in her eyes...the way she looks at you."

"How is it she looks at me?" He leans his head back with an arched eyebrow.

"I—"

How does she look at him? Like he's her whole world. Like she loves him. *Like I do.*

"The same way I do," I blurt without thinking.

"Hmm." He smirks, leaning his forehead on mine. "Does that mean you want more, too? Because that's all I want, all I can think about."

"Liam..." *I need to tell him.*

"We'll work through it. I know we will. I just need you to promise one thing to me."

"What?" I breathe.

"Don't leave," he whispers, his lips impossibly close. "Everything else I can handle. I can wait."

"But—"

"Promise me," he insists.

"I promise."

Upon hearing that word, he kisses me fervently. The same sensations from before flow into my body and cloud my judgement.

I won't leave him again; I know that. Going through life without him is an endless punishment that I won't bear to go through once more. But this time around, Liam will be the one to leave.

And when it happens, my heart will be ripped right out of my chest, and there won't be anything else left to salvage.

THIRTY-NINE

Willow

IT'S NERVE-WRACKING, REALLY.

Today is the 24th of December, which means Nana is long gone, and Liam is expecting Dylan and me to arrive at any moment. But what's eating away at me is the fact that a couple of days ago, he was adamant to take samples for a DNA test.

Stupid me gave in, of course. How could I refuse?

But I've been panicking ever since.

From waking up in the middle of the night because of horrifying nightmares to being startled by a door closing and having a random panic attack. I've been a bloody mess.

This means I have to tell him. And I have to do it before that damn letter with the results arrives. He's been so understanding, so loving, that it pains me. But for the life of me, how the hell do I tell him the truth?

Because of the holidays, when we went earlier in the week, they told us we would only receive the results by Tuesday the 26th. The torture.

"We're here," I mumble with my hands still attached to the wheel. Though, the car is already fully parked.

"We've been here for five minutes," Dylan counters, some sassiness in his voice. "I've been talking to you, and you don't answer."

"Sorry. What did you say?"

"Will I have presents in his house? Can Santa find me here?"

"You know Santa can find us anywhere," I answer. "Don't you want to go?" He nods eagerly, satisfied by knowing Santa is an all-knowing figure.

With that, I get out of the car and round it, opening the passenger door and unbuckling him. When his feet finally settle on the ground, he holds my free hand as I lock the car with the other before we walk together to Liam's building.

He lives in one of these fancy apartments in the higher part of the city with a beautiful view over the city centre as it lowers down towards the river. The entrance, elevators, and hallways are all squeaky clean in beige and white tones and marble floors.

"Wow," Dylan mutters, looking around. "The ten floor? Wow!"

I chuckle at the way he says the floor wrong as the elevator doors close in front of us, and starts going up. My insides bubble with nervousness. It doesn't matter how many times we're together and he reassures me this is to last, my body is on edge, my nerve endings stand to attention, and the anticipation eats away at me.

Will this feeling ever change? Ease down? Probably, I hope.

Instead of having to walk down the corridor to the apartment number he had told me it was, we're both surprised by a grinning Liam waiting for us in front of the metal doors.

"You scared me," I whine, clutching my chest.

"Sorry. After you rang the bell, I just couldn't wait for you to get up here." He beams. "Come on!"

His excitement is enough to lift my mood and ease some of my worries–for now. So, we follow him down the corridor to the front door of his apartment before he opens the door and beckons us inside. Dylan jumps right in, looking around him, while I take a few cautious steps inside.

The apartment is modern and slick. It still feels homey with a few things here and there, a few pillows, table centrepieces and a few portraits scattered around the place.

"Wow, this is so cool!" Dylan shouts. "So much better than our house."

"What are you on about?" Liam asks, tilting his head. "Your house is better, even homier and just a tiny bit more crowded. It's just what a home should feel like." He steals a heated glance at me. "I love it there, that's why besides working and sleeping, I've been around more often than not."

"Thanks, Liam," I say, blushing. "But, Mister Wow, here, is amazed because this house looks way more expensive than ours." I glare at him.

But Dylan, the shameless kid he is, just ignores me and keeps inspecting the place.

"I do love your house way more than I like it here," Liam whispers to me the moment Dylan disappears into the kitchen area. "Give me your bags; let's put them in the bedrooms."

When I nod, he yells to Dylan, "Don't touch anything without one of us by your side."

To which my kid yells back an "okay." *What even?*

The blond man in front of me takes the overnight bags I brought and walks in the opposite direction of the hallway. I follow, taking in the house. When we reach the first door, he opens the door and stays by the entrance, looking at me with a shy expression.

If there is one thing that Liam isn't, it's shy. So, I curiously peek in, looking around the room, and I swear my heart jumps right into my throat.

The bed frame, covered with some dark and light blue sheets, a striking contrast to the white walls. On the opposite end, there's a chest of drawers with a few stuffed animals on top, and right next to it, there are some shelves with children's books.

I'm speechless. There's no way this has always been like this. He must've changed it after learning about Dylan's existence.

My eyes burn with unshed tears at the thoughtfulness of this man.

"This used to be my office," he chimes in, his voice wavering. "Well sort of, but recently, I decided to change it a little in the hope Dylan could spend the night sometimes." He looks at me sheepishly. "This is where he'll be sleeping."

On impulse, I hug him tight, thanking him for this. There are no possible words that could express how grateful I am.

"This space is because I want to spend time with the both of you." His breath fans over my hair. "You have no idea how much I wanted this to be my first Christmas with my family."

His family. *We're his family.*

I swear my legs buckle from his words alone. This man knows how to rock my world in every possible way.

Oh god, I can't even deny it any longer. My feelings for him.

"What's wrong? Was it because I called–"

"No." My voice comes out weak. "I just wasn't expecting it. I'm-"

Suddenly, I can't speak because Liam cuts me off with his lips. They're soft and tentative at first, but as soon as I sigh and melt into his embrace, it grows in intensity.

Tongues meet in a delicate dance, and I can't fight the moan that escapes my lips. That's enough for a grunt to leave Liam's throat and for his hands to move from my face to grip the curve of my waist, bringing me impossibly close to him.

Automatically, my arms snake around his neck, my fingers digging into his dark blond locks. His hair is as soft as I remember.

There are so many racing thoughts going through my brain, but I can't honestly focus on a specific one. Everything comes running back to one person. Him and everything related. We fit together in all the right places, making me feel like this is meant to be.

Like we're meant to be.

As we both come up for air, Liam doesn't hesitate to rest his forehead on mine. Our breaths mix as our eyes flutter open. I notice how his pupils are blown out of proportion, and the thought makes a warm fuzzy feeling grow at the bottom of my tummy–the kind I hadn't felt in years, not since our last time together.

"I can't get enough of you," he whispers.

But then, a sudden thought crosses my mind, making me pale. Distancing myself from him quite abruptly but still holding his shoulders, I blurt, "Where will I be sleeping?"

"In my room," he answers, smiling.

Then he grabs my hand and tugs me to follow him to the next door. It's the master bedroom with a walk-in closet and a private bathroom. Just like the rest, it's modern with light colours, mainly white and different shades of grey.

"Oh, no. I don't want you sleeping on the couch or anything," I comment, and he laughs.

He comes forward until our bodies meet, but he doesn't stop there, forcing the both of us to walk this time—him forward and me backwards.

"There's no way you'll sleep on my small and uncomfortable couch!" The offended tone in his voice is loud and clear.

"Well, I don't want you sleeping there either," I counter.

"I'm sure there's a very obvious solution," he taunts in a whisper before bumping his nose against mine.

"Yeah? What is it?"

"There's a big, comfortable, king-sized bed right next to us, which we could both sleep comfortably in."

Looking to my right-hand side, I take in the huge bed. When the realisation dawns on me about what he's suggesting, I gasp and swat his chest.

"What are you insinuating, Liam Davis?"

"Well, it's just sleeping, we don't—" He stops himself. "I mean–I wasn't–I don't–" He rubs his hand across his face before giving me a guilty look. "I just want to be close to you. Hold you, that's it. But I–I can sleep on the couch."

Having him this embarrassed, for once in his life, makes me chuckle and cup his cheeks.

"It's fine," I say, caressing his cheek. "Let's do whatever feels right at that moment," I whisper.

My statement makes him look at me with hope twinkling in his eyes. "Right." He nods. "I can work with that," he says, inching closer and closer. I close my eyes, expecting a kiss.

One that never comes because of a little tornado called Dylan bursts into the bedroom.

"I want to watch The Grinch," he screeches.

I sigh in frustration, letting my head fall onto Liam's chest while he laughs.

"Let's go then, buddy." Liam swoops Dylan into his arms and pulls me with them towards the living room.

Liam sets up the movie for us, and we watch two Grinch movies before I notice it's close to dinner. I ask him just to give me a short orientation tour around the kitchen so I can cook dinner, but he refuses right away, getting up from the couch himself and cooking dinner for all three of us while I watch the rest of the movie with Dylan.

He's snuggling with me by the time Liam calls us to the table. He flashes me a proud smile as soon as we sit down, serving us a traditional Christmas dish here in Portugal—boiled cod. It looks and smells so good, I'm amazed.

He used to be a mess in the kitchen, but I guess living on his own has taught him quite a few tricks. The boy I fell in love with, all of those years ago, has become a man.

I shouldn't be surprised, but I still am.

"Mummy, not fish!" Dylan whines, pleading with his eyes.

"Oh, man," Liam mumbles. "You told me fish was fine!" Panic lacing his voice.

"And it is," I reassure him. "Don't be easily manipulated by a six-year-old!" Then I turn to Dylan. "Well, if you want Santa to come and leave your presents while you sleep so you can open them tomorrow morning, you have to eat your fish *and* vegetables." I narrow my eyes at him.

He scrunches his face and grumbles something I can't decipher but nods anyway, waiting for Liam to serve him and for me to take the bones out of the fish for him. He eats in silence with an ever-present scowl, and we just laugh at his attitude.

I can't even get mad at him.

"I'm done," he mumbles with a full mouth and a clean plate.

I don't understand what the hell kids have against vegetables and fish. I love it, personally.

When we're all done, Liam tells me to get Dylan ready for bed while he puts the dishes in the dishwasher, letting me know he'll meet us shortly. So, in the extra bedroom Liam owns in this beautiful apartment, I get Dylan into his PJs, then force him to brush his teeth, and once he is finally ready, I settle on the bed next to him, getting ready to read him a Christmas story. That's exactly when Liam slips into the room.

He sits down next to Dylan, on the opposite side of the single bed, and I start reading with our little boy right in-between us.

Once I finish the story, Dylan looks at me with big puppy eyes and asks, "Mum, tell me my favourite story."

I blush fervently and glance at Liam before looking back at Dylan.

"Not tonight, baby; it's getting late."

"Please," he begs. "Liam doesn't know it yet, and I love when you tell me about how these two best friends meet. It reminds me of me and Abby." His half-smile is enough to melt my heart. Of course, I give in.

I start narrating the story to him—well, them. The story of this young girl that, around Dylan's age, used to go to the park every day with her mother and older brother.

"They used to play together, but as time went by and her brother started to make more friends, she slowly got left to entertain herself. It'd make her both happy and sad. Happy because it meant her brother had friends and sad because she still had none."

"Until..." he presses, and I laugh a little.

"Until this bright blue-eyed boy approached her with a small flower in his hand and gave it to her. She stopped the tears that were silently falling down her cheeks and took it without uttering a word to him. She was shy, you know, so she didn't know what to say. But he did...he told her—"

"You're too pretty to cry," Liam interrupts me, completing what I was going to say.

"Exactly." I gulp, looking sheepishly at his intense eyes.

Have I been subconsciously telling stories about Liam and me? *Totally*. Have I been doing it consciously, too? *Probably*.

When Dylan started asking me for happy stories, all I had were our memories. So, I used them.

"And then," I continue. "The young boy sat down by her side and kept her company for the rest of the afternoon, making her laugh all the time, doing her bidding and mostly just keeping her happy. He kept her happy just by being close, and they became the best of friends." Dylan sighs in contentment, eyes fluttering while snuggling between us.

"Now, time for bed, baby," I mutter.

He squirms under the sheets until he finds a comfortable position, and I kiss his forehead. "Good night, baby. Merry Christmas. I love you," I whisper.

"Goodnight, Mummy. I love you, too," he whispers back.

I stand up and wait for Liam to say good night, too. He probably remembers that afternoon that we met when we were just shy of six years old. Especially since he remembers exactly what he told me back then.

"Goodnight, buddy." Liam gently pats his hair before leaning down to kiss his forehead. "Merry Christmas."

"Merry Christmas," he mutters, his eyes already closing. "Goodnight, Daddy."

I freeze as the axis in my world shifts while looking at my unbothered kid, uttering those words as if it was just his normal routine. He just called Liam "Daddy" as if it wasn't the first time those words came out of his mouth.

FORTY

Willow

DYLAN'S SOFT SNORES START TO GROW IN STRENGTH AND DEPTH, letting us know he's falling asleep fast—and deep—but we're both rooted in place, looking at the six-year-old as if he's an alien.

Barely moving, in his spot right next to me, Liam's head twists and so does mine as we look at each other with wide eyes. This is surreal.

I know kids are more intelligent than we give them credit for, and they're often underestimated, but this is mind-blowing. How much my kid has been aware of what has been happening around him has me flabbergasted. And the way he said it with so much ease and confidence. He is sure of his words—of his feelings. And while I should be happy, it makes me dread that result now more than ever. I could be breaking two hearts instead of one with that DNA test, and the fact that I can break my son's heart feels like a stab to mine, too.

"He…" Liam trails off, a sparkle in his blue depths. The heaviness of his emotion shining through them pierces me.

Opening the bedroom door, I usher him outside before we wake Dylan. As soon as the door clicks shut, Liam harshly grabs my cheeks with both hands, his face close to mine. Unshed tears swim in his eyes as the biggest and broadest smile covers his face.

Yet, we're walking opposites. While I still have a slice of apprehension preventing me from fully enjoying this moment, the man in front of me oozes happiness and pride from every pore in his skin.

"He called me Dad," he whispers, and I gently nod. "He–" he stops himself, deep in thought. "Oh god, I'm speechless."

"I am, too," I comment quietly. "I never thought he would suspect this. I was planning a conversation with him after the results, but I never expected this. He is just too clever for his own good."

"Thank you," Liam whispers, pecking my lips.

"What for?" I lean my head back, to have a better look at his face.

"For this." His thumb grazes my cheek, wiping a tear I didn't even know was falling. "For giving me Dylan, for giving me a family."

My heart skips a beat.

"I'm so scared," I confess. "I'm terrified you'll hate me if–"

"Lo," Liam stops me. "We've talked about this. I could never."

"But–"

"I'll wait. Your time, your rules, yeah? It doesn't matter the outcome."

"I'm so sorry."

"Don't be." He kisses my forehead, hugging me tight. "We've overcome so much, and, in the end, everything worked out. You and Dylan are in my life; that's all that matters."

"But I kept him from you...I was young, alone, scared, and so hurt, but it still was wrong. I shouldn't have–" I hesitate, looking down at my feet, but he tilts my head up, forcing me to look at him.

"I understand," he mutters, resting his forehead on mine. "It's all in the past now."

"Liam," I call for him, my voice wavering the moment his hand grips my hip.

"I love you," we both say at the same time.

The sound of his grave voice uttering the exact same words in-sync is enough to send a shiver down my spine. It must have done the same to him because as soon as I look into his eyes, the dark shade seizing his irises makes me take a staggering step back.

With his eyes doing all the talking and a serious expression, he takes one step forward. Then another and another.

He doesn't stop until my back is plastered against the wall and his chest is pressed against mine, trapping me in. With his body touching mine everywhere, it burns from the inside out. My stomach twists and coils with every second that passes, the tension between us thickening. It's unexpected and pleasurable—something I had forgotten all about.

It's bringing my body back to life. *He's* bringing my body back to life.

"Liam," I moan as his fingers caress the skin on my collarbone.

"Do you want me to stop?" he asks, now reaching my jaw before gripping it gently.

"No." I almost choke on the word.

I close my eyes and bask in the feeling of his touch. It's tentative, delicate and feels foreign and familiar at the same time.

"If you say stop, I'll stop right there and then. It doesn't matter how far gone we are."

"I know," I whisper.

And I do. His hand stopped moving when he asked me this, showing me that even though he is the one instigating, I'm in control of the situation.

"I missed you." His whisper echoes in my ear. "I missed you so damn much."

His voice is shaky and raspy, travelling straight down into the bottom of my belly. For the first time in years, urgency hits me, and I clench my thighs together in a failed attempt to ease some of the pressure there. But his naughty hand lowers down from my hip to my butt, groping me.

God, this is intense.

I haven't felt this way since...

"Liam, I haven't—"

"Shh," he cuts me off. "Don't worry. Just know that I would never hurt you. You know that, right?" I nod with closed eyes. If I look at him right now, I might just break down.

"Come here," he mutters, lowering his hands to the back of my thighs and pulling me up into his hold. It forces me to wrap my legs around his waist and the moment my core presses against his erection, I gasp as my body sizzles with internal fireworks and blinding lights.

"I know," he groans onto my neck. "I feel it, too."

He starts walking, carrying me to his bedroom while kissing me. I only realise we've arrived when he starts lowering me to his bed, letting his own body fall on top of mine. Still, he is cautious enough to balance his body weight on his elbows, careful not to crush me.

"Are you sure?" he asks, his eyes peeking up at me through his thick lashes.

"Yes," I answer, bringing his hands down to the hem of my blouse. "Please, don't stop."

I'm drunk on his touch, way too submerged in this sea of pleasure and unable to let go of it. For years, I had come to terms with the fact that I'd never feel anything like this again. No one could ever make me feel like this, and the hope that we'd meet again had left my body and soul long ago.

And yet here I am. *Lost in him.*

"I love you," he repeats while taking my shirt off.

Right when I am about to tell him the same words back, his lips press to my chest—right over my heart—stopping me. He keeps going, lowering to my belly, and my self-awareness awakens.

Stretch marks. My hands grab him in a frail attempt to stop it, but he swats my hands away. "No," he grumbles. "Don't you dare do that. Not with me." One kiss over my stomach. A second right next to my belly button, and it follows with light kisses peppered right over my lower belly, where most of the proof of my pregnancy lies. "You're not to cover yourself from me. Not ever. You're beautiful."

His hands lower to my jeans, a mischievous grin on his face as he slowly unbuttons them. The way his fingers slowly and gently graze my skin is intoxicating.

"Oh my," I moan as my fingers slip through his hair.

Then, he grabs the waistline and pulls it down, slowly and unbelievably seductively undressing me. In an instant, I'm on his bed, lying in just my underwear, completely exposed. Instead of feeling uncomfortable, I feel loved. Cherished.

Liam has never made me feel uncomfortable—and there's no other way I can feel when he looks at me like he's looking at the tastiest food on earth. Like I'm his whole world.

As he is mine.

To even us out, he starts undressing by taking his shirt off first. My eyes devour his body, watching as his muscles tense and relax with every movement. The slacks follow, leaving him only in his boxer briefs.

Lowering back down on top of me, he kisses my forehead, each eye, my nose and lastly my mouth, where he licks my bottom lip, as a way to ask for entrance.

In no time, we're both panting messes as our tongues dance together. The intensity grows to the point that his hand lowers to my core, massaging my clit, and I start tugging at his boxers.

"Ahh, fuck," he groans before taking off his boxers and pulling my panties down while I take off my bra.

The moment he presses against me again, I gasp into his mouth, the feeling of skin on skin overwhelming me even more. We're completely glued together and fully naked, a mess of tangled limbs, grazing skin, and frenzied grinding.

Taking me by surprise, Liam rolls us over, so I'm straddling him. With one forearm pressed against my bum, he drags his body back against the headboard of the bed.

"I want you to be in control," he mutters while leaning onto his side to open the bedside drawer.

When he straightens back up, there's a condom in his hand. He looks me in the eye while tearing the foil open, attentively gauging my reaction. Is he afraid I'll get scared and bolt? Or that I'll start to panic?

Maybe I should, but at this moment, as I stare back into his eyes, I'm serene and sure about this decision. The respect, understanding, and trust he's shown me, which he has also cultivated in me, is a huge part of this. It wouldn't feel right with anyone else.

"You can choose if, when, and how. I want you to be sure–" I shut him up by kissing him harshly while grabbing his dick, slowly stroking it up and down.

After an initial hiss upon my sudden touch, he chuckles, kissing me back. After a few moments, he stops my hand to put the rubber on. Then he gropes my ass, bringing me closer to him again, manoeuvring my hips to grind on him.

I moan at the feeling, snaking my arms around his neck as he buries his head in my neck.

"You feel so good already," he groans. "I don't know how the hell I managed this long without you." I lift my hips a little, aligning with his shaft. "I can't live without you."

As those words find a home in my heart, making it flutter, I start lowering myself slowly. It's agonising and divine at the same time. The both of us moan loudly as he enters me.

Finally, the intrusion is welcomed. Warmth spreads through my veins as we tightly hold onto each other.

My heart is bursting with love and happiness. I feel full, not only physically but also emotionally. Never before have I felt this connected to someone, in every way possible.

"Oh, Liam." I still my movements for a few seconds, allowing both of our bodies to get reacquainted with each other.

"I know, baby. I know." His hold on me squeezes for a moment, and it's then that I understand...This intensity, these overflowing feelings will never lessen.

This is it for me. I start to move again, keeping a slow pace. Up and down. With my hands on his shoulders, I open my eyes to look at him. Our eyes meet, and the amount of electricity and emotion coursing through both of us is too much.

With one hand on my hip and the other at the base of my neck, we focus on each other, taking and giving whatever we can to prolong this moment. We're being loud—I know we are, but right here and now, nothing else matters.

"I...love...you," he mumbles between his shallow breaths.

I say it back, leaving no space for questions or doubts. Though, it becomes hard to stay anything else as the crippling emotions take over. My brain shuts down, allowing the organ in the middle of my chest to take over the wheel.

I let go, fully giving in to my love and desire for him as my pace quickens and so do our sounds. They become frantic, messy, and stunted.

"Lo, I won't be able to hold–" I cut him off with a kiss. *I know* because I'm not lasting either.

The exact moment our tongues touch and his hand squeezes my bum, shivers run up my spine, spreading this strong tingling sensation through my body. My gut squeezes as does my core, forcing an orgasmic moan out of me.

Liam's body trembles underneath mine, followed by a loud growl that he tries to muffle by burying his head in my neck. He thrusts up harshly a few times before finally stilling underneath me, his body slowly relaxing.

Losing all of the strength in my body, I let my full weight fall onto him, and he squeezes me against him, sliding us down and covering us with the sheets.

We stay quiet, lying down in his bed, holding each other. The only sounds filling the bedroom are our harsh breaths, still recovering from the exertion of the act, and the light ticking of a watch close by.

As I slowly come back down from the high, thoughts start to invade my brain. It's been even better than I remembered, and it's robbed me of words. Completely.

"God, was it ever like this before? I don't remember it being this intense." He sighs against my hair while his fingers keep running up and down my back.

"I agree," I mutter. "It's different now. So much better. I–" I clear my throat before continuing, "I never thought I could do this again in my entire life and enjoy it. I–"

Liam's thumb and index grip my chin, cutting me off. He tilts it up, gently beckoning me to look up at him.

"I am honoured you chose me," he whispers, pecking my lips.

"There's no one else in this universe I could do any of this with. I've realised that now."

He grins, kissing me again.

After a few minutes, he begrudgingly stands up to dispose of the condom, coming back to bed immediately after and diving under the sheets. He tangles his body with mine, cuddling me.

We talk for hours, catching up with everything that has happened through the years we've been apart. I tell him about Dylan; all of the funny stories and all of his firsts, promising to show all of the pictures and videos I've taken so far. He confesses how diving into school after I left was his saving grace, allowing him to graduate one year early. The guilt tries to eat away at me at his confession, but he quickly snaps me out of it with kisses and tickles.

We talk until my eyes feel heavy and start to close on their own accord. The Sandman finally sprinkles some of his magic dust, lulling me into dreamland after one entire week of nightmares. And while Liam's body warmth keeps me safe, right before sleep takes over, I still faintly hear the words he mutters in my ear, "I love you, Willow. I never stopped."

FORTY-ONE

Liam

MY EYES FLUTTER AS I SLIP BACK INTO CONSCIOUSNESS.

For the first time in years, there is a lightness inside, just like a balloon filled with helium that floats carelessly through the sky. That's the effect Willow has on me. She will always influence my mood.

I love her. And the fact that we fucking said it at the same, just like the first time we confessed our true feelings for each other, is just too much of a coincidence for my heart.

Last night was the best night of my life.

I stretch my left arm to wrap it around her waist and snuggle, but my eyes snap open at the realisation that the spot next to me is empty.

"Lo?" *Did she leave?*

Looking around my bedroom, wondering if her things are still scattered around my bedroom or picked up. I notice her overnight bag by the door and her jeans neatly folded on the black imperial concubine, close to my walk-in closet.

She's still here.

My conclusions are confirmed when I hear some mischievous giggling outside. The sound is ethereal, waking my foggy brain right away and making it way easier to get out of bed. First, I put some boxers on—Dylan's awake, too.

I probably need a shower, but to be honest, I don't want to wash away what happened last night. It's ridiculous, but there's a part of me that is insanely holding on to it, afraid she'll slip through my fingers *again.*

Once my feet step into the bathroom, the doorbell rings, and I freeze. *Who the fuck is it?*

They wouldn't appear uninvited, right?

I only snap out of my inner thoughts when I hear rushed footsteps and a frantic Willow calling after him to not open the door, but it's too late.

The clicking of the lock sounds, and Dylan greets whoever it is cheerfully, "Hello, who are you?"

Shit!

I hurriedly knot my shorts' strings that were hanging on the back of the door and run outside. When I reach them, I stop in my tracks.

It's deadly silent with my parents gaping at a dishevelled Willow in just a baggy T-shirt of mine and a curious Dylan, tilting his head at them. My heart thrashes inside, echoing through my ears.

"Well, well," my father tuts. "This is quite a surprise."

Willow gasps, hastily grabbing Dylan's arm.

"What?" another male voice hear speaks, but I ignore it, focusing on Willow's abnormal stance.

With her breath hitching, she stumbles back until a soft thud sounds from her back hitting the wall.

What's happening?

I step between her and my family, not even sparing them a glance and ask, "Lo, what's wrong?"

"Mummy, breathe."

My hands hover over her, but I stop myself as her breaths turn shallow, one hand pressing Dylan hard against her and the other clutching her throat so tight I doubt she can even breathe.

"Ahh, fuck!" someone curses, but I'm so focused on the woman panicking in front of me that I tune it out.

"No, no. Please, no," she chants over and over again with tears in her eyes, looking straight through me into the dark void that's taking over her brain.

"Baby?" I turn to her, reaching for her shoulders.

She recoils, and I retract my hand right away.

"Willow? Baby?" I call.

Finally, her eyes snap back to mine, just now awakening from the daze she was in. Then, mumbling something incomprehensible, she rushes to the bathroom, pulling Dylan behind with her.

I'm about to follow them when my father calls me. The door clicks shut behind her and the lock turns, letting me know I just missed my chance.

Fuck.

Turning around, I see my parents with the other person who had abandoned me—Mason. I guess this is a year for reunions, not that I wanted to see them today. But fuck, a whirlwind of mixed emotions hits me upon seeing him after all of these years.

He looks slightly better than the last time I seen him. Though from the aftermath of doing drugs non-stop for so long, he looks way older than just twenty-five. Still, he's put on some weight and has some more colour on his skin. What concerns me are the looks in all three sets of eyes, all focused on me. Mason and our mother's are wide-eyed and seemingly surprised. While my father's is the same as usual…angry.

"Weren't you supposed to come for New Year only?" I can't help the snark lacing my words.

"We wanted to surprise you," my father claims.

"Except we're the surprised ones," my mother comments, a hint of disbelief in her voice. Then she corrects her stance, straightening her spine while her face morphs into a distant, cold expression. "What is this?"

"This is my house," I bark out the words. I am my father's son, after all. "And you're not supposed to be here today," I comment, trying to snap out of my light daze. "You were supposed to come for New Year."

"What's this, Liam?" my father asks, completely disregarding my comment about them being here early.

He glares over my shoulder in the direction Willow just fled towards, letting me know to whom he is directing his anger. Just the realisation of it, of someone targeting Willow, makes my blood boil.

I am about to answer back when he beats me to it, "Excuse us!"

The man who raised me under the unattainably high expectations he created pushes past my body, entering the living room and making himself at home. My mother mimics him, walking inside with a poker face, and my brother hurries after them, not even looking me in the eye. Good, if he starts to act like them now, I might not answer rationally.

"I called you," my father informs me, a tightness in his voice, giving away more than he wants to. In response, I can't help but huff.

"What now?" I ask, clearly irritated. "As you can see, I was busy!"

"Oh, we understand now. It's loud and clear." The bite in his voice is strong, only feeding my annoyance.

"Wasn't it clear we were supposed to spend the 31st and the 1st of January together instead?" I ask. "Since when is it acceptable to appear unannounced in someone else's home? To cause all of this ruckus, on top of it all!"

"What part of 'surprise' have you not understood, boy?"

"John," my mother chimes in hesitantly. "How about we all sit down and talk? Surely, Liam has an explanation."

There is zero will or patience in me to deal with them and their prejudice. Sure, my parents provided me with a lifestyle just a few can brag about, but when it came to everything else, it was very lacking. The love, support, and *understanding*—especially the latter.

We never came first to them. They surely don't come first to me.

In my brain, I'm checking in on her; it's an automatic response.

Yes, I'm choosing her.

In reality, I shouldn't need to choose one or the other. But if it comes down to it, there's one thing I am sure of…I'm not letting her go again. Not after everything.

Without bothering to answer his wife, John Davis glares at me, wanting me to back down and bend to his will. Except, I'm not the same kid who left for college. I've been living on my own ever since I started college, free from their control.

I'm not handing it back to them now—not anymore. That's why I ignore them as I walk down the corridor to the door she disappeared into.

"Lo?" I call, knocking on the bathroom door. "Baby, what's wrong? Let me in."

The wood blocks my view but doesn't smother the sounds coming from inside. Short and uncontrolled breaths fill the room, alongside Dylan's soft whispers. It doesn't matter that I keep calling her—she doesn't answer.

How can I break her out of it?

"Dy, buddy?"

"Yes," his answer is delayed and hesitant.

"Is Mummy having a hard time breathing?"

"Y-yes," he stammers in a shaky voice.

Bloody hell. She must be having a panic attack again.

"Don't cry, buddy," I tell him. "Let's try and help her, yeah? Can you do as I say?"

"She won't speak," he warns me. "She never does when this happens."

So, this happens often. Of course, she has trauma. Panic attacks are common. Why the fuck didn't I make the connection?

Flashbacks from his birthday and her teacher helping her out flood my mind. She was a mess and couldn't even speak; she's probably the same now.

"Can you unlock the door?" I try.

"She's holding the key too hard," he mumbles, seemingly struggling with something.

"Got it," he says.

His footsteps are faint and not even a full minute later, he opens the door for me. Slipping inside, I lock it again—just in case someone tries to snoop in. This time around, I keep some distance as I crouch in front of her.

"Baby," I call her. "You need to take slow and deep breaths."

All the while, he snuggles against her side, and she holds him back just as tight.

Oh, good. She lets him touch her.

"Buddy?" The clever boy I hope is my son looks at me through shiny eyes. He is so worried it hurts. "Touch Mummy's cheeks and tell her to look at you." He does and surprisingly, she locks eyes with him.

My heart soars at the small victory. Their bond is so strong, and I can't even feel jealous. I am just proud. She is giving him the kind of love I never got, even through the hard times she has had to face.

"Tell her to breathe with you," I instruct.

He does as I say, but she fails to do it, her breath still hitching as fat tears stroll down her face. He looks at me, hopeless and in want of direction.

"Ask her to look at you again and name the colours she sees." When he hesitates, I insist, "Go on, buddy."

"Blu–" She hiccups, and he coos her to go on. "B-brown." Another hiccup and one less sob. *Another win.* "White." A deep breath in and a long exhale. Yes.

"One more, Mummy," he encourages her.

"Grey," she mumbles, looking at Dylan's small-sized sweatpants. "T-thanks."

The hoarseness in her voice sounds like she's been shouting and singing at a concert non-stop. Panic attacks exert people's bodies in a way many don't realise. And watching the only woman I have ever loved having one first-hand for the second time in two months awakes a part of me I never knew existed.

It's primal—monstrous, even. It creates a rage inside like never before. All I want is to go back to Lisbon, the city we used to live in, and find the piece of shit who hurt her this bad. Or fucking travel in time, back to that night, so I can right all of my wrongs. To get home earlier—fuck, not even leave in the first place. Just so I could be there and fucking walk her home!

I want to keep her under my arm and never let go again, making sure she is one hundred percent safe.

"Baby," I call, but she looks away from me. Ouch. "What's wrong?"

When I try to touch her, she still flinches, and fuck, it hurts. It hurts that I'm not a safe haven for her like Dylan is.

"Lo?"

"I never wanted this to happen," she cries, sobbing again. "I swear!"

"Whatever it is, baby, we'll—"

"No!" I startle at the loud boom of her voice. "You don't understand," she wails. "I can't—you'll hate me!"

"You know I won't."

"Please, you need to know I would never do anything to hurt you." I nod, agreeing. *I know that now.* "Not willingly," she emphasises.

"Let's do something," I intervene, not wanting her to dwell on something she shouldn't and instigate another panic attack. "You and Dylan get dressed and give me an hour. I'll meet you at your house, and we'll spend the rest of Christmas together. You'll tell me on your own time and terms. Yeah?"

"Yes, please," Dylan chimes up. "Let's go, Mummy."

She's sceptical, and even though I can't understand why, I need her to believe me. I'll be there.

"Trust me," I beg. "I love you, that won't change."

With a weak nod, she unlocks the door and flees to my bedroom, where their bags are. As soon as my bedroom door clicks shut, I grip the bathroom sink, taking a deep breath. Fuck, not even assisting Dr Shawn during long surgeries is as draining.

It hurts, though, how easy it is for someone to snap their fingers and burn her world down. It's even worse to not be able to help—at all.

I'm useless. How can one simple second be enough to burst the bubble of happiness we've finally reached? *Fucking hell.*

Once I am finally calm and collected, I walk back to the living room, to face my obnoxious parents and send them on their way. If they don't leave, I will.

Thankfully, there's a corner preventing them from seeing the front door directly, which means she might be able to leave undetected once she's ready.

The only person sitting on my couch is my brother. His body twitches once in a while, his hands constantly shaking as his eyes barely focus on something specific. Is he still in withdrawal? He shouldn't if what my mother said on our phone call was true.

My parents pop up from the kitchen, my father seething, "How could you?"

"How could I what?" I counter, not even bothering to hide the edge in my voice.

I do not have the patience for this.

My parents look like they're about to blow up with how red their faces are, and my poor brother looks more stressed with each passing second. I bet he's craving some white powder to sniff—especially with those two hounding his every move again.

"After everything we've done for you–" my father booms.

"And after what that despicable girl did," my mother shrieks. "How could you forgive her?"

"It isn't your business, is it?" I can't help but snide. "We talked and solved everything. You don't know what happened, and I—"

"We don't?" My father cuts me off, that signature sarcasm of his. "Are you sure?"

A heaviness falls upon my chest. What?

"What the hell are you on about?" I ask, exasperated. "Look, I'm not interested in the twisted games you like to play. That girl back there went through hell and back for that kid. And yes, maybe she didn't make the best decisions, but she did the best she could with the little she had."

"Did she tell you the truth, then?" he taunts. "That the kid isn't yours?"

I go completely still, hand hanging mid-air as I look at him wide-eyed. How does he—

A whimper catches my attention, and I see my brother rocking back and forward on the couch, his hands clutching the roots of his hair tightly. All of this fighting must be triggering him and worsening his cravings.

"Let's stop this! Mason is not–"

"Oh, so you don't know! Not really, do you?" An evil laugh escapes my father's mouth. "So fucking naïve! She's manipulating you, and you're falling for it!"

"She told me," I counter. "Except, it could be mine, too. We'll be sure soon."

"Good, then." The patronising tone in his voice makes me want to punch him. He's never been so lucky to be my father before.

But this isn't news. He's always been cold and detached, intervening only to get his way. Appearances came first, and the family came second. It hasn't changed one fucking bit.

"We'll finally know which one of you is the father, then."

My mother's words feel like a bucket of freezing water over my head. My heart drops to my feet as my brain struggles to comprehend these words.

And because I can't keep up fast enough, my father chimes in right afterwards, "Yes, we'll need to know which one of you will ask for full custody."

What?

"No, no, no," a soft wail sounds behind me. "Oh no!"

I turn just in time to see my girl crying—again—while opening the front door.

"No one's fucking doing that," I growl, that primal instinct to protect her—*them*—coming out.

"Watch me," my father challenges me, pushing his chest out and trying to look taller than me. While I have inherited my mother's blonde hair, everything has been given to me by this excuse of a man in front of me. And I've never regretted my ancestry as much as this day. "That little whore is the fucking problem, and I'll get rid of it."

When I look back, she's still there like a statue, still gripping the door.

"Come here and admit everything!"

When he stalks in her direction, I step in front of him, blocking access to her. "Babe," I call her. "Get home, and I'll meet you—"

"It wasn't enough that you screwed both of my sons—destroying one's life and distancing the other from his family—you had to keep this child a secret?"

"What?" I croak.

"You heard it right. That kid is most likely your nephew!"

"You're crazy," I chuckle darkly, not believing him for one second.

"Am I? Then why else would she leave without telling you about the kid? Huh?"

My hands, which were pressing against my father's chest, fall limply to my sides. My face contorts in confusion as I glance back at Mason. He's still rocking back and forward, hands covering his head like he's protecting himself from unbearable pain.

My brother? Willow?

It can't be. They barely spent time together—or talked for that matter—since he was never home. He's claiming that both of them cheated, but...she would never.

Cheat? Nah, that's ridiculous, and I know it. I—*shit.*

"Mummy, let's go home. Please." I snap out of it as Dylan's incessant requests fall upon deaf ears. Turning around, I see her crouching down, barely able to breathe.

"Willow?" I call weakly. "What is this all about?"

She wouldn't. *I know it.*

When her swollen eyes lock on mine, they knock the breath out of me at the pain mirrored in them. She's hurting so damn bad, but...

"I wouldn't," she mumbles through her sobs. "Not..." And with a shaky breath, she hastily stands up and pulls Dylan with her, slamming the door behind her.

Not? *Not what?*

I should go after her, and fuck, I want to! But my body refuses to hear my brain, staying rooted in place.

Dumbfounded.

It takes me a second, a second too long to put the pieces together as snippets of what she's told me fit together. All of those times she was afraid to tell me such an important part of everything, afraid I'd hate her alongside her need to try and find the proper way to tell me—whatever it was. And just today...the way she told me she wouldn't do anything like that to me, not willingly.

Not willingly!

I spin, facing my brother, and his gaze is already locked on mine. He looks gutted...like he's been carrying the weight of the world around his shoulders—*no.*

He looks guilty.

My vision turns red as all the information falls into place. That protectiveness that stays hidden most of the time takes over every fibre of my body as my brain conjures cruel images of plausible scenarios.

"What the fuck did you do to her?" I roar, charging towards him.

It's a weird state of consciousness, as for the first time, I give in to some of my darkest urges. My hands grab the collar of his shirt, slamming his back against the wall.

"Tell me," I growl. "I want the fucking truth. What did you do to her?"

"Liam, stop." My mother's shouts fall on deaf ears. "He's your brother!"

Brother? The man in front of me has been reduced to nothing in my eyes. Such a monster couldn't be related to me. He's all drugs and addiction, bad choices and unforgiveable actions. A dangerous criminal. At this point, there is nothing else to salvage.

"He did nothing!" my father bellows behind me. "She threw herself at him!"

A hand–probably his–grips my shoulder tightly with a harsh push backwards, and it only spurs me on, the rage bubbling to the surface as I suddenly push my arm back, elbowing whoever is behind me. A scrunching sound is followed by a grunt, and the hold on my body disappears.

On any other day, I would have cared, but not now. Years of pent-up anger and bottled-up feelings are now coming out. For so long, I had blamed her for everything that has happened, and I'm just realising now that it was directed at the wrong person all along.

Willow was raped. And my brother–*my blood*–was responsible for it. The perpetrator. A criminal. A fucking rapist. And my parents? They're just as evil for knowing what transpired and not holding him accountable for his actions. Mason has been roaming around freely without suffering the consequences of what he's done. All the while that young girl was left to fend for herself in this cruel world.

Coming to this conclusion, it's placing me on the edge, just on the brink of losing control.

"Did you force yourself on her?" The heaviness in the words floats around us as he gulps.

The way he looks away is enough to give me the answer. And while it's what I expected, it's absolutely not what I want. Still, I push through because I need to hear it from his mouth.

"Yes or no?" My forearm slides up, pressing against his neck.

"Y-yes," he stammers, his eyes red and shiny with tears.

I knew it.

"What did you do to her?" Mason starts to choke, but I don't budge.

This is *why* she was so afraid to tell me who did it. I get it now because...how would she be able to break it to me? "*Hey Liam, I know he looks like you, but that's because he can also be your nephew.*"

"I want to hear you say it," I growl.

"Liam, stop this madness," my mum shrieks again.

"Madness?" I shout. "Madness is the fact that you never cared to stop him before, and you think he's worth defending now?"

"I finally convinced your father to help him–"

"You should have helped him then," I shut her off. "Maybe then, he wouldn't have done what he did."

She doesn't answer, glazing down in shame. It's a low blow since I know she always fought with John because of Mason. She disagreed with the ways my father dealt with the issues, but being completely dependent on him and having her place in their community secured was more important to her, so she always did as he ordered. Letting my father become the wedge that tore my brother apart from his family.

Now? Now, it's too fucking late for amends.

Turning my attention back to Mason, I demand, "Confess, and I might go easy on you. What did you do?"

"I–I had sex with her," he admits.

I growl at his choice of words. *Sex, my ass!*

I had sex with her last night, with consent. *Her consent.* My forearm presses tighter against his throat as the burning flames of wrath order my brain to inflict pain, to make him suffer as much as she did.

Loathing and remorse rise to the surface, too. I know this is pointless because it won't erase what she went through, but it's the only thing bringing me a fraction of relief in this moment. Because my own brother, a man I adored and looked up to, was able to hurt the love of my life beyond repair.

"Did she want it?" No answer comes out, and it only spurs me on. "Tell me!"

"N-no," he croaks.

I let go of him, my arms falling limply to my sides as a huge crack grows in my heart. It's one thing to know, but to hear it..."So, you raped her."

"Baby brother, I was high. I didn't–"

The familiar cracking sound of a bone breaking rings throughout my apartment. My knuckles sting upon impact, but the pain is welcomed, a feeble distraction from the real hurt within.

One more. Two. Three.

Not even when he's on the ground–unconscious–do I stop. There's no going back now as everything comes out. All of the anguish I endured throughout these years and the recently gained guilt are unleashed, trying to make up for the fact that she wasn't safe. Not even from my own family–my own blood.

A trauma so strong she still has panic attacks about it. The kind of emotional scarring that never leaves, and all because of *him.*

"*Stop*! You'll kill him!" My mum's high-pitched voice rings in my ears, and I finally stop.

Her sobs are followed by a strong body pulling me away from my brother. I know it's my father, and even though I don't want him to touch me–hell I don't want anyone touching me–this time, I let him.

"Look what you've done." She glares at me before kneeling before him. "This was never supposed to happen," she grits. She's speaking to me, but looking at him, surveying his injuries. "I have failed him time and time again. I had just gotten your father on board with helping him, and now this...We were going to make it better," she sobs, holding on to him.

When I don't answer her rant, she adds, "My poor boy, he just wanted to get back on track."

Her sobs are exaggerated and honestly, they're starting to piss me off.

"I–I deserved it," Mason croaks as he rouses.

The fact he is still conscious is both relieving and disappointing. The last thing I want is to go to jail, but every drop of sympathy I had left for my brother has vanished. Nothing–*nothing*–justifies what he did. Especially his little brother's girlfriend. What kind of sick man does that?

"*No*!" our mother wails, clutching him in her arms. "You were sick. Now, you want to make things right; that should be enough."

"Make things right?" I bark. "Then why was dad threatening to ask for Dylan's custody? That's not making things right!"

"What would you prefer?" my dad growls, making me turn to look at him. We look so much alike, yet we are so different. "Have your brother thrown into prison instead? That would ruin our lives, on top of his!"

"So, ruining hers is the solution? Wasn't all the pain she went through already enough? To go through a pregnancy and raise a child in her teenage years that *could* be her rapist's kid?"

My father's mouth snaps shut as his eyes widen in reaction to my booming words. My head feels like it's going to burst soon. If I look as raging as I feel, it must be a terrifying sight.

"Nothing he can do will make it up to her–to *them*! And if it's up to me..." I turn to my brother. "You'll rot away in jail for a long time for this shit. Mark my words."

"You can't possibly be serious, boy." My father swoops in once again, walking towards me. "We've given you everything, and you're going to side with that girl?"

I laugh sarcastically. "How can you possibly ask that?"

"She probably fucking asked for it," he booms. "She entered the house late at night with only him inside! She went straight into the wolf's lair and didn't expect anything to happen? She couldn't be that naïve!"

"What are you saying?" My voice is quiet, deadly, while my blood boils inside me. "She entered our house, lured in by my brother when she was expecting me to arrive at any given moment and should have expected to be forced to do what she didn't want to? She went there because I was supposed to be there!"

"Well, I—"

"Get out," I grit the words out. There's nothing they can say to change my mind.

If my brother wanted to make things right, he would have gone to the police right away to confess what he did, not hide behind the drugs and now put the responsibility on my parents to make it all go away. Because that's all my parents are good for—making problems disappear.

They have this perfect family picture on the outside, but they're completely rotten on the inside.

And I want nothing to do with them. *Nothing.*

They keep silent as they help Mason back on his feet, and I fight the urge to beat him to a pulp once more. When they don't move after I've told them to get out twice, I scream, "Get the fuck out!"

"We'll see if you keep talking to us in that tone once I cut you off," my father snarks back.

"Shove the fucking money up your ass!"

"Watch your mouth," he snarls while my mother slowly walks my brother to the front door.

"Or what?" I counter, getting in his face. "Want to take a swing? *I dare* you."

We stare off for a while, daring each other to make a move or stand down, and thankfully, the man in front of me takes a step back. He shakes his head, showing his disappointment, but I am way past caring for it—caring for them.

He stomps after the other two, slamming the door shut, and all the adrenaline travelling through my body slows down as my alert state wears down.

As some fatigue hits, my brain reels with thoughts of everything that just transpired, properly processing the information. All of these years, I've been angry at her for disappearing, for abandoning me while I needed her. For leaving me after I gave her the best of me.

I was so fucking wrong.

For so long, I've been furious at the wrong person instead because my brother was the one who forced her away. By hurting her so much she couldn't even look me in the eye and confide what had happened.

So young and hurt...so alone.

Everything makes sense now: the panic when seeing me again, the constant hesitancy in not telling me what transpired, and telling me I'm not the father despite Dylan being my twin. She wasn't being selfish.

She was protecting me.

Bloody hell, I love this woman so damn hard. She deserves everything.

"What the fuck am I doing?" I mutter to myself. "She's out there alone, and I'm here stuck in my head."

She probably thinks I hate her; she probably thinks I believe them...

I need to go to her and make things right.

I need to show her that I do believe her and that I *fucking love her.*

FORTY-TWO

Willow

I KNEW THIS WOULD HAPPEN. I STILL DID WHAT HE ASKED OF ME because…how can I say no to him? I love him so much. *Too much.*

And in the end, just like I imagined, he let me go because he didn't believe it.

How could he? It's his family, and I can't compete with that…

"Mummy?" Dylan calls me, pulling on my sleeve. "I'm tired," he whines.

We've been walking around the city for an hour, and I honestly don't know what to do. Will he be waiting by my car at his building? Or by my house? Will he be fully out of my life from now on? Will they join forces to take Dylan from me?

I shiver in fear just from the thought. It feels like if I make a decision, it will be final, and I am too triggered to face him and too scared to lose him.

"I'm sorry, baby. Let's go sit down a little bit, okay?" I pull him up onto my arms and carry him to the bench across the street.

"Mummy?" I hum in response, holding him to my side while he plays with the ends of my hair. "Why did we have to leave?"

"I am so sorry, baby. We wanted to give you the best Christmas, but things didn't go as planned. Liam's parents don't get along with me. I am so, so sorry."

"It's fine." He sniffles. "Can we go back?"

"I–I don't know," I confess. "It's up to Liam. How about Mummy calls a cab so we go home, for now? Then we can talk to Liam later and maybe visit him again." He nods, burying his head into my side.

It's hard to keep my composure while my brain keeps attacking me with old memories. Seeing Mason after all of these years has opened up the hole I have been trying so hard to fill.

He was just there like nothing ever happened, like he didn't strip me of my dignity and step on it afterwards. Like he didn't vanish into thin air and leave me to pick up the pieces of everything he destroyed.

At that moment, it felt like someone opened my chest and squeezed my heart to ashes.

And by now, after the confusion that I saw in his eyes has worn off, Liam is probably siding with them, blaming me for everything.

We'll need to know which one of you will ask for full custody.

No other words could scare me as much as those. I'd still rather go through all the pain again than lose my son. They took everything from me that night. I lost the person I was, the person I loved most in life, and even most of my family. Knowing I have Dylan has been my rock, my strength to go forward, and I won't let them take that away from me as well.

I'll run away again if I have to.

Warm fingers brush my soaked cheeks, and I open my eyes to find Dylan looking at me with a miserable expression. My poor baby, having to go through all of this and constantly watching me break down. He deserves better than this.

"Don't be sad, Mummy." Dylan climbs onto my lap, hugging me. "It's Christmas. We have to be happy!"

I let out a shaky laugh at his attempt to cheer me up. "Yes, you're right."

"Willow?" a male voice calls from a distance.

I freeze, afraid of looking up to see who it is. At least, only until Dylan shrieks the person's name.

"*Athur*!"

He jumps off my lap and runs to my Portuguese and Literature professor. Well, *former professor* since the semester has finished.

Arthur ruffles Dylan's hair before crouching down to his height. My son wastes no time jumping into his arms, and he picks him up, unfazed. Then he slowly comes my way, and as the distance closes in, I see a frown forming on his face. Probably due to my bloodshot eyes and swollen face.

"What's wrong?" he asks, sitting down next to me.

I shake my head, not wanting to talk about, it but Dylan beats me to it. "We were at Dad Liam's for Christmas. Some persons appeared and were mean to Mummy. She cried, and we left."

Well, that's a light way to put it. My eyes blur, but I dab them, not wanting to cry again.

"Is that all that happened?" he asks, sceptical of my silence.

Doesn't he know kids are too pure to lie? He just doesn't know the details that made me so upset.

"*He* was there," I whisper.

"As in..."

"Yes." I nod. "He's Liam's brother."

I look at him, waiting for a reaction, but there's none. That's when I remember that he already knew everything. He was the first one to know.

"They were shocked to see me there and blamed me for everything right away," I mumble.

At that, Arthur's attention snaps back to mine, his eyes fiery with rage.

"*They what?*" His tone is borderline menacing.

"Yeah, but I don't want to get into it in detail." I tilt my chin down towards Dylan.

He nods but keeps silent for a while, looking at the street and the scarce people that wander around. Mostly families that are going for an early stroll before Christmas lunch or others that are supposed to be on their way to spend it with someone else.

After a little while, he finally asks, "Why didn't you go home?"

"There's no one there today," I confess. "And I'm afraid that a certain *someone* could be there, waiting for me or might show up later."

"I see," he mutters. "It's almost lunchtime."

I know. *Oh god, what am I going to do?*

Upon seeing the panic in my eyes, his expression softens. His dark brown eyes swirl with concern, and he offers, "Well, how about you come and have lunch with me?"

Dylan looks at us for the first time, still on Arthur's lap. And from the looks of it, he is silently begging me to say yes.

But I can't.

"I couldn't intrude."

"I'll be by myself today," he admits shyly. "Your company would definitely make the day better, and I'll take you home as soon as you want. Yeah?"

I hesitate for a second, but then slowly nod. There's no harm in accepting his help, right? He has proved time and time again that this is a harmless relationship—a friendship. And up until very recently, I've lacked those. While I'm grateful for Ethan and Hazel, the connection that developed between us is different.

I nod again, and Arthur doesn't waste any time in helping me up and guiding me to his car, all the while carrying Dylan in his arms.

I swear, my kid takes advantage of people the best way he can. He makes them adore him, unable to resist his cuteness.

"Where were you, if you're just heading home now?" I ask, curiosity getting the best of me. "Uh, only if you want to tell me," I add, blushing.

We walk side by side at a leisurely pace. The Christmas lights and decorations are everywhere, surrounding us. Dylan's eyes sweep around the street in awe of the sight, and even I appreciate it. It makes me feel slightly lighter.

"It's fine," he assures me. "I went to my sister's grave. I always do on the holidays; she used to love them."

"Oh, I'm sorry for bringing it up."

"Don't worry."

It turns out his house is within walking distance, taking less than ten minutes to arrive. But from here, I know the cemetery is at least an hour walk, leaving me wondering about his need for walking so much on such a day. Is he...lonely? He must be.

Inside his house, I notice it is open-concept and am immediately hit with that woodsy scent that follows him everywhere. The decoration is simple and modern, but the dark furniture gives it an edge, just like him.

Fortunately, the tall windows counter it, allowing sunlight to stream through. It's somehow balanced, and even though it's my first time here, I feel comfortable.

"Welcome," he mumbles, closing the door behind us. "The house is half messy because I wasn't expecting anyone, but I have enough food for the three of us. Let me just heat it."

With that, he finally places Dylan down and heads to the kitchen, still in plain sight. My boy, instead of clinging to me, rushes up to the couch and sighs in relief. I let him be for a while since he no longer seems too concerned with me.

"Do you want help?" I ask Arthur, hoping I can occupy my mind with something like setting the table.

"Nah, go and sit down for a bit."

Begrudgingly, I obey and snuggle up with Dylan on the couch. After a few minutes, he calls us to sit down by the table, presenting us with a generous platter of roasted lamb and potatoes, plus a pot of rice and a bowl of salad.

"This was all for yourself?" I ask, shocked.

He rubs the back of his neck in embarrassment. "Yeah, I–I don't like cooking too often, even though I'm pretty good at it. So, I tend to do it in big quantities, hoping for it to usually last me a day or two."

"That's clever," I comment. "Especially when you have a demanding, hungry kid and little time to cook or bake," I joke.

Dylan sticks his tongue out, and I fake glare at him, nodding for him to start eating his food. Throughout the entirety of lunch, Arthur keeps the conversation light-hearted and constantly interacts with Dylan. It has a huge calming effect on me.

After the meal, Dylan begs for a movie, and Arthur gives in right away.

Truth is, I don't want to go home either. At least, not yet.

I know I'm avoiding the inevitable, but after the stress from earlier this morning, I need to set my head straight before I can face whatever is heading my way. And if I so much as look at Liam, I'll break down.

That's why we stay and watch the cartoon movies that are playing on the TV. We get engrossed in it, and time flies by. I only realise I've been here for too long when the light inside dims into an orange hue. The sun is setting.

Dylan has fallen asleep on my lap long ago, and Arthur sits down on a leather recliner, right next to us.

"Arthur?" I whisper. "I think it's time I head home."

He nods, standing and gently scooping Dylan up in his arms, allowing me to get up.

"Let's get you home," he whispers back.

Just when we start to walk, my phone rings, and I hastily pick it up, trying not to wake Dylan.

"Where are you?" Liam pants on the other side of the call.

"I—" I freeze. Of course, he was going to call. What do I do now? Because I don't know if I have the guts to hear what he has to say to me.

"I'm so fucking worried; why aren't you home? I've been knocking and calling for hours, and you're not here."

Worried?

"I–we're fine." I settle on those words as my eyes blur.

"Come back home, please," he pleads. "We need to talk about this."

"I can't," I admit in a shaky voice. "Not today, *please.*"

"Fine," he sighs. "But please come back home. It's getting late, and I'm worried. I'll leave."

Why is he being so kind? Is he not mad?

"Thank you," I stutter.

"I'll wait, Willow. I'll wait."

"I–"

"Text me when you get home so I'm not worried."

"O-of course," I mumble.

He hangs up, and I sigh in relief.

"Everything alright?" Arthur asks, bringing my attention back to him and my sleeping kid.

"Yes." I smile weakly. "It will be."

I'll make sure of it.

He carries Dylan to the car, strapping him down safely next to me in the back. The drive is quick, only around twenty minutes until we get to my house. For most of the ride, we keep silent, seemingly with the understanding that I need it.

And, of course, my brain keeps dragging me back to think of Liam and all of my fears. After everything and how passionate we were last night, it's safe to say I'm ruined for any other man that walks the earth.

At this point, it no longer matters if he decides to never look me in the eye; if he chooses to just be there for Dylan–god, I hope he does–I'll never be able to get over him.

He's my beginning, my middle, and my end. Liam is not just part of my heart, he *is* my heart, and I will love that man until the day I die.

"We're here," Arthur announces.

"Thank you, for everything," I say sincerely.

"Always," he states. "I mean it, Willow. If you ever need someone... I'm a friend. Please don't hesitate."

I nod and smile. He seems pleased with my answer, getting out of the car and rounding it to open the door for me. I unbuckle my kid and transfer him to my neck, he stirs, slightly opening his eyes and automatically clutching my neck, burying his head in my chest. It tells me right away, it'll be one of those nights, where we'll only rest if we're attached.

With a quick goodnight, I step into the darkened house, walking upstairs straight into my bedroom. I'm exhausted, and my eyes feel heavy but I'm sure I won't be able to sleep that much.

The anxiety has lessened but I still see his face every time I close my eyes. He's walking around, free to do whatever. Free to hurt other women and not pay for what he's done or might do.

It's unbelievably unfair to be blamed for something I didn't want.

Why do we keep being the ones asking for it? Why are men able to get away with their actions, by blaming them on us?

This has to stop. Men need to be accountable for their actions and for what happens inside their minds.

I just hope, in my heart, that Liam sees me and understands I would never do what his parents accused me of. I just hope he sees the truth and believes me.

Because at this point, I don't know if I could survive the world without him in my life.

FORTY-THREE

Willow

I BLINK THROUGH THE PIERCING BRIGHT LIGHT COMING IN THROUGH my bedroom window, reaching out for Dylan's sleeping body. His absence brings me to consciousness way faster than is natural, and I sit up. He's not here, and I hope Nana has already arrived to be with him downstairs. Otherwise, I'll freak out.

"Dylan?" I call, expecting him to pop his head in from behind the door.

When he doesn't, I panic, and without being able to think about anything else, I rush downstairs.

However, once I reach the ground floor, I'm rooted to the spot at the sound of hushed giggles coming from the kitchen. My body relaxes, recognizing my boy's sounds anywhere.

"That's disgusting," Liam's voice sounds, making me tense all over again.

He gags, and Dylan laughs louder. "It's delicious," he claims proudly. "Come on, try some more."

It's a quarter past seven. How is Liam here already?

Curiosity gets the best of me, and I peek through the kitchen door. The sight makes my heartbeat skyrocket. Dylan's on Liam's lap, trying to force him to taste a pancake with Nutella, syrup, and pineapple in the mix. It's one of the things he loves to eat, even though it definitely is disgusting.

I've tried it and hated it, but hey, we all have a weird food combination we love—mine is chips with yoghurt.

Liam tastes it again, and his face contorts into a deep frown. It's clearly visible how much he is not enjoying it.

"Hmmm," he pretends to enjoy it, but I can see the twitch in his mouth and how much his eyes are narrowed. What is he doing? "It's good."

I mentally facepalm myself. He'll force him to eat it every time from now on.

I freeze as my brain just realises what I thought. From now on? Who's to tell me this isn't the last time I see them together? He's probably here to say his goodbyes—for good.

"You're up," Liam breathes.

My eyes snap up to his, wide and expectant. Waiting for the moment the shoe drops because...how can it not?

"I–" I stumble over my words, not knowing what to say under his intense gaze.

This is the moment I've been dreading, and right now, there's no way I can escape it.

"Remember what we've talked about?" Liam mumbles into Dylan's ear.

He nods eagerly before jumping off his lap and heading my way. He hugs my hip and quietly tells me he'll be waiting for us in the living room while watching a movie. Throughout the whole ordeal, I'm speechless. My brain is reeling with questions I'm afraid to ask because it will open the door for a conversation I absolutely don't want to have.

"Lo?" Liam calls me in a surprisingly gentle and warm tone.

Still, I can't bring my eyes to his. Focusing on his shoulder, chin, or hands is way easier than the ocean-like irises that keep begging me for attention.

"Can we just get it over with?" In contradiction with my words, my voice wobbles.

"What do you mean?" He stands and slowly walks to me.

His movements are so measured, so slow, that it feels like he is approaching a cornered animal.

"I know you must hate me," I confess when he takes another step, stopping right in front of me. "You probably believe them, so just..." I cut myself off to breathe, wringing my hands together in stress. "Get it over with."

"Look at me." Two fingers gently grip my chin, tilting it up, and I shut my eyes tightly. "Baby..."

There's a desperate edge to his voice now. I've never heard him call me baby this way, and it shatters my resolve. Giving in to him like a kid gives in to candy, I finally stare into his breathtaking eyes. They're so deep and vibrant, overflowing with so many different emotions. I see concern, guilt, and regret, and I recognise them because I feel them, too. But what strikes me the most is that he isn't angry or showing hate towards me.

Automatically, my tense body relaxes.

"Never," he whispers slowly. "Ever," he emphasises. "In a million years would I doubt you. I know you avoid confrontation like the plague, and I know you'd rather run away than have it all blow up in your face, but if there is one thing I know, it's that you wouldn't lie. Not to me and certainly not about this."

Reeling but not letting his words sink in, I open my mouth to argue—to defend myself—until I realise I don't need to.

He believes me.

"But your parents said–"

"Fuck what my parents said," he cuts me off. "I want to know what you say instead."

"I–"

"Can you tell me what happened?" Pulling my hand towards the kitchen stool, he forces me to sit down on his lap. His hands grip my waist, manoeuvring me until we're both comfortable, and he places his chin on my shoulder, intertwining our fingers in front of my stomach.

It's astonishing how easily he knows what I need. The need for the proximity of his body to feel safe, and yet, not being able to face him while I recall the worst night in my life. Taking a deep, encouraging breath, I start, "We were supposed to meet that night, but you weren't there. I was going to go back home, but your brother said I could wait inside, that you'd be back soon, and I believed him."

My hands start shaking involuntarily, and he cups them, trying to get them to stop. When they finally cease, his thumbs start to draw little circles over my skin. It calms me down some more, enough to keep track of what I have to say.

"I sat on the couch, watching some TV to kill time while waiting for you. After a couple of minutes, he came and sat down next to me. At first, he was silent and kept his distance, so I let it go, but then he started throwing out some weird comments. How cute I was when I stuttered and how the good girl appearance suited me so well..."

His chest vibrates, and a low growl forms in his throat as his hold on me tightens. Through a shaky whisper, I confess, "He came on to me. I tried to stop him–" A sob cuts off my words. "I swear, I tried!"

"Shh," he coos when the sobs intensify, his hand finding my cheek. "I am so sorry, baby." He turns my head to the side, resting his forehead on mine. "I should have been there. I was out to buy us some condoms, but the goddamn shop was closed, and it took me so long. Then when I got home, there was no sign of you, and the house had been robbed. I didn't even know you were inside the house, I–" He stops himself for a second. "When you told me you had been attacked, I assumed it had happened in a dark alley on the way to your house..."

"How could I tell you that your brother was the one that–"

"I know, baby," he hushes me. "I know now. I'm sorry I was so angry at you. I had just assumed you stood me up. Then when you started ignoring me for those weeks before you disappeared, I was going crazy; I didn't know what to think."

"I need you to believe me, Liam. What your parents said, I...I didn't want it. I cried and begged him to stop. I even screamed it, but he never stopped."

His eyebrows twist in agony before his eyes shut tightly. This must be so hard to hear, but he asked me to tell him the truth and it hurts just as much to admit it. The pain was and still is unbearable. I was torn open and broken—not only physically but spiritually.

"I believe you. Always." Then with a sigh, he continues, "My parents...they're horrible people. My brother was and is sick, and they keep on enabling him instead of making him accountable for his actions." His voice rises a little, showing me the annoyance of being reminded of his family.

"I'm sorry for everything. For ignoring you and then leaving."

"I wish you would have told me back then..." he trails off, half lost in his thoughts. "You wouldn't have gone through all of this alone. I would have believed you and been there with you every step of the way."

I can only nod in understanding, but still...while I can't change the past and make the right decision, I don't know how I would have been able to face him back then either.

"It hurt, but I understand you, and I forgive you if you forgive me," he mutters, his thumb caressing my lips. Our faces are so close I can breathe in his exhales. "And we better forgive each other because I love you so fucking much. I never stopped, and I never will."

"Yeah?" I ask, hopeful.

"Fuck yeah," he exclaims. "I want to try; we need a chance to have it all, and I'm not going to waste it. There's no life for me without you and Dylan in it."

Fresh minty breaths fan my face with a light hint of pineapple. It's comfortable and familiar. It's home.

"Neither am I," I agree with him. "But what about this mess with your parents? They won't let it go this easy.... And–" I stop myself to bring my voice down to a whisper, "We still need to pick up the paternity test."

"Well..." He leans back, creating some distance between us, while digging something from his back pocket. "How about we deal with one thing at a time, hmm?"

With that, his hand comes back into view, between our bodies, holding a white envelope.

"Is that..." I trail off, attempting to grab it, but Liam dodges me.

"I need to say," he chimes in, catching my attention again. "If you want to be sure, I won't stop you. It's your choice, and I will understand either way, but I need you to understand mine as well."

Then, doing the unthinkable and with his eyes set on mine, he tears it in half. I gasp, attempting to grab it. He lets me grab it, but doesn't let go, holding it between us with his eyes scorching mine in an intense stare.

"Wha–" I trail off, shocked. "How could you do that?"

"Because," he grits, finally letting the papers go. One of his hands traces my skin, up my arm until it reaches my neck. Gently, he splays it over the nape of my neck, bringing our faces impossibly closer again. "I don't fucking care what that DNA test says, what's written on that paper will not define what I feel for him nor my relationship with him. I am Dylan's father whether blood agrees with it or not."

Tears flood my eyes, blurring my sight, and my lips and chin tremble with the wave of emotion that hits me. This man, this man right here in front of me, means everything to me, and I love him so, so much.

Without thinking twice, I lunge towards him, wrapping my arms around his neck and kissing him. I kiss the hell out of him because, dang, he deserves it and so much more.

"I love you." Once again, we breathe the magic words to each other at the same time and end up chuckling.

With a naughty smirk, he holds me up and sits me down on the counter with his hips wedged between my legs. My cheeks blush violently as memories from two nights ago invade my head, mixing with the fact that I haven't been in this position since we were sixteen and horny.

We're just not sixteen anymore.

Liam notices and with a smirk, he kisses my cherry-reddened cheeks.

"Repeat with me," he mutters as his hands slide up my waist. "He's ours."

"He's ours," I repeat, tasting the words in my mouth.

The heaviness of the meaning isn't lost on me as tears start to flow freely. How can he be so calm and sure of this? How can he want to move forward without having confirmation?

"Baby, don't cry," he coos. "Everything's alright."

I stutter and trip over my words, not being able to form anything. His touch, his comfort, only propels me to sob harder. It's intense, crippling.

"Hey, look at me. Come on." His thumbs make quick work of wiping underneath my eyes. "There's no reason to be crying, Willow. Look at me, baby. What did we agree on?" he asks.

"No matter the outcome, it won't change anything," I mumble between a couple of hiccups.

"Exactly," he mutters. "No matter the outcome...he's ours."

"He's ours," I repeat, trying to sink those words into my mind.

"Are you done talking? I'm bored," Dylan interrupts us.

We both laugh, and without wasting time, Liam picks him up and carries him to where I am standing. His free hand wraps around my waist, bringing me to his chest, face to face with Dylan. He smiles wide at me, and I can't help but return it and wrap both my arms around them.

"That's it," he hums in contentment. "A family hug."

We stand there in silence, hugging tightly, enjoying the feeling of being together and the warmth and love that oozes out of us. When we finally slightly let go, Liam looks at me with an emotional glaze in his eyes before turning his attention to Dylan.

"I know I wasn't here before, and I'm sorry for that, but I'm here now, and I won't go away ever again. I love you, *son*, so much."

Dylan's bottom lip trembles, and he latches himself onto Liam's neck.

"I love the both of you, too," I add before hugging both of them.

After that, our son tries to usher us to the living room to watch the movie with him. However, looking at the torn paper pieces in my hands, something jabs at my heart.

"Go ahead, boys," I mutter nonchalantly.

They both nod, and Liam gives me a knowing look before directing Dylan out of the kitchen. I rush to the opposite end of the kitchen, hiding from the hallway. As my hands slowly open the envelope and unfold the papers, it heats my skin as if those light sections of the letter had the biggest secret of the world burning their way to freedom.

He wouldn't be mad, would he? If I took a peek? It is *my* choice, after all—those were his words. It doesn't matter who his father is, and the fact that Liam doesn't care either makes my heart swell with love, but there's still this little fly who keeps close to my ear, nagging me about it.

Not being able to fight the urge, I place both halves together and look through them in search of the part that has the information I yearn for. It's silent here—with both of them no longer close by—and it's deafening as I see the words I've been wanting to see for years now.

Words that, even though they change nothing in our hearts, can define everything in court—if needed.

From left to right, my eyes keep going, reading on and soon, they unfocus for the thousandth time today with the emotion of knowing after so many years of doubt, of wondering. After so many years of hoping to have one specific outcome and now being able to read the scientific proof, to see the truth with my own eyes, it's liberating.

It seems unreal, but it's pretty much real. That I have my entire heart—*and family*—here with me. I am completely happy because I am home.

Because home is where your heart is.

EPILOGUE

Liam

FUNNY TO THINK HOW MUCH FOUR YEARS CAN CHANGE ONE'S LIFE.

If someone had told me all those years ago that I'd find her again and gain a family from that encounter, I would have laughed in that person's face. But here I am, still wrapped around Willow's little finger and doting on my nine-year-old.

From an empty walking corpse, finding them was like having the breath of life blown straight into my mouth. Don't get me wrong, it doesn't mean it was easy. There have been a few bumps on the road.

From Johanna's incessant attempts to get together at the beginning—even after my rejection—and my father's futile attempts to get my brother off the hook when the man himself admitted to his wrongdoings...it's been a rollercoaster.

At first, Willow didn't want any problems with my parents, knowing they had the money to overpower us legally, but the law states that when a minor is sexually assaulted, they can only report it until their twenty-third birthday. After that, the statute of limitations applies. For a moment there, I thought we would never have closure from this or have my brother pay the consequences of his actions.

But with her therapist's help, we did it. And before my father could even swallow us whole with his power, my brother admitted to everything and said he'd accept any sentence that the judge thought fitting. The bare minimum.

John Davis has not stopped harassing us, though. It's a never-ending cycle that—according to him—will only end when he's sure Dylan is not my brother's. It makes me insanely mad because I *am* his father.

I may not have seen the DNA test with my own eyes, but I knew it from the moment she got out of that kitchen that day. It was her widest and brightest smile—an unforgettable memory. Another hint was the fact that my father's attempts at custody requests, grandparent rights and so many other crazy court notices we've been receiving, haven't affected her. *At all.*

And fuck, it turns me on as much as it makes me proud. My girlfriend—soon to be fiancé, *I hope*—has grown so much and fought so hard. While I know she has been doing it long before I came back, watching it up close has been inspiring.

I want to marry the hell out of her. This ring has been burning all my pockets for over a month now, but nothing ever feels like the right—or perfect—moment. We're both officially done with school. Willow is going to start next fall as an elementary teacher in Dylan's old school, and I'm already finishing up my last residency as a paediatric cardiologist. *It's time.*

"You think it's time?" Her round coffee irises look up at me through the dark blue hues of the aquarium. We've made it a tradition to come once a year since it was one of our first significant times together—as a family.

Still, my eyes widen in reaction to her words.

Did I say that out loud?

"W-what?" I stutter.

"I was thinking..." she trails off, looking at our boy with his head plastered against that damn thick glass. "He's been calling you Dad since that Christmas. With your dad asking for custody, claiming Mason is the father, to me, it would make sense if—"

"I told you I don't care about seeing the result," I cut her off. "He's mine, no matter what those papers say, and my father can fuck off with his entitlement."

"No," she groans, pulling me back by my hand.

That's another one of her conquests; there have been several. From her nightmares vanishing to maybe just once or twice a year to barely having that extreme sensitivity to touch or sudden noises. Willow has been doing so much better.

Partly because of the wonderful people that surround her. From the shy, closed-off girl she was, she's become a social butterfly, strengthening the bond she created with her college friends.

Ethan and Hazel are still a constant presence in our lives. They come around almost every other weekend and most of the holidays, too. So much so that Dylan calls them aunt and uncle. Ethan is the calmness of the three, and Hazel is slightly more guarded but still has that spunk in her personality. But the both of them have always been very protective of Willow. Even after all of these years, Hazel's greeting signature to me is the cut-throat move, just to make sure I'm on my best behaviour.

And while it can be silly to some, it makes me proud to know she has found people that love her and want to protect her just as much.

Even that professor of hers...with time I've come to put my jealousy aside and understand them—*their bond.* Arthur and Willow share the same kind of pain, and while I wish I could be her only one for everything, I have to accept the fact that this kind of pain, I won't be able to understand—not to the extent he does.

He is a fucking good friend, always calling to check up on her and everyone else. Not even the three hundred kilometres between them has kept him away, not really. Though, my less rational side surely doesn't mind the distance.

But my favourite? The way she is more secure in herself—no longer stuttering, no more skittish moments, and she has slowly learned her own way of standing up to others. Even myself—and I fucking love it.

"That's not what I meant." She chuckles with a roll of her eyes.

There's that recognisable hint of annoyance in her voice. It usually comes alongside some of her secret sassiness—which I also love—and I can't help but feel the urge to entice it even more by irking her up. My hands lower to her backside, kneading her soft curves before I harshly grope her ass and bury my nose in her neck. "What did you mean, then?"

"Stop being crass, Liam." She tries to pull me away, unsuccessfully.

At that moment, Dylan turns back, looking for us, twisting his face as soon as he sees us. "Ewww," he mouths to me, and I laugh through a shrug before wrapping my arms around her upper back and hugging her tight.

"What did you mean, love?"

My words seem to finally do the trick as she smiles wide and wraps her arms around my neck. Her back is facing Dylan, but she knows I've got my eye on him. I always do, and she trusts me completely. In itself, it means the world to me.

"I was thinking we should finally change his birth certificate." Her lips move, slowly enunciating every word with care, and her peach-coloured cheeks tighten from her shy smile.

With my eyes set on hers, I don't move.

"What?"

"His birth certificate," she repeats. "Not only would it make it official, but I also think it would send your father a message. Maybe... he'll back off."

I scoff, "He won't."

"Still," my beautiful girlfriend insists. "I want him to have your name, too, and I'm sure he wants it. We can also ask him if it makes you more comfortable."

I'm still at loss for words, looking at her.

"Dylan, baby," she calls.

He visibly huffs before slowly turning back to us and begrudgingly walking toward us.

"Mum," he hisses. "Don't call me baby in public."

"Right," she giggles, unaffected.

"Daaaad," he groans, and I finally snap out of my stupor, chuckling nervously. "Tell her not to call me baby. I'm no baby."

"Sorry, bud. She's the boss." I shrug my shoulders.

Willow ignores us, looking slightly down at him to say, "I was telling your dad I think it's about time you have his surname, too. What do you think?"

His eyes widen, looking at her, then at me. Then at her again, and I'm suddenly terrified. What if he doesn't agree? What if, despite calling me dad, he doesn't see me as one?

Fuck. I've never had my confidence wavering this hard.

"Oh," he mumbles, now deep in thought. "Will I no longer have yours?"

My heart somersaults, and I think Willow's does, too, with the way she instantly lets go of me and hugs him to her. He's squished against her chest—that's how tall he is.

"No, no," she coos. "You'll have both of our names. Both of us, *always.*"

He keeps quiet for a long time, deep in thought as fear creeps inside me.

What if he doesn't want it?

"Why haven't we done that yet?" he asks instead, the light blue hues of his irises curiously peeking up at me. It's still daunting at times, how much we look alike.

I shrug, not really knowing why. I guess it never crossed my mind before. The only thing that would change would be the papers. In my life, my head, and my heart, Dylan is my kid. There aren't enough papers in this world that can tell me otherwise.

"I've thought about it often," Willows mumbles. "But I wanted you to understand what it means and have a say in it, too." Then she glances at me before continuing, "I feel like it's time."

"When can we do it?"

"Oh, um..." she trails off.

I'm still in the same place, looking at them. At a loss for words and movements. I have probably turned into stone by now.

"Whenever you both want," she finally answers.

"I...yes." Still wordless.

"Dad," Dylan calls, coming up to me.

He pulls on my arm, motioning his hand for me to bend down to his height. And finally, I move.

"The ring," he whispers.

What?

"What?" I stutter, dumbstruck.

"The ring," he hisses. "Ask her now."

Oh. *Oh*!

"Now?" I ask, and he nods eagerly. "Yeah, yeah."

"Everything alright, boys?"

Looking directly at her, my throat bobs up and down with nerves. *Now?* I mean, I have been carrying it around for a while...Nana and Jake have been making sure to let me know that they expect it soon, leaving hints and jabs here and there. but...right now?

She's gorgeous. Her dark brown locks are long and flowing over her arms and back. The fair skin is flushed on her cheeks from the warm temperature inside. There's an aura in here. The walls of this aquarium are pitch black with the only light coming in through the big central water tank.

It creates these ever-moving blue hues, covering everything around her. The way the shadows created by the water move over her face, highlighting her cheekbones and that special glint in her eyes, draws me in because, in so many ways, she's like water. Transparent, pure, and capable of creating life.

She created Dylan and unintentionally brought me back to mine. Just like water, I need her to survive.

"Daaaad," he groans.

"Yes," I answer hastily. "Everything's...peachy."

She's sceptical, though, suspicion clear in her eyes.

"If neither of you wants to add the surname, it's—"

"*No*!" We both cut her off at the same time.

Bewildered at our—*my*—awkwardness, I take the courage to do what I've been wanting to do for a while. It never felt like the perfect moment before because of this. This is where it was always supposed to happen.

My knee lowers, hitting the ground just as my hands fumble with the inside pocket of my jacket. Willow gasps, and from the corner of my eye, I see Dylan's excited jumps.

"Willow," I start as soon as the box hits my fingertips. "For years, I was told to be patient because time heals and dwindles feelings for those who no longer are part of our lives. Well, they lied." I laugh nervously, looking at her shiny eyes. "There wasn't a year, month, week, or day where you've been less loved by me. Even when we were apart, and goddamn those were the longest seven years of my life, but they were worth it. *So fucking worth it.* Do you know why?"

She shakes her head, her hand covering her mouth, not hiding her light sobs.

"Because it brought me back to you. Having you *and* Dylan in my life made all of that pain worth it. There's no other option for us than being stuck together, and I can't see my life without being able to call you my wife. So, will you marry me?"

With both hands on her face and Dylan excitedly telling her to say yes, she keeps quiet for a moment. The silence becomes deafening and heavy in a room where I know everyone else is focused on us. I don't care; my sole focus is her. It always will be.

"Yes," she hiccups the word out, and everyone cheers. Loud.

I don't know anyone else in here, but they are cheering like they're my best friends. And inside, I am, too.

All tension dissipates from my body, and I stand up, getting the ring out and sliding it onto her finger. Then I kiss her, and our mouths mould together perfectly, lighting my body up with fireworks. It never gets old.

"Eww," Dylan groans. "Stop." Wedging between us, we chuckle, hugging him tight.

Our journey wasn't easy, but this is. Loving her is easy—and that's what's supposed to happen when you love your soulmate.

"W-wait," she stutters, pulling us slightly apart. "So, you don't want to change the surname's situation?"

I deadpan. "I just asked you to marry me, and you think I don't want my son to have my surname?"

"Well–"

"Yes, I want to," I answer her.

"I do, too," Dylan chimes in. "I should have had it to begin with."

My heart must have grown twice in size because it feels like it's bruising my ribs with how hard and fast it's beating. My head feels light with the amount of happiness floating through me.

There's nothing that can beat this feeling. Not the ghost from our past, or the threats from our future. If we stick together, nothing can tear down what we have built.

Right here and now, I have everything I have always wished for. It was a long, windy, and steep road, but in the end, I knew it was leading me to her.

Deep down, I've always known I would always find my way back to Willow.

BONUS #1

Willow

Electric blue fills in my hazy mind.

Otherwise, I'd be panicking by now.

The light-headedness helps me stay afloat. If I was fully conscious, everything would be done. This is serious.

Liam stands in front of me, the hottest I've seen in years, reminding me fully, how he could be doing much better out there. Instead, he chose me. *We chose each other.*

His blond hair is lighter, due to sun exposure during these sunny days of summer. And, unlike every other day, it is also perfectly combed and held in place with some hair wax. It has grown, nearly hitting his shoulders now.

His suit sits perfectly on his tall frame, the sandy-toned pants hug his muscles, while the matching jacket frames the white button. The outfit is completed by a little set of dried wildflowers, that match my bouquet.

Never, in a million years, I had hoped this day would come. The day we become husband and wife.

"From the moment I set my eyes on you when we were five years old, I knew. Right then and there, filled with tears and snot over being abandoned by your big brother," A few chuckles sound from my side, cutting him off for a few seconds. "I knew that there was no one else but you for me in this world."

His words draw me in, finally blocking the rest of the world. *It's just the two of us.*

My cheeks feel cold from the fat tears streaming down my face and for once I am glad, I took Hazel's advice. This woman wouldn't take a no for an answer and almost ate me alive when I insisted on using my regular makeup.

But now, as I ugly cry in front of the love of my life, as he professes his vows to me, I am thankful. To be honest, it's a miracle I am still standing up.

Our hands are locked in together, tight, as the comforting energy flows through him to me. Liam has become my rock, and a life without him is unfathomable.

"That was proved in the seven years we have spent apart. I tried—and failed—to fill the void you had left in my heart. And that was because you were the only one who could heal my broken heart and restore my damaged soul. I thought for a long while that I would never be whole again, but you proved me wrong. That night, everything changed. I found my way back to you and on top of that, I gained a son; a *family*. I love you. I always have and I always will, after all, we are two halves of a whole: soulmates."

His voice is firm and confident, hiding the nervousness that I can see in his eyes—that I can feel in his shaky hands.

His eyes lock on mine, expectantly and I freeze, taken aback by the emotion in them. As the silence stretches, it's only when someone annoyingly coughs that I stop the trance we are in. Sparing my right-hand side a glance, I notice my brother, sitting right in front of me with wide eyes and tilting his head maniacally.

A pull on my dress, makes me look to the opposite side. "It's your turn, Mum," Dylan hisses.

The chapel is small but still, the silence is so deafening that its acoustic makes his words quite audible to everyone.

"Oh god," I startle, realising that it's my turn to speak. Everyone chuckles and I add, "How am I even going to top that?"

There aren't a lot of people here with us. But it is just as we wanted it. The small group of guests, filling in the small chapel, make up the rest of the world. Overall, we might have around thirty guests. Forty, tops.

Most of the guests are coworkers on my and Liam's side, but there are a few who are the most important for both of us. At the front row, on my side, I have Nana, and Jake alongside Ethan who is followed by Hazel. All four of them are on baby duty, taking care of the most recent addition to the family. *Jeremy.*

Not long after I graduated and got a job as a primary school teacher, we found out I was pregnant. While I was terrified, having just recently landed a job, Liam was ecstatic. Over the moon with excitement.

Thankfully, the school I am working for was amazing about it, since I was able to finish the school year before giving birth, not affecting my contract for that season.

It was magical, the pregnancy.

It was a different experience from the first time. For Jeremy, I constantly felt protected, supported, and loved. Liam was relentless, always there for me and the baby once he was out. It made me as happy as it broke my heart, that all of that eagerness was his way of filling the little void of missing all of that with Dylan.

And Dylan.... He turned out to be the best big brother I could ever expect him. He shares, he talks to him and even tries to play.

Behind my family and two closest friends, is Arthur. My old university teacher and best friend, sitting right next to my old boss, Shilah. She came with her husband and daughter. In the third row, we have a not-so-little Abby with her mother—unfortunately, her parents recently divorced. Out of these people, only two are blood-related but they have become my family.

My parents' and Liam's parent's absence speaks volumes but we both agreed they were not to be invited.

This day is for *us.* To celebrate our love. *Our family.*

"I am a firm believer that we all have our half out there," I start with a shaky voice. That is when Dylan moves permanently to my side, holding my trembling hand. "And that no matter what circumstance throws at you, fate will always gravitate that one person back to you. I was lucky enough to meet mine at the age of five," I chuckle, nervously. "However, I had lost hope. Losing you made me realise that you were it and that I could never find you again. But that pushed me through, thinking you'd still be happy. Look at how wrong I was..."

"Baby," Liam whispers, wiping the tears running down my cheeks. "You don't-"

I shush him, "But the universe knows what is doing. The fates ended up bringing you back to me. And I am so grateful because as my other half, you are my happiness. The love of my life."

Keeping my eyes trained on the blue irises that always carry me to a calm ocean, I continue, "I can't say there was an epiphany where I realized that I loved you because every time I look back on our memories, the feeling has never changed, it only grew. Even throughout all those years, we were apart, nothing changed. When we locked eyes again, everything came rushing back in. As I looked into your eyes, I was reminded that there isn't any other soul in this universe that could make me this happy; *this whole.* In you, I found my best friend, my companion, my lover, my soulmate, and my home. *I love you, forever and always.*"

A harsh tug on my arm forces my face to land on his hands, and instantaneously, my eyes close welcoming the incoming kiss he's about to force on me.

"Mr Davis, not yet," the priest tuts, his words forcing our faces apart.

Liam grunts a begrudging agreement just as Dylan exclaims, "My time to shine!"

He jumps to the middle of us, like he often does, opening the wedding ring box and showing it to the guests before turning to us, the widest smile on his face.

Everyone chuckles at his antics. We quickly exchange the preset catholic vows as we place each other's rings on their rightful fingers.

"You can now kiss the bride," the priest announces as everyone stands up to applaud.

Liam lunges for me, twirling me and dipping me before smashing his lips onto mine.

"Come on."

"Liam, we have the first dance soon," I hiss.

This man's impulsivity has changed nothing over the years. On most days, it is blissful to break the routine that always threatens to cast shadows over our relationship, but on a day like this...

Everything is planned out to the last detail. Why is he steering off track?

People will be worried, wondering why we are not opening the party with our first dance.

"I know baby, we'll be just in time for it, don't worry," he calmly answers.

His eyes twinkle with the kind of mischief he always shows off when he is planning something. Very often a surprise, but what could it be on this day?

If he is looking for a hidden corner to seduce me, in a moment we're so tight on time, I swear I'll–

"Liam, I told you we are not having sex while all these people are looking for us an-"

"Shush," he cuts me off. "I *will* fuck you somewhere in here tonight, that you can be sure of. But this is not it...yet," he smirks. *Ugh, that smirk is my undoing.*

Being reckless is not part of my DNA, God knows it isn't. But Liam always manages to get me to agree with his crazy ideas. Deep down, I enjoy it. He reminds me that we still are young and free. Despite having a family and responsibilities, we can afford to let go occasionally.

"Then wha-" my voice dies in my throat just as we turn the curb, leaving Jake's property.

In front of us stand the two last people I'd thought I'd see today.

"Willow," the brunette woman whispers in front of me.

Shiny brown eyes stare at me, a world's worth of emotion in them, just as I stagger back one step. Her face is slightly contorted in a tiny pout, though she barely looks her age.

Almost like the years haven't gone through her, not since I left.

"No, Liam-" With another step back, I try to leave but his hand tightens on mine, gently tugging me to him.

"Baby, I'm here," he whispers while his other hand cradles my cheek. "I won't leave you alone. My parents can't be salvaged but yours still can, how about we give them one last chance?"

He is right.

One thing I have learned from therapy is I should have let my brother and parents know everything. I was a minor and traumatised. Telling them everything and allowing them to take things from there should have been the right path.

But I refused to admit the truth out loud to myself, let alone someone else. It was harsh on everyone and I wasn't fair either. Forcing Jake to not do anything about it, refusing to tell my parents the truth, and worse, leaving Liam without telling him...

There were several serious mistakes on my side too. I can't make them accountable for everything, either.

Maybe it's time...

With a slight nod, I notice Liam's tension leave his body, before he adds, "I'm right here," he whispers. "You can do this."

"Hi Mum," I greet her. Just then, I hear footsteps and see my father walk up to us too. "Dad..."

Monica, my mother takes a few steps towards us, just as my father reaches us. Her hands stretch, attempting to hold mine and I can't help but take a step back, forcing my back against Liam's strong chest.

Understanding my reluctance she lowers her hands while straightening her spine, "We didn't mean to intrude but we couldn't let this day pass without at least trying... We know now... everything."

"Yes," she breathes out. "The truth is out now."

"Now I understand why Jake and your grandmother were so angry with us," she starts. "We couldn't understand. While you looked traumatised, you never fully admitted what happened, we thought it was just your fear of facing the consequences for being reckless. But we should have known, we should have," she chuckles humourlessly.

"You were never reckless," Stephen, my father chimes in for the first time, his quiet voice laced with pain.

"If you had told us, Willow, we would have-"

"But I didn't," I cut her off. "I was too scared."

"We should have known," she disagrees. "The signs were all there... Oh dear, I am so sorry."

Monica breaks out crying, a sob freeing itself from her throat, just as Stephen holds on to her. Then he emotionally adds, "*We* are sorry."

"I know," I quietly add, Liam's hand squeezing mine, letting me know he is still here. "Everyone made mistakes but I still think you should have stood by me."

"Yes," Liam whispers to my hair, pleased I am standing up to myself.

"We should have," Stephen adds. "But you need to understand that, the way we were raised-"

"That excuse won't work with me," I cut him off, tilting my chin up and looking into both sets of eyes, one at a time. "The woman that raised one of you is the same one who welcomed me with open arms. The same woman that with just one look at me, she knew. She knew and never needed to ask or have me tell her about it. She believed in me and helped unconditionally, *for years.*"

"It was different back when-"

"—and," I cut in again, wanting to be heard on top of everything else. "Now that I am a mother, I can't bear the possibility of thinking that my kids can't come to me when they need me. I would bend over backwards if it meant I was giving my kids what they needed from me."

"You are right," Monica wails, hastily grabbing my hand. "We realised that too late. And while we can't excuse our behaviour in the past, all we can ask is for you to give us a second chance. A chance to show you how much we regret everything and want to make right by you."

Sparing Liam a glance he nods, telling me to do whatever I want because he wouldn't be any other way. My other half, my better side. He is always encouraging me to go beyond my limits, step over my comfort zone and never regret anything in life.

"I don't know if..." I pause, trying to find the correct words. "I am not sure if I will ever be able to fully forgive you."

"Oh no," she cries harder, holding onto Stephen, just as he looks at me with his shiny dark green eyes.

I notice the moment hope starts to abandon them and it stings.

"But, I..."

"Go on," Liam encourages me.

"I don't think I can live the rest of my life without my family whole again. Especially now, that Nana's health is rapidly decreasing... I want her to see everyone together and happy. It's also important that Dylan and Jeremy have at least one set of grandparents. So, I am glad you decided to try and make amends. Thank you."

The couple in front of us nods, unsure of how to act and my body melts into Liam's afraid of the next step. I miss my parents. I miss hugging them but I am not sure how to go about it.

A light bump on my shoulder catches my attention, looking up I notice the most handsome set of blue eyes looking right back at me, "Go hug them."

"Right," I chuckle nervously.

All it takes is a couple of steps for them to rush to me and hug me at the same time. It's tight and warm and it sends the right rush of emotions through my body.

Flashbacks from my happy childhood, all the good moments come rushing back into me as I finally break down crying in their arms. Years of pent-up sadness and disappointment releasing. It's almost palpable as I feel it abandoning my body, showing me how much I need this.

One last step that my heart needed in its recovery journey.

"Let's get inside, people are waiting for us," Liam chimes in after a while.

We all nod, as I run back and latch myself to him. *My safe place.*

Dylan, as always, is giving everyone a show, dancing like he is the star of this event. Ethan, Jake, and Nana's attention are fully on him, while Hazel holds a laughing Jeremy in her arms. They're all distracted, missing the two people following after Liam and I, until we're right by their sides.

My brother and grandmother do a double take before their mouths silently open agape. With the tense silence surrounding us, it's the usual oblivious and happy person cutting it off, "Who are you?"

Liam chuckles, and everyone else's bodies visibly relax. "Son, meet Monica and Stephen, your grandparents."

"Hi Dylan," Monica bends slightly, to match his growing height. "I'm your Nana!"

"I already have a Nana," he bluntly answers, stunning everyone into silence. "Are they your parents?" He asks Liam.

"They're mine," I finally answer.

"Nana?" He calls *my* grandmother. While being eerily silent until now, she finally takes her eyes off Monica and Stephen, sparing my son a glance. He takes a few steps closer to her and bends, whispering to her ear–loudly, "Is this the pretentious bitch you're always talking about?"

Several gasps sound, mine included. A couple of choking sounds to my left and I notice Jacob trying to contain his laughter. With my ear and neck burning with embarrassment, I start, "Dylan, you can't speak like-"

"I said what I said," Nana cuts me off. "Don't blame the boy for my words."

Always the first to defend him. And me too.

Nana has been the rock for this little family I have created. From treating Liam like her own grandson–thus making Jake jealous several times–to caring for Dylan and Jeremy so deeply. I couldn't have asked for better people to surround me.

Everything has been...easier. Lighter. *Happier.*

"I am working on being better," Monica admits.

Stealing her a glance, I can see the regret all over her face. It's visible she is trying.

"You better, or I'll bust your ass. You will never be too old for that," Nana scolds.

Everyone chuckles lightly, the tension finally dissipating. With a small smile, I look at Dylan, his sparkly blue eyes wide and curious, assimilating everything around him.

He's a pre-teen now and just around twenty inches shorter than me. No doubt, I'll soon be surpassed by my firstborn. The mere thought squeezes my heart, it was hard as it is, to watch him start middle school last autumn.

"Baby," Liam's soothing voice catches my attention. "Let's go."

"Where?" I ask. "I can't handle any more surprises."

He smirks with a mischievous glint in his eyes. But just as his mouth opens to answer me, Dylan beats him to it, "I want to go too, what is the surprise?"

Liam's mouth snaps closed just as his eyes widen when he looks at Dylan. *Oh my god!*

"Well-" Liam starts but he's cut off by my brother.

"Dy, Buddy... Stop being a Mummy's boy and leave your parents alone for a moment."

"I'm not!" He whines. "And I have. I want in too, at least once today."

"I'll save you a dance," I kiss his cheek. "Is that okay?"

He side-eyes me, before huffing a yes. Just then Abby shows up, stealing his full attention. Dylan brightens up the moment he sets eyes on her and I am so thankful he was fast to make friends in this city. In a flash, he's off his seat and starts running after her.

"Let's go," I am hastily pulled by my husband.

It's weird, that after all of these years. After all this suffering, I managed to find my way back to him. After everything we managed to heal enough to forgive and love each other unconditionally.

With a quick look at everyone, I see my parents and Nana fussing over Jeremy, while Jake, Ethan, and Hazel hold the same knowing smirk in their eyes. *Oh god, they know.*

"You're mad," I complain as we walk away from the guests. "The house is full of people. Someone can catch us!"

His intentions were clear the moment Dylan left him speechless. Their relationship is still growing and developing but it is obvious that Dylan still scares him sometimes maybe because they're too much alike.

"Let them," he growls, pulling me inside the bathroom with him.

Locking the door, he turns to me, his eyes dark with desire. With slow movements, his gaze scours over me, like a predator scours their prey.

"I can't bear to look at you in this dress anymore. I need to fuck you in it." His hand lands on the side of my neck, just as he presses his body to mine, lighting it up.

"You're being crude," I warn.

"You secretly love it," he breathes out against my mouth and I shudder. *I do.*

The past few years leading to this moment have been a rediscovering of my sexuality. And Liam has been the perfect partner for it. He has always been patient with my timings and respectful of my limits while still being open-minded and willing to help me push my limits into new realities.

I have won back the control that had been taken from me. It has been quite an enjoyable journey with this man by my side.

His head moves towards me, grazing his lips over mine. We're so close, tangled in each other, with the warmth of his body invading mine.

"I'll be everything you want, baby. Crude and dirty. Sweet and romantic."

"You are everything I want," I whisper.

"Good," he smirks. "Because I can't wait any longer to consummate our marriage."

I shriek when his hands suddenly grip my waist and lift me in the air. My reflex is to hold on to his neck, just as he sits me down on the counter right next to the toilet sink.

"Someone can get in!" My words are weak and trembling from the soft caress his hands place on my legs, slowly bunching my long skirt up.

"I locked the door," he whispers, looking straight into my eyes. "Relax, love. I'll make you feel good."

His strong fingers outline the limit of my stockings before venturing further up, into the apex of my legs. It forces a gasp out of me.

"That's it," he coos. "Feels good, doesn't it?"

"Y-yes," I stammer with a heaving chest.

"You're so beautiful." Hot gushes of breath fan my neck, while the cold counter cools my bottom. It's a heavy contrast on my straining body, but so pleasant at the same time.

It only heightens he finds my core, pushing my lingerie to the side and caressing my folds.

"Always so wet for me," he growls.

The impatience is clear in the way his voice wavers.

"Liam, I need you," I beg, needing the coil in the bottom of my belly to be soothed.

"I'm right here," he answers, and the sound of his zipper opening sounds.

His head grazes my entrance, eliciting a quiet moan from me. Only this man can get me to such a high state of vulnerability and not have me worried. In his hands I am *safe.*

"Wait," I exclaim, pushing his chest slightly away. He looks at me confused and I add, "I am not on the pill yet."

"We can have twenty kids, for all I care." He growls, his cock still grazing my core, teasing me. *Torturing me.* "But I can go get one if you want to."

"I want what you want," I admit, letting him take the lead.

His hand grabs my chin and lightly squeezes, making me look at him. His eyes are locked on mine, his mouth slightly open, with a hair's worth of space between us.

He is beautiful like this. Dishevelled hair, swollen lips, and eyes hazy from desire. So transparent and raw.

The eye contact has been crucial for me. It's a grounding detail that I need, to keep me in the present. It allows me to enjoy it to the fullest and reminds me of who is here with me, who's making me feel so good. So happy. So full.

"I want to fuck my *wife* seven ways into Sunday, with nothing between us," he whispers just as he pushes in.

"Oh god-" He swallows my moan with a ravishing kiss.

My back slowly hits the mirror, just as he fills me to the hilt but I don't care anymore. Just as always, Liam is capable of taking me beyond my limits, making me forget all my fears and worries, and allowing me to live in the moment just like he does.

Worrying about nothing but the two of us, and how perfectly together we fit.

"I love this," he groans, leaning back and watching me intently. His eyes move from my flushed face to my bouncing chest and keep lowering to the area we are joined together. "I love seeing you fall apart in my hands, and completely let go."

"Oh Liam," I moan, his words make it so much more intense.

"The trust you have in me turns me on so fucking much. Fuck!"

He speeds up, getting lost in the moment, just like I do.

Still, as we come apart together, I can't help but remind myself of how lucky I am, to have found him again.

We were strong enough to heal and fix everything. Strong enough to find our way to happiness and save our family.

It's all I could ask for. Liam is my everything. *Liam is my home.*

BONUS #2

Jake

Being the entertaining uncle that I have been for the past sixteen years has been amazing. Conducting fun sleepovers where the boys don't need to clock in by eight or nine in the evening and being able to let out my childish side without being judged is just my thing.

But the past day has not been fun. At all.

Being the responsible parent where I need to be the one cooking, dressing, making sure they are in school on time or go to bed early enough—it's fucking torture.

Remind me to never impregnate a woman. *Ever.*

"Come on Dy. You're sixteen, help me out, man!! I whine.

"Aren't you the parent tonight?" The little—not so little—spawn of the devil teases by lifting one eyebrow. "I am just watching," he smirks.

I've created a monster. *Little shit.*

"Watching what? Me killing the three of us tonight? Can't you take pity on your *Funcle* and help while your mother is busy birthing another little shit, just like you?"

Instead of answering me, he plops down on the couch, placing his feet on the table. This kid is testing me tonight, he knows damn well his mother doesn't want him doing that.

"It's my turn to watch cartoons," Jeremy whines.

"Tough luck bro, I am watching my show." Dylan counters back, replacing the remote on the other side of the couch, away from his little brother.

They've been at each other's throats all day and I swear I don't fucking know how the hell my sister puts up with this.

I'll need to be carried out in a straitjacket by the time they return. *I am not kidding!*

"Give me the remote, little shit!" Jeremy yells, jumping into Dylan's belly.

Fuck. I need to be aware of what I say in front of Jer, he is in his copycat stage.

Rushing to them, I pick the younger kid up, before Dylan can retaliate.

"Fuck!" The curse comes out when Dylan still manages to pinch his brother on his leg. "Jeremy," I call ignoring the angering teenager behind me.

Placing Jeremy on the lone puffy chair, I warn. "You can't say curse words, they're bad!"

"But you just said it!" He cocks his head to the side.

I sigh, exasperated.

Not only is this kid right. I am also pushing my luck.

It's not like I can be a reliable authoritative figure after spending all these years, teaching them to be sneaky and sassy.

This is my karma. And she's a bitch, coming back to bite me in the ass when I need these two to behave the most.

If only Nana was still here to help.

They would have been in bed by now and the house wouldn't be hanging on a fucking thread. I have broken way too many plates and mugs, the dishwasher doesn't even work–I am sure I am the problem since it was working this morning.

But fuck, I'd give everything to have that woman back.

If there was someone other than Willow that these two obeyed right away, it was Nana.

"Do you think it'll take much longer for the baby to be here?" Dylan asks, keeping his focus still solely on the TV.

I fucking hope not.

"I am going to call your dad and see if he has news and afterwards, you two will go straight to bed. How about that?"

"Pleaseeeeee!" Jeremy whines, jumping and holding onto my arm, hanging his body on it. "I miss Mummy!"

I do too buddy. *I do too.*

Instead of having the opportunity to call my brother-in-law. My phone rings in my pocket, and I use my free hand to pick it up, "Hello?"

Both boys rush to me and lean in, trying to listen to anything.

"He's finally here!"

The three of us yell upon hearing the words we wanted.

"You guys can come for a quick visit only because she must get some sleep after. Those two need to go to sleep too, but I know they won't be able to before they see their little brother."

"Everything's alright with both?" I ask.

"It was longer than Jeremy's and she struggled a lot more this time around. The little shit didn't seem keen on getting out, but my wife is a wonder woman and made it seem easy."

"Liam, watch your language," my little sister's tired voice sounds and my chest swells.

Happiness. Pride. Excitement.

All of those, course through my veins, getting me anxious to get there.

"We'll be there in twenty," I inform Liam before hanging up on him.

"Let's go see Mummy and meet the baby!"

"Let's go!" Dylan exclaims, jumping into action right away.

"Mummy!" Jeremy screeches, jumping out of my hold and running to her bed.

Luckily, Liam picks him up before he can reach her, carefully sitting him next to her.

"Buddy, we need to be careful with Mummy for a few weeks. Be gentle, ok?"

Jeremy nods and slowly sits down by his mum's side. She's holding our newest family member against her chest while her other arm stretches so her second son can tuck himself against her. I come closer as well, standing next to the bed and leaning over her shoulder with Dylan right in front of me, peeking too.

The baby is partly covered by the hospital's blue blanket. Only the top part of his bare head is showing, along with his tiny hand sticking out in a clutched fist.

"Does he have a name yet?" Dylan asks, focusing on the baby.

My baby sister looks at him with a gentle smile on her face—as she always has. I may be the older brother, but she's the one I look up to. The way her heart has stayed gentle and kind through all the pain, and the way she finds strength and resilience to keep going. The strongest person I've ever met.

"Not yet, we wanted to wait for you guys, and decide together."

"Bumblebee?" Jeremy chimes in, touching my newest nephew on the nose.

"Don't be stupid," Dylan sighs, annoyed. "We can't use a car name on a car!"

"Dylan, don't offend your brother."

"Sorry, mum."

"How about Derek?" Liam tries.

"Ugh, no!" I counter. "Jake?"

"We're not naming him after you," he snickers, side-eyeing me before sitting down on the chair next to Willow's bed.

"Well, it's a damn pretty name!" It doesn't matter what I say. No one values me in this family.

"Not for my brother." Dylan scrunches his nose.

He extends his hand, grazing his index on the kid's fist. It opens and closes encasing his finger in his tiny hold. It makes Jeremy giggle when he softly tugs his older brother's hand, surrendering everyone to his cuteness.

It doesn't last long, though.

The newborn baby suddenly tugs Dylan's hand rather harshly for someone who has been out of the womb for less than five hours, provoking a loud "ouch" out of my sixteen-year-old nephew. As if that wasn't enough, he almost hits his head on Willow's.

Then a wail breaks out, making the baby fuss and cry right after.

"He kicked me!" Jeremy cries, holding his ribs.

"Jesus Christ," I mutter, picking him up before things take a turn for worse.

All the while, Liam is trying to pry the baby's hand off Dylan's finger, *unsuccessfully.*

"He's not letting go of me," Dylan whines, tugging his finger.

When he does, the soft wails turn into loud cries and soon the once cute baby turns into a satanic banshee.

"I can't-" Liam grunts.

"Stop," Willow sighs, annoyed. "Let me try. Please, neither of you move."

"But he's hurting me!"

"Don't be a crybaby," I taunt him.

He glares at me with his finger still stuck in the—*born from hell*—baby's hand.

He is still shrieking when Willow manages to pry his fingers off, finally releasing Dylan. Then, she calmly adjusts him, closer to her chest. She lowers the hospital gown, popping one of her boobs out and I can't help but look away startled. I mean, she's still my baby sister.

She's unfazed about it, though, focused on getting him to eat. The kid stops crying as soon as his mouth latches to the nipple, slurping and gurgling sounds filling the space between us. *Damn.*

Liam and Dylan ignore me, hypnotised by the tiny creature holding on to milk for dear life.

"Babies are little monsters when they're hungry," I comment, positioning myself behind them, doing the same. Jeremy's head leans against my chest, most likely doing the same.

Fuck. He's so wrinkly and ugly.

"JAKE!" Willow gasps her eyes jumping to mine, wide in disbelief.

"Oh shit, did I say that out loud?"

Everyone is laughing except for my dear sister, who looks mad.

"Whoopsies?" I smile awkwardly.

"Babies are wrinkly when they're born," Liam agrees. "But they're still cute. Especially mine."

"Let's agree to disagree."

"Now that you mention it..." Dylan trails off. "He is kinda ugly."

Willow frowns, "No, he isn't. He looks just like you."

"You wish, mum," Dylan counters. "I know I am the favourite, but I'm not even blonde and by watching his bald head, he'll be just like dad. *Blonde.*"

"Oh shush, he's just a baby." She waves us off. "He'll grow into a handsome boy."

It's official. I've heard this sentence three times by now. Nothing can beat a mother's love.

"Yeah, yeah. Cute and annoying, if he follows his brothers' steps." I deadpan. "Still no name?"

"We're so indecisive."

"I don't blame you, what could you name such a wild baby?" Everyone chuckles at my words.

Dylan was calm but all smiley and gooey. Jeremy cried a lot at first but became a shy kid. He's more outgoing only with people he is comfortable but this one... He was a struggle to be born according to Liam, and has already created havoc in a matter of minutes.

"Yeah, out of the three of them, he is the wildest one. Didn't give me a break at all during the pregnancy and it's not slowing down now."

"OH!" Dylan exclaims, having his eureka moment. "How about Wilder?"

Silence follows, as everyone ponders, all eyes on the little famished dobby look-a-like. It's a good suggestion though. The temperamental side of Liam seems to have been passed down to all his offspring and so far, this one seems the worst one.

If he is the wildest one of the three, it's a suitable name.

"I dig it," I comment first.

"Oddly enough, I like it too." Liam agrees.

"Are you guys sure? Isn't it a little... unconventional?"

"What's unconventional?" Jeremy asks.

"Out of the ordinary," Dylan deadpans."

"What is ordinary?" Jeremy asks.

"Not normal," I finally answer, putting a rest on the continuous questions.

"I mean, what's even normal about us?" Dylan continues. "Teenage parents, who reunited after how many years and now keep trying for a girl, but end up with temperamental boys, instead. Not to mention the irresponsible uncle in the mix? Unconventional is good. And it suits the little gremlin. He's been a bad boy from the start."

"Who are you calling irresponsible?" I smack his head.

He groans in pain, but then looks at me, mischief in his eyes. "We were supposed to be in bed already."

Oh, it's on!

"Your dad called and-"

He smirks. "We weren't in bed when Dad called."

The nerve of this kid.

"I was trying to get you to-"

"Jake, you're too permissive." Willow's head shakes and Liam tries not to laugh at me.

"These little shits ignore me and do as they wish. You don't have kids, you have demons!"

Desperation is a reality. *They'll drive me crazy.*

All the years I have yearned for kids of my own, evaporate into thin air whenever I have my nephews for more than a couple of hours.

"It's your fault, you always wanted to be the cool uncle. No one takes you seriously," Willow tuts, unimpressed.

"Excuse me for being fun to hang out with. It's-"

"Dylan," my sister cuts me off. "Please do as your uncle says when you guys go back home. We need things to go smoothly when we're back home. You're sixteen, you're old enough to know when to behave."

Her tone is assertive, but not harsh and Dylan nods instantly.

"Of course, Mum," he answers in such an innocent voice I almost see a halo forming on top of his head. "I just wanted to tease him a bit, he needs to get ready for when he has his kids."

"As if," I scoff.

"With the number of women you pull, I am still surprised no one has shown up with a baby at your door, yet."

"Because I wrap it up," I answer. "I'm responsible."

Liam scoffs, "I did it too, and look at the sixteen-year-old right in front of you."

"In your situation, it's called fate dear brother-in-law. *Destiny.*"

"Wow, the womanizer believes in destiny?" Willow jokes, chuckling.

Then, she straightens herself raises Wilder's and places him on her side with his face on top of her shoulder, softly patting his back.

"With your story, who wouldn't, Lo? Look at how far you've gotten!" I kiss the top of her head. "I am so proud of you!"

I am.

And jealous too. I, too, once had this kind of love and relationship. *Or so I thought.* But unlike my little sister and brother-in-law, we were not meant to be. Fate wasn't on our side like it was on theirs and I envy them a whole lot for it.

Instead, my fate is to be a never-ending bachelor, who is too scorned to trust that someone could ever love me for who I am. *If she didn't, who would?*

But I don't let the useless sadness linger in my heart for too long. Not when it comes to my sister. This woman right here went through hell and back. She withstood every curve life threw at her and turned it into something good, whether it was a lesson or growth. She took the bad and turned it into love and prosperity.

That's something not everyone can do, I know I wouldn't.

Willow found her way back to her soulmate and found her happy ending. For years, we thought Nana was the glue keeping us together but I've realised it wasn't. It's my sister.

No one can fill in her shoes or her place in this family.

She's the heart and soul, giving us all the strength and inspiration we need.

Willow may not create havoc in her wake like a hurricane, but she's just as resilient. Like the flowers that bloom in the desert. They're beautiful and delicate creations that grow despite the hardships they have to face.

The End

BACK TO LIFE – PREVIEW

ONE

Arthur Adell

Looking around, I force myself not to cringe at the shitty state of the building. There is more visible cement and mould than the white paint that was used to cover these walls. But then again, what is it that one can expect from a place that survives solely on charity? As much as Safe Haven provides a safe environment for dozens of kids, it doesn't make miracles in comfort.

I help out, monetarily and as a handyman, but there's only so much that it is enough for. Every day there are new young adults, and worse, teenagers, coming here asking for help. The fact that they can keep afloat is a miracle in itself.

Hopefully, I can help fix this one bit soon as well.

And there are arseholes like the one in front of me, who could have it all and refuse it. Instead, he keeps frequenting the centre and while he helps as much as he can, I know it's still a burden for the staff.

What they use to help him out, could be used for someone else, that's for sure.

The old wooden chair squeaks under my weight as I lean forward, setting both my elbows on the table separating me from Thomas.

"How's the boyfriend?" I ask in a playful whisper, trying to start the conversation through the easier route.

"Meh," he answers, nonchalantly. But I see it, the way his bright blue eyes twinkle with mischief and his lip tugs up on one side. "He was too clingy for me, I got fed up."

Jesus fucking Christ. Kids these days, change relationships like I change boxer briefs. Way too damn fast.

"And here I thought he was the one?" I joke and he chuckles, shaking his head. "I was expecting to be introduced and hoping to scare the shit out of him?"

"Ha, you wish," he counters, leaning back on the old chair showing off the old and frayed T-shirt.

I keep buying him new clothes, and this brat keeps refusing to use them, keeping the old and worn-out stuff.

"I scared him just fine on my own," he smirks but I see it doesn't reach his eyes, and his next words just confirm it. "With my trust issues."

I laugh along, not meaning it. But touching the subject will only make him clam up on me, and that is the last thing I want.

Knowing him for a while now, I already know what's the best way to keep him here, talking to me and opening up. Even if he keeps using sarcasm as his armour when he doesn't need to. Not with me.

But Thomas is right, he does have trust issues, a consequence of what his family has put him through for years on end. While I'd like to think he trusts me fully, deep down he must be thinking that' eventually, I'll disappoint him too, just like everyone else.

Too damn bad, I want to prove him wrong.

"Until when will you refuse to come to live with me, T?"

The blond kid in front of me huffs, annoyed at my insistence. Or is it persistence?

We've been going in circles for months now. But it seems as If I have rubbed off on him. *Too much may I add.*

"You have no obligation to take me in or even help me, I'll manage old man, stop being a thorn in my ass."

"You're being stupid, boy," I hiss. "I've been your godfather for three years now. From the moment you stepped into this place asking for help, not knowing how to make your family accept you, through all of those shitty moments in-between until your dad threw you out the moment you turned eighteen. You're close to turning nineteen now, remember?"

Once I moved here, after a month of barely getting through life with nothing but work to keep my dark brain occupied, a flyer from this place literally fell on my feet. It felt like a sign from Alexa. If not... A way to honour her and her memory.

It was perfect, an institution that was opened to help all kinds of kids in need, whether in partnership with orphanages or to someone who might need this place as a safe place.

I've seen it all, teenagers who run away from home after one of hundreds of beatings, having no safer place than this one to come. Or kids who starve at home but because they don't want to be put in the system they come here for free meals or snacks.

One thing that I have learned since I started volunteering here is that not everything is black and white. Sometimes, it's not just as simple as going to the Police to report what's happening.

Unfortunately, more times than not, justice—and the system—don't work in the kid's best interests.

"Yes," he grits out, looking away from me. Choosing, at this exact moment, that the bland and decaying room is more interesting than me. He's probably remembering how he begged me to let him stay at the centre and show everyone how he could turn his life around, by himself.

I promised to give him one year. And that deadline is almost over.

In these three years, I've learned just how full of life and love Thomas can be, and how he could be doing great things if he wasn't focusing on the wrong side of life. The darker one.

Ha, the hypocrisy is not lost on me. And yet, I want to see this kid thrive and have a normal life. I can fucking give him that.

"How about a loan?" I ask desperate, not really meaning it. "You come live with me and you go to University, you can study whatever the fuck you want, I told you. I'll pay your tuition and you'll pay me back once you have a proper and steady job, how about that?"

"And rent? Food?" He glances at me before looking back down. "Just...no"

Fuck this. And fuck his dad that taught him to be so fucking proud. *That prejudiced piece of shit.*

"Fuck that," I growl, "who do you think donates enough to this centre so that they can feed you and all the other kids? Do you think me making you a home-cooked meal will make you or me less of a man?"

"No, but-"

"No fucking buts," I tell him, trying to reason. "You're my only family in this damned city too, kiddo. Come on," I urge.

"Let me think about it," he sighs.

My body sags, whether from dejection or relief, is still unknown.

"Alright," I agree, hopeful this time around, he will think it through and will let me love him the way his parents should have. "I have an afternoon class in a few hours, do you need a ride?"

"Nah," he waves me off. "Mary needs me to fix the lights on the boy's shower room and some other stuff."

"I'll see you tomorrow, then?"

"Maybe," he counters, wiggling his eyes.

"No crazy shit, T," I warn. "And call me if you need, whatever time!"

"Got it, old man."

"I fucking mean it," I call out as he turns his back on me.

The last thing I see is his hand lifting from his forehead, in a salute movement, as he turns the corner, out of the spacious but rather empty living room we were hanging out in.

I am too fucking old for school. Even as a Professor. Especially as a Professor.

Rather curious to think that I feel right at home at Safe Haven, with broken kids, and feel misplaced and annoyed on University grounds, where just as similar—at least some—are trying to make someone out of themselves.

You were one of them at some point too, arsehole. Still... I hate this.

Well, Arthur, it's either this or staying home driving yourself crazy.

What's worse, is the fact that this year, school started right on my birthday. *Another year without her.* I'd rather be anywhere else but here today.

At least, no one else knows what day it is...

"Happy birthday, Mr Adell!" The Dean's secretary chirps from her desk.

Or maybe not.

Her exaggerated happy voice irks me and not in a good way. I, often, have to fight the urge to snap at her. It's not necessarily her fault I'm a bitter and moody arsehole. *But it is what it is.*

"Thank you, Miriam," I answer curtly, just as I always do.

It doesn't make her eagerness waver. *No.* She keeps on smiling brightly and batting her eyelashes at me. *What's that supposed to do?*

"Do you have all my paperwork?"

"Here, Sir."

The hairs on my neck rise and for the worst reason ever. How I fucking hate it when women call me *Sir.* Maybe it's my stupid brain jumping into unnecessary and chauvinistic conclusions, that every time women use this word their tone changes. *Or is it all in my head?*

Miriam stands up from her chair and raises both arms, holding up the beige paper cover to me. Her extended arms are quite close to each other, squeezing her chest and giving me a full view of her cleavage.

Fucking hell.

Snatching the papers from her hand, I grunt something similar to a thank you and walk away from the situation, heading towards my classroom.

The first day of school in September usually means freshmen. All of them seem to consistently come from La-la-land, with their heads on the clouds, assuming that University is just a continuation of High School.

Instead, they fall from their high horses once they see the amount of work they'll have to do if they want to graduate and have a degree.

With my head deep in thinking, I barely manage to notice a young girl—a student—dramatically waving at me while skipping in my direction.

"Hello Mr Adell," she greets, breathless, as if those light jumps could have been enough to tire her. Ha, s*uch a fragile flower.*

"Hello? Do I know you?"

"Oh, uh, no-" she chuckles nervously, threading her fingers through her long brown hair as her body keeps lightly swinging from one side to the other, a shy smile on her face. "My name is Taylor, I was wondering if I could attend your classes as an external student. I tried to enrol but there were no more spots."

"What is your degree about?"

"Ahm," she stammers, glancing down as her cheeks start to redden. "Social studies, but-"

"Then, my subject is not even required for you to graduate."

"No, but I really like Literature, and-"

"No," I answer.

"Oh," her mouth opens.

Then it closes and opens once again. It's not only her cheeks that are dark red now but all of her face and neck. The embarrassment visibly taking over.

"There are students who need this class to graduate, let's not undermine their deserved spot in my class, yeah?"

"But I won't bother anyone, I won't even speak! *Sir*, please..." She emphasizes that stupid word and I shudder in disgust.

"It's Professor Adell," I correct her. "And my answer is still no. Excuse me, but I have a class to teach."

With that, I leave her dumbfounded in the building's grey corridor, walking to the classroom where all of my students—hopefully—are waiting for me.

As soon as I open the doors to the classroom, I start to talk, without even sparing the seating students a glance, "Good morning. I am Professor Adell and I will be your teacher for the semester."

My bag settles on the table, as does the paperwork, once I reach it. Turning my back on the students, I write my surname on the board—yes even with a short surname, some still write it wrong.

"Not Mr Adell, nor my name—if you end up finding it out—, especially not Sir or Mr You can only call me Professor Adell—it'll save you all—*and me*—a lot of trouble."

As I finally turn around and watch the three rows of students sitting on the opposite side, all of them are looking at me. A few blankly, others with gaping mouths. Especially the girls.

There are a lot of girls... *Again.*

I hate the first day of school. I hate my birthday.

No, scratch that, *I hate my fucking life.*

Lying to myself won't get me anywhere. It doesn't matter how long it's been. There's still this heavy void that's feeding on me. One more year and nothing has changed. One more year and I am still as miserable as the year before.

To be honest, every new school year only reminds me of what I needed and never knew I wanted. *A love like theirs.*

But that's something I can't have. Because let's be real, who would be able to love an arsehole like me? *No one.*

The door bursts open as someone shows up, looking frantic.

"Oh my gosh, I am so sorry I am late!" The voice is undoubtedly female, resonating through the silent classroom. "Someone decided to fucking jump into the train line when the train was going through and almost died! We got stuck for forty-five minutes before the paramedics arrived and tended to the person. I am so, so, so sorry!"

My eye twitches at the sound of cursing inside my classroom. Is it hypocritical? Probably, since I curse every five minutes on a regular day—outside of work. But hearing it, inside my classroom and by a female... A student no less, makes me want to smash something.

Instead, I take a deep breath. Trying—and failing—to not become annoyed.

Sparing the *hurricane-girl* who dares bursting into my classroom a glance, I am rooted in place.

For the first time in years, my heart speeds up, warming me up. The heat creeps up my neck, unsettling me. In over ten years of teaching only one other person has caught my attention and for the completely wrong reasons—Willow.

She was a sheer image of the face that haunts my dreams at night. A living reminder of my dark past. And all I wanted was to hurt her enough to make her quit my subject. Not seeing her again, meant bliss in my fucked up brain.

But upon meeting Dylan, and seeing her single mother struggles, she quickly became a dear friend and the emotional support I had lacked until then. After her, I've never dared spare a glance at any other student. *Until now.*

A toffee brown-skinned girl stands at the entrance, panting as if she has just run a marathon to get here. Her long hair is braided tight on her scalp, with a few golden beads in between, decorating them. They're all directed to the same point, the top of the back of her head where they are joined together, falling over in a big ponytail.

The hairstyle, matches her outfit, a casual tight crop top, that shows her midsection. It's paired with washed-out jeans that hug her curves snugly, and a pair of beige high heels.

Who the fuck comes to school in heels?

It's only when a cough sounds from where the rest of her classmates are sitting, that I snap out of my reverie.

"Sit down," I grunt, avoiding looking at her again by fumbling with my paperwork.

No, she is not the only black woman in my classroom, nor the first I have ever taught. While one can't say that racism no longer exists–because it does, unfortunately–Europe is less problematic about race in comparison to other areas of the world.

Here in Portugal, regardless of your race, if a Portuguese citizen has good grades and struggles financially, the government will certainly provide a scholarship.

Then why is she the first one to catch my attention?

No, Arthur. Students are strictly off-limits for a reason.

She does as I ordered, unbothered by my harsh tone or the scowl on my face, plopping down on the first row.

I start the class by passing a couple of sheets from the list of books they'll have to read this semester, as well as the two main projects they'll have to work on, in the writing skill part of the subject.

"Those papers are to be returned to my desk by the end of the class. Copy by hand, take pictures whatever you prefer to do but those papers are due on my desk before the bell rings."

A small murmuring starts between the students but I ignore it, as I hand out the papers to the first row, purposely avoiding the girl who got late to my class.

"Now, I know you haven't had the time to start your readings yet but a class is a class. So today, we're informally debating about a book." Everyone groans in annoyance at my words as I walk back to my desk. "Let's talk about José Saramago and his book, Baltazar and Blimunda."

The slow murmur slows to a stop, as everyone suddenly gets quiet. It stretches as I quickly look at the different faces crowding the classroom.

Why the fuck do I teach again?

"How many of you have read the damn book?" I can't help but snap, earning a few startled bodies.

At least, half the students raise their hands.

"Alright, then what do you remember from it?"

"The Convent of Mafra's construction is depicted in the story," a blonde kid grunts while slumping further down on his chair.

"What century?" I ask but he shrugs.

"Eighteenth," a girl somewhere in the third or fourth row speaks.

"Yes, what else?" Silence, *again.*

From the corner of my eye, something catches my attention. The girl who had the nerve to arrive late has her chin resting on her hand, as her eyes are unfocused, slightly aimed up. *Is she daydreaming while I am asking questions about a book?*

"You," I call, loudly.

She startles and looks at me with wide eyes. When no one else speaks she looks around and behind her, confused. *Yep, definitely daydreaming.* Why does this feel like a deja vu?

When she notices all eyes—mine included—are focused on her, she meekly asks, "Me?"

"Yes," I snap. "Miss..."

"Keita," she answers confidently. "Zuri Keita."

"Miss Keita, what do you know about the book we were just talking about?"

"Are you really putting me on the hot seat because I was late? I will get you that damn justification tomorrow," she counters back with gritted teeth.

"I am putting you on the *hot seat* because you are daydreaming in *my* class. If you're not paying attention, may as well leave."

Deja-fucking-Vu. Sick, twisted bastard.

Crossing my arms, I lean back against the desk, watching intently as her eyebrows twist in a frown and her lips set in a grim and thin line.

"Daydreaming?" She scoffs loudly, earning a few gasps from her classmates and an intrigued, quirked eyebrow from me. "I was trying to remember more details of it."

"Well then," I taunt. "Don't keep to yourself, share with us."

"Baltazar was working in the Convent's construction and fell in love with Blimunda after meeting her. I remember she had a clairvoyance gift, which allowed her to see inside people, like their souls or auras. Not sure, but these two commoners met an alchemist priest who was working on the construction of a flying machine. However, in the period the story is set in, there's a regulatory entity called the Inquisition that chases down and eliminates everything they decide to be considered against their devotion. In the end, the priest flees and Baltazar gets arrested and convicted to burn for sorcery because he was caught flying the machine. Is that succinct enough?"

Not bad.

"That's the impartial perspective yes, but I was expecting something more insightful," I taunt.

Miss Keita rolls her eyes, and I can barely hide the satisfaction that surges through me. My lips twitch at the same time my stomach flips upon her reaction. How warped can one be? My body is lighting up just from irking her up.

"Right," she grits. "Thankfully, the author harshly criticises that period's society, especially the government—a monarchy may I add—and the church. Not that things have improved that much ever since, but the corruption and the clout back then were out of this world.

The representatives of the church took advantage of the religion to control the people. The trials and Autos-de-fé are detailed, and a clear example of the cruelty that existed through that period. Especially how ignorant, bigot and xenophobic people were back then. Unfortunately, a lot still are."

Pretty good answer.

At least she knows what she's talking about doesn't seem to be in here just because it is considered to be one of the easiest subjects. With the satisfaction of her correct answer, this time around, I allow my lips to tug a tiny bit at the edges but give nothing else away.

"Too many in my opinion," I agree with her. She freezes for a second so I add, giving her the recognition she deserves. "Well done Miss Keita."

She seems to be a strong-willed girl, and she knows her literature.

Good.

My student—*why does that word taste bitter in my mouth?*—slowly nods before looking down at her notebook and I add, "Just try and look focused next time, it shouldn't be hard."

There is a snickering sound but I ignore it just this once, focusing my attention on the wall behind the students. Anyone else would have been berated by snickering at me but her? It wouldn't be satisfying if she hadn't had the last word. *Or sound.*

ACKNOWLEDGEMENTS

Diving into this journey was never part of the plan. Writing was never supposed to become something so real and intense, something that I can't go without. Not anymore.

It started as an escape and quickly turned into a passion. And I am truly happy that found a new part of me that I didn't know I was missing. However, none of this would ever be possible without the amazing people in my life. Some were brought to me through the worlds of books, others have been with me through thick and thin and never stopped believing me. That's why I can't finish this book without mentioning them and showing my gratitude.

Thank you to Pedro, the love of my life, the one that even without being able to speak the language, always motivated me into achieving all of my goals. You're my best friend and my biggest supporter.

Thank you to Val, the best friend the world of books brought into my life. A true friend. Never in a million years would I think I'd find you, the kindest, bluntest person ever. You're there always and for everything, no exceptions, no condition and I wouldn't want it any other way. The Ice Queen of my heart.

Thank you to L. A. Cannon, Dai and Danique, the three other women that stumbled into my life through what we most had in common: books. I'll make sure to keep you by my side at all times. You are amazing friends, putting up with me during the most annoying times, never negating me the help I needed. You're trustworthy, kind and honest in a cutthroat world.

Without being able to forget sweet Steph, which without owing me anything, was able to help out a huge ton when I was in dire need of beta readers before sending out the draft to my editor. You were such a rockstar and a life saver!

Lastly, but just as important, my editor, Kirsty. Girl, you were godsent. I was terrified of finding a Grinch that would tear my work through the mud but you were graceful in sending through your suggestions and such a talented editor. I hope we can continue working in a near future.

To all my current and future readers. The biggest thank you. Without you this book wouldn't have seen the light of day. I hope I did you proud.

Obrigada,
Mel Véran

ABOUT THE AUTHOR

On the edge of reaching the "Big Thirties" (just two years away from now), the author is Portuguese and works as a certified Tourist Guide. Not only that, she is also a history and music addict and loves to travel around the world.

She is happily committed her job, her fiancé and her four-pawed child, her twelve year old dog. Writing is a recent passion that has turned her world upside down and has given her the opportunity of publishing this book, her debut.

Hopefully reading the book will make you as happy as it made her while writing it.

Instagram: **@melv.author**
TikTok: **@melvauthor**
Facebook: **Mel Veran**

www.ingramcontent.com/pod-product-compliance
Lightning Source LLC
LaVergne TN
LVHW010535160826
845677LV00013B/2888

* 9 7 8 9 8 9 3 3 6 7 4 9 0 *